The History of British Women's Writing, 1945–1975

The History of British Women's Writing
General Editors: **Jennie Batchelor** and **Cora Kaplan**

Advisory Board: Isobel Armstrong, Rachel Bowlby, Helen Carr, Carolyn Dinshaw, Margaret Ezell, Margaret Ferguson, Isobel Grundy, and Felicity Nussbaum

The History of British Women's Writing is an innovative and ambitious monograph series that seeks both to synthesise the work of several generations of feminist scholars, and to advance new directions for the study of women's writing. Volume editors and contributors are leading scholars whose work collectively reflects the global excellence in this expanding field of study. It is envisaged that this series will be a key resource for specialist and non-specialist scholars and students alike.

Titles include:

Elizabeth Herbert McAvoy and Diane Watt (*editors*)
THE HISTORY OF BRITISH WOMEN'S WRITING, 700–1500
Volume One

Caroline Bicks and Jennifer Summit (*editors*)
THE HISTORY OF BRITISH WOMEN'S WRITING, 1500–1610
Volume Two

Mihoko Suzuki (*editor*)
THE HISTORY OF BRITISH WOMEN'S WRITING, 1610–1690
Volume Three

Ros Ballaster (*editor*)
THE HISTORY OF BRITISH WOMEN'S WRITING, 1690–1750
Volume Four

Jacqueline M. Labbe (*editor*)
THE HISTORY OF BRITISH WOMEN'S WRITING, 1750–1830
Volume Five

Holly Laird (*editor*)
THE HISTORY OF BRITISH WOMEN'S WRITING, 1880–1920
Volume Seven

Mary Joannou (*editor*)
THE HISTORY OF BRITISH WOMEN'S WRITING, 1920–1945
Volume Eight

Mary Eagleton and Emma Parker (*editors*)
THE HISTORY OF BRITISH WOMEN'S WRITING, 1970–Present
Volume Ten

History of British Women's Writing
Series Standing Order ISBN 978-0-230-20079-1 (hardback)
(outside North America only)

You can receive future titles in this series as they are published by placing a standing order. Please contact your bookseller or, in case of difficulty, write to us at the address below with your name and address, the title of the series and the ISBN quoted above.

Customer Services Department, **Springer Nature**, Cromwell Place, Hampshire International Business Park, Lime Tree Way, Basingstoke, Hampshire RG24 8YJ, UK

The History of British Women's Writing, 1945–1975

Volume Nine

Edited by

Clare Hanson

and

Susan Watkins

palgrave
macmillan

Clare Hanson and Susan Watkins

History of British Women's Writing
ISBN 978-1-137-47735-4   ISBN 978-1-137-47736-1 (eBook)
DOI 10.1007/978-1-137-47736-1

Cover credit: Homer Sykes Archive / Alamy Stock Photo

Printed on acid-free paper

This Palgrave Macmillan imprint is published by SpringerNature
The registered company is Macmillan Publishers Ltd.
The registered company address is: The Campus, 4 Crinan Street, London, N1
9XW, United Kingdom

Contents

Series Editors' Preface

One of the most significant developments in literary studies in the last quarter of a century has been the remarkable growth of scholarship on women's writing. This was inspired by, and in turn provided inspiration for, a post-war women's movement, which saw women's cultural expression as key to their emancipation. The retrieval, republication and reappraisal of women's writing, beginning in the mid 1960s, have radically affected the literary curriculum in schools and universities. A revised canon now includes many more women writers. Literature courses that focus on what women thought and wrote from antiquity onwards have become popular undergraduate and postgraduate options. These new initiatives have meant that gender – in language, authors, texts, audience and in the history of print culture more generally – are central questions for literary criticism and literary history. A mass of fascinating research and analysis extending over several decades now stands as testimony to a lively and diverse set of debates, in an area of work that is still expanding.

Indeed so rapid has this expansion been, that it has become increasingly difficult for students and academics to have a comprehensive view of the wider field of women's writing outside their own period or specialism. As the research on women has moved from the margins to the confident centre of literary studies it has become rich in essays and monographs dealing with smaller groups of authors, with particular genres and with defined periods of literary production, reflecting the divisions of intellectual labour and development of expertise that are typical of the discipline of literary studies. Collections of essays that provide overviews within particular periods and genres do exist, but no published series has taken on the mapping of the field even within one language group or national culture.

A History of British Women's Writing is intended as just such a cartographic standard work. Its ambition is to provide, in ten volumes edited by leading experts in the field, and comprised of newly commissioned essays by specialist scholars, a clear and integrated picture of women's contribution to the world of letters within Great Britain from medieval times to the present. In taking on such a wide ranging project we were inspired by the founding, in 2003, of Chawton House Library, a UK registered charity with a unique collection of books focusing on women's writing in English from 1600 to 1830, set in the home and working estate of Jane Austen's brother.

Jennie Batchelor
University of Kent

Cora Kaplan
Queen Mary, University of London

Acknowledgements

We are grateful to the General Editors of this series, Cora Kaplan and Jennie Batchelor, for their guidance and support throughout the production of this volume and to the anonymous external reader for suggestions for improvement. The production process has been carried out with exemplary professionalism by the editorial team of Paula Kennedy, Ben Doyle, Peter Cary, Tomas Rene and Camille Davies at Palgrave. Our greatest debt, however, is to our contributors, who have enthusiastically embraced this project and whose depth of engagement with post-war women's writing is evident on every page. Their responsiveness, professionalism and good humour have made the editing process a pleasure and a privilege. We are also grateful to the editors of Vol 10 of the *History of British Women's Writing*, Mary Eagleton and Emma Parker, for their generous support and astute advice. We have found working together a pleasure and each of us would like to take this opportunity to thank the other for the ongoing conversation that co-editing the volume has involved.

We are grateful to the Homer Sykes Archive / Alamy Stock Photo for permission to reproduce the cover photograph.

Notes on Contributors

Leanne Bibby is Senior Lecturer in English Studies at Teesside University and has previously taught at Leeds Beckett and Leeds Trinity Universities. Her research specialisms include contemporary women's writing and the relationship between literature and historical narrative.

Kristin Bluemel is Professor of English and Wayne D. McMurray Endowed Chair in the Humanities at Monmouth University. She is author of articles and books on twentieth-century writers and artists including Dorothy Richardson, Stevie Smith, Inez Holden, Virginia Woolf, Gwen Raverat, and Joan Hassall. She is currently co-editing a collection titled *Rural Modernity: A Critical Intervention* and writing a monograph on twentieth-century British women wood engravers.

Catherine Butler is Senior Lecturer in English Literature at Cardiff University, where her academic books on children's literature include *Four British Fantasists* (Scarecrow/ChLA, 2006), *Teaching Children's Fiction* (Palgrave, 2006) and *Reading History in Children's Books* (with Hallie O'Donovan; Palgrave, 2012). She has also edited several academic collections, and produced six novels for children and teenagers, as well as some shorter works, of which the most recent is *Twisted Winter* (A&C Black, 2013).

Sandra Courtman is a former Programme Director for Arts and Humanities at the University of Sheffield. Since 2015, she has been working as a freelance researcher, teacher and creative writer. She has a portfolio of publications on Caribbean and Black British writing and her research focus is on the apparent paucity of West Indian women's writing during the immediate post Second World War period.

Deborah Chambers is Professor of Media and Cultural Studies at Newcastle University. Her research areas include media cultures; women and journalism, media and intimate relationships; changing homes and media technologies. As well as her work on *Women and Journalism* (Routledge 2004, with Linda Steiner and Carole Fleming), her books include *New Social Ties: Contemporary Connections in a Fragmented Society* (Palgrave 2006); *A Sociology of Family Life: Change and Diversity in Intimate Relations* (Polity 2012); *Social Media and Personal Relationships* (Palgrave 2013) and *Changing Media, Homes and Households* (Routledge 2016).

Jane Dowson is Reader in Twentieth-Century Literature at De Montfort University, Leicester. Her publications include *Women, Modernism and*

British Poetry 1910–39 (2002), *Women's Writing 1945-60: After The Deluge* (ed.2003), *A Cambridge History of Twentieth-Century Women's Poetry* (co-authored, 2005), *The Cambridge Companion to Twentieth-Century British and Irish Women's Poetry* (ed. 2011), and *Carol Ann Duffy: Poet for our Times* (2016).

Mary Eagleton was formerly Professor of Contemporary Women's Writing at Leeds Beckett University, UK. She has published extensively on contemporary women's writing, feminist literary theory, and feminist literary history. Titles include: ed. (with Emma Parker) *The History of British Women's Writing, 1970-Present* (2015); ed. *Feminist Literary Theory: A Reader* (3rd revised edition, 2011); *Figuring the Woman Author in Contemporary Fiction* (2005); and ed. *A Concise Companion to Feminist Theory* (2003). She has published essays on, among others, Doris Lessing, A.S. Byatt, Margaret Drabble, Hilary Mantel, Carol Shields, Margaret Atwood, Alice Walker, Diana Athill, Emma Tennant and Zadie Smith. She is the founding Chair of the Contemporary Women's Writing Association and the founding co-editor of the Oxford University Press journal, *Contemporary Women's Writing*.

Katie Gramich is a Professor of English Literature at Cardiff University, specializing in Welsh women's writing. Her publications include *Rediscovering Margiad Evans: marginality, gender and illness* (Cardiff: University of Wales Press, 2013), a translation of Kate Roberts' *Feet in Chains* (Parthian: 2012) and *Twentieth-century women's writing in Wales: land, gender, belonging* (Cardiff: University of Wales Press, 2007). With Professor Claire Connolly at University College Cork and Dr Paul O'Leary at Aberystwyth University, she runs the Wales-Ireland Research Network.

Gabriele Griffin is Professor of Gender Research at Uppsala University, Sweden. She is also Visiting Professor at Abo Akademi University and at the Gender Institute, London School of Economics. Her work centres on feminist research methodologies and on women's cultural production, specifically theatre. She is Co-ordinator of the Nordforsk-funded Centre of Excellence, Nordwit. Recent publications include *Cross-Cultural Interviewing* (ed., Routledge, 2016) and *Research Methods for Reading Digital Data in the Digital Humanities* (Edinburgh UP, 2016).

Clare Hanson is Professor of Twentieth Century Literature at the University of Southampton. She has published widely on the short story and on twentieth-century women's writing and is the author of *Hysterical Fictions: the Woman's Novel in the Twentieth Century* (Palgrave 2000), *A Cultural History of Pregnancy: Pregnancy, Medicine and Culture in Britain, 1750–2000* (Palgrave 2004) and *Eugenics, Literature and Culture in Post-war Britain* (Routledge 2012). Between 2010 and 2012 she was co-editor of the OUP journal *Contemporary Women's Writing*. Her current research explores the relationship between genetics and the literary imagination.

Phyllis Lassner is Professor in the Crown Family Center for Jewish Studies, the Gender Studies and Cook Family Writing Program at Northwestern University. In addition to articles on interwar and wartime women writers, she is the author of two books on Elizabeth Bowen, *British Women Writers of World War II, Colonial Strangers: Women Writing the End of the British Empire, Anglo-Jewish Women Writing the Holocaust,* and most recently, *Espionage and Exile: Fascism and Antifascism in British Spy Fiction and Film.* She created and edits the Northwestern University Press Series, "Cultural Expressions of World War II" and was awarded the International Diamond Jubilee Fellowship at Southampton University.

Elizabeth Maslen is a Senior Research Fellow of the Institute of English Studies, University of London and at Queen Mary, University of London. Her recent books include *Life in the Writings of Storm Jameson* (Evanston: Northwestern University Press, 2014); a revised and enlarged edition of *Doris Lessing* in the Writers and their Work series (Mary Tavy: Northcote House Publishers in conjunction with the British Council, 1994 and 2014).

Kaye Mitchell is Senior Lecturer in Contemporary Literature at the University of Manchester and Co-Director of the Centre for New Writing. She is the author of two books – *A.L. Kennedy: New British Fiction* (Palgrave, 2007), and *Intention and Text: Towards an Intentionality of Literary Form* (Continuum, 2008) – and editor of a collection of essays on the British author Sarah Waters (Bloomsbury, 2013) and of a special issue of *Contemporary Women's Writing* (OUP, 2015) on experimental women's writing. Her current work-in-progress includes a monograph on the politics and poetics of shame in contemporary literature, for which she received a Humboldt Foundation Research Fellowship for Experienced Researchers in 2014-15, and a co-edited collection on British avant-garde writing of the 1960s.

Kerry Myler is a Senior Lecturer in Contemporary Literature and Programme Leader for English Literature at Newman University, Birmingham. Her research interests include: Doris Lessing and anti-psychiatry; women's writing and mental illness; female sexuality in post-war and contemporary women's writing; women's bodies, sexuality and motherhood in literature and popular culture. She is an executive committee member of the Contemporary Women's Writing Association.

Sue Vice is Professor of English Literature at the University of Sheffield. Her most recent publications include *Representing Perpetrators in Holocaust Literature and Film,* co-edited with Jenni Adams (2013), *Textual Deceptions: False Memoirs and Literary Hoaxes in the Contemporary Era* (2014), and her critical study of Barry Hines's writing, co-written with David Forrest, will be published in 2017.

Diana Wallace is Professor of English Literature at the University of South Wales. Her teaching and research focus mainly on women's writing, historical fiction and the Gothic. She is the author of *Female Gothic Histories: Gender, History and the Gothic* (University of Wales Press, 2013), *The Woman's Historical Novel: British Women Writers, 1900-2000* (Palgrave, 2005) and *Sisters and Rivals in British Women's Fiction 1914–39* (Macmillan, 2000).

Susan Watkins is Professor of Women's Writing in the School of Cultural Studies and Humanities at Leeds Beckett University. She is the author of *Twentieth-Century Women Novelists: Feminist Theory into Practice* (Palgrave 2001) and *Doris Lessing* (Manchester University Press 2010) and co-editor of *Scandalous Fictions: The Twentieth-Century Novel in the Public Sphere* (Palgrave 2006) and *Doris Lessing: Border Crossings* (Continuum 2009). She was Chair of the Contemporary Women's Writing Association from 2010-2014 and co-editor of the *Journal of Commonwealth Literature* from 2010-2015.

Chronology

Year	Events	Works
1945	VE Day marks the end of the war in Europe; USA drops atomic bomb on Hiroshima and Nagasaki, Japan; Landslide Labour victory with new government led by Clement Attlee; VJ day marks the end of the Pacific conflict; Family Allowances Bill; BBC radio expands with the Light Programme added to the Home Service	Elizabeth Bowen, *The Demon Lover;* Vera Brittain, *Account Rendered;* Sylvia Lynd, *Collected Poems;* Una Marson, *Towards the Stars;* Betty Miller, *On the Side of the Angels;* Nancy Mitford, *The Pursuit of Love;* Ruth Pitter, *The Bridge: Poems 1939-1944;* Kathleen Raine, *Ecce Homo;* Mary Renault, *The Middle Mist;* Anya Seton, *My Theodosia;* Edith Sitwell, *The Song of the Cold;* Elizabeth Taylor, *At Mrs Lippincote's*
1946	Royal Commission on Equal Pay tentatively recommends equal pay for teachers and civil servants; New Towns Act; National Health Service Act; National Insurance Act	Frances Bellerby, *Plash Mill and Other Poems;* Enid Blyton, *First Term at Mallory Towers;* H.D., *Trilogy;* Denise Levertov, *The Double Image;* Ruth Pitter, *Pitter on Cats;* Kathleen Raine, *Living in Time;* Kate Roberts, *A Summer Day and Other Stories*
1947	School leaving age raised to 15; India granted independence; Town and Country Planning Act; Nationalisation of coal industry	Clemence Dane, *Call Home the Heart;* Storm Jameson, *Before the Crossing* and *The Black Laurel;* Elizabeth Taylor, *A View of the Harbour*
1948	National Health Service established; Apartheid imposed in South Africa; SS Empire Windrush brings 492 West Indian immigrants to Tilbury Docks; Olympic Games at Wembley Stadium in London; The Children Act; Nationalisation of the railways	Enid Blyton, *Second Form at Mallory Towers;* Elizabeth Bowen, *The Heat of the Day;* Margaret Irwin's *Elizabeth: Captive Princess,* the second in her trilogy of historical novels about Elizabeth I; Mary Renault, *The North Face*

(Continued)

Year	Events	Works
1949	Independence of the Republic of Ireland; North Atlantic Treaty Organisation (NATO) is founded; Clothes rationing ends	Georgette Heyer, *Arabella;* Marghanita Laski, *Little Boy Lost;* Nancy Mitford, *Love in a Cold Climate;* Jean Plaidy, *Murder Most Royal;* Stevie Smith, *The Holiday;* Elizabeth Taylor, *A Wreath of Roses*
1950	*The Archers* starts on BBC radio; *Watch with Mother* starts on BBC Television; The Korean War begins (and concludes in 1953)	Georgette Heyer, *The Grand Sophy;* Rose Macaulay, *The World My Wilderness;* Doris Lessing, *The Grass is Singing;* Ruth Pitter, *Urania;* Barbara Pym, *Some Tame Gazelle;* Stevie Smith, *Harold's Leap*
1951	Conservatives win General Election, Winston Churchill becomes prime minister for the second time; Festival of Britain in London 3 May-30 September; Eirene White, Labour MP, introduces bill to make possible divorce by consent. Forced to withdraw it	Storm Jameson, *The Green Man;* Sylvia Raman's 'Women of Twilight' begins a five month run at the Vaudeville Theatre; Elizabeth Taylor, *A Game of Hide and Seek*
1952	Death of George VI and accession of Elizabeth II	Barbara Pym, *Excellent Women;* Han Suyin, *A Many-Splendoured Thing*
1953	Coronation of Queen Elizabeth II; Over 300,000 new homes built	English translation of Simone de Beauvoir, *The Second Sex;* Jeanette Dowling and Francis Letton, *The Young Elizabeth* is performed 504 times in this, the year of the Queen's coronation; Margaret Irwin, *Elizabeth and the Prince of Spain;* Rosamond Lehmann, *The Echoing Grove;* Barbara Pym, *Jane and Prudence;* Mary Renault, *The Charioteer*

Year	Events	Works
1954	End of rationing	Margot Bennett, *The Long Way Back;* Frances Cornford, *Collected Poems;* Marghanita Laski, *The Offshore Island;* Kamala Markandaya, *Nectar in a Sieve;* Iris Murdoch, *Under the Net;* Nayantara Sahgal, *Prison and Chocolate Cake;* Rosemary Sutcliff, *The Eagle of the Ninth;* Sylvia Townsend Warner, *The Flint Anchor*
1955	National Council of Women, conference on single women; Commercial television begins in Britain; Claudia Jones founds *The West Indian Gazette*	Elizabeth Jennings wins the Somerset Maugham Award for *A Way of Looking;* Kamala Markandaya, *Some Inner Fury;* Ruth Pitter is the first woman to receive the Queen's Gold Medal for poetry; Rebecca West, *A Train of Powder*
1956	Report of the *Royal Commission on Marriage and Divorce;* Suez Crisis; Hungarian uprising is followed by USSR's invasion of Hungary; Britain opens first nuclear power station	Lucille Iremonger, *West Indian Folk Tales;* Janet McNeill, *Tea at Four O' Clock;* Kathleen Raine, *Collected Poems;* Kate Roberts, *The Living Sleep*
1957	Report of the Royal Commission on Mental Illness and Mental Deficiency; First 'H' Bomb tests in the Pacific; Mary Stott invited to edit the *Guardian* Women's Page, which she continued until 1972	Georgette Heyer, *Sylvester;* Stevie Smith, *Not Waving But Drowning;* Muriel Spark, *The Comforters* and 'The Party through the Wall', first performed on the BBC's Third Programme

(Continued)

Year	Events	Works
1958	Notting Hill race riots; National Council of Women, conference on working mothers; Campaign for Nuclear Disarmament established and the first Aldermaston March took place	Christine Brooke-Rose, *Out*; Veronica Hull, *The Monkey Puzzle*; Storm Jameson, *A Ulysses Too Many*; Ann Jellicoe's *The Sport of My Mad Mother* at the Royal Court theatre; Elizabeth Jennings, *A Sense of the World*; Doris Lessing's *Each His Own Wilderness* at the Royal Court theatre; Joan Littlewood's production of Shelagh Delaney's *A Taste of Honey* at the Theatre Royal, Stratford East; Mina Loy, *Lunar Baedeker & Time-Tables*; Penelope Mortimer, *Daddy's Gone A-Hunting*; Philippa Pearce, *Tom's Midnight Garden*; Mary Renault, *The King Must Die*; Muriel Spark, *The Go-Away Bird and Other Stories*; Muriel Spark's 'The Interview' first performed on the BBC's Third Programme
1959	The Enforcement of Morals Act, Lord Devlin; Mental Health Act; Obscene Publications Act; Marjorie Proops takes over the advice column of the *Daily Mirror* as Agony Aunt	Frances Cornford wins the Queen's Gold Medal for poetry; Menna Gallie, *Strike for a Kingdom*; Karen Gershon, *The Relentless Year*; Beryl Gilroy writes *In Praise of Love and Children*, which has to wait until 1994 to be published; Jacquetta Hawkes, *Providence Island*; Marghanita Laski, *The Offshore Island*; Kate Roberts, *Tea in the Heather*
1960	The Pill introduced in USA; *Coronation Street* starts on ITV television; Acquittal of Penguin Books for publishing unexpurgated edition of D. H. Lawrence's *Lady Chatterley's Lover* after trial	Victoria Holt, *Mistress of Mellyn*; Jenny Joseph wins Eric Gregory award; Doris Lessing, *In Pursuit of the English*; Sylvia Plath, *The Colossus*; Lynne Reid Banks, *The L-Shaped Room*

Year	Events	Works
1961	*Sunday Telegraph* first published; Britain applies for membership in the EEC; Film *A Taste of Honey* released; *Songs of Praise* first broadcast; Birth control pills become available on the NHS; Trial of Adolph Eichmann	H.D., *Helen in Egypt;* Georgette Heyer, *A Civil Contract;* Attia Hosain, *Sunlight on a Broken Column;* Elizabeth Jennings, *Song for a Birth or a Death;* Denise Levertov, *Selected Poems;* Barbara Pym, *No Fond Return of Love;* Muriel Spark, 'The Danger Zone' and *The Prime of Miss Jean Brodie;* Katharine Whitehorn, *Kitchen in the Corner: Cooking in a Bedsitter*
1962	Liberal Party revival in the UK; Commonwealth Immigrants Act; Race riots in West Midlands; The Welsh Language Society is founded; Introduction of student grants; The Net Book Agreement survives a challenge from the Registrar of Restrictive Practices	Joan Aiken, *The Wolves of Willoughby Chase;* Phyllis Bottome, *The Goal;* Doris Lessing, *The Golden Notebook;* Menna Gallie, *The Small Mine;* Ann Jellicoe's *The Knack* first performed at the Royal Court Theatre; Naomi Mitchison, *Memoirs of a Spacewoman;* Penelope Mortimer, *The Pumpkin Eater;* Mary Renault, *The Bull From the Sea;* Muriel Spark, 'Doctors of Philosophy' first performed; Sylvia Wynter, *The Hills of Hebron*
1963	Suicide of Sylvia Plath; The Beatles release their first album; Profumo Affair – John Profumo resigns after being caught with call-girl Christine Keeler; Prime Minister Harold Macmillan resigns	Hannah Arendt, *Eichmann in Jerusalem: A Report on the Banality of Evil;* Anita Desai, *Cry the Peacock;* Margaret Drabble, *A Summer Bird-Cage;* Nell Dunn, *Up the Junction;* Betty Friedan, *The Feminine Mystique;* Norah Lofts, *The Concubine;* Sylvia Plath, *The Bell Jar;* Edith Sitwell awarded C.Litt from the Royal Society of Literature; Muriel Spark, *The Girls of Slender Means*

(Continued)

Year	Events	Works
1964	Violent clashes between mods and rockers at Clacton and Brighton; BBC Two begins broadcasting; Last execution takes place in the British Isles; Labour Party defeats the Conservatives	A.S. Byatt, *The Shadow of the Sun;* Elizabeth Jennings, *Recoveries;* Ann Quin, *Berg*
1965	Sir Winston Churchill dies; Moors murders – Ian Brady and Myra Hindley are charged; The death penalty is abolished	Anita Desai, *Voices in the City;* Margaret Drabble, *The Millstone;* Sylvia Plath, *Ariel;* Edith Sitwell, *Selected Poems;* Muriel Spark, *The Mandelbaum Gate*
1966	Unemployment rises sharply; Election of Gwynfor Evans, the first Plaid Cwymru MP; Sybille Bedford publishes her report on the 1963-5 Frankfurt Auschwitz trial	Louise Bennett, *Jamaica Labrish;* Bryher, *This January Tale;* Angela Carter, *Shadow Dance;* Maureen Duffy, *The Microcosm;* Elaine Feinstein, *Collected Poems and Translations;* Karen Gershon, *We Came as Children;* Elizabeth Jennings, *The Mind has Mountains;* Kamala Markandaya, *A Handful of Rice;* Naomi Mitchison, *Return to the Fairy Hill;* Flora Nwapa's *Efuru* is the only novel by a woman to be published (rather than republished) in the African Writers Series; Jean Rhys, *Wide Sargasso Sea;* Stevie Smith wins the Cholmondley Award and publishes *The Frog Prince;* Muriel Spark, *Doctors of Philosophy*
1967	Abortion Act; Family Planning Act; The Sexual Offences Act decriminalises homosexuality in England and Wales (for men over 21 not in the armed forces)	Angela Carter, *The Magic Toyshop;* Margaret Drabble, *Jerusalem the Golden;* Nell Dunn, *Poor Cow;* R. D. Laing, *The Politics of Experience;* Kate Roberts, *Fairness of Morning;* Fay Weldon, *The Fat Woman's Joke*

Year	Events	Works
1968	Reintroduction of International Women's Day; Theatres act abolishes censorship in the theatre; Enoch Powell, 'Rivers of Blood' speech; Anti-Vietnam War demonstrations	Angela Carter, *Several Perceptions;* Storm Jameson, *The White Crow;* Helen MacInnes, *The Salzburg Connection;* Iris Murdoch, *The Nice and the Good;* Ruth Pitter, *Poems, 1926–1966;* Red Ladder Theatre founded
1969	Passing of the Divorce Reform act abolishing the concept of matrimonial offence; British troops sent into Northern Ireland; First issue of *Shrew* magazine	Jane Arden, 'Vagina Rex and the Gas Oven' staged at the Drury Lane Arts Lab; Angela Carter, *Heroes and Villains;* Caryl Churchill, 'Lovesick' (radio drama); Margaret Drabble, *The Waterfall;* Maureen Duffy, 'Rites' and *Wounds;* Elizabeth Jennings, *The Animals' Arrival;* Ursula K. Le Guin, *The Left Hand of Darkness;* Doris Lessing, *The Four-Gated City;* Stevie Smith wins the Queen's Gold Medal for poetry
1970	Passing of the Equal Pay Act; Voting age reduced from 21 to 18; Passing of the Matrimonial Proceeds and Property Act; Family Planning Association obliged to make contraception available to unmarried women; National Council for the Unmarried Mother and her Child, set up in 1918, renamed the National Council for One-Parent families; The first National Women's Liberation Movement conference held at Ruskin College, Oxford; Publication of Eva Figes's *Patriarchal Attitudes;* Publication of Germaine Greer's *The Female Eunuch*	Jane Arden, *Vagina Rex and the Gas Oven;* Agatha Christie, *Passenger to Frankfurt;* Mena Gallie, *You're Welcome to Ulster;* Karen Gershon, *The Pulse in the Stone: Jerusalem Poems;* Elizabeth Jennings, *Lucidities;* Mary Renault, *Fire from Heaven;* Muriel Spark, *The Driver's Seat*

(Continued)

Year	Events	Works
1971	Immigration Act, Commonwealth citizens lose their automatic right to settle in the UK; Introduction of internment without trial in Northern Ireland; Women's Street Theatre Group founded	Angela Carter, *Love;* Elaine Feinstein's translation of the poems of Marina Tsvetayeva; Judith Kerr, *When Hitler Stole Pink Rabbit;* Juliet Mitchell, *Woman's Estate;* Doris Lessing, *Briefing for a Descent into Hell*
1972	Bloody Sunday/the Bogside Massacre in County Derry, Northern Ireland; Northern Ireland placed under Direct Rule from Westminster; Cambridge colleges Churchill, Clare, and King's admit women students; First issue of *Spare Rib*	Beryl Bainbridge, *Harriet Said;* Angela Carter, *The Infernal Desire Machines of Doctor Hoffman;* Caryl Churchill, *Owners;* Buchi Emecheta, *In the Ditch;* Elizabeth Jennings, *Relationships;* Jennifer Johnston, *The Captains and the Kings;* Daphne du Maurier, *Rule Britannia;* Mary Renault, *The Persian Boy;* Anne Ridler, *Some Time After and other Poems;* Nayantara Sahgal, *The Day in Shadow;* Stevie Smith, *Scorpion and other Poems;* Elizabeth Taylor, *The Devastating Boys*
1973	Britain joins the European Economic Community; Virago Press founded; Establishment of the Women's Theatre Group (later becomes Sphinx Theatre Company); First Women's Theatre Festival, London; Establishment of *Red Rag: A Magazine of Women's Liberation;* Commercial Radio begins	Beryl Bainbridge, *The Dressmaker;* Ruth Fainlight, *The Region's Violence;* Anna Kavan, *Ice;* Kamala Markandaya, *The Nowhere Man;* Penelope Mortimer, *The Home;* Sheila Rowbotham, *Woman's Consciousness Man's World;* Mary Stott, *Forgetting's No Excuse;* Fay Weldon, *Down Among the Women*

Year	Events	Works
1974	Contraception made free to all women; Passing of Employment Protection Act which provided for paid maternity leave and protection during pregnancy; Founding of the Women's Aid Federation to support women and children experiencing domestic violence; Oxford colleges Brasenose, Jesus, Wadham and Hertford admit women students; Gillian Reynolds becomes the first woman to present the news on BBC Radio	Beryl Bainbridge, *The Bottle Factory Outing;* Angela Carter, *Fireworks: Nine Profane Pieces;* Jenny Joseph, *Rose in the Afternoon;* Doris Lessing, *The Memoirs of a Survivor;* Penelope Lively, *The House in Norham Gardens;* Juliet Mitchell, *Psychoanalysis and Feminism;* Ruth Pitter awarded CLitt by Royal Society of Literature; Anne Stevenson, *Travelling Behind Glass, Correspondences: A Family History in Letters*
1975	Passing of the Sex Discrimination Act; Matrimonial Causes Act; Disability Discrimination Act; End of internment without trial in Northern Ireland; Establishment of the Monstrous Regiment Theatre Company; Establishment of Gay Sweatshop; Angela Rippon is the first woman to read the main evening television news bulletin on BBC1	Beryl Bainbridge, *Sweet William;* Judy Bloome, *Forever;* Christine Brooke-Rose, *Thru;* Elaine Feinstein, *Children of the Rose;* Karen Gershon, *My Daughters, My Sisters and Other Poems;* Naomi Mitchison, *Solution Three;* Charles Reznikoff, *Holocaust;* Stevie Smith, *Collected Poems;* Fay Weldon, *Female Friends*

Introduction

Clare Hanson and Susan Watkins

Mapping the territory

The period between 1945 and 1975 was one of major social change in Britain. At the end of the Second World War, the country was bankrupt and the bomb sites that scarred the urban landscape were emblems not only of physical destruction but also of a damaged social and political fabric. However, planning for a better future had already begun during the war, partly in response to the poverty and suffering caused by the Great Depression, the cause of much of the 'want, disease, ignorance, squalor and idleness' that Beveridge identified in his 1942 report as obstacles to social progress. Building on Beveridge's recommendations and as part of the post-war consensus, both Labour and Conservative governments passed legislation that ensured expanded educational opportunities for all, free healthcare, the provision of family allowances and social insurance. The long-term impact of the Welfare State is hard to assess but it undoubtedly lifted many out of poverty and the historian Carolyn Steedman suggests that it also had more intangible psychological benefits. In her memoir *Landscape for a Good Woman* (1986) she links it with a broader social narrative that recognised the rights of the marginalised and that 'told me, in a covert way, that I had a right to exist, was worth something'.[1] While the war triggered progressive domestic reconstruction, it also brought global transformations. It precipitated the decline of Britain's status as a global superpower, as evidenced by the Suez crisis when Britain was forced by America to withdraw its forces from Egypt. This period also saw the end of the British Empire, with India's independence in 1947 followed by that of Sudan, the Gold Coast, Malaya, Jamaica, Trinidad and Barbados. As Britain relinquished its colonial powers, the arrival of the iconic ship the *SS Empire Windrush* at Tilbury Docks in

© The Author(s) 2017
C. Hanson and S. Watkins, *The History of British Women's Writing, 1945–1975*,
History of British Women's Writing, DOI: 10.1057/978-1-137-47736-1_1

1948 marked the beginning of mass immigration from the former colonies, inaugurating the move towards a multi-cultural Britain.

The staging of the Festival of Britain in 1951 signalled a determination to build a better economic and cultural future as it celebrated the achievements of British science and technology alongside architecture and the arts. The coronation which followed two years later was hailed as inaugurating a 'new Elizabethan' era of growth and prosperity, a mood captured in A.S. Byatt's novel *The Virgin in the Garden* (1978) which probes the parallels and disjunctions between the England of the Virgin Queen and the post-war present. The loosening of austerity, the end of rationing and the building of new homes generated an optimism on the domestic front which was fissured by unease over the Conservative government's foreign policies. The Suez crisis was a particular flashpoint for politicians of all stripes who argued that rather than invading Egypt, Britain should intervene in relation to the illegal Soviet invasion of Hungary. Suez prompted anti-war protests and together with the government's decision to build a hydrogen bomb, led to the inauguration of the Campaign for Nuclear Disarmament in 1957.

The 1960s saw a further liberalisation of social attitudes in the wake of the 1961 Profumo Affair when the Secretary of State for War was forced to resign over an affair with the call girl Christine Keeler, exposing the hypocrisy of the political establishment. The Labour government elected in 1964 embarked on a series of progressive measures, abolishing the death penalty in 1965 and legalising homosexuality in 1967, while abortion was legalised in the same year and in 1969 the Divorce Act allowed couples to divorce on a no fault basis. Importantly for sexual liberation, the contraceptive pill was licensed in the UK in 1961, although it was only available to married women prior to 1968. The rise of the counter-culture brought increased openness about sex and sexuality and fed into a questioning of gendered identities that had been kick-started by the publication in the US of Betty Friedan's *The Feminine Mystique* (1963), which was also read widely in the UK. As Angela Carter commented, although 'false prophets, loonies and charlatans' abounded in the counter-cultural milieu of the 1960s, this was for her a moment of 'unprecedented public philosophical awareness' that made it possible to question for the first time 'the nature of my reality as a woman. How that social fiction of my 'femininity' was created, by means outside my control, and palmed off on me as the real thing'.[2]

The contours of British women's writing in this period have been obscured by two influential narratives. The first is a literary-historical understanding of twentieth-century literature which privileges the twin peaks of modernism (1900 – 1940) and postmodernism (dating from the late 1960s – 1990), the implication being that literature which falls outside these parameters lacks both experimental force and high literary value. The second is the conceptualisation of British feminist history in terms of a first wave dating from the late nineteenth century to around 1930 and a second running from the late sixties to 1990, together with a belief that, as Elizabeth Wilson puts it, 'there was no feminism between 1945 and 1968' as the aspirations of women mysteriously 'withered away'.[3] There is, of course, some truth in these accounts but they are problematic not just because they over-simplify but because they have the potential to consolidate prejudices against particular kinds of literature and history. In this respect, a number of critics have recently begun to assess the limitations of the modernism/postmodernism axis for understanding the scope of twentieth century literature, albeit against a backdrop of what Douglas Mao and Rebecca L. Walkowitz term the 'expansionist' tendency of twenty-first century modernist criticism.[4]

Challenging the usefulness of these categories for reading mid-century literature, critics have developed critical frameworks which adopt alternative points of reference in relation to period and style. One is the middlebrow, a kind of writing famously derided by Virginia Woolf as 'neither one thing nor the other', suspended between high and low literary culture, the despised other of modernism.[5] Repudiating Woolf's repudiation, Nicola Humble argues in her influential study of the feminine middlebrow that this genre extends beyond high modernism well into the 1950s and that it was 'a powerful force in establishing and consolidating, but also in resisting, new class and gender identities'.[6] Similarly, the contributors to Erica Brown and Mary Grover's edited collection *Middlebrow Literary Cultures: the Battle of the Brows* (2011) explore the politics of middlebrow literary production between 1920 and 1960, taking as a starting point the editors' contention that the term is the product of deep anxieties about 'cultural authority and cultural transmission'.[7] Taking a different tack, Kristin Bluemel has made the case for intermodernism as a category which can help to make sense of the forces and forms that produced non-modernist, mid-twentieth-century literature, a theme she pursues in her contribution to this volume. For Bluemel, the concept of intermodernism enables a recovery of the aesthetic, material and ideological investments of writers who cannot be assimilated to modernism and whose position is 'eccentric' in terms of politics and style.[8] Such writers forge flexible political alliances during the Second World War and the Cold War, embracing genres that fall outside the formal aesthetic of modernism, including spy thrillers, documentaries and historical fiction.

Marina MacKay and Lyndsey Stonebridge also challenge the literary-historical preoccupation with modernism and postmodernism in the introduction to their edited collection *British Fiction after Modernism: the Novel at Mid-Century* (2007). Arguing that a focus on the writing of the mid-century reveals complex continuities between earlier and later periods, they make the claim for the Second World War as the major turning point of the century in Britain, positioning it as a 'domestic and geopolitical watershed' that remains 'inescapably present in public culture and popular memory'.[9] On the home front, the war brought a progressive post-war settlement but it also triggered the end of empire and of Britain's status as a superpower, transformations that had major implications for a literature which had to negotiate both post-war trauma and national decline. Maroula Joannou's

Women's Writing, Englishness and National and Cultural Identity: The Mobile Woman and the Migrant Voice, 1938-1962 (2012) similarly avoids the usual period demarcations of twentieth-century literary history and considers the writing of the 1950s alongside that of the 1940s and the immediate pre-war period. For Joannou, this time-span enables her to look more closely at the long-term ramifications of the war and it allows for a more fine-grained understanding of the impact on women of post-war displacements and the dissolution of empire. Joannou's study is notable in that it not only challenges period boundaries but shifts the focus to women writers, thus producing what she refers to as a different 'literary cartography' of the period.[10] A focus on gender also shapes Phyllis Lassner's work on wartime and post-war women's writing. *British Women Writers of World War II: Battlegrounds of their Own* (1998) explores the inter-relations between gender, space and genre, arguing that women writers 'tested the ideological and aesthetic grounds of traditional genre definitions in relation to their own ideologies and the language of wartime representation', an argument she extends in her essay for this collection.[11] Her subsequent study *Colonial Strangers: Women Writing the End of the British Empire* (2004) explores women writers' engagement with the intertwined legacies of fascism and colonialism, while *Anglo-Jewish Women Writing the Holocaust: Displaced Witnesses* (2009) assesses British memoirists and writers of the Holocaust, arguing that their work has been neglected because they have been identified not as survivors of the camps and ghettoes but as refugees, a point which is taken up in Sue Vice's essay on responses to the Holocaust in this collection.

A further pioneering study concerned exclusively with women's writing is Deborah Philips and Ian Haywood's *Brave New Causes: Women in British Postwar Fictions* (1998), which demonstrates the importance of themes such as the working woman, reproduction, the crisis of the country house and delinquency for women writers of the 1950s. Philips and Haywood argue that fiction of this period does not abandon the marriage plot but 'provide[s] a large degree of relative autonomy for the development of the working heroine and her problems and achievements'.[12] The book is unusual in its consideration of popular and middlebrow writing and Philips's *Women's Fiction 1945-2005: Writing Romance* retains this focus on women's popular fiction, arguing that '[t]he novels discussed here belong to genres of fiction that are rarely reviewed or cited in critical studies, and most are not considered as worthy of entry into the feminist canon. These are, however, the titles that women read'.[13] Susheila Nasta's edited collection *Motherlands* (1991) is also ground-breaking in its exploration of black and minority ethnic women's writing from Africa, the Caribbean and South Asia from the period 1945 to 1975. The concept of 'motherlands' allows the collection to explore the idea of mother nations, mother figures and relationships between mothers, daughters and sisters, and migration or exile from the mother-land. The focus is not exclusively on British writers, since the aim is to explore women writers who share experiences of double colonisation, a subject which is taken up in Sandra Courtman's essay for this collection.

As indicated above, a number of post-war women writers have been associated with postmodernism on the grounds of their deployment of a ludic, self-referential style and/or their scepticism towards Enlightenment metanarratives. David Lodge, for example, argues that Muriel Spark was a postmodernist *avant la lettre*,[14] while Linda Hutcheon singles out Angela Carter's fiction as exemplary in its engagement with a range of postmodern issues, offering a reading of the early story 'The Loves of Lady Purple' in support of this view.[15] The postmodern aspects of Lessing's *The Golden Notebook* (1962) and *The Four-Gated City* (1969) have also been much debated, as critics have linked the fractured form of these texts with a decentring of the subject and with a radical questioning of the stability of language.[16] Yet as critics from Bernard Bergonzi to Dominic Head have pointed out, although postmodernism flourished elsewhere it was met with caution in British literary circles where a commitment to realism and liberal individualism remained strong.[17] For Head, this leads to a distinctively British postmodernism which reworks the realist contract rather than rejecting it, retaining a commitment to degrees of referentiality. If postmodernism was modified by realism in this way, Patricia Waugh suggests that women writers also viewed the postmodern aesthetic from a position of critical distance. She argues that although the postmodern emphasis on the marginal and the oppositional was congenial to women writers, they were less invested in the deconstruction of the autonomous and bounded subject as many did not conceptualise subjectivity in this way. For her, women's writing exists in 'a contradictory relationship to both the dominant liberal conception of subjectivity [...] and to the classic "postmodernist" deconstruction of this liberal trajectory': rather than investing in defining or deconstructing the isolated ego, it is engaged in discovering 'a collective concept of subjectivity which foregrounds the construction of identity *in relationship*'.[18] Doris Lessing's contention that her 'Children of Violence' sequence is a study of the individual conscience in its relationship to the collective can be seen as emblematic of this understanding of identity as inherently relational, forged in and through connection with others.[19] Waugh's analysis, then, highlights the tension between the deconstructive energies of postmodernism and the reconstructive ambitions of British women writers whose work both coheres with and exceeds the aesthetic category of postmodernism.

Gender in transition

The post-war period is often seen as retrogressive in terms of gender politics as women are thought to have returned to the home to take up their roles as wives and mothers, an assumption fixed in popular memory by iconic images of domesticity in post-war advertising. However, the return to domesticity is a myth which was first challenged by Elizabeth Wilson in her sociological study *Only Halfway to Paradise* (1980). Wilson's research showed that married women continued to enter the workforce in considerable numbers, the proportion of married women in the workforce rising to 21 per cent in 1951, 32 per cent in 1961, and 47 per cent in 1972.[20] Moreover in the immediate post-war period, far from discouraging women to work, the government put out an appeal for women workers who were needed in industries such as clothing, textiles, iron and steel and in professions such as nursing and midwifery. What was distinctive – and damaging – about this period was the way in which women's paid work was delimited by government and policy makers. Influential post-war planners like William Beveridge and Richard Titmuss argued that the traditional division of labour between men and women should remain intact, with women staying at home to raise their families, perhaps doing part-time work when children were at school, only returning to full-time work when they had grown up.[21] In other words, it was assumed that women's careers should always be secondary to the needs of their families. This model of 'women's two roles' was a lynch-pin of post-war policy, reflecting a conservative ideology of motherhood which had become more, not less, entrenched after the dislocations of wartime. Its pervasiveness is captured in Doris Lessing's story 'To Room Nineteen' as the main protagonist Susan Rawlings reflects that 'children needed their mother to a certain age, that both parents knew and agreed on, and when these four healthy, wisely brought-up children were of the right age, [she] would work again'.[22] She has accepted a framing of her role in terms of subordination to the needs of her family and a relinquishing of autonomy: the cost of conforming to this model is revealed when after attempting and failing to establish a literal and metaphorical space of her own, she commits suicide by gassing herself.

Contemporary debates about woman's dual role focussed almost exclusively on middle-class women like Lessing's protagonist. As Wilson notes, working-class women were used to combining paid work with motherhood but what changed after the war was that middle- and upper-class women abandoned the idea of 'marriage as a career', wanting marriage, motherhood *and* a career. As one woman put it, 'the point for me [...] was that the women older than me chose *either* a career *or* marriage. [...] [But] *we* said, I and my friends, we would be mothers *and* women in our own right.'[23] Ironically, the most important factor that militated against such an ambition was the steep drop in the number of domestic servants which was caused by gradually increasing affluence and wider opportunities for working-class women. The result was the proletarianisation of middle-class women, who were forced to undertake domestic labour that would have been unthinkable to a previous generation. It was this, combined with the failure of successive governments to provide childcare, that led to many feeling imprisoned in the home, suffering from what Berry Friedan was to dub 'the problem with no name'.[24] Friedan argued that millions of women suffered from the frustrations invoked by the poet Anne Stevenson in her sequence *Correspondences*, which articulates 'the anger, the confusion, the misery and the doubt' associated with post-war marriage and motherhood. As Jane Dowson notes in her essay for this collection, Stevenson also commented that 'the hysteria at the end of this poem is one many of us felt in the fifties and sixties' and indeed hysteria is a prominent motif in post-war women's writing, as mental illness and breakdown are represented as the almost inevitable corollary of subjection to the feminine mystique.[25] The best-known examples are Sylvia Plath's visceral account of breakdown in *The Bell Jar* and Lessing's phenomenological exploration of madness in *The Four-Gated City*, both of which invoke the stifling, obliterating quality of domestic space which the protagonists fear they will never escape. While Plath's Esther Greenwood is 'reconditioned' through psychoanalytic treatment and assimilated to domestic femininity, Martha Quest's tortuous, exhilarating journey into madness in *The Four-Gated City* points to the possibility that so-called 'breakdown' can act as a crucible for change and a re-making of the self, in line with R.D. Laing's arguments in *The Politics of Experience*.[26] As Leanne Bibby suggests in her contribution to this collection, many women writers depict breakdown as the source of insights which, though painful, can have a generative potential and which in many respects pave the way for second-wave feminism. The post-war emphasis on the traditional family generated opposition from within, preparing the ground for the critique of the nuclear family that was central to the work of second-wave feminists such as Juliet Mitchell and Sheila Rowbotham.

Publishing women writers

John Feather views the British publishing industry of the 1950s and 1960s as 'stable, contented and perhaps a little smug'.[27] One example of this conservatism is the Net Book Agreement, which easily survived a challenge from the Registrar of Restrictive Practices in1962.[28] Feather sums up the British reading public after WWII, as seen by publishers, as follows:

> British book readers were predominantly middle class and well educated, which in itself is hardly surprising. More alarming was the fact that over one-third of the population never read books at all, and that, of those who did read, nearly half obtained their books from libraries rather than bookshops.[29]

Although this may offer a rather traditional / conservative picture of the reading public, Feather also suggests that precisely because social changes were beginning to affect the world of publishing publishers began to analyse their markets very closely for the first time; from mid-century onwards they responded to these findings with concerted efforts to promote reading and buying books and cater for changes in British culture and society. Outputs increased: in 1950 the number of new titles exceeded 10,000; by 1960 over 17,000 and by 1970 23,000.[30] Literary censorship in effect gradually disappeared after the acquittal of Penguin books for publishing an unexpurgated edition of *Lady Chatterley's Lover* in 1960. Theatre censorship was finally abolished in 1968. However, as Kerry Myler argues in chapter 6, this liberalisation 'also raised the question of the double standard. For female authors there had to be a careful negotiation of this new territory of representation – their own sex and bodies – not only in terms of what could be written but also what could be written about women *by* women' (p. 109).

The growth of paperback publication created new markets amongst the reading public in the UK. Paperbacks were now not merely cheap reprints of previously published hardback books only intended for those with more modest incomes. Iain Stevenson suggests that the idea that '[h]ardbacks were bought by the better-off middle classes...while paperbacks were bought by the poorer classes', resulting in a 'significant difference in taste and appreciation of quality' is a 'crude and snobbish segmentation [that] was never even partially true'.[31] Specialist book clubs and imprints for genre fiction expanded throughout the 1960s. As Susan Watkins's discussion of the publishing history of science fiction in chapter 15 suggests, magazine publication, as well as frequent reprinting from magazine to anthology and sometimes to paperback, affected conventional ideas about authorship: pseudonymity was a marker of the low status of science fiction and often obscured women's involvement in the genre, as well as being a reflection of their subordinate status *within* that genre.

The interplay between novel forms and novel markets can be seen in the particular cases of some women writers who were at the top of the best seller lists. In 1977 the publisher Paul Hamlyn began publication of republished titles from the Heinemann and Secker and Warburg backlist in what have since become known as 'omnibus' editions. Each 1000-page hardback book contained four or five of an author's novels and was sold for a reasonable price of £3.95. The print run was 50,000 and the books were sold in W. H. Smith and via Octopus agents. The deliberate mix of titles is noteworthy: from 'literary' authors to best sellers. For example, five of Georgette Heyer's novels: *These Old Shades, Sprig Muslin, Sylvester, The Corinthian,* and *The Convenient Marriage* were packaged and sold in this way in a series which also included authors such as Evelyn Waugh, F. Scott Fitzgerald, H.G Wells, Ernest Hemingway, Graham Greene, C.S. Forester and Raymond Chandler. The reprinting of the Regency romances of Heyer (as Diana Wallace argues in chapter 14 this was a genre Heyer could be said to have invented) alongside Chandler's hardboiled detective fiction, the naval warfare novels of Forester and what were to become classics of American and British literature suggests the loosening of hierarchies of genre. The series sold almost four million copies and made a profit of over £2 million.[32] New readers lapped up this new format.

The situation for women working in publishing was also changing to some extent. Although Iain Stevenson argues that '[t]he tendency of some trade publishers to "employ" young women of high social status (and possessing trust funds) as "interns" for little or no salary still persists today', subsequently he suggests that these ' "Samanthas" (as I have heard them called)' were gradually replaced by women who expected 'proper jobs and prospects' and 'transformed the way publishing was done'.[33] In *Stet*, her 2000 memoir of her fifty years in publishing from 1948 onwards, Diana Athill explains her reluctance to question institutional sexism and poor pay as follows: 'it was *only* the mixed vanity and lack of confidence of the brainwashed female which held me there in acceptance of something which I knew to be unjust and which other women, whom I admired, were beginning actively to confront'.[34] The founding of Virago in 1973 can rightly be seen to mark the point when this confrontation becomes explicit.

Global connections

Contrary to views of this period as one of warm beer and nostalgic affection for little England, the majority of the writers discussed here are committed international thinkers, whether they are invested in re-constructing and rethinking what it means to be European after the Holocaust, negotiating a new relationship with the US and the USSR as the Cold War emerges, questioning ideas of 'internal empire' within the UK, or forging a culture that includes the contradictions of women migrants' lives. Some of the changes within the publishing industry discussed earlier were important in facilitating what we term the proto cosmopolitanism of writing at this time. The rise of 'educational' publishing of paperbacks in the rapidly decolonising countries that became part of the Commonwealth was motivated, as Gail Low has shown, by a mixture of commercial and philanthropic considerations. She argues that '[o]ver the succeeding two post-war decades, colonial territories became the site where education fuelled the publishing boom and was pursued by commerce in the name of a new modernity'.[35] Companies like Oxford University Press and Heinemann established subsidiaries that initially acted as distributors of British textbooks, then printed local editions of existing books and finally commissioned local new writers. Series like Heinemann Educational Publishing's African Writers Series moved between 'literary' and 'educational' publishing and were extremely successful, although Low has argued that there was a danger that the series 'became synonymous' with African writing, with writers second-guessing what would 'fit' within its remit.[36] As Sandra Courtman argues in chapter 11, the only woman writer whose writing was first published (rather than reprinted) in the AWS in the 1960s and 1970s was Flora Nwapa; the dominance of male writers in the series makes clear that it is important, as Low argues, to ask 'who produced African writing, for whom and on what terms'.[37]

For Courtman, the 'gender bias and patriarchal gate-keeping' (p. 198) of the series tended to marginalise important writers of the period.

The medium of radio also provided a home for writing from the Caribbean in the BBC's *Caribbean Voices* programme, broadcast from 1943-58; however, Caribbean *women's* writing was severely under-represented. Originated by the Jamaican poet and broadcaster Una Marson, in the late 1940s and 1950s Gladys Lindo, the BBC agent in Trinidad, acted as editor and selected material for broadcast in London. Low argues that 'out of nearly four-hundred contributors to the series they [women] comprised a little less than twenty percent'[38] and that Lindo chose according to her editor, Henry Swanzy's likes and dislikes (the latter including 'sweetly pretty poems by...spinster ladies'.[39] Courtman's chapter makes clear how important writers like Beryl Gilroy, Louise Bennett and Buchi Emecheta worked and wrote outside the male-dominated networks of affiliation created by ventures such as the African Writers series and Caribbean Voices.

Relationships between the UK, Europe, the USA and the USSR were also changing in this period, as the effects of WWII were gradually replaced by the emerging Cold War. What Elizabeth Maslen, in this volume, refers to as 'the loss of a shared moral perspective' (p. 213) haunts writers like Muriel Spark, Doris Lessing, Naomi Mitchison and Storm Jameson, who saw Europe's place in the wider world changing fundamentally as the second half of the twentieth century unfolded. Writers like Spark and Jameson investigate what became known as the Holocaust in novels including Spark's *The Mandelbaum Gate* (1965), in which the central female character briefly attends the 1961 trial of Adolph Eichmann. Hannah Arendt's thesis about the 'banality of evil'[40] is in this text almost embodied in the *apparently* incidental appearance and treatment of the trial transcripts in the novel, which generate what Vice refers to in chapter 9 as a 'self-justifying rhetorical form' (p. 166). Yet the connections between the protagonist, Barbara Vaughan's self-questioning about her religion, 'ethnicity' and culture, the situation in a divided Jerusalem in 1961 and the legacy of the Holocaust gradually become clear as the book progresses.

Storm Jameson's *The Moment of Truth*, published in 1949 and written between October 1947 and February 1948, is similarly concerned with the European dilemma, but set in the near future. All of Europe has been conquered by Russia and a small group of people wait in the north of the UK for the last plane to the USA. Each of these characters has assumed they would be one of the passengers, when instructions arrive ordering others to be transported instead. The question of who gets a seat on the plane results in a dilemma for each individual: leaving for the US would mean waging war against the UK and its people. Staying would mean either submitting to the Russians or trying to create a resistance movement. At this point one of the characters reveals that he is a Communist, and will assist the invading forces. The group has to decide what to do with him. Arguably, the subject of individual ethics and decision-making in the context of atrocity is, in the immediate post-war environment, such a sore spot that it has to be transported into the future. If, here, Jameson projects forward into a Cold War world where the UK is caught between the two ideological 'blocks' of the USA and the USSR, the moral dilemmas remain at the level of the individual framed by her particular context.

Jameson was not the only writer to feel the formal effects and pressures on genre and mode caused by the horrific material generated by WWII and its aftermath. In *The Golden Notebook* (1962) Lessing's heroine, Anna Wulf, is living off the proceeds of an early novel, *Frontiers of War*, but struggling with writer's block. She feels unable to write another book because she has lost her belief in the value and purpose of art and literature. In the preface to the 1972 edition of the novel Lessing writes that the reasons for the block are 'linked with the disparity between the overwhelming problems of war, famine, poverty, and the tiny individual who was trying to mirror them'.[41] An awareness of the magnitude of the issues facing humanity is one of the motives for Lessing's turn to science fiction, which enables her to locate these challenges in the context of evolutionary time and cosmic space. Exploiting the estranging possibilities of the genre, Lessing jettisons realist narrative and the conception of the subject it entails, reimagining and extending the boundaries of subjectivity, while Naomi Mitchison's science fiction explores the porous boundaries between humans and other species. In modelling such alternative subjectivities these writers anticipate the concerns of twenty-first century posthumanism, which similarly calls in question both the humanist conception of the subject and human exceptionalism.

The period covered by this volume was one of major transitions as Britain moved from post-war exhaustion to affluence and an opening up of wider opportunities across social classes, while simultaneously negotiating the pressures of decolonisation and a new world order. It was a period shadowed by revelations about the scale of the Holocaust and haunted by the threat of nuclear catastrophe but it was also one energised by rapidly developing technologies, including information and space technologies. In many respects, it was a period in which modernity was rebooted and intensified, supported by communications networks which enabled the movement of economic and social capital across the developed world. There has recently been a surge of interest in the cultural transformations impelled by these changes and post-war literature is emerging as a vibrant critical field: this volume is intended as a contribution to this debate. There is still some way to go in relation to the representation of female authors in literary history and we hope that the essays in this collection will draw attention to the richness and diversity of women's writing as it participates in post-war cultural reconstruction.

The structure of the volume

The volume is divided into four main sections: 'Part One: Changing Forms'; 'Part Two: Reconstructing Gender'; 'Part Three: Global Politics'; 'Part Four: Expanding Genres'. The first section, 'Changing Forms', considers the importance of women writers' interventions in relation to the politics of form. The four chapters in this section cover fiction, poetry, drama and journalism, each considering the tensions between different modes of writing. Mitchell (chapter1) explores the dichotomy between realism and experimentalism in fiction, arguing that this narrowly formalist opposition fails to do justice to the complexity of women's writing in this period. Dowson (chapter 2) charts women poets' struggles with gendered poetic conventions and reveals the subtle ways in which they contested and subverted the forms available to them. Griffin (chapter 3) reads women writers' well-made plays for their political subtexts and posits a link between the political transitions of the period and the subsequent emergence of alternative theatre and experimental performance. Chambers (chapter 4) charts the way journalists created a 'counter public sphere' in which issues especially pertinent to women were presented to a wider audience, opening up a vital channel for feminist debate.

'Reconstructing Gender', the volume's second section, focuses on transformations in attitudes to gender and sexuality in the period. Eagleton (chapter 5) explores the relations between gender and class, noting the tension between the professional ambitions of the 'clever girls' who profited from post-war social mobility and the constraints they experienced when they married and had children. Myler (chapter 6) tracks the impact on women's writing of the lifting of censorship and the advent of the contraceptive pill, tracing the complex interplay between the politics of sex and the politics of representation in female-authored texts which address sex, desire and reproduction. Meanwhile Bibby (chapter 7) argues that second-wave feminism and literature were closely interconnected as writing became a form of feminist activism, creating imaginative spaces for an increasingly radical re-thinking of patriarchy and of the female subject position.

Part Three, 'Global Politics', consists of five chapters which all examine, in different ways, women writers' engagement with global politics. In chapter 8, Bluemel explores what she characterises as 'the ambiguous intimacy of peacetime to wartime' (p. 142), theorising a post-war women's literary tradition that negotiates between war and peace, the public and the private, the imperial past and the postcolonial future. Stressing the way in which this writing crosses thematic and formal boundaries she positions it as post-war intermodernism. Vice (chapter 9) opens up the question of women writers' response to the Holocaust at a time when the term itself was not widely used; nonetheless, she finds evidence of the earliest developments of Holocaust consciousness in the work of writers who witnessed war-crimes trials or who were themselves refugees. In chapter 10, Gramich explores the analogy between the internal colonies (Northern Ireland, Wales and Scotland) and the overseas empire, assessing the impact of economic decline and changing social structures on women writers of the so-called 'Celtic fringe'. Courtman (chapter 11) focuses on women writers who were born elsewhere but whose writing had a transformative impact on British literature and culture as they negotiated the discourses of patriarchy and empire, shaping new forms to accommodate complex cultural transitions. Maslen (chapter 12) takes Storm Jameson and Doris Lessing as exemplary figures who register the profound and long-lasting effect of two world wars, the rise of Fascism in the inter-war period, the bombing of Hiroshima and Nagasaki and the scale of the Holocaust. Positioning their work as both 'witness literature' and 'tragic realism', she stresses both the depth of its engagement with twentieth century history and its continuing relevance.

The final section, 'Expanding Genres' focuses on the importance of women's work in popular forms. Lassner (chapter 13) draws attention to the significance of spy thrillers written by women which articulate anxieties about political and social change in the Cold War while subverting the gendered conventions of the genre. Wallace (chapter 14) examines the richness of historical fiction which moves between the categories of Modernism, realism and the middlebrow as it probes social and historical constructions of gender, race and sexuality. In chapter 15, Butler explores the ways in which class and gender norms are inscribed and contested in children's literature, noting too the broadening of the subject matter which became available to children in this period. Finally, Watkins (chapter 16) assesses the distinctive contribution of women's science fiction, which offers critiques of sex/gender norms and at the same time questions the orthodoxies of the post-war scientific thought.

Notes

1. Carolyn Steedman, *Landscape for a Good Woman: A Story of Two Lives* (London: Virago, 1986), p. 122.
2. Angela Carter, 'Notes from the Front Line' in *The Collected Angela Carter, Shaking a Leg: Journalism and Writings,* ed. by J. Uglow (London: Chatto & Windus, 1997), pp. 37–38.
3. Elizabeth Wilson, *Only Halfway to Paradise: Women in Postwar Britain: 1945–1968* (London: Tavistock Publications Ltd, 1980), p. 2.
4. D. Mao and R. L. Walkowitz, 'The New Modernist Studies', *PMLA* 123: 3 (2008), 737–748. As they point out, the remit of such criticism has been extended temporally (modernism is construed as encompassing the period from the mid-C19th to the 1950s and 1960s), spatially (it is conceptualized in what Susan Stanford Friedman calls 'planetary' terms) and vertically (modernism now encompasses high and low cultural forms). See Susan Stanford Friedman, 'Planetarity: Musing Modernist Studies', *Modernism/Modernity* 17:3 (2010), 471–499.

5. Virginia Woolf, *The Death of the Moth, and Other Essays* (London: Hogarth Press, 1942), p. 115.
6. Nicola Humble, *The Feminine Middlebrow Novel, 1920s to 1950s: Class, Domesticity and Bohemianism* (Oxford: Oxford University Press, 2001), p.3.
7. *Middlebrow Literary Cultures: the Battle of the Brows,* ed. by Erica Brown and Mary Grover (Basingstoke: Palgrave Macmillan, 2011), p.1.
8. *Intermodernism: Literary Culture in Mid-Twentieth-Century Britain* ed. by Kristin Bluemel (Edinburgh: Edinburgh University Press, 2009), p. 5.
9. *British Fiction after Modernism: the Novel at Mid-Century* ed. by Marina Mackay and Lyndsey Stonebridge (Basingstoke: Palgrave Macmillan, 2007), p.6.
10. Maroula Joannou, *Women's Writing, Englishness and National and Cultural Identity: the Mobile Woman and the Migrant Voice, 1938-1962* (Basingstoke: Palgrave Macmillan, 2012), p. 2.
11. Phyllis Lassner, *British Women Writers of World War II: Battlegrounds of their Own* (Basingstoke: Palgrave Macmillan, 1998), p. 2.
12. Deborah Philips and Ian Haywood, *Brave New Causes: Women in British Postwar Fictions* (London: Leicester University Press, 1998), p. 21.
13. Deborah Philips, *Women's Fiction 1945 – 2005* (London: Continuum, 2006), p. 1.
14. David Lodge, 'Rereading *Memento Mori* by Muriel Spark', *Guardian,* 5 June 2010, <http://www.theguardian.com/books/2010/jun/05/memento-mori-muriel-spark-novel, > [accessed 10 January 2015]
15. Linda Hutcheon, *The Politics of Postmodernism* [1989] (London: Routledge, 2002) p.31. 'The Loves of Lady Purple' was published in Angela Carter, *Fireworks: Nine Profane Pieces* (London: Quartet Books, 1974)
16. For a detailed discussion of this topic see Molly Hite, *The Other Side of the Story: Structures and Strategies of Contemporary Feminist Narratives* (Ithaca, NY: Cornell University Press, 1992)
17. See Bernard Bergonzi, *The Situation of the Novel* [1970] (London: Macmillan, 1979) and Dominic Head, *The Cambridge Introduction to Modern British Fiction, 1950 – 2000* (Cambridge: Cambridge University Press, 2002)
18. Patricia Waugh, *Feminine Fictions: Revisiting the Postmodern* (London: Routledge, 1989), p. 10.
19. Doris Lessing, 'Preface' to *The Golden Notebook* [1962] (London: Granada, 1972), pp. 13–14.
20. Wilson, *Only Halfway to Paradise,* p. 41.
21. Wilson, *Only Halfway to Paradise,* pp. 48–49.
22. Doris Lessing, *Collected Stories Volume One: To Room Nineteen* [1978] (London: Triad Panther, 1979), p. 346.
23. Correspondent quoted in Wilson, *Only Halfway to Paradise,* p. 47.
24. See Betty Friedan, Chapter 1 'The Problem That Has No Name' in *The Feminine Mystique* [1963] (London: Penguin Modern Classics, 2010).
25. Anne Stevenson, 'Writing as a Woman' in *Women Writing and Writing About Women* ed. by Mary Jacobus (London: Croom Helm, 1979), p. 172, p. 177.
26. See R. D. Laing, *The Politics of Experience and the Bird of Paradise* (London: Penguin, 1967) which argues that psychosis is analogous to a voyage of discovery.
27. John Feather, *A History of British Publishing,* 2nd edition (London: Routledge, 2005), p. 199.
28. The Net Book Agreement regulated the retail price at which books could be sold to the public so that booksellers were obliged to sell books at the prices specified by the publishers.

29. Feather, *A History of British Publishing*, p. 198.
30. Feather, *A History of British Publishing*, p. 199.
31. Iain Stevenson, *Book Makers: British Publishing in the Twentieth Century* (London: The British Library, 2010), p. 155.
32. Stevenson, *Book Makers*, p. 220.
33. Stevenson, *Book Makers*, pp. 199–200.
34. Diana Athill, *Stet* (London: Granta, 2000), p. 56.
35. Gail Low, *Publishing the Postcolonial: Anglophone West African and Caribbean Writing in the UK 1948-1968* (London: Routledge, 2012), p. 30.
36. Low, *Publishing the Postcolonial*, p. 92.
37. Low, p. 92.
38. Gail Low, 'Publishing Histories', in *A Concise Companion to Postcolonial Literature*, ed. by S. Chew and D. Richards (Chichester: Wiley-Blackwell, 2010), p. 214.
39. Gail Low, '"Finding the Centre?" Publishing Commonwealth Writing in London: The Case of Anglophone Caribbean Writing 1950-65', *Journal of Commonwealth Literature*, 37:2 (2002), pp. 21–38 (p. 31).
40. Hannah Arendt, *Eichmann in Jerusalem: A Report on the Banality of Evil* (London: Faber and Faber, 1963).
41. Doris Lessing, Preface to *The Golden Notebook* , pp. 7–21 (p. 12).

Part I
Changing Forms

1
Post-War Fiction: Realism and Experimentalism

Kaye Mitchell

Introduction: the realism vs experimentalism debates

In the second half of the twentieth century, debates about literary style frequently came back to what was represented as a central tension – either animating or stultifying, depending on your perspective – between realism and experimentalism. One argument of this chapter is that an attention to the richness and diversity of women's writing in this period might complicate – and thus render more sophisticated and nuanced – our understanding of the meanings and functions of 'realism' and 'experimentalism', thereby challenging one particular, entrenched version of twentieth-century literary history. The mid-century sees the publication of the later novels of Ivy Compton-Burnett (1884–1969), an author who might be read as 'reactionary', part of what Rubin Rabinovitz describes as 'a general Victorian revival' in the post-war period,[1] and yet who – in works such as *Manservant and Maidservant* (1947) – uses her brittle, acerbic dialogue to expose and lampoon domestic tyranny, thus '[defamiliarizing] what appears to be natural'.[2]

At the other end of the span of time covered in this collection, and seemingly at the other end of the realism/experimentalism spectrum, Angela Carter (1940–1992) publishes her early fiction, and in novels such as *The Magic Toyshop* (1967) and *The Infernal Desire Machines of Doctor Hoffman* (1972) displays the growing preoccupations with fantasy, fairy tale and theatricality (puppet theatres, circuses, utopian and dystopian worlds) and with the demythologisation of gender that would come to characterise her later work and pave the way for a distinctly feminist brand of postmodernism; yet Carter's work too, precisely because of its politics, might be read as '[rooted] in social reality', thus making it 'realist' in the broad sense that Andrzej Gasiorek intends (more on this anon).[3] In the three novels that would come to be known as the 'Bristol trilogy' – *Shadow Dance* (1966), *Several Perceptions*

© The Author(s) 2017
C. Hanson and S. Watkins, *The History of British Women's Writing, 1945–1975*,
History of British Women's Writing, DOI: 10.1057/978-1-137-47736-1_2

(1968) and *Love* (1971) – Carter engages with the political and material realities of the 1960s counterculture (the sexual revolution, beatnik culture, the war in Vietnam) and with the more entrenched historical realities of male violence against women, yet in each case filters these through the fantastic and/or disturbed imaginations of her central characters. Thus the horribly scarred Ghislaine in *Shadow Dance* appears to Morris, in his 'state of guilty fear', as 'a vampire woman, walking the streets on the continual qui vive, [...] and the moment she saw him she would snatch him up and absorb him, threshing, into the chasm in her face';[4] Annabel, in *Love*, is described as being 'like a child who reconstructs the world according to its whims', choosing 'to populate her home with imaginary animals because she preferred them to the drab fauna of reality';[5] in *Several Perceptions*, Joseph's ex-girlfriend becomes, in his distorted, vengeful memory of her, a 'Witch woman. Incubus. Haunter of battlefields after the carnage in the image of a crow. [...] His Madonna of the abattoir.'[6] Contra a more positive vision of post-war welfare provision and urban reconstruction, Carter presents a city of decay and dereliction, populated by the homeless and hopeless, with individual domestic spaces (Lee and Annabel's room in *Love*; the abandoned houses that Morris and Honeybuzzard break into, in *Shadow Dance*) transformed into lurid or nightmarish sites of fear and fantasy. Contra the more optimistic and galvanic qualities of the radical political movements of the 1960s, Carter offers an array of characters who are variously marginal, disoriented, haunted, suicidal and dispossessed. These often macabre visions prefigure the more overtly Gothic and Surrealist influences of Carter's later, more obviously 'experimental', fiction.

In between Compton-Burnett and Carter lie the haunting wartime stories of Elizabeth Bowen, the stark anti-novels of Christine Brooke-Rose, the surreal explorations of inner and outer landscapes of Anna Kavan, the late flowering of Jean Rhys in her subversive rewriting of *Jane Eyre*, *Wide Sargasso Sea* (1966), the claustrophobic, marginal worlds of Ann Quin's fiction, and the penetrating humour of Muriel Spark. The variety and inventiveness of works such as these precludes any easy distinction between, or categorisation as, 'realism' or 'experimentalism'.

Nevertheless, writing in 1969, David Lodge famously proffered the image of the novelist 'standing at a crossroads', compelled to choose between 'the realistic novel' ('the road on which he stands') and 'the two routes that branch off in opposite directions from the crossroads': the 'non-fiction novel' and 'fabulation' (a term taken from Robert Scholes' *The Fabulators*).[7] If Lodge remained relatively optimistic about both a situation of 'cultural pluralism' and the tenacious grip of the realist novel upon the English literary imagination,[8] others of the period were much less so. The over-riding critical vision of the novel of the 1950s (and early 1960s) is of an unadventurous return to realism that distinguishes this period from the modernism that preceded it and the postmodernism that succeeded it. Thus Rabinovitz, writing in 1967, asserts that: 'By the early 1950s the dominant critical attitude had become anti-experimental, and very soon afterwards this attitude also predominated among most English novelists'.[9] In a survey of contemporary novelists – via their reviews of their peers' works and their public statements on the state and purpose of literature – Rabinovitz finds a rejection of modernist techniques of formal experiment and a tendency to '[turn] instead to older novelists for inspiration'.[10] He concludes, pessimistically, that, 'the novelists of the 1950s have not produced fiction which approaches the quality of the novels of the writers whom they have imitated. Nor, for that matter, is their work as good as the fiction of the writers whom they have rejected.'[11] Bernard Bergonzi, just three years later, painted a similarly bleak picture, describing 'the dilemma of the contemporary novelist' as the fact that 'he has inherited a form whose principal characteristic is novelty, or stylistic dynamism, and yet nearly everything possible to be achieved has already been done',[12] and identifying a kind of stylistic stagnation in the mid-century.

This debate about style, then, was also an argument about quality and about the future of British fiction, with the likes of Rabinovitz and Bergonzi claiming that British fiction was, in the 1950s and 1960s, backward-looking and parochial, arrested, in its refusal of experiment; and authors such as C. P. Snow and Kingsley Amis arguing, in contrast, that 'experimental' fiction was exhausted, amounting to little more than (in Amis's oft-quoted phrase) 'obtruded oddity'.[13] More recent perspectives, however, have tended to critique the narrowly formalist representation of realism and experimentalism as dichotomous that emerges in the 1960s and 1970s. Indeed, in a recent reassessment of 'mid-century fiction', Marina MacKay and Lyndsey Stonebridge suggest that this false dichotomy has ramifications for the reception and critical legacy of authors of this period:

> Thinking about mid-century fiction precisely *as* mid-century fiction is also an attempt to get beyond the formalist distinction between experimental and realist fiction that has dominated accounts of this period and which has also, and not always merely incidentally, stamped many mid-century writers as irretrievably and disastrously minor.[14]

One of the first works to unpick the distinction is Gasiorek's *Post-War British Fiction: Realism and After* (1995), in which he works towards a view of realism as 'flexible, wide-ranging, unstable, historically variable, and radically open-ended' and asserts that, 'part of my undertaking in this book has been to dispute that a clear-cut realism/experimentalism divide has much validity in the post-war period.'[15] Significantly, Gasiorek's understanding of realism is 'historical' rather than 'formalist', as it constitutes, for him, 'a general cognitive stance *vis-à-vis* the world' rather than 'a set of textual characteristics', and might express itself via different narrative forms in different eras.[16] What he evolves, then, is a broader understanding of 'realist fiction' as offering 'representations that are plausible by virtue of their rootedness in social reality' and 'a general orientation to an external world that it attempts to represent'.[17] These ideas of 'rootedness in social reality' and 'orientation to [the] external world' might offer different entry points into thinking about the work of women writers in the period 1945–1975. They might also help to trouble the polarisation of the critical debate around experiment, for in the works that form the basis of my discussion a 'realist' style is frequently disrupted by forays into fantasy, extended elaborations of interiority, instances of abrupt self-reflexivity, or forms of symbolism which render the familiar as uncanny or unsettling in some manner; in turn, the work of some of the more 'experimental' writers that I will be considering can still be read as rooted in, and commenting on, 'social reality'.

And yet, the critical discussions of realism versus experimentalism in the 1960s and early 1970s were conducted almost entirely through readings of work by male authors. While Iris Murdoch and Muriel Spark receive an occasional – though often dismissive – mention,[18] it is male novelists and critics whose voices dominate the debate and whose work is taken as representative of the state of English fiction as a whole (Rabinovitz's 'survey' of the field of 1950s fiction, for example, offers three extended case studies – of Kingsley Amis, C.P. Snow and Angus Wilson – as the basis for sweeping claims about the wider literary scene). The realism vs. experimentalism debate, then, remains a largely masculinist discourse of stagnation vs. progress, or integrity vs. 'oddity' (depending on your viewpoint), and while the wider politics of realism and experimentalism are frequently debated – the question of how ideologically conservative or radical these aesthetic choices on the part of novelists might be[19] – the specific gender politics are rarely considered.

In what follows I hope to redress this balance somewhat. In addition, while accepting Rita Felski's assertion that, 'it is impossible to make a convincing case for the claim that there is anything inherently feminine or feminist in experimental writing as such',[20] I will consider the broader gender politics of experiment, and the particular uses (and different degrees) of literary experimentalism by women writers in this period.

Realism, domesticity and gender: Elizabeth Taylor

While Amis's comment on the 'obtruded oddity' of literary experiment was unnecessarily reductive, he did make the crucial point that 'experiment' is often too narrowly construed as *formal experiment*, while 'adventurousness in subject matter or attitude or tone' is not viewed as experimental.[21] Christine Brooke-Rose, despite representing quite a different standpoint vis-à-vis experiment, nevertheless makes a not dissimilar point when she claims that, '"experiment" is often regarded as "merely" formal, tinkering with technique ..., tinkering with the signifier irrespective of the signified'.[22] In this section, I offer brief readings of two novels by Elizabeth Taylor (1912–1975), an author who produced superficially 'realist' fiction, often with a domestic focus, but whose texts might be read as more 'experimental' than they first appear, precisely because of their subversive dissection of the symbolism and power dynamics of domestic spaces and domestic relations. Taylor, in the words of a 2007 profile in *The Atlantic*, is 'best known for not being better known';[23] an English author who produced a steady output of novels and short stories between 1945 and 1976 (the posthumous *Blaming*). She has suffered both from sharing her name with a more famous public figure (the film *National Velvet* was released in 1944, one year before the novelist Taylor's first novel was published), and from a rather dismissive critical reception which has tended to treat her – and contemporaries such as Rosamond Lehmann, Elizabeth Bowen and Barbara Pym – as definitively middlebrow writers, with a focus on domesticity, marriage and the lives of middle-class women.

In Taylor's *At Mrs Lippincote's* (1945), a borrowed house in wartime provides the backdrop to the slow decline of an unsatisfactory marriage between Roddy and Julia. At the novel's close, following the revelation of Roddy's infidelity, Julia exclaims: "Here we are then! ... Husband and wife, alone together. On either side of – not our hearth but a borrowed one."[24] Throughout, the unfamiliarity of the house serves as an expression of Julia's own sense of unease with the role of dutiful officer's wife allotted to her. Early on, she sits in the garden watching the light fading and 'the house standing forward in a more solid and menacing outline', and thinks:

It was safe enough sitting out here in the garden, nothing could harm her, but in the house, with the light beginning to fail, there was always the fear not of the room in which she sat but of the other rooms where she could not be and which, once it was dark, she could scarcely bring herself to visit.[25]

This failure to feel at home is more profound than a dissatisfaction at wartime evacuation and the need to live in someone else's home (a home that is definitely *unheimlich*, haunted as it is by Mrs Lippincote's photographs, memories and, periodically, by her rather wayward and unpredictable daughter). It expresses, rather, an unfocused but pressing desire on Julia's part, a restlessness which seems to her husband simply a 'refusal to accept' what he sees as necessary 'rules', without which 'everything became queer and unsafe'.[26]

For Julia, however, this is expressed more profoundly and positively as a desire for connection, communication, fleeting intimacy: 'To myself, I seem like a little point of darkness with the rest of the world swirling in glittering circles round me. How I *long* to draw some of the brightness to me!' And yet, 'other people's lives remain an illusion' and 'what little treasure and brightness you may bring home to yourself ... changes at once to darkness, is absorbed by your own shadow.'[27] In its brief but illuminating forays into

Julia's 'inquisitive', mobile consciousness, *At Mrs Lippincote's* mimics some of its more obviously experimental modernist forebears; meanwhile, Julia's 'struggle with the house', and that house's 'disintegration' imbue the realist representation of domestic space with anxieties about violence, instability and the porousness of the boundary between the private and the public – particularly as far as women are concerned.[28]

This is even more pronounced in *A Wreath of Roses* (1949), a novel that begins and ends with a startlingly violent act, but which explores also the relative tumult of the inner lives of three women: unmarried Camilla, her married friend Liz (now a mother), and Liz's former governess, Frances, in whose house they spend the summer. Again, despite its realist, middlebrow credentials, the novel employs quite dramatic shifts of focalisation to take us into the inner lives of its characters. Frances's interior monologue in particular – relayed through a kind of free indirect narration that approaches stream-of-consciousness style – hints at the fundamental violence underlying the everyday:

> An English sadness like a veil over all I painted, until it became ladylike and nostalgic, governessy, utterly lacking in ferocity, brutality, violence. Whereas in the centre of the earth, in the heart of life, in the core of even everyday things is there not violence, with flames wheeling, turmoil, pain, chaos?[29]

Most strikingly, the novel takes us into the mind of a murderer, a young man with whom Camilla unwittingly becomes involved. In sinister ramblings in his diary, he notes how, 'We are all like icebergs; underneath where the greater parts are hidden it is dark and unreachable. That hidden part is our secret thoughts and our childhood, our dreams and our fears.'[30] Yet if Richard is a fairly predictable locus of disorder and evil in the novel, Frances's inner monologues show that 'turmoil' to be more widespread and more ingrained in the domestic and everyday. It is Camilla's sense of herself as a frustrated spinster – in need of a husband, home and family – which makes her easy prey for Richard's advances, yet the various domestic spaces and relationships in the novel are portrayed ambivalently at best. Early on in the novel, Liz exclaims that, '"Marriage is such a sordid, morbid relationship!"' before expressing her disappointment with her own,[31] while Camilla jokily reads aloud a passage on 'The Solemnity of Wedlock' in a book found at Frances's house, which offers a bleak view of marriage for the bride: '"She looks around, and unless she loves – loves long and deeply and worthily – she sees a blank and dreary void, and her heart aches with a dumb, dull pain ..."'.[32] Later, watching a couple with a child in the park, Camilla muses on their married life together: 'There they were for the rest of their time, separated from one another, but also, because of one another, separated from the world.'[33] The alienation that characterises Richard's particular pathology, then, is found to be more pervasive and entrenched, at the heart of home and family.

In turn, the novel's domestic spaces offer little by way of comfort or respite. Camilla's own childhood home was 'a dark Victorian house' with 'muffled rooms, too many books' and a 'cerebral atmosphere', which she 'accepted ... though I was being choked by it.'[34] Liz feels like a stranger in her marital home, unable to supplant the long-established housekeeper. Frances's house should be a refuge for all three women, but in fact their physical proximity only produces tensions, revealing fissures in their relationships. The plot's denouement occurs in an abandoned cottage, where Camilla and Richard take shelter from the rain, but when Richard says, "Let us pretend we are married to one another and coming to live here in this house", Camilla replies: "It would invite disaster to live in a house like this."[35] And after Richard's confession of murder, she thinks: 'He is like this empty, cobwebbed house ... Room after room is full of echoes, there's nothing there', the abandoned, once-welcoming domestic space now a signifier for a disturbed mind. Behind the idyll of the much-desired marital home, lies only decay and disappointment; behind the everyday, lies something darker and more insidious: 'Parting the leaves to look for treasure, love, adventure, she inadvertently disclosed evil, and recoiled.'[36]

Emergent experimental tendencies: Murdoch, Spark

In a recent overview of the 'British experimental novel', Jennifer Hodgson suggests that the 'emergent experimental tendency' of the mid-century is also evident in 'more "mainstream"' writers like 'Muriel Spark, Doris Lessing, Iris Murdoch, John Fowles and William Golding'.[37] In this section, I consider those 'tendencies' in two crucial 1950s publications: Iris Murdoch's *Under the Net* (1954) and Muriel Spark's *The Comforters* (1957).

In her first novel, *Under the Net* (1954), Murdoch (1919-1999) offers a picaresque tale of the adventures of writer and translator Jake, which yet laces its humorous set pieces with more profound meditations on language, truth and the artistic enterprise. An academic philosopher – she studied and subsequently taught at Oxford University, and published several works of philosophy, notably *The Sovereignty of Good* (1970) – Murdoch brought her concerns with the moral life, attentiveness and philosophical realism into the fictional universes she created.

Throughout *Under the Net*, we find an emphasis on theatricality and artifice – whether this is the film studio facades, representing ancient Rome, which provide a surreal backdrop to a political meeting that turns violent; or Mister Mars, the performing dog inexpertly kidnapped by Jake in a scene that plays out like staged farce; or Anna's strange mime theatre, its performers bearing masks that are 'grotesque and stylized, but with a certain queer beauty'.[38] In this world, the duplicitous surface of things bespeaks the unreliability of a 'reality' that Jake moves through haphazardly, never sure where his escapades will take him next. As he tells the reader at the outset, after learning that he is to be kicked out of his current lodging: 'This was what always happened. I would be at pains to put my universe in order and set it ticking, when suddenly it would burst again into a mess of the same poor pieces'.[39]

If Jake's 'universe' is made up of the relatively banal bits and pieces of harsh reality – his need for a job, income, lodging – then it is also shot through with strong elements of fantasy and imagination (witness, for example, Jake's bus journey towards the end of the novel, which is illuminated by his existential stream-of-consciousness: 'through this shaft of nothings we drive onward with that miraculous vitality that creates our precarious habitations in the past and the future...').[40] The philosophically inflected conversations between Hugo and Jake, which give the novel its title, pivot on Hugo's belief that, "The whole language is a machine for making falsehoods".[41] Indeed, in their discussion of 'what it meant to describe a feeling or state of mind' – a task in which the omniscient realist narrator is all too often engaged – Hugo asserts that, "these things are falsified from the start":[42]

"But suppose I try hard to be accurate," I said.
"One can't be," said Hugo. "The only hope is to avoid saying it. As soon as I start to describe anything, our conversation for instance, and see how absolutely instinctively you ..."
"Touch it up?" I suggested.
"It's deeper than that," said Hugo. "The language just won't let you present it as it really was."[43]

Jake subsequently fictionalises these discussions and publishes them as a novel-in-dialogue entitled *The Silencer*, in which 'Annandine' (the Hugo character) declares that: 'All theorizing is flight. We must be ruled by the situation itself and this is unutterably particular. Indeed it is something to which we can never get close enough, however hard we may try as it were to crawl under the net.'[44]

The integration of these relatively extended discussions tacitly presents them as a commentary on the difficulties (technical, stylistic, ethical, aesthetic) of translating experience into language. While not exactly 'metafictional' in the manner of later, more obviously postmodernist works, *Under the Net*, through its very title, draws attention to the slippages of meaning and communication with which the novelist must contend and to the impossibility of grasping experience in all its ineffability. In later works such as *The Black Prince* (1973), Murdoch would go further in her explorations of language and falsehood, contingency, perspectivism and the 'naturalistic' presentation of character,[45] but even this first novel includes elements of a kind of literary self-consciousness at odds with more traditional realisms. It is unsurprising, therefore, that Dominic Head reads Murdoch's work as a 'bridge' and 'point of continuity' between old (liberal humanist) and new (postmodernist) perspectives in the post-war period and notes 'the importance of contingency to her moral thought'.[46] This endorsement of 'contingency' is most evident in Murdoch's 1961 essay, 'Against Dryness', in which she states the need for 'a renewed sense of the difficulty and complexity of the moral life and opacity of persons', and suggests that, 'through literature we can rediscover a sense of the density of our lives', an understanding that 'reality is not a given whole', and 'a respect for the contingent'.[47] But in Hugo's assertion, in *Under the Net*, that 'nothing consoles and nothing justifies except a story – but that doesn't stop all stories from being lies'[48], we see a prefiguring of the hope expressed in 'On Dryness' that the greatest (most uncompromising) literature can in fact 'arm us against consolation and fantasy'.[49]

If Murdoch provides a 'bridge' between old and new, then her contemporary Muriel Spark (1918-2006) similarly treads a 'third path' between those false oppositions of realism and experimentalism, combining 'a self-reflexive focus on novelistic technique, including modes of metafictional play, with a probing investigation of the moral, psychological, and institutional dimensions of human conduct'.[50] The acerbically witty Scottish novelist and Catholic convert, best known for *The Prime of Miss Jean Brodie* (1961), but who also produced, in the course of her lifetime, short stories, poems, plays, and studies of Mary Shelley and John Masefield, is, in Marina MacKay's evocative summation, 'an amphibious figure'.[51] This is perhaps particularly the case in her first novel, *The Comforters* (1957), in which the more or less realist narrative is interrupted in its plot when one of the protagonists, Caroline, starts hearing the tapping of a typewriter and voices apparently commenting on the action and/or repeating her own thoughts:

> Just then she heard the sound of a typewriter. It seemed to come through the wall on her left. It stopped, and was immediately followed by a voice remarking her own thoughts. It said: *On the whole she did not think there would be any difficulty with Helena.*[52]

And as Caroline falls asleep she hears the words: 'At this point in the narrative, it might be as well to state that the characters in this novel are all fictitious, and do not refer to any living persons whatsoever.'[53] As she explains to her priest:

> I think it is one person. It uses a typewriter. It uses the past tense. It's exactly as if someone were watching me closely, able to read my thoughts; it's as if the person was waiting to pounce on some insignificant thought or action, in order to make it signify in a strange distorted way.[54]

Tellingly, Caroline is writing a book entitled '*Form in the Modern Novel*', but confesses that she is 'having difficulty with the chapter on realism'.[55]

The Comforters enacts this 'difficulty', as Caroline, realising that she is a character in a novel, sets out to frustrate her author's manipulative designs. While 'The Typing Ghost' forms only one strand of the story here,[56] the novel evinces a general anxiety about the status and worth of fiction, with the mystery surrounding her boyfriend Laurence's grandmother described as an 'artificial plot' by Caroline (who aims to 'spoil it' and 'hold up the action of the novel'), poets referred to in passing as 'professional liars', the nasty Mrs Hogg described as 'not a real-life-character, … only a gargoyle', and Caroline herself ultimately accused of literary misrepresentation by 'the character called Laurence Manders'.[57] Although these metafictional meditations are presented with typical Sparkian levity,[58] they can also be read as commentary on the novel's wider questions of faith (Caroline, like her author, is a recent Catholic convert), dogma, deception and submission to authority – whether that authority is an omniscient novelist or an omniscient God;[59] tellingly, the least sympathetic character here, Mrs Hogg, routinely described as monstrous and evil, is roundly deplored for 'her fanatical moral intrusiveness, so near to an utterly primitive mania', and we are told that, 'Georgina's lust for converts to the Faith was terrifying, for by the Faith she meant herself'.[60] If 'realistic novels' are, in Spark's own judgment, 'more committed to dogmatic and absolute truth than most other varieties of fiction',[61] then *The Comforters* appears to deploy its elements of *non-realism* as an attempt to undercut any impression of dogmatism or absolutism.

Both *Under the Net* and *The Comforters* might be thought of as 'problematic novels' in Lodge's sense: while generally adhering to the 'reality principle', they nevertheless offer more self-reflexive meditations on fictionality, the manipulations of authorship, and the workings of authority, thus 'making the reader *participate* in the aesthetic and philosophical problems the writing of fiction presents, by embodying them directly in the narrative'.[62]

Radical influences: Brooke-Rose, Quin

Rabinovitz notes how, 'during the 1950s, when the *nouveau roman* was emerging in France, most English novelists had returned to traditional forms',[63] yet for some women writers in the longer period under consideration here, the *nouveau roman* was a crucial influence. Indeed, Spark suggested that Alain Robbe-Grillet, the French writer and one of the foremost practitioners and theorists of the *nouveau roman* in the mid-century, had 'influenced [her] a good deal', lending her work 'a certain detachment', particularly *The Driver's Seat*, which she described as 'very Robbe-Grillet, except I have more characters.'[64] Nevertheless, and despite the unemotive, coolly objective style of the narrative in which a young woman, Lise, carefully orchestrates her own murder, *The Driver's Seat* remains rooted in a particular social reality, raising 'disturbingly far-reaching questions about the threat of sexual violence against women who seek to assert control over their own lives in the manner advocated in the feminist discourse that was contemporary with Spark's novel', and displaying once again the 'tension between innovation and representation – reflexivity and reportage – in the author's oeuvre'.[65] In this section I will look at two examples of 1960s novels bearing the imprint of radical influences including, but not limited to, the *nouveau roman*: Christine Brooke-Rose's *Out* (1964) and Ann Quin's *Berg* (1964).

In a 1958 essay on Beckett, Brooke-Rose (1923-2012) lauds what she terms 'anti-novels', which can 'turn the form inside out, hold it up, perhaps, to ridicule, and give it a thorough beating, or at least an airing' as ' indispensable to our knowledge of the form.'[66] Brooke-Rose's commitment to '[turning] the form inside out' – often with the kind of humour that 'ridicule' suggests – arguably contributed to her decision to move to France in 1968, where she lived and worked for the rest of her life; as a critic, author and Professor (at the University of Paris-Vincennes), she championed playful, experimental, self-reflexive (and occasionally lipogrammatic) writing, but found herself, in the words of one obituary, 'increasingly invisible in Britain'.[67] In her work – particularly in 1960s works such as *Out* (1964), *Such* (1966) and *Between* (1968) – Brooke-Rose responds to Robbe-Grillet's injunction to novelists, in 'Towards a New Novel' (1956), to produce a new kind of literature that will do away with false symbolism and approach the object-ness of objects head-on, without superfluous 'animistic or domesticating adjectives'.[68]

In *Out* this stripped-back object-ness of objects – evoked via an emphasis on their spatial or geometric arrangement and relation to each other – is especially evident. The narrator becomes, consequently, a point of observation, a position within the geometric arrangement of objects, even an object among other objects, rather than a fully fleshed-out person of depth and psychological verisimilitude (an impression compounded by the use of impersonal descriptions such as 'the left foot', rather than, for example, *his* left foot).[69] A typical passage reads:

> The rectangular frame of the verandah [sic] is itself still held in the rounded frame formed by the line of the eyebrow and the line of the nose, to the left of the nose with the right eye closed; below, there is the invisible but assumed line of the cheek, which becomes visible only with a downward look that blurs the picture.[70]

In the style of Robbe-Grillet, objects are treated equally – not singled out or presented as symbolic or standing for something else, not aestheticised. The description of objects also involves a degree of defamiliarisation, as they are presented as objects in a field of vision, but are not necessarily contextualised or identified according to their function. In addition, throughout the text, there is an obsessive emphasis on looking, with repeated references to the blue eye that squints, but is mobile, and the 'pale fixed eye',[71] but also to microscopes, telescopes, periscopes, and other ocular devices. This placing of the world under a microscope conjures an atmosphere both clinical and affectless – an impression intensified by the preoccupation with physical, biological and medical detail; the surrounding world and its inhabitants are scanned for symptoms and disorders (signs of the obscure but sinister 'malady'), rather than being presented aesthetically or appraisingly. In turn, the prose itself evinces an affectless passivity ('Sexual intercourse takes place on the kitchen chair. It is satisfactory.'),[72] despite the emotive character of the content (the novel's concern with racial prejudice, poverty, illness and disempowerment, for example). That affectless quality of *Out* is partly due to the relative absence of (representation of) interiority or psychological detail; when that detail does occur – for example when the protagonist mentally composes a letter complaining about his treatment, while waiting at the Labour Exchange, the thoughts are mixed up with the external description, often in the same sentence, so that the boundaries between inner and outer world blur:

> The fly has left the mottled floor, frightened, perhaps, by the banging of metal cupboard doors and filing cabinets. The sound in the air, however, is mottled with human voices. It is all the more astonishing in view of the fact that your head gardener seems to be, to all appearances, himself an ex-Ukayan.[73]

The last sentence here ('It is all the more astonishing ...') returns us to the letter, the inner monologue, and to a quite different situation (the protagonist's rude treatment at the hands of Mrs. Mgulu's head gardener) abruptly, without explanation or contextualisation.

Brooke-Rose's formal innovation should not, however, be seen either as obscuring the content of her fiction or of divorcing her texts from 'reality'; she does more than simply 'tinkering with the signifier'. In *Out*, the experimental elements of the text enhance and extend a plot in which a key reversal of racial power relations has occurred, following 'the displacement' and the spreading of a 'malady' that disproportionately affects white people.[74] Here it is white people (the 'Colourless')[75] who are treated as slaves and servants, seen as sickly, poor and disempowered, and who are stereotyped and discriminated against: 'the Ukayans have long had a bad reputation as workers, you know', says one character; and 'you people look so alike you know', announces another.[76] In turn, that prejudice is often denied in familiar ways: 'I mean I'm not one for prejudice in these matters. One of my best friends was a Uessayan of Ukay extraction'.[77] Familiar attitudes and events are inverted, revealing their fundamental absurdity and delivering a political message that both emerges from and critiques reality. Form and content interact, then, in the denaturalization of narrative and of reality.

In the same year that Brooke-Rose published *Out*, Ann Quin published her first novel, *Berg*.[78] A British writer associated with experimental

contemporaries such as B.S. Johnson and Rayner Heppenstall, Quin (1936–
1973) rather fell into obscurity after her death by suicide in 1973; however,
in recent years Dalkey Archive has republished her novels alongside a
biography of the author by Robert Buckeye (*Re: Quin*, 2013), while in 2014
the Cinecity festival in Brighton (Quin's hometown) exhibited a film set
installation for an imaginary screen version of *Berg*, to celebrate the fiftieth
anniversary of its publication.[79]
    As the novel's epigraph tautly informs us: 'a man called Berg, who changed
his name to Greb, came to a seaside town intending to kill his father ...'.[80]
A simultaneously farcical and sinister tale follows, in which Berg's paranoid
imaginings colour and distort his outer reality ('They're waiting, the birds,
outside to tear me to shreds'),[81] as his attempts at parricide become ever
more doomed and pathetic and he fails to achieve self-actualisation as 'a
man of action conquering all.'[82] As Hodgson identifies, *Berg* brings together
a number of competing influences, including the 1960s reinvention of the
Oedipus myth (now 'employed to describe the ways in which the anarchic productivity of unconscious desire is sublimated and regulated'), the
anti-psychiatry movement (centred on the work of R. D. Laing), a now
decaying English seaside town music hall tradition, ideas of carnival and
transgression, and the Theatre of the Absurd.[83] Together, these influences
aid Quin in her attempts 'to convey the artificiality and estrangement of the
conditions of modern life'.[84] That impression of estrangement is achieved
via a narrative that blurs the distinctions between fantasy and reality, irrationality and rationality, past and present, moving in and out of Berg's twisted
consciousness and oscillating between third and second person and a kind
of free indirect narration, in a jumble of images and thoughts that sometimes fails to cohere into sense:

> Time meaningless for you exploring the mysterious regions of mountains,
> lakes, jungles within a blanket territory. I pull my eye through a keyhole,
> on a string the days are declared; thoughts are switchbacks uncontrolled.
>   ... Idea and image juxtapositioned, spinning between myth and
> rationality, the odd years spent at a right angle; if I over-reach, can I be
> sure of reclaiming a movement outside habitual movement?[85]

Quin's later novels (*Three*, 1966; *Passages*, 1969; *Tripticks*, 1972) would continue her project of exploring 'the colonisation of consciousness' by the
discordant voices of an estranging modern culture,[86] while Brooke-Rose's
experimental writing of the 1960s would lay the groundwork for what
would come to be seen as her most difficult novel, *Thru* (1975) – a novel
which, claims Andrew Williamson, 'baffled its contemporary critics and has
continued to baffle for over thirty years'.[87] Brooke-Rose herself admitted
the difficulty of this novel, claiming that 'I want the reader to participate',
that is to engage with the text in a more than superficial or passive way;[88]

but this constantly shifting text, with its unattributed dialogue, use of diagrams and experimental typography, deployment of structuralist narratology, and intense self-reflexivity (it may be taking place in a creative writing class or in a theory class and/or may be the product of such a class) offers few footholds for understanding. For Brian McHale, *Thru* is 'a text of radical ontological hesitation: a paradigmatic postmodern novel',[89] but for women writers of this period, there is arguably no such thing as a 'paradigmatic postmodern novel'. The disparate works of Murdoch, Spark, Kavan, Brooke-Rose, Quin and Carter might all be read as positing quite diverse species of 'ontological hesitation' in their troubling of reality and of the relation of word to world: how to compare the science fictional 'slipstream' landscapes of Kavan's *Ice* (1967) with the vulgar bedsit-land of *Berg*? Or the artful philosophising of *The Black Prince* (1973) with the affectless prose of *Out* or the linguistic ebullience of Brigid Brophy's *In Transit* (1969)? Or the slyly manipulative social comedy of Spark's *The Prime of Miss Jean Brodie* (1961) with the surreal gothic of Carter's *The Magic Toyshop* (1967) – which in turn would constitute a transitional text en route to the more fantastical dystopian visions of *The Infernal Desire Machines of Doctor Hoffman* (1972) and *The Passion of New Eve* (1977)?

Conclusion: the past, present and future of experiment

MacKay and Stonebridge blame the false polarisation of realism and experimentalism for the diminished legacies of certain mid-century 'realists', and Hodgson suggests something similar about the ways in which 'the experimental novel' has been found 'lacking' and '[dismissed] … to the peripheries of literary history.'[90] This dismissal, however, is perhaps particularly the case for women authors. Brooke-Rose famously asserted that:

> It does seem … not only more difficult for a woman *experimental* writer to be accepted than for a woman writer (which corresponds to the male situation of experimental writer vs. writer), but also peculiarly more difficult for a *woman* experimental writer to be accepted than for a *male* experimental writer.[91]

And she notes the tendency for women experimental writers to be marginalised as 'minor' members of a particular movement and/or defined by their relationships with male writers of that movement. Advising women authors 'to slip through all the labels, including that of "woman writer"', Brooke-Rose nevertheless concedes that the 'price' of this 'is to belong nowhere'.[92] This refusal to belong might be an advantage, but it can also result in a failure to achieve recognition, as the exclusion of women writers from the twentieth century debates on realism versus experimentalism suggests.

Women experimentalists still face particular challenges – not only marginalisation. Experimental literary practices such as the disavowal of authorial authority, the use of cut-ups or plagiarised material to contest notions of originality, the wholesale incorporation of low-brow or popular cultural material, the rejection of coherence, linearity and rationality, the deployment of explicitly sexual or violent content, the use of vernacular language, deliberate obscurantism, the refusal of craft, or the embracing of out-and-out subjectivism – these are all practices that might be read quite differently in the work of male and female authors, respectively, and more work is needed to think through the finer details of the wider gender politics of experiment.[93] Felski claims 'there exists no necessary relationship between feminism and experimental form', but maintains that '[a]n exploration of avant-garde form can constitute an important part of an oppositional women's culture'.[94] The texts considered in this chapter bear out *both* these points, suggesting that there is a need for a new, more nuanced critical language to talk about women's experimental writing – one that moves on from the French feminism-influenced criticism of Ellen Friedman (reiterated in Friedman and Fuchs' landmark *Breaking the Sequence*), with its assumption that, when women experimentalists '[subvert] the forms of conventional narrative, they subvert the patriarchal structure these forms reflect'.[95] It is possible to contest this too-facile analogy, while also insisting on the value of revisiting and re-evaluating the experimental practices of women authors in the period 1945-1975; this chapter constitutes just one in a growing number of contemporary re-evaluations.

Notes

1. Rubin Rabinovitz, *The Reaction Against Experiment in the English Novel, 1957–1960* (New York: Columbia University Press, 1967), p. 78.
2. Andrzej Gasiorek, *Post-War British Fiction: Realism and After* (London: Edward Arnold, 1995), p. 24.
3. Gasiorek, *Post-War British Fiction*, p. 183.
4. Angela Carter, *Shadow Dance* [1966] (London: Virago, 1994), p. 39.
5. Angela Carter, *Love* [1971] (London: Vintage, 2006), p. 34.
6. Angela Carter, *Several Perceptions* [1968] (London: Virago, 1995), p. 15.
7. David Lodge, 'The Novelist at the Crossroads', *Critical Inquiry*, 11 (1969), 105–32, (p. 118, p. 119).
8. Lodge, 'The Novelist at the Crossroads', p. 117.
9. Rabinovitz, *The Reaction Against Experiment*, p. 37.
10. Rabinovitz, *The Reaction Against Experiment*, p. 2.
11. Rabinovitz, *The Reaction Against Experiment*, p. 168.
12. Bernard Bergonzi, *The Situation of the Novel*, 2nd edition (Basingstoke: Macmillan, 1979).
13. Kingsley Amis, 'Five novels by West Indian and Indian authors' [review], *Spectator*, 200: 565 (2 May 1958), quoted in Rabinovitz, p. 40.
14. Lyndsey Stonebridge and Marina MacKay, 'Introduction: British Fiction After Modernism' in *British Fiction After Modernism: The Novel at Mid-Century*. ed. by Stonebridge and MacKay (Basingstoke: Palgrave, 2007), pp. 1–16 (p. 3).

34   *Kaye Mitchell*

15. Gasiorek, *Post-War British Fiction*, p. 14.
16. Gasiorek, *Post-War British Fiction*, p. 14.
17. Gasiorek, *Post-War British Fiction*, p. 183.
18. Bergonzi, for example, asserts that Iris Murdoch 'is largely lacking in the essential novelistic [gifts] ... of insight, sympathy and true imagination (as opposed to an endlessly ramifying fancy)' (p. 48).
19. See, for example, Catherine Belsey's representation of realist literature as 'a predominantly conservative form' and her suggestion that 'the experience of reading a realist text is ultimately reassuring' – rather than challenging or subversive. Catherine Belsey, *Critical Practice* (London: Methuen, 1980), p. 51. Gasiorek, by contrast, maintains that 'there is no necessary link ... between realism, however it is conceived, and any given political position', (vi).
20. Rita Felski, *Beyond Feminist Aesthetics: Feminist Literature and Social Change* (Cambridge, MA: Harvard University Press, 1989), p. 5.
21. Amis, 'Five novels', p. 565.
22. Christine Brooke-Rose, 'Illiterations' in *Breaking the Sequence* ed. Ellen G. Friedman and Miriam Fuchs (Princeton: Princeton University Press, 1989), pp. 55–71 (p. 64).
23. Benjamin Schwarz, 'The Other Elizabeth Taylor', *The Atlantic*, September 2007. <http://www.theatlantic.com/magazine/archive/2007/09/the-other-elizabeth-taylor/306125/>.
24. Elizabeth Taylor, *At Mrs Lippincote's* [1945] (London: Virago, 2006), pp. 213–14.
25. Taylor, *Lippincote's*, p. 37.
26. Taylor, *Lippincote's*, p. 105.
27. Taylor, *Lippincote's*, p. 110.
28. Taylor, *Lippincote's*, pp. 31, 32.
29. Elizabeth Taylor, *A Wreath of Roses* [1949] (London: Virago, 2011), p. 34.
30. Taylor, *Wreath*, p. 78.
31. Taylor, *Wreath*, p. 10.
32. Taylor, *Wreath*, p. 33.
33. Taylor *Wreath*, p. 127.
34. Taylor, *Wreath*, p. 74.
35. Taylor, *Wreath*, p. 199.
36. Taylor, *Wreath*, p. 204.
37. Jennifer Hodgson, '"Such a Thing as Avant-Garde Has Ceased to Exist": The Hidden Legacies of the British Experimental Novel' in *Twenty-First Century Fiction: What Happens Now*, ed. by Sian Adiseshiah and Rupert Hildyard (Basingstoke: Palgrave, 2013), pp. 15–33 (p. 24).
38. Iris Murdoch, *Under the Net* [1954] (London: Vintage, 2002), p. 40.
39. Murdoch, *Under the Net*, p. 9.
40. Murdoch, *Under the Net*, p. 275.
41. Murdoch, *Under the Net*, p. 68.
42. Murdoch, *Under the Net*, p. 66.
43. Murdoch, *Under the Net*, p. 67.
44. Murdoch, *Under the Net*, p. 91.
45. Note, for example, *The Black Prince*'s inclusion of framing devices such as an 'Editor's Foreword' and four postscripts by 'dramatis personae' which complicate and in some cases contradict the already unreliable (or at least disingenuous) main narrative. Iris Murdoch, *The Black Prince* [1973] (London: Vintage, 1999).
46. Dominic Head, *Modern British Fiction, 1950–2000* (Cambridge: Cambridge University Press, 2002), p. 257.

47. Iris Murdoch, 'Against Dryness', in *The Novel Today* ed. by M. Bradbury [1961] (London: Fontana, 1990), pp. 15–24 (pp. 22–3).
48. Murdoch, *Under the Net*, p. 91.
49. Murdoch, 'Against Dryness', p. 22.
50. David Herman, '"A Salutary Scar": Muriel Spark's Desegregated Art in the Twenty-First Century', *Modern Fiction Studies*, 54:3 (2008), 473–86, (p. 473–4).
51. Marina MacKay, 'Muriel Spark and the Meaning of Treason', *Modern Fiction Studies*, 54:3 (2008), 505–22, (p. 506).
52. Muriel Spark, *The Comforters* [1957] (London: Virago, 2009), pp. 34–5.
53. Spark, *The Comforters*, p. 59.
54. Spark, *The Comforters*, p. 53.
55. Spark, *The Comforters*, pp. 47, 48.
56. Spark, *The Comforters*, p. 146.
57. Spark, *The Comforters*, pp. 93, 113, 126, 186.
58. For example, Caroline's assertion that the voices have gone quiet during her stay in hospital because 'the author doesn't know how to describe a hospital ward', is followed, on the very same page, by a highly serviceable and convincing description of that hospital ward. (Spark, *The Comforters*, p. 147).
59. Patricia Waugh suggests that, 'Acceptance and simultaneous subversion of both her faith and the novel form provide [Spark's] fictional base. They facilitate her satirical treatment of the irrationalities of a world where everyone has forgotten God, through the stylized creation of fictional worlds where absolutely no one, and certainly not the reader, is allowed to', Patricia Waugh, *Metafiction* (London: Methuen, 1984), p. 121.
60. Spark, *Comforters*, pp. 132, 133.
61. Robert Hosmer, 'An Interview with Dame Muriel Spark', *Salmagundi* 146/147 (2005), 127–58, (p. 147).
62. Lodge, 'The Novelist at the Crossroads', p. 123.
63. Rabinovitz, *The Reaction Against Experiment*, p. 2.
64. Hosmer, 'An Interview', p. 135.
65. Herman, '"A Salutary Scar"', pp. 475, 476.
66. Christine Brooke-Rose, 'Samuel Beckett and the Anti-Novel', *London Magazine*, 5:12 (1958), 38–46 (p. 38)
67. Stuart Jeffries, 'Christine Brooke-Rose obituary', *Guardian*, Friday 23 March 2012. <https://www.theguardian.com/books/2012/mar/23/christine-brooke-rose1>.
68. Alain Robbe-Grillet 'Towards a New Novel' in *Snapshots and Towards a New Novel*, trans. by Barbara Wright [1956] (London: Calder and Boyars, 1965), p. 53.
69. Christine Brooke-Rose, *Out* in *The Christine Brooke-Rose Omnibus* [1964] (Manchester: Carcanet, 1965), pp. 7–98 (p. 37).
70. Brooke-Rose, *Out*, p. 29.
71. Brooke-Rose, *Out*, p. 13.
72. Brooke-Rose, *Out*, p. 69.
73. Brooke-Rose, *Out*, p. 44.
74. Brooke-Rose, *Out*, pp. 62, 151.
75. Brooke-Rose, *Out*, p. 44.
76. Brooke-Rose, *Out*, pp. 38, 81.
77. Brooke-Rose, *Out*, p. 39.
78. It was her first published, but not the first she had written. See: <http://annquin.com/?page_id=9> [accessed 3 November 2015].
79. See http://www.cine-city.co.uk/projects/berg/.

80. Ann Quin, *Berg* [1964] (London: Marian Boyars, 2009), prelims.
81. Quin, *Berg*, p. 55.
82. Quin, *Berg*, p. 23.
83. Jennifer Hodgson, 'If You Don't Mind We'll Leave My Mother Out of All This: Liberating Oedipus in *Berg*', from unpublished PhD thesis, Durham University, 2013, unpaginated.
84. Hodgson, 'If You Don't Mind'.
85. Quin, *Berg*, pp. 7–8.
86. Hodgson, 'Avant-Garde', p. 22.
87. Andrew Williamson, '*Invisible Author?* Christine Brooke-Rose's Absent Presence', *Contemporary Women's Writing*, 4:1 (2010), 55–72.
88. David Hayman and Keith Cohen, 'An Interview with Christine Brooke-Rose', *Contemporary Literature*, 17 (1976), 1–23, (p. 8).
89. Brian McHale, 'The Postmodernism(s) of Christine Brooke-Rose' in *Utterly Other Discourse* ed. by Ellen Friedman and Richard Martin (Normal, IL: Dalkey Archive Press, 1995), pp. 192–213 (p. 200).
90. Hodgson, 'Avant-Garde', p. 21.
91. Brooke-Rose, 'Illiterations', p. 65.
92. Brooke-Rose, 'Illiterations', p. 67.
93. For more on this topic, see my article: 'The Gender Politics of Experiment', *Contemporary Women's Writing*, 9:1 (2015), 1–15.
94. Felski, *Beyond Feminist Aesthetics*, p. 31.
95. Ellen Friedman, '"Utterly Other Discourse": The Anticanon of Experimental Women Writers from Dorothy Richardson to Christine Brooke-Rose', *Modern Fiction Studies*, 34:3 (1988), 353–70 (p. 355).

2
Lyric, Narrative and Performance in Poetry

Jane Dowson

Introduction: 'Rid me of this old sound-box'

The lyric was the dominant mode of poetry in this post-war period but was particularly challenging for women due to the critical establishment's scepticism towards eliding 'woman' with 'poet'. We find poets struggling to grasp an individual female subjectivity, to reconcile their identities as writers and wives, mothers or spinsters, and thus to find a personal voice that was authentic. Additionally, literary women defined themselves against the weakest practitioners of the lyric who tended to conservative or trite formalism. The most dynamic poets often eschewed the lyric in favour of a dramatic persona by which to vent their concerns about social injustices or global turbulence. A few daringly fictionalised the first person pronoun to explore female identity. Some poets disrupted the lyric form altogether as a means to disturb and find a place within a male-dominated lyric tradition. This chapter also records the scarce but brave public poems and skilful uses of a narrative voice that warrant more recognition in the annals of this period's literary activity.

In 1949, Meum Stewart explained how *The Distaff Muse: An Anthology of Poetry Written by Women* had originated in a paper called 'Feminine Poetry' that she had planned to read on the radio but was unable to do so due to some 'emotional hitch' in the BBC. She explained further that when 'Various Contributors' had rebelled against naming her anthology *Feminine Poetry*, she realised that they were all of a generation who knew that praise was never given to a woman unless it could be said '"She writes like a man"'.[1] Twenty years later, David Cecil commended Ruth Pitter's verse forms as 'those of the mainstream English poetic tradition' and claimed, 'It would be possible to argue that Ruth Pitter is a man's poet'.[2] In 1975, Margaret Byers regretfully concluded from her survey of British poetry since 1960

© The Author(s) 2017
C. Hanson and S. Watkins, *The History of British Women's Writing, 1945–1975*,
History of British Women's Writing, DOI: 10.1057/978–1–137–47736–1_3

'[Women poets] write without distinctive style – without style at all – and are tolerated as chameleons in whatever adopted skin they sport'.[3] While an indistinct style partly typifies the post-war poetics of gentility,[4] it is crucial to read women's poems in the context of a conservative, obdurate and elite literary academy. As Richard Greene notes regarding Edith Sitwell's (decidedly unfeminine) experimental work, 'even the most sympathetic critics did not know what to make of the fact that a woman was arguably the outstanding English-born poet of her day [the 1950s].'[5] Al Alvarez also acknowledged the existence of 'The London old-boy circuit' of the 1950s and Martin Booth believed that 'old-boy-networking'[6] explained women's absence from anthologies between 1964 and 1984. To illustrate, in 1974, an editor omitted women from an anthology of modern poets 'due to the fact that Britain in the last fifteen years has not produced a woman poet of real stature'.[7]

One path to being published and approved was as an honorary man but critics persisted in essentialising and sidelining women according to the stereotype of a sentimental and formally tame verse. In 'Miss Snooks, Poetess' Stevie Smith parodies the promotion of decorous verse by women '[Who] went on being awfully nice / And took a lot of prizes'.[8] Literary poets were thus caught between demonstrating their prowess in masculine forms and developing a more original but unfeminine poetic voice. Frances Cornford was acutely conscious of the 'awful word poetess', of needing to 'cut the umbilical cord between the poem and the writer[9] and also of the need to achieve a 'more casual tone of voice'.[10] One critic celebrated Anne Ridler's 'very English religious experience firmly located in an English garden',[11] but in 1972 Ridler cried, 'O Muse, who should be heavenly, break / My voice, make me a new one! / Rid me of this old sound-box, / Trap of exhausted echoes / And coffin of past power.'[12] As Ridler intimates, the apparent social and technical conformity that initially rewarded poets was something of a death knell for they were largely excluded from literary histories and overlooked by feminist critics.

The following roll call redresses the oversight and homogenisation of the number of poets 'of stature'. Since publication and recognition were frequently delayed, they are grouped generically rather than by age. H.D. (Hilda Doolittle) (1886–1961), Mina Loy (1882–1966) and Sylvia Townsend Warner (1893–1978) were all technically progressive and although published in their lifetimes, critical acclaim gathered momentum after their deaths. Poets publishing at the end of their lives, Lilian Bowes Lyon (1895–1949), Frances Cornford (1886–1960), Elizabeth Daryush (1887–1977) and Vita Sackville-West (1892–1962), tended to a genteel tone and tight formalism that can obscure their distinct techniques and the complexity of their underlying impulses. With Stevie Smith (1902–71) and Sylvia Plath (1932–63) as the most original voices, poets in the prime of their careers – registered by strong publishing histories – span a broad age range, timespan, and are stylistically individual. They defined themselves against both social and aesthetic feminine moulds while rarely addressing female subjectivity. They include:

Frances Bellerby (1889–1975), Karen Gershon (1923–1993), Phoebe Hesketh (1909–2005), Elizabeth Jennings (1926–2001), Denise Levertov (1923–97), Kathleen Raine (1908–2003), Ruth Pitter (1897–92), Anne Ridler (1912–2001), E. J. Scovell (1907–99), Edith Sitwell (1887–1964) and Sheila Wingfield (1906–1992). Poets starting off tend to be more female-centred and colloquial on a spectrum between the formally cautious and the linguistically innovative. Here we can include Anna Adams (1926–2011), Fleur Adcock (b. 1934), Patricia Beer (1924–99), Anne Beresford (b. 1929), Jeni Couzyn (b. 1942), Maureen Duffy (b. 1933), Ruth Fainlight (b. 1931), Elaine Feinstein (b. 1930), Molly Holden (1927–81), Frances Horowitz (1938–83), Libby Houston (b. 1941), Nicki Jackowska (b. 1942), Einor Jones (b. 1950), Jenny Joseph (b. 1932), Lynette Roberts (1909–95), Carole Rumens (b. 1944), Anne Stevenson (b. 1933) and Rosemary Tonks (b. 1932). Una Marson's (1905–65) *Towards the Stars* (1945), her last published work but the first to be published in London, presented a voice that was distinctly Caribbean and distinctly female. In retrospect, she can be deemed a contributor to the evolution of Black British poetry as a powerful underground movement. Much of the movement's power lay in its performance whereby it built up solidarity within black communities. Marson handed on the baton of female Caribbean poetry to the highly performative Louise Bennett (1919–2006), although Bennett's work was only published through Jamaican presses during this period. In 1945 she studied at London's Royal Academy of Dramatic Art and reached a broad public through her work for the BBC Subsequently, she travelled between America, Jamaica and Britain yet her conscious preference for Jamaican oral dialect idioms gained lasting popularity. Her wit, humour, and dramatic techniques set an example for Guyanese-born Grace Nichols (b. 1950) who arrived in Britain in 1977. Nichols also became popular and influential, combining or switching between oral dialect and standard English, between strategies for performance and for the page.

Major poets, Eavan Boland (b. 1944) and Eiléan Ní Chuilleanáin (b. 1942), emerged in Ireland and while their skilful blending of personal and national histories can be put in productive dialogue with many poets, they would not wish to count as 'British'. However, Boland's reflection, 'I had no clear sense of how my womanhood could connect with my life as a poet',[13] is aired in private or retrospectively by many. According to Betty Friedan, women at this time 'were taught to pity the neurotic unfeminine, unhappy women who wanted to be poets or physicists or presidents.'[14] This chapter outlines the ways in which poets tried to forge an individual yet impersonal poetic method and it finds a cohering aesthetic in their alienation from social prescriptions for women. Whether ventilating public or private concerns they tend to objectify, fictionalise, dramatise, or pluralise the speaking voice. Several poems constitute a specifically female stream of writing about displacement, war, injustice, materialism, love, marriage and motherhood. Into the 1970s, a few evoke the possibility of poetically exploring the nature of 'womanhood' itself while others transgress the parameters of lyric expression altogether.

'Less a / stranger here than anywhere else': women and poetic decorum

The suppression of what Eavan Boland calls 'womanhood' manifests in several poets who, like her, struggled to connect their lives with their writing. Kathleen Raine illustrates what Al Alvarez describes as the predominantly genteel mode: 'academic-administrative verse, polite, knowledgeable, efficient, polished, and, in its quiet way, even intelligent.'[15] A student of Natural Sciences at Girton College, Cambridge, Raine was much admired for her scholarship, evocation of ancient mysteries and precise observations.[16] She published her *Collected Poems* in 1954, won several awards and in 1968 was unsuccessfully proposed for the Chair of Oxford Poetry. She took an avowedly anti-feminist stance and proudly refused to allow her work in anthologies of women's poetry. However, an unpublished essay recounts that when she was fourteen she sublimated her 'womanhood' due to her father blocking a relationship with a man she loved: 'But rightly or wrongly, that was the beginning, for me, of the parting of the ways of the life of the heart and the life of the mind. ... The way of womanhood wrecked by my early but real heartbreak, my life's energies were directed, perforce, into other channels, and the writing of poetry became a simple harmless substitute for life'.[17]

Raine indicates that her poetry avoided the expressive mode as a means of psychic survival. Other women, too, eschewed the personal through adopting conventional subjects and formalism. E. J. Scovell hid her gender through initials and her ordered verse was universally lauded for its timelessness and tonal reticence.[18] Vita Sackville-West's book-length pastoral *The Garden* that 'gives some permanence to ancient ways quickly disappearing',[19] won the Heinemann Prize in 1946, but was far removed from her very unconventional bisexuality and turbulent passions. Ruth Pitter's stoical observations of landscape and people in a jaunty iambic beat thinly gloss her chronic personal suffering: 'It was all so desolating, / Tragic yet Loving: grievous and quite all right.'[20] Positioning herself outside any social norms or poetic tradition, Stevie Smith bravely projected her alienation into an idiosyncratic mix of voices. In the four-lined 'Wretched Woman', the voice that chastises her 'lack of household craft' could be Society, the husband, the housewife herself, and, most potently, all three.[21]

It was the incomers who boldly flexed the conventions of English verse to a natural speaking voice. New Zealand-born Fleur Adcock, who had a 'mobile childhood', being educated in Britain during the Second World War and moving permanently there in 1963, asserts, 'Being an outsider is actually a useful thing for a writer. It sharpens the perceptions',[22] and poses the question, 'are women natural outsiders?'[23] Using Shakespearean 'rhyming iambics' self-consciously,[24] Adcock's witty internal monologues expose social inhibitions, particularly between men and women. Her first collection (1964) was published in New Zealand but the next four (1967, 1971, 1974, 1979) by the prestigious Oxford University Press, indicating the esteem for her careful yet individual poetic measures. The American settlers H.D., Sylvia Plath, her friend Ruth Fainlight and Anne Stevenson – who would be Plath's biographer - brought a 'mid-Atlantic imagination', shimmying between the roles of observer and participant.[25] Stevenson migrated to Britain in 1954 and reflects, 'I was still lost, rootless, countryless, unable to feel my way into or out of the academic setting (Cambridge, Glasgow, Oxford) in which my husband clearly belonged.'[26] In 'England' she strips the country's rural and urban landscapes of romance with the ambivalent sentiments of liminality: 'No one leaves England enamoured, / but England remembered invites an equivocal regret'.[27] Plath's settings, whether rural Devon, Yorkshire or London, are backdrops to exploring her inner torments and her floral symbols bleakly defamiliarise archetypal femininity. In 'Poppies in July', the flowers are 'little hell flames', and she complains, 'And it exhausts me to watch you / Flickering like that, wrinkly and clear red, like the skin of a mouth. // A mouth just bloodied. / Little bloody skirts!' The Bee poems, set in the context of an idyllic English village, consist of unsettling questions, dense metaphors and colour-coding – 'Pillar of white in a blackout of knives' – to express and explore her unfathomable psychic disorientation.[28]

English-born poets who emigrated also found release from the stranglehold of literary conservatism. Following Mina Loy some decades earlier, in 1948 – when English poetry was 'all in the doldrums'[29] – Denise Levertov moved to America where she developed a free and political lyric voice. Like Smith, Plath and Adcock, she made an aesthetic out of her displacement: 'and though I am a citizen of the United States and less a / stranger here than anywhere else, perhaps, / I am Essex-born'.[30] Several poets found inspiration and a confidence through translating the work of other poets, particularly female poets. Frances Cornford produced *Poems from the Russian* (1943) and Elaine Feinstein translated the passionate and adventurous work of Marina Tsvetayeva (1971). Later, Ruth Fainlight brought the Portugese Sophia de Mello Breyner to British readers (1983, 1986). Levertov, Plath, Feinstein, Gershon and Fainlight negotiated a Jewish heritage as well as the English literary tradition. However, Fainlight attributes her conflicted subjectivity to her sex – being eclipsed by the fame of her husband and brother – rather than to her nationality or religion. In a frequently self-deprecating voice she hints at the synchronicity of writing and self-realisation: 'The wound I won't allow to heal – but flaunt, / Preserve, admire, and call it art'.[31]

Public Voices: 'fume-crazy croaking sibyl[s]'

Al Alvarez describes how the principle of gentility – a 'more or less' belief that life is orderly, people polite, emotions and habits decent and controllable and that God is good – collided with two world wars, the threat of nuclear war and new science: 'It is hard to live in an age of psychoanalysis and feel oneself wholly detached from the dominant public savagery.'[32] The challenge of finding an authentic and engaged public voice was particularly acute for women. Edith Sitwell's letters record her strong reactions to the news of nuclear bombings and she was never shy of public performance, but she told Stephen Spender in 1946: 'a woman's problem in writing poetry is different to a man's. That is why I have been such a hell of a time learning to get out of my poetry. There was no one to point the way. I had to learn everything – learn, amongst other things, not to be timid. And that was one of the most difficult things of all.'[33] The poets in this section 'keep themselves out' through multi-vocality, personifications, dense symbolism and collective pronouns, yet the best pieces are more directly informed by the poets' inner terrains. Sylvia Plath famously put holocaust imagery in dialogue with her intensely personal self-explorations in 'Daddy', 'Lady Lazarus', 'Mary's Song' and elsewhere. Profound personal reactions to the trials of Nazi war criminals that divulged harrowing details of Hitler and the Third Reich permeate Stevie Smith's 'The Leader', Ruth Pitter's 'Victory Bonfire' and Anne Ridler's 'Into the Whirlwind'. Ridler's 'Reading the News' merges individual with collective responsibility and establishes an interface between private and public spheres: 'All these years we have watched the statesmen talking, / The hopeful signing letters to *The Times*, / And while we dragged our feet, the road was leading / To famine, torture camps and atom bombs.'[34] In her visionary 'The Flowering of the Rod', H.D. switches between first and third person pronouns and her motifs of a culture's death and resurrection also pertain to her own mental breakdown.[35]

The largely neglected long narrative poems by Sitwell, H.D., Sheila Wingfield and Lynette Roberts are woven with allusions from classical and Christian mythology that stage the 'dominant public savagery' as an epic of the human race. The speakers lament the inhumanity of violence but they also utter visions of universal love, arguably a particularly female orientation. In a letter, Sitwell described the bombing of Hiroshima as '*the most gigantic event since the Crucifixion took place*'[36] and her volume, *The Song of the Cold* (1945) begins with 'Three Poems of the Atomic Age'. In 'The Shadow of Cain', the apocalyptic vision, strident rhythm and impassioned tone attempt to render the enormity of war: 'And everywhere / The great voice of the Sun in sap and bud / Fed from the heart of Being, the panic Power, / The sacred Fury, shouts of Eternity / To the blind eyes, the heat in the wingèd seed, the fire in the blood.'[37] Contemporary readers find such lines overworked, yet they were applauded at the time of publication. In *Gods with Stainless Ears*, Roberts more accessibly blends symbols from the elements, myth and her local landscape in Wales. Written during the war but published in 1951, the sequence has the choral features of *Under Milk Wood* by her friend and fellow poet, Dylan Thomas, coupled with filmic narrative shifts between long shots and close-ups. Wingfield's lesser-known epic, *Beat*

Drum, Beat Heart (1946), consists of four parts like a musical score and drew G. S. Fraser's approval since 'the emotions get expressed indirectly through her grip on the outer world'.[38] Fraser implies that such a grip is unusual for a woman and overlooks how the four parts, 'Men at War', 'Men At Peace', 'Women in Love' and 'Women in Peace', self-evidently explore gendered experience. The title, *Beat Drum, Beat Heart*, marks and distils how war can intensify and awaken fear, love, and a zest for life. In Part Three, one framing voice is that of a querulous yet self-abasing woman poet: 'Bending my ear to catch / The oracle, at the same time it's I, / Fume-crazy croaking sibyl, who predict it.'[39]

Lacking role models, but motivated by strong egalitarian impulses, women spoke of social injustices, usually under cover of the dramatic monologue. True to an atmosphere 'in which all political optimism and idealism seemed childish',[40] Sitwell recorded, 'How strange is the point of view that makes people believe Democracy should flatten people down, instead of pulling people up' and in 'A Song of the Cold' prophetically denounces the cold hearts of the rich, 'the High Priests of the god of this world, the saints of Mammon, / The cult of gold?', and envisions universal kinship: 'Give me your hand to warm me. I am no more alone.'[41] In various dialects, Ruth Pitter's narrative characterisations celebrate the heroic spirit of the vulnerable, such as the deserving Mrs Crow, the 'Old Nelly' poems or the protagonist of a Hardyesque monologue, 'The Stolen Babe'. 'A Father Questioned' is a Blakean dialogue between Innocence and Experience that obliquely links economic with domestic oppression: 'O father, who was the noseless man, and the child / With angel eyes and face all covered with sores? / What was the woman screaming? why did they take her / Away, and where? Had someone hurt her father?' The child also asks why the unemployed are hungry, when the shops are full of food, and why they have to become soldiers and die.[42] Patricia Beer responds to a news report about the wrongful shooting of a deaf 65-year-old Cypriot and in 'Paralytic' even Sylvia Plath directs her pain to the moving internal monologue of a crippled man.[43] 'Susan Miles', the pseudonym for Ursula Roberts (née Wyllie), published a book-length polyphonic social satire *Lettice Delmer* in 1958, but the composition date of this dramatic novel in verse is still unknown.

Technically, Stevie Smith's poems can be hard to periodise, but they express the same egalitarianism as her contemporaries – 'Oh no no, you Angels, I say, / No hierarchies I pray'.[44] As here, a prosaic idiom often transgresses genre boundaries and she often fractures verbal moulds altogether. Initially refused by publishers, Smith published two poetic novels, and her first poetry publications (1937, 1938, 1942) received mixed receptions but her collections during this period (1950, 1957, 1958, 1966, 1971, 1972), a *Selected Poems* in 1962 and her posthumous yet landmark *Collected Poems* in 1975, indicate that her uncompromising individuality and linguistic playfulness gained attention and frequently respect – famously from Philip Larkin.

In the multi-vocal 'Our Bog is Dood', the faux-naïve voice of children destabilises any centre of truth or authority and satirises religious factions: 'Each
one upon each other glared / In pride and misery / For what was dood,
and what their Bog / They never could agree.'[45] Her indifference to poetic
authority mediates her challenges to the misuse of power while she wields
the dramatic monologue to disturb predictable sympathies. In 'Death-bed of
a Financier', the man divulges his mistreatment of resources: 'Deal not with
me as I have dealt on earth', he prays.[46] 'The Death Sentence', in the voice of
a man convicted, was published before the death penalty was abolished in
1965 and 'Angel Boley', based on the 1966 Myra Hindley child murder case,
shockingly scrutinises the psychological processes of the abuser.[47] 'Valuable',
composed after 'reading two paragraphs in a newspaper', confronts the low
self-esteem in girls who 'cheapen' themselves and conceive illegitimate
babies[48] and 'B.B.C. Feature Programme on Prostitution' (published in *Poetry
Review* Winter 1967) poetically responds to a documentary that broadcast
the views of prostitutes, their clients and the clergy. Characteristically, Smith
refuses any fixed moral standpoint but is scathing about cultural aspirations
to wealth: 'So they all admitted money was the thing', to have 'enough
for the telly', 'pink lampshades', 'buying a place of your own and being
respected'.[49] 'Drugs Made Pauline Vague' is a startling dramatization of a
husband and his mistress duping the wife, but in 'Pad, Pad', it is the man
whose heartbreak renders him speechless.[50]

Lyrics of self-exploration: 'the drama of blood, lust and death'

The conscious friction between their writing and their 'womanhood' sparks
the best poets' literary dynamism and they increasingly centred female perspectives and experience. Although Sylvia Plath became a touchstone for the
popular but demeaned term 'confessional', she sought a personal yet representative poetic method, insisting, 'it shouldn't be a kind of shut up box and
mirror-looking, narcissistic experience.'[51] In 1959, after regretting 'the rigid
formal structure' of a new poem, she realised, 'How odd, men don't interest
me at all now, only women and women-talk. Must try poems. DO NOT
SHOW ANY TO TED. I sometimes feel a paralysis come over me: his opinion
is so important to me.'[52] A few weeks later she determined: 'My main thing
now is to start with real things: real emotions, and leave out the baby gods,
the old men of the sea, the thin people, the knights, the moon-mothers,
the mad maudlins, the Lorelei, the hermits, and get into me, Ted, friends,
mother and brother and father and family. The real world. Real situations,
behind which the great gods play the drama of blood, lust and death.'[53]
The 'real emotions' of her bitterness are manufactured into exaggerated
metaphors of animals that plunder and devalue Hughes's poetic purse. 'In
'Daddy' she claims, 'If I've killed one man, I've killed two' and reduces masculine symbolic language to 'your gobbledygoo'.[54] 'The Colossus', also the

title of her first collection (1960), famously stands for both the men in her life and the overbearing weight of the male literary tradition: 'Thirty years now I have laboured / To dredge the silt from your throat' – the anagram of 'slit' marking an unsubtle killer instinct that is sharply unfeminine.[55] In 'The Disquieting Muses' she confronts the unwelcome inheritance of femaleness and in 'Stillborn' displaces harrowing maternal metaphors to symbolise both her writer's block and release from it.[56] She assertively speaks for other women about her injuries in 'Burning the Letters' or 'For a Fatherless Son': 'You will be aware of an absence, presently, / Growing beside you, like a tree'.[57] It was the posthumous *Ariel* (1965) that established her reputation although it is hard to discern between critical esteem for her highly coloured poetics, feminist approval for her provocative treatment of a sex war, and salacious interest in the theatre of her biography due to the tragedy of her suicide.

In 'Writing as a Woman', Anne Stevenson finds in Plath's autobiographical novel *The Bell Jar* (1963) a source for her own self-realisation: 'I've regarded *The Bell Jar* as an honest, often brilliant account of a woman's confrontation with a society many of whose values are an insult to her integrity'.[58] It leads Stevenson to advocate the possibility of reconciling 'woman' and 'poet' if 'our theme is women's survival and self-discovery'.[59] Accordingly, her poem, 'Generations', about her grandmother, mother and herself, exposes 'three degrees of self sacrifice',[60] and 'The Takeover', grapples with the angelic women who 'have locked themselves up in my house', and from whom, like Virginia Woolf before her, she has to break free.[61] 'The Women', written in Yorkshire, 1956, when she was stuck with the wives of her husband's fellow officers, dramatises how their lives consist in waiting for their men to come home and Stevenson comments, 'although I didn't know it I was going through a bell jar experience of my own'.[62] The bell jar symbolises 'a vacuum composed of self-cancelling values', that include middle-class social vacuity, domesticity, the ambition to write, and the will to succeed. Images of nothingness pervade the poem: the tables are 'lifeless' and 'The room is a murmuring shell of nothing at all. / As the fire dies under the dahlias, shifting embers / flake from the silence'. However, 'echoes of ocean curl from the flowered wall' and hint at a life beyond the women's limbic confines. As Stevenson concludes: 'One way out of the dilemma of the woman/writer is to write poems about the dilemma itself.' She also believes that, '"I" is not the foundation for art – you need a craft at the expense of the self.'[63] Following her first collection, *Reversals* (1969), in her sequence, *Correspondences* (1974), she 'learned how to put experience into poetry without "confessing it"', by using the epistolary form, and believed, 'All the anger, the confusion, the misery and the doubt I experienced during the fifties and sixties went into it.'[64] Based on letters she found in archives, the saga of an American family, 'not unlike my own, but not my own', traces the entrapment experienced by women across several generations. The youngest, Kay, a version of the poet, ends up in an asylum and the poem concludes as she beseeches her mother to take her away: 'I'll try, I'll try, really, / I'll try again. The marriage, / The baby. The house. The whole damn bore! // Because for me what the hell else is there? / Mother, what more? What more?'⁶⁵ Stevenson explains, 'Kay's *feelings*, her mixed love and hatred for her child, her sense of imprisonment in her house, her impulse to fly, to escape to drink or to an anonymous city – these feelings *have* been mine. ...The hysteria at the end of this poem is one many of us felt in the fifties and sixties'.⁶⁶

Stevenson's frank revelations resonate through the period as women find in poetry a means to verbalise the missing self-actualization described by Friedan in *The Feminine Mystique* (1963). Frances Cornford depicts home and family life conventionally but her papers reveal a persistent melancholy, debilitating depressions and her fight to write when no profession, 'requires the expense of spirit as domestic life does on a woman'.⁶⁷ Three decades later, Fleur Adcock echoes, 'I find it hard to imagine how anyone, but particularly a woman, can be both a domestic partner and a writer'.⁶⁸ Denise Levertov's 'Folding a Shirt' and 'Poem', written in London, 1946, chillingly anticipate Simone De Beauvoir's polemic indictment of domesticity as, 'holding away death but also refusing life':⁶⁹ 'With folded clothes she folds her fear, / but cannot put desire away, / and cannot make the silence hear'; 'The undertone of all their solitude / is the unceasing question, "Who am I?"'⁷⁰ Ruth Fainlight asks the same question but is unemotional, nonspecific and keeps the reader at bay. This self-containment is reflected in the tight control of form and language, although she crafts by cadence rather than strict metre. In 'Unseemly', the rational logic self-consciously jars with the profound discord it describes: 'I left my race and family / To learn about myself; that / was my explanation. So I became / Unseemly and dishonourable. // I called myself a poet, reasoning / That poets are inhuman'.⁷¹ At one remove from the lyric 'I', 'Disguise' dramatically describes a woman painting her body black and ends: 'But she was painted out, / A ghost, a negative, / Released by this disguise / From everything (yes: / Life, Death, Love, / Him; everything).'⁷² Jenny Joseph, who is less hampered by literary propriety and more freely colloquial, nevertheless decries 'self-expression'.⁷³ She professes wanting to explore the world, not 'the labyrinth of my own mind', and consciously depicts the weather, seasons and daily circumstance because they affect everyone. However, she complains, 'The use of dailiness got me dubbed a "domestic" poet which I not only resent but disagree with'.⁷⁴ She articulates her 'bell jar' clash between personal integrity and polite society in 'An exile in Devon' where she encounters a genteel woman with two fair children but 'Her complete niceness makes me very lonely'. Wishing the woman's facade would crack through some kind of suffering, the poet befriends her own pain: 'I ache for the misery that I fight against'.⁷⁵ Her popular 'Warning' offers a fantasy of uninhibited seniority but also portrays 'the sobriety of my youth' as stiflingly mundane: 'But now we must have clothes that keep us dry / And pay our rent and not swear in the street / And set a good example for the children. / We must have friends to dinner and read the papers.'[76] The regular iambic pentameter of this quatrain mimics the humdrum conformity that jostles with personal choice, mediated through the free verse and uneven lines of other stanzas.

The incompatibility between womanhood and writing is most acutely depicted where poets rupture idealisations of motherhood. Plath's ironic tone and displaced symbols vehemently desentimentalise pregnancy in 'Metaphors' – 'I'm a means, a stage, a cow in calf' – and 'Morning Song': 'The Midwife slapped your footsoles', 'All night your moth-breath / Flickers among the flat pink roses'.[77] Echoing Friedan's discovery of 'the problem that has no name', Stevenson describes how after the birth of her first baby and then twelve years of moving around (1957–1969), 'no doctor could diagnose my ailment ... I was in a state of appalling numbness'.[78] She believes she speaks for thousands of educated women with small babies who followed in the wake of an enterprising husband and underwent the same depressions, sense of failure, and mental collapse if not divorce. While 'The Spirit is too blunt an Instrument' celebrates the baby's intricate form, in 'The Victory' Stevenson refutes Wordsworth's ethereal depiction of new-born innocence with a bluntly visceral account: 'The stains / of your cloud of glory / bled from my veins'. The poem's title and angry tone resentfully predict how maternal love will bleed her dry, a condition more intense and bitter in 'The Suburb'.[79] Jeni Couzyn also marvels at the creation of her child, yet independently concurs: 'When my daughter was born I was forced to die to the idea of myself as poet. My need to write, and the impossibility of writing with a young child, caused me great anguish, as it has so many women before me.'[80] The phrase, 'the skull beneath the skin', in Fainlight's 'A Child Asleep' echoes T. S. Eliot's 'Whispers of Immortality' and also the macabre metaphors of her friend Plath. The mother projects her own sense of inevitable suffering onto her boy: 'I cannot spare him for I am not spared.' It is followed by 'The Screaming Baby' in which 'the cringing woman must adore or kill him' and then by 'Infanticide' in which someone does kill the child.[81] Mediated through third person pronouns, Elaine Feinstein's 'Calliope in a Labour Ward' speaks of all women's self-abandonment in childbirth and motherhood: 'grunting in gas and air / they sail to a / darkness without self'. [82] These lines also exemplify how poetry can rescue women from the abyss by talking about it.

In editing an anthology of love poems by women in the 1960s, Jeni Couzyn was struck by the recurrence of pain and loss, observing, 'Marriage is the contract by which women poets sign away their right to work'.[83] In 'The Ache of Marriage', Denise Levertov avers, 'We look for communion / and are turned away', [84] and in Stevenson's witty but cynical 'The Marriage' the awkwardness of fitting bodies together is a metaphor for a couple's psychological and emotional mismatch: 'All would be well / if only / they could face each other'. Disillusion informs 'The Affair' and 'The Demolition' in which the extended metaphor of a house signifies complete breakdown: 'They have taken to patching the floor / while the roof tears'.[85] Joseph's 'Women at Streatham Hill' reveals how women repress their desires and the narrative lyric, 'Dawn Walkers', cinematically presents a cityscape in which girls leave 'beds where love went wrong or died or turned away', then sympathetically zooms in on one woman who chases her runaway man in vain.[86] Through internal monologues that combine self-expression with observation, Fleur Adcock adeptly presents how a couple's apparent civility masks anxieties and power dynamics about love and sex. In 'Knife-Play' the speaking female admits her hurt at the man's contempt but refuses to capitulate to it. The female is the agent in 'Advice to a Discarded Lover' and scorns the rejected man's 'self-pity'. While the short 'Lament' captures mutuality, 'Folie à Deux' and 'Kilpeck' are comi-tragic dramas of couples acting out social rituals that evade the realms of feeling and the 'sweet obvious act' of sex.

Conclusion: 'What the hell else is there?'

Referring miserably to 'The marriage, / The baby. The house.', Anne Stevenson's fictional Kay cries 'what the hell else is there?' In a climate of polarised and confused constructions of what 'woman' means apart from her feminine roles, the poets discussed in the previous section stand out for consciously negotiating and tackling the vexed equation between their sex and their writing. They rarely, however, own or articulate a distinctly female subjectivity. Jenny Joseph uses the speaking 'I' in 'Mirror, Mirror' but the self it reflects is merely shadowy.[87] In Ruth Fainlight's 'Two Blue Dresses', the mirror warns her young self of 'The probability / Of loneliness'[88] and in Sylvia Plath's paradigmatic 'Mirror', the looking glass also speaks: 'the woman bends over me, / Searching my reaches for what she really is.' Furthermore, 'In me she has drowned a young girl, and in me an old woman / Rises toward her day after day, like a terrible fish.'[89] The many poems on ageing register how women are haunted by the inexorable rise of the 'terrible fish'. Not only is the concept of woman terrible or blank, but there is no viable alternative to her socially assigned roles. Plath's 'Spinster' depicts a woman's journey away from men to total isolation through symbols of the elements and seasons; in winter, she barricades herself against 'mutinous weather' where 'no mere insurgent men could hope to break / With curse, fist, threat / Or love, either.'[90] Fleur Adcock's frequently anthologised 'Against Coupling' recommends independence but has an air of irony and her less jovial 'Miss Hamilton in London' mocks the woman's prim appearance then exposes the 'thrusting black spears', of her painful loneliness.[91] Edith Sitwell, Ruth Pitter, Elizabeth Jennings and Stevie Smith never married and this social marginalisation might explain the personas of eccentricity adopted by Sitwell and Smith. Jennings's poems were more conventional and gained her entry to the otherwise all-male grouping, 'The Movement'. However, her deceptively tidy formalism and lyrical closure are containers for the hidden turmoil we find in her private papers: 'I am so sick of being called "lucid", "delicate", "not outreaching my grasp" etc. Critics are always criticising one for not being what they want one to be. ... I'm not quiet and restrained.'[92] Her self-explorations conceal as much as they reveal, particularly about her frustrated love affairs. She is most personal in the poems informed by her experiences of depression, suicide attempts and mental hospitals, collected in *Recoveries* (1964) and *The Mind Has Mountains* (1966). Smith, too, suffered depression and tried suicide,[93] confessing to the personal origin of her most famous work: 'I felt too low for words (eh??) last weekend but worked it all off in a poem ... called "Not Waving but Drowning."'[94] This multi-vocal lyric stands as an emblem of the internal dramas behind so many women's poems. Lidia Vianu notes Fainlight's 'strong desire to restrain the grief while constantly talking about it', and charges her: 'Your emotions are coated in a wrapping of decency, but they rage inside the poem.' Fainlight admits, 'The whole project of writing poetry is an attempt to understand oneself. If I could define myself so easily, so definitively, I would not (would not need to) write poetry'.[95] However, 'Lilith', a revisionary narrative about the creation and fall of Adam and Eve, projects a feminist perspective on sex inequalities: 'Lilith's disgrace thus defined / Good and evil. She would be / Outside, the feared, the alien, / Hungry and dangerous.'[96] Although the cadences are controlled, we glimpse the 'specifically female anger' that Fainlight admits was the impetus for many poems.[97]

Unlike the networks between modernist women before them or the closer association between more contemporary poets, these poets largely operated alone. Only occasionally, did they find inspiration through the work of their contemporaries or predecessors – Ridler and Scovell were professional friends, Plath called herself 'a desperate [Stevie] Smith addict', and Plath's work inspired Stevenson, and, accelerated by her death in 1963, it undoubtedly ignited Fainlight's and other poets' feminist and creative impulses. Frequently, however, women distanced themselves from others in order to avoid the pejorative homogenising of 'women's poetry'. Tellingly, Couzyn observed that during the 1960s and 1970s anthologists favoured the demure Patricia Beer as a token woman, 'because she can be relied on never to embarrass the reader with anything too "female".'[98] Couzyn's comment indirectly acknowledges the increasing prevalence of more freely female-centric expression. From 1970, the Women's Liberation movement fed into, and was fed by, consciousness-raising poetry that was published by the new feminist presses.[99] This poetry reads as a collective protest against women's social and literary marginalization. As Michèle Roberts put it: 'In adolescence, increasing alienation from myself and from the view of femininity purveyed by the late 1950s / early 1960s culture drove me and my writing underground. ... I came out as a poet when I found the Women's Liberation Movement in 1970 and realised that I wasn't mad so much as confused and angry.'[100] However, just as 'femininity' and 'poetry' had been conceptually antithetical, a reactionary academy polarised 'literary' and 'feminist', and Roberts did not publish a poetry volume until 1986. Veronica Forrest-Thomson (1947–75), who published three books of linguistically innovative work before her untimely death, was fiercely academic and theorised her principles in *Poetic Artifice*, published posthumously. Interested in the Tel Quel avant-garde in Paris, particularly Julia Kristeva, her play with language is deconstructive, interrogating the interdependence of language, authority and identity. 'Through The Looking-Glass' expresses the desire for an identifiable self along with the choice to fashion it. The speaking female appropriates fairy-tale to a feminist consciousness: 'Mirror, mirror on the wall / show me in succession all / my faces, that I may view / and choose which I would like as true.'[101] Nicki Jackowska and Rosemary Tonks also experimented with densely symbolic lyrical expression and, with Forrest-Thomson, paved the way for the daringly feminist innovations of Wendy Mulford, Carlyle Reedy and Denise Riley.

In summary, one version of this period is of quiet poets who are justly acclaimed for their technical skill and precise perceptions but of little interest as *women* writers. However, the private or retrospective disclosures of many reveal a 'bell jar' consciousness that railed against the pressures to be genteel, to succeed in roles that did not suit their intelligence and educations. Collectively, they left a legacy of differing models of female-authored poetry, veering between the stylistically conservative and radical, the gender-shy and the feminist. While there is no tidily linear development, there are some shifts in the status and nature of women as poets. In the post-war years, conventionality was rewarded – Pitter and Cornford were the first women to receive the Queen's Gold Medal for Poetry in 1955 and 1959 respectively. However, more daring and more female-centric work received plaudits from the 1960s – Smith received the Cholmondley Award in 1966 and the Queen's Gold Medal in 1969. Sitwell and Pitter gained prestigious C.Litts from the Royal Society of Literature (1963, 1974) and other significant garlands went to Jennings, Joseph and Plath's *Ariel*.[102] Women featured in radio broadcasts, but apart from Jennings, were rarely visible as editors or reviewers. Hence the initiatives for segregated publishing outlets, magazines and anthologies that would expand and flourish in the following decades.

Notes

1. Meum Stewart, 'Prefatory Note', in *The Distaff Muse: An Anthology of Poetry Written by Women* ed. by Clifford Bax and Meum Stewart (London: Hollis & Carter, 1949).
2. David Cecil, 'Introduction', in *Ruth Pitter: Homage to a Poet* ed. by Arthur W. Russell (London: Rapp & Whiting, 1969).
3. Margaret Byers, 'Cautious Vision: Recent British Poetry by Women' in *British Poetry Since 1960: A Critical Survey* ed. by Michael Schmidt and Grevel Lindop (Manchester: Carcanet, 1972), pp. 74–84 (p. 84).

4. See the Introductions to *The New Poetry* ed. by Alvin Alvarez (Harmondsworth: Penguin, 1962) and Martin Booth, *British Poetry 1964–84: Driving Through the Barricades* (London: Routledge & Kegan Paul, 1985).
5. Richard Greene, *Edith Sitwell: Avant Garde Poet, English Genius* (London: Virago Press, 2011), p. 320.
6. Alvarez, *The New Poetry*, p. 21; Booth, *British Poetry*, p. 63.
7. Geoffrey Summerfield, Introduction, *Worlds: Seven Modern Poets*, (Harmondsworth: Penguin, 1974).
8. Stevie Smith, 'Miss Snooks, Poetess', Poetry (November 1964), *Me Again: The Uncollected Writings of Stevie Smith*, ed. by Jack Barbara and William McBrien (London: Virago, 1988), p. 226.
9. 'Views and Recollections of a Sunday Poet' (27 March, 1956); 'Notes for a talk on *Woman's Hour*' (BBC, 4 November 1959), *Literary Papers of Frances Cornford*, Department of Manuscripts, London: The British Library, Add. Mss. 58387.
10. 'Reading at Cambridge Literary Circle' (2 October 1953), *Literary Papers of Frances Cornford*, Add. Mss. 58386.
11. John Williams, *Twentieth Century Poetry: A Critical Introduction* (London: Edward Arnold, 1987), p. 71.
12. Anne Ridler, 'For a New Voice', *Some Time After and Other Poems* (London: Faber, 1972), p. 9.
13. Eavan Boland, *Collected Poems* (Manchester: Carcanet, 1995), p. xi.
14. Betty Friedan, *The Feminine Mystique* (New York: Dell Publishing, 1963), p. 11.
15. Alvarez, *The New Poetry*, p. 23.
16. See Grevel Lindop, 'Kathleen Raine: The Tenth Decade', *PN Review*, 27: 2 (2000), 36–50.
17. Kathleen Raine, 'Love, Cambridge, Poetry: Extracts from an Unpublished Essay' in Lindop, 'Kathleen Raine', pp. 37–9.
18. Peter Scupham, 'Shelf Lives 9: E. J. Scovell', *PN Review*, 26: 3 (2000), 26–8, 27.
19. Elizabeth W. Pomeroy, 'Within Living Memory: Vita Sackville West's Poems of Land and Garden', *Twentieth-Century Literature*, 28: 3 (1982) 269–89 (p. 270).
20. Ruth Pitter, 'The Brothers: A Dream', *Collected Poems* (London: Enitharmon, 1996), p. 269.
21. Stevie Smith, *Collected Poems* (London, Allen Lane, 1975), p. 264.
22. Fleur Adcock, in *Six Women Poets* ed. by Judith Kinsman (Oxford: Oxford University Press, 1992), p. 53.
23. Jeni Couzyn, *The Bloodaxe Book of Contemporary Women Poets* (Newcastle upon Tyne: Bloodaxe, 1985), p. 202.
24. Fleur Adcock, 'In Memoriam: James K. Baxter', *Selected Poems* (Oxford: Oxford University Press, 1983), pp. 51–2.
25. Melanie Petch, 'The Mid-Atlantic Imagination' in *The Cambridge Companion to Twentieth-Century British and Irish Women's Poetry* ed. by Jane Dowson (Cambridge: Cambridge University Press, 2011), pp. 82–96 (p. 93).
26. Couzyn, *The Bloodaxe Book*, p. 187.
27. Anne Stevenson, *Travelling Behind Glass: Selected Poems* (Oxford: Oxford University Press, 1974), pp. 22–4.
28. *Sylvia Path: Collected Poems* ed. by Ted Hughes (London: Faber, 1981), pp. 203, 176).
29. William Packard, 'Interview with Denise Levertov, 1971' in *Denise Levertov: In Her Own Province* ed. by Linda W. Wagner (New York: New Directions, 1979),

pp. 1–21 (p. 8). See also, P. Giles, 'American Literature in English Translation: Denise Levertov and Others', *PMLA*, 119: 1 (2004), 31–41.

30. Denise Levertov, 'A Map of the Western Part of the County of Essex', *Selected Poems* [1961] (New York: New Directions, 2004), p. 20.
31. Ruth Fainlight, 'Poem' [*The Region's Violence* 1973], *New and Collected Poems* (Tarset: Bloodaxe, 2010), p. 120.
32. Alvarez, *The New Poetry*, p. 25.
33. *Selected Letters of Edith Sitwell* ed. by Richard Greene (London: Virago, 1998), p. 280.
34. Anne Ridler, *Some Time After and Other Poems*, p. 32.
35. H. D. *Trilogy* [1944–46] (Manchester: Carcanet, 1988).
36. Edith Sitwell, 10 August 1945, in Richard Greene, *Edith Sitwell: Avant Garde Poet*, (London: Virago, 2012), p. 318. [Sitwell's italics].
37. Sitwell, in *Edith Sitwell: Selected Poems* ed. by John Lehmann (London: Macmillan, 1961), p. 108.
38. George S. Fraser, 'Preface' to Sheila Wingfield, *Collected Poems 1938–83* (New York: Hill and Wang, 1983), p. xv.
39. Wingfield, *Collected Poems*, p. 49.
40. Kenneth Allott, *The Penguin Book of Contemporary Verse* [1950] (Harmondsworth: Penguin, 1962), p. 29.
41. Sitwell in *Edith Sitwell: Selected Poems* ed. by Lehmann, pp. 96–100, (p. 99).
42. Pitter, *Collected Poems*, pp. 221–2.
43. Patricia Beer, *Collected Poems* (Manchester: Carcanet, 1990), pp. 19–20; Sylvia Plath, *Collected Poems*, p. 266.
44. Smith, 'No Categories', *Collected Poems*, p. 258.
45. Smith, *Collected Poems*, p. 265.
46. Smith, *Collected Poems*, p. 271.
47. Smith, *Collected Poems*, pp. 286, 530–1.
48. Smith, *Collected Poems*, pp. 447–8.
49. Stevie Smith, *Me Again: The Uncollected Writings of Stevie Smith* (London: Virago, 1983), pp. 242–3.
50. Smith, *Collected Poems*, pp. 266, 253.
51. Sylvia Plath, 'The Poet Speaks', Argo Record Co., (No RG455 LM, 1962).
52. 20 and 28 January 1959, in *The Journals of Sylvia Plath* ed. by Ted Hughes, (New York: Dial Press, 1982), pp. 293, 295.
53. Plath, 25 February 1959, *Journals*, p. 298.
54. Plath, *Collected Poems*, pp. 222–4.
55. Plath, *Collected Poems*, p. 129.
56. Plath, *Collected Poems*, pp. 74–6, 142.
57. Plath, *Collected Poems*, pp. 204–6.
58. Anne Stevenson, 'Writing as a Woman' in *Women Writing and Writing About Women* ed. by M. Jacobus (London: Croom Helm, 1979), pp. 159–76 (p. 159).
59. Stevenson, 'Writing as a Woman', p. 173.
60. Stevenson, 'Writing as a Woman', p. 166.
61. Anne Stevenson, *Travelling Behind Glass* (Oxford: Oxford University Press, 1974), pp. 50, 9–10. Virginia Woolf, 'Professions for Women', *Selected Essays* [1942] (Oxford: Oxford University Press, 2008), pp. 140–5.
62. Stevenson, 'Writing as a Woman', p. 166.
63. Stevenson, 'Writing as a Woman', pp. 163, 188.
64. Stevenson, 'Writing as a Woman', p. 172.
65. Stevenson, *Correspondences: A Family History in Letters* (London: Oxford University Press, 1974).

66. Stevenson, 'Writing as a Woman', p. 177. [Stevenson's italics].
67. Cornford, 'Views and Recollections of a Sunday Poet'.
68. Couzyn, *The Bloodaxe Book*, p. 202.
69. Simone de Beauvoir, *The Second Sex* [1949] (London: Vintage, 1997), p. 471.
70. Denise Levertov, *Collected Earlier Poems, 1940–1960* (New York: New Directions, 1979), pp. 6–7.
71. Ruth Fainlight [*To See the Matter Clearly*, 1968], *New and Collected Poems*, p. 75.
72. Fainlight [*The Region's Violence*, 1973], *New and Collected Poems*, p. 106.
73. Couzyn, *The Bloodaxe Book*, p. 170.
74. Couzyn, *The Bloodaxe Book*, pp. 169–70.
75. Jenny Joseph, *Rose in the Afternoon and Other Poems* (London: Dent & Sons, 1974), p. 17.
76. Joseph, *Rose in the Afternoon*, p. 16.
77. Plath, *Collected Poems*, pp. 116, 156–7.
78. Stevenson, 'Writing as a Woman', p. 166.
79. Stevenson, *Travelling Behind Glass*, pp. 17, 16, 11–12. She appropriates William Wordsworth's phrase 'trailing clouds of glory' from the 'Ode: Intimations of Immortality from Recollections of Early Childhood'.
80. Couzyn, *The Bloodaxe Book*, p. 215.
81. Fainlight [*To See the Matter Clearly*, 1968], *New and Collected Poems*, p. 54.
82. Elaine Feinstein, *Collected Poems and Translations* [1966] (Manchester: Carcanet, 2002), p. 3.
83. Couzyn, *The Bloodaxe Book*, pp. 17–18.
84. Levertov, *Selected Poems*, p. 30.
85. Stevenson, *Travelling Behind Glass*, pp. 42–4.
86. Joseph, *Rose in the Afternoon*, pp. 8, 60.
87. Joseph, *Rose in the Afternoon*, pp. 64-5.
88. Fainlight [*The Region's Violence*, 1973], *New and Collected Poems*, p. 99.
89. Plath, *Collected Poems*, p. 173.
90. Plath, *Collected Poems*, p. 49.
91. Adcock, *Selected Poems*, pp. 33, 9.
92. Jennings to Michael Hamburger (3 August 1953). Leeds: Leeds University Library, The Brotherton Collection, Michael Hamburger Correspondence.
93. See 'Too Tired for Words' [1956], *Me Again*, pp. 111–18.
94. Smith, Letter to Kay Dick, 25 April, 1953, *Me Again*, p. 294.
95. Lidia Vianu, 'Four interviews with Ruth Fainlight', *Desperado Essay-Interviews* (Bucharest: Editura Universitatii din Bucuresti, 2006). <http://lidiavianu.scriptmania.com/ruth_fainlight.htm,> [accessed 24 June 2015]
96. Fainlight [*To See the Matter Clearly*, 1968], *New and Collected Poems*, p. 95.
97. Couzyn, *The Bloodaxe Book*, p. 130.
98. Couzyn, *The Bloodaxe Book*, p. 15.
99. See *Without Adam: The Femina Anthology of Poetry* ed. by Joan M. Simpson (London: Femina Press, 1968).
100. Michele Roberts, 'Questions and Answers' in *On Gender and Writing* ed. by Michelene Wandor (London: Pandora, 1983), p. 64.
101. Veronica Forrest-Thomson, 'Through the Looking Glass', *Collected Poems and Translations* (Bristol: Shearsman Books, 2008), p. 221.
102. J. Higgins, 'Awards', *British Poetry since 1960* ed. by Schmidt and Lindop, pp. 253-9.

3

Look Back in Gender: Drama

Gabriele Griffin

The phrase 'look back in gender' was popularised by playwright and critic Michelene Wandor in her assessment of 'sexuality and the family in post-war British drama'.[1] It was in part a feminist riposte to the overweening association of post-war drama with John Osborne's 1956 play *Look Back in Anger* which became synonymous with the notion of the 'Angry Young Men' (*not* women!) that has dominated readings of the theatre, and indeed of film, of the 1950s ever since.[2] 'Post-war', in Wandor's first and a subsequent volume[3] as elsewhere, takes the 1950s as its starting point, largely ignoring the fact that five years of post-war preceded it.[4] Spanning thirty years of drama from 1945-1975, this chapter follows the development of women's work for the theatre decade by decade. In each section I shall briefly sketch the political and social context before exploring how these affected women dramatists' work.

The late 1940s

The second half of the 1940s, the transition period from war to peace as Wandor has described it,[5] was characterised by rationing and austerity on the one hand, and a series of political changes designed to reform Britain. Importantly for women who would be one of the major beneficiaries of these developments, the period saw the embedding of the welfare state, inaugurated in some respects by the 1944 Butler Act which established free secondary education for all. It was followed by the Family Allowances Act of 1945 which guaranteed payment to all mothers with more than one child; the 1945 National Insurance Act; the 1946 National Health Service Act (implemented in 1948); the 1947 Town and Country Planning Act (which became important in the context of council housing); the 1948 National Assistance Act; the 1948 Children Act, and a number of other acts which, altogether, established a potentially fairer system of distribution of resources

© The Author(s) 2017
C. Hanson and S. Watkins, *The History of British Women's Writing, 1945–1975*,
History of British Women's Writing, DOI: 10.1057/978-1-137-47736-1_4

for the benefit – means-tested or otherwise – of all. This state reform was accompanied by the nationalization of major industries in the wake of Labour's unexpected landslide election victory in 1945 (coal in 1947; aviation first in 1939, then reformed in 1946; British Railways in 1947; Cable and Wireless in 1947; electricity and gas in 1948),[6] and by the beginnings of the end of the British Empire (India gained independence in 1947) and the now iconic arrival of the ship, the *Empire Windrush,* from the West Indies into Tilbury in 1948, signalling the commencement of mass immigration into Britain from the (increasingly former) colonies.

Britain was thus set on a course of improvements on the home front but there is little sense of this in the play *Call Home the Heart,*[7] by Clemence Dane (1885–1965)[8] which was first performed at the St James's Theatre in London on 10 April 1947 and had 44 performances.[9] At the time, *The Times* suggested that 'The conflict in this serious and satisfying play is less between persons than between reality and unreality ...', and it described the story as being about 'homecoming from the war'.[10] It accurately states that one of the central characters, Lydia, daughter of Mr and Mrs Frazer, 'who hardly knew her husband [Colin] before he was taken prisoner, has fixed her thoughts romantically on another man [Roylance], known as briefly, who has been posted missing. Today, after five years, the two return together, and Lydia must face not one stranger but two.' *The Times* review then moves on to suggest that at the heart of the play is Lydia's parents 'impossible marriage', something which 'happens every day'.

Reading the play now, it strikes one somewhat differently. Formally in many ways it retains the characteristics of the well-made play of the pre-World War II era. It is in two acts, takes place over a 24-hour period and in one setting, the Frazers' house, adopts a chronological approach, and ends with the retention of the status quo of the marriages that have come under duress in the course of the play, Lydia's to Colin, and Mr and Mrs Frazer's. It has extensive, detailed stage directions (the whole of the first page is given over to this, for example), designed to produce verisimilitude, and features a drawing room and porch with all the accompanying furniture that one might expect to find in an upper-middle class household. In other words, the play's setting is the typical home of a bourgeois family – the kind of household and family that will come under attack in 1950s drama. But what is really striking about this play, and which is wholly absent in its review in *The Times* cited above, is that it features a family which has been *repeatedly* through wars by which all the characters have been deeply affected. Lydia, the daughter, did 'war-work' abroad in Alexandria and was injured when the boat on which she was coming home was torpedoed and sank. She has won a medal for saving a number of children whilst half-drowning. She is convalescing from her ankle injury and suffers from post-traumatic stress. Haunted both by her near-drowning experience and by the fact that her husband Colin has spent two years in a prisoner-of-war camp and Roylance

Hutchinson, a man with whom she had a romantic entanglement, has been reported missing, presumed killed, she has repeated nightmares. In these the sinking of the boat and the issue of her relation to Colin and Roylance are intertwined as moral dilemmas. On the boat, two nurses decided to stay with the worst injured soldiers who were housed under deck and in consequence drowned. This moral dilemma about saving oneself *versus* keeping one's promise to others at the expense of self is also evident in the question of Roylance and Lydia's 'marriage of true minds' to which 'no impediment' should be admitted *versus* Lydia's actual marriage to Colin. The play employs nightmarish soundscapes (alarms sounding with increasing intensity) which would have been particularly salient for London audiences who had been through the Blitz and repeated refrains such as 'the war is over' and 'resurrection' to create a sense of the intensity and resilience of Lydia's post-traumatic stress.

Set against Lydia's troubled return to the bosom of her bourgeois family, is the presence, completely unremarked upon in *The Times* review, of Svava, a refugee from Warsaw, whom, according to the stage directions, '*no one could mistake ... for an Anglo-Saxon*'[11] in terms of her appearance, and who is cast in the role of unpaid servant by Lydia's mother. Svava has lost all of her family except her mother who remains in Poland: her three sisters married 'Pole Jews' and are 'All dead', whilst her husband died of starvation in a camp, and her father died after being forcibly moved off his land by incoming Russians.[12] Svava explains her name as being a 'Valkyr. One of the swan-maidens on the battlefield. They carry away the dead. In Warsaw I often did so, like my name, and I dug many graves.'[13] She is described as manifesting hoarding and secret-eating behaviour, an effect of her war-time deprivation. But the family who has taken her in ignore her history. As Lydia says: 'Never dared ask [about her story] – just as I've never dared see the Belsen film. Every night would be a nightmare.'[14] At one point Svava castigates the family for their attitude: 'For what do you know, in this safe, rich island, where it is green even in winter? So much less than I know – you lucky people!' Colin takes exception to this stance: 'I don't quite care to take that. Look, Svava, I've been in several camps since Singapore. Some weren't nice. And I'm one of thousands.' To which Svava replies: 'I answer – Warsaw was my *home*.'[15] Roylance, the man whose health has been ruined through torture in the camp where he was with Colin because he 'would conduct a personal war'[16] by protesting against the camp's conditions, is cast as the only person who truly understands Svava. He explains her attitude to Lydia who, of course, in contrast to Svava, still has a home, even if it is damaged: 'She has nothing left, not even hope. She's free to embrace the moment. That's happiness.'[17] Tellingly, Roylance who is dying from his war injuries, leaves with Svava who decides to look after him.

Just as all of the surviving younger generation are variously and deeply damaged by the war (David is dead, Lydia is physically and mentally scarred, both Colin and Roylance have to come to terms with their camp experiences, Svava is displaced, and Hetty, a woman of working-class background who had a relationship with David and is mother to his illegitimate son), so are the older generation affected. As Mrs Frazer says at one point: 'I've not had half my life. Four years gone in the last war, and now another six ripped out.'[18] Much of the play's preoccupation is with what the war has done to the Frazers, including the mother. Played by Sybil Thorndyke in the St James's production, her depiction of Mrs Frazer is described in the *Times* review as 'Nothing is missing – absurdity, egotism, sentimentality, genuine hurt, in fact the whole hotchpotch of qualities that is known here as Mrs Fraser [*sic*] and elsewhere by the names of many other women.'[19] *The Times's* phrasing here makes clear the low esteem in which this character – representative, it would appear, 'of many other women' – is held. But when she says, 'This white in my hair – that's you [Lydia], not David [the son]. It came when I thought you'd been drowned. David killed, your father absorbed in the hospital ...', her suffering becomes apparent. Lydia's orientation, as in many texts of the early twentieth century, is towards her father, and as Mrs Frazer miserably diagnoses: 'I don't exist for you any more than I do for him.'[20]

Mrs Frazer who also has to find a new role for herself post-war, ultimately saves the day when the question arises of what should happen with Hetty's son, their grandchild. Upon the discovery that he is that grandchild, the family immediately, unthinkingly and without concern for Hetty, the clearly competent and loving mother, decide to adopt. Hetty refuses this, making an impassioned plea for the need of state provision for single mothers,[21] thus reflecting the mood of the time to effect comprehensive governmental reforms – but ones that do justice to all, including single girls and their children.[22] As Hetty needs to work to earn a living, Mrs Frazer's offer to start a crèche and baby-sit the child saves the day. By the end of the play all the women have working roles: Lydia is thinking about going back into publishing (a job she did before her war work), Hetty works in a factory as she has done throughout the war, Mrs Frazer is opening a crèche in her home, and Svava is going off to care for Roylance. And, although one might argue that at least the last two of these jobs are extensions of the conventional feminine care roles that were to come under increasing attack from the 1950s onwards, nonetheless a world of change has been inaugurated.

The 1950s

That change was to gather pace in the 1950s. In critiquing the reception of 1950s drama as the provenance of angry young men, Susan Bassnett has argued that this narrative might be retold by engaging with 'women dramatists who wrote prolifically and successfully for the commercial stage of the period.'[23] Bassnett's point is well taken since, as Clare Hemmings has suggested, 'how feminists tell stories matters in part because of the ways in which they intersect with wider institutionalizations of gendered meanings.'[24] Bassnett draws on Maggie Gale's work on *West End Women* to highlight that women, not least writers such as Agatha Christie and Enid Bagnold who were widely known for writing in other genres such as fiction as well, wrote successfully for the stage. 'Successfully' here means that their plays had extended runs in commercial West End theatres. Sylvia Raman's *Women of Twilight*, for example, which Gale discusses,[25] had 235 performances at the Vaudeville Theatre between November 1951 and April 1952. Jeanette Dowling and F. Letton's *The Young Elizabeth*, perhaps unsurprisingly, had 504 performances in 1953, the year of Elizabeth II's coronation.[26]

The 1950s tend to be heralded as a period of optimism, inaugurated by the Festival of Britain in May 1951and followed by Elizabeth II's accession to the throne on 6 February 1952. The post-war rebuilding of the country and the post-war labour shortage led to a steady rise in female employment and to a new prosperity, following the gradual removal of rationing in the early 1950s.[27] Simultaneously, however, from 1951 the decade was ruled by a series of Conservative governments who supported rearmament in the face of the Korean war, decided on the manufacture of the hydrogen bomb (February 1955) and saw a series of international crises, especially in the middle of the decade, such as the Suez crisis in 1956 and the invasion of Hungary by Soviet troops in the November of that same year, leading to significant disenchantment among the Communist left, including in Britain. Partly in response to the explosion of the first British hydrogen bomb in May 1957 in the Pacific, the Campaign for Nuclear Disarmament (CND) was established in February 1958 which, later that year, organised the first Aldermaston protest march. Politically, the 1950s were thus characterised by a profound conservatism taking hold as well as new forms of anti-conservative forces such as CND emerging.

The views of both sides were aired through the expanding technological empire of the British Broadcasting Corporation. After World War II BBC radio included the Home Service, the Light Programme and from 1946, the Third Programme. This became a space for women writers who had a voice in the drama slots. In the second half of the 1950s, Muriel Spark and Doris Lessing (as much as Caryl Churchill did in the late 1960s and early 1970s) wrote radio plays but those spaces were soon competing with television as the new form of home entertainment: 'Television made steady progress from its base at Alexandra Palace, north London – broadcasting for 30 hours each week by 1950, and 50 by 1955. Families rushed to buy sets to watch the Queen's coronation in 1953.'[28] One might argue that two kinds of drama emerged: one still very much focussed on the bourgeois family or its remnants, featuring 'mature adults' at its centre, often in conflict with the younger generation; the other, a theatre of the younger generation, coming of age in post-war Britain, often from the lower-middle classes and critical of the pre-war generations but in a state of angst and resentment, and without a teleological sense of progression in their lives.

Muriel Spark's radio plays, and in particular 'The Party Through the Wall' and 'The Interview', very much belong to the first category of drama.[29] Central to both, as to much of Spark's work, is a sense of faded gentility, of the downward mobility of those once comfortably off, and of the impacts this situation has on the plays' central female characters. Both plays have small casts, featuring three characters, two women and a man. In 'The Party Through The Wall', Ethel Carson, a woman in her fifties, who, however, dresses 'young' (in 'a now-white duffle coat over pink velvet corduroy jeans') has come to live in London's Kensington in a street of bomb-damaged houses where she seeks peace for her 'nerves'. It is never made clear whether her 'nerves' are a function of the war and she is in effect also 'war-damaged', or whether there are other causes. But she is described as having been 'an unusual person from the time of [her] youth',[30] suggesting that she may have always been what used to be described as 'neurasthenic'. In 'classic', ironic Spark mode, Ethel is constructed as 'devoted to art and to all spiritual matters'; her weekly routines involve Tuesdays at the 'Kensington Cabbalah Study Group', Wednesdays spent on 'automatic writing', time with her 'Dream Prognostication Circle' and her 'Astral-Radiation Trance Club'.[31] The activities, told by the over-bearing male narrator, a Dr Fell who lives next door to Ethel, undermine Ethel's credibility as they suggest that she is susceptible to 'hokum'. And, indeed, an initial difference is set up between her and her 'nervy' condition, and the narrator, Dr Fell. He is supposedly a retired medical man specializing in 'nervous cases'. Science is here seemingly set against spirituality, but Fell's reliability is increasingly called into question as his living circumstances take on sinister dimensions; it is suggested that he is a serial killer who murdered his sister and has possibly done away with Ethel, too. The notion that both characters suffer from some mental disorder is reinforced in the way in which they are made to mirror each other's sentences and actions. She talks about others getting on her nerves, so does he. Telling the listener that Miss Carson eventually left, Fell says: 'I could not leave her alone ... Indeed, she would not leave me alone ...'[32] Since Fell is the narrator and has both the first and the last word, he dominates the play. But the construction of the characters as partly mirroring each other in their strained mental condition reduces that difference – women and men seem to be equally deluded and unreliable witnesses.

The mental decline of older women is also at the heart of 'The Interview' which features the elderly Dame Lettice, her live-in 'companion-secretary Miss Bone ('Tiggy') and Dame Lettice's nephew Roy. It is never quite clear whether Dame Lettice is suffering from dementia and hence has imaginary conversations with her nephew, or whether she replays actual conversations that took place in the past in her mind. The play alternates between conversations between Dame Lettice and Tiggy, and between Dame Lettice and her nephew. As Dame Lettice comes out of her conversations with her nephew, she endlessly calls for Tiggy who at one point says: 'I don't get any time to myself on this job. That's the worst of living in.'[33] Writing at a time when the (female) carer role is increasingly under scrutiny, Tiggy's dilemma of how to 'live with' Dame Lettice's fading mental capacities reads rather poignantly.[34] Dame Lettice is in the process of dictating her memoir to Tiggy but never gets much beyond the first sentences as her memory waxes and vanes. Significantly, and like Ethel Carson in 'The Party Through the Wall', she is invested in 'the supremacy of the world of the imagination, a world in which literally anything can happen', which she sets against 'the mundane facts of everyday life'.[35] Tiggy, possibly to ward off the stress of having to deal with someone whose memory is deteriorating, constantly rehearses precisely these facts[36] for 'The Quiz',[37] a show in which she hopes to win a prize that will set her free financially. Like Roy, Dame Lettice's nephew, who appears to be at least partially financially dependent on his aunt and thus seemingly forced to do as she pleases, Tiggy is dependent on her for her income. The play gathers its dramatic tension from the shifting perceptions it creates regarding facts versus imagination and whose interpretation prevails, Dame Lettice's or Tiggy's. As in 'Party Through the Wall', a death is suggested as is the possibility that Roy's departed spirit 'haunts' the two women but as in the former play, so here the question of what has actually occurred is ultimately left unanswered. Neither the facts nor imagination help in resolving the mystery fully.

Cross-generational issues, already described in *Call the Heart Home* as 'The battlefields of home' where 'Our parents order our lives. ... And we revolutionize theirs',[38] gained greater prominence in the 1950s, particularly in its second half. One *Times* correspondent maintained of the theatre productions in 1958 when *A Taste of Honey,* by Shelagh Delaney (1938-2011)[39] and *The Sport of My Mad Mother*, by Ann Jellicoe (1927-)[40] were staged, that 'Stage parents come in for punishment.'[41] Younger generations, and characters from beyond the bourgeois family, started to come into focus, both at Joan Littlewood's Theatre Royal, Stratford East, set up in 1953 and at the newly opened Royal Court Theatre.[42]

Joan Littlewood's[43] production of *A Taste of Honey* became a West End hit with an initial run of 27 performances at the Theatre Royal, and a subsequent run at the Wyndham's and then to the Criterion, of 368 performances.[44] In contrast, *The Sport of My Mad Mother*, staged at the Royal Court Theatre, had only 14 performances. As Jellicoe herself said: '*Sport* was what Philip Locke called a '"*flop d'estime*", which was very accurate and it was quite a painful experience.'[45] The critics loved it, the audience did not. The success of Delaney's play may in part be explained by the ways in which it conformed to certain standard tropes of theatre. *A Taste of Honey* was very much in the realist vein, presenting identifiable social problems in the conventional form of a two-act play in which 'motherhood itself is a central theme'[46] and heteronormative gender roles are only partially put under pressure. Single mother Helen, irresponsible, decidedly un-maternal, living off men, and her teenage daughter Jo who becomes pregnant by a black boy in the course of the play, have a tempestuous relationship, structured by Helen's fraught interactions with men and her readiness to abandon her daughter in an instant in pursuit of those men and pleasure. The play explicitly questions the 'naturalness' of motherhood[47] as the only unfailingly caring person is gay art student Geof who seeks to support Jo through her pregnancy. As Jo says to him: '[Motherhood] comes natural to you, Geoffrey Ingham. You'd make somebody a wonderful wife.'[48] However, Helen returns to Jo when she is abandoned by her domineering lover Peter and ousts Geof. When Helen learns that the baby is by a black man, she once more abandons Jo, now completely alone and ignorant of Geof's departure. The play not only deals with the issues of teenage pregnancy and single motherhood, thwarted educational ambition (Jo's) in an age of expanding education for all, and rootlessness, but also, importantly, highlights racial[49] and homophobic prejudice, not least on the part of women who themselves are socially marginalised but are not readily empathetic towards others. In many ways it reproduces the notion of the lonely rootless urban female figure, dependent on men yet unable to find commitment, the *flâneuse* of the late nineteenth/early twentieth century, familiar from the short stories of Katherine Mansfield, for instance, and who re-appears later in the writings of Jean Rhys.

The Sport of My Mad Mother pushes some of the issues such as male violence and unwanted motherhood raised in *Taste* into the London gangland of the early 1950s Teddy Boys, a world structured by the rhythmic swell of rising violence and remission, and in which Greta, a threatening female figure, seems to rule. The play, though conventionally divided into three acts, is experimental in style and lyrical in its use of language. It has extended sections of chanting, of repetition of words, of characters working themselves into a frenzy, with the characters being described as 'Chorus' at times, making the play reminiscent of *The Bacchae*. Set outside in a London back alley in which gang members constantly threaten and physically attack each other and outsiders, the world depicted is one of a peer culture of menace. This is as far removed from the bourgeois drawing room as one may get and Aleks Sierz, unsurprisingly, views *Sport* as a precursor of in-yer-face theatre.[50] Greta's pregnancy and birth-giving at the end of the play is interwoven into a cycle of destruction and regeneration, with a final unceremonious direct address to the audience to 'clear out. I'm blowing this place up. We'll have a bonfire: bring your own axes. All right everyone off! Off!'[51]

In some respects, the peer-group tribalism of *The Sport of My Mad Mother*, its title reminiscent of Shakespeare's 'As flies to wanton boys are we to th' gods,/they kill us for their sport.'[52] seems to be the antidote to Doris Lessing's 1958 play 'Each His Own Wilderness',[53] also staged at the Royal Court Theatre – for one reading only.[54] That play returns the audience not so much to the drawing-room as to the entrance hall, a threshold space

that people pass through and which symbolises the flux in family relations. Unlike most other later plays by women, especially from the 1970s
and under the influence of second-wave feminism when mother-daughter
relations formed one core theme of enquiry, this play explores a mother-
son relationship. Here the mother, Myra, is constructed as a free-thinking
independent woman whose life largely takes place outside the home in pursuit of various political causes. Her son Tony, by contrast, just out of Army
Service, longs for conventional home life. The play opens with '*an H-bomb
explosion. CURTAIN UP on the sound of blast. Silence. Machine-gun fire. The
explosion again.*'[55] This soundscape turns out to be a recording, prepared by
Myra for a demonstration against nuclear armament. Tony is the antidote to
Jellicoe's Teddy Boy characters in *The Sport*. Conservative, order-loving, cynical and prone to infantile outbursts, he resents his mother's lack of attention
to him. Myra, on the other hand, feels that her time to do her own thing
has come. As she says to Tony: 'I've never wanted security and safety and
the walls of respectability – you damned little petty-bourgeois. My God, the
irony of it – that *we* [politically engaged women] should have given birth
to a generation of little boys and office clerks and ...'[56] Myra is invigorated
by the political battles she engages in. Tony, however, in many ways like
Jellicoe's Teddy Boy characters, represents a generation deeply affected by
the war (he and his mother survived the bombing of their house though
being buried alive for several hours) who has lost faith in the powers of
politics to change things for the better. He accuses Myra:

> Do you know what you have created ... A house for every family ... That's
> socialism. ... To every man his front door and his front door key. To each
> his own wilderness.[57]

Tony's desire to be 'ordinary and safe'[58] jostles uneasily with his sense that
the rising welfare state has created an interior, quasi-domestic wilderness,
a jungle of political and other kinds of factionalism, emblematised by his
own fraught relation with his mother. He wants to preserve their home but
she sells it off in order to set him – and herself – free from conventional
constraints.

The 1960s

Freedom from conventional constraints was certainly one of the watch
phrases of the 1960s. 1961 was the year of the Profumo Affair which led to
the then Secretary of State for War, John Profumo, being forced to resign in
1963 over his involvement with call girl Christine Keeler. Under a Labour
government from 1964, the death penalty was abolished in 1965, the 1967
Sexual Offences Act legalised homosexuality, the Abortion Act of the same
year made abortion under certain circumstances legal, and the 1969 Divorce

Reform Act made divorce an easier proposition. The 'swinging sixties' as they became known went together with a rapid expansion of youth culture and its commercialization. Importantly, in 1968 theatre censorship was finally abolished.[59] But the 1960s were also the period of CND demonstrations, 'mods' vs 'rockers' seaside-resort clashes, sit-ins at the London School of Economics and other universities, and anti-Vietnam war demonstrations. Jellicoe produced 'The Knack', 'a comedy with one set, four actors, about sex: it's absolutely cast iron [guaranteed to succeed].'[60] The play centres on the relationship between three young men and a woman, a peer group of sorts, which heralds the emphasis on the younger generation that continued in the 1960s. The three men are all sexual banter; when Nancy appears she becomes the focus of their sexual competitiveness. The play makes uncomfortable reading since the third act is dominated by Nancy's accusation that she has been raped and the men's, specifically the sexually most predatory one, Tolen's, assertion that 'In all his dealings with women a man must act with promptness and authority – even, if need be, force.'[61] Tolen's lines that 'Her saying that we have raped her is a fantasy. She has fabricated this fantasy because she really does want to be raped; she wants to be the centre of attention',[62] are meant to be comical but strike one as extremely misogynistic and sexist. Given feminist interventions around coercive sex at the time, 'The Knack' seems to come precisely from an era when men's sexually predatory dominance over women was taken for granted and women's sexual freedom was constructed as a threat to male 'authority' over women.

Generational authority and peer group exchange are the focus of Muriel Spark's 1961 radio play 'The Danger Zone',[63] described in the text as 'an elemental drama'.[64] It features a group of youngsters who take to the mountains whilst their parents fret about what they get up to. As one parent says: 'all the youngsters from the age of sixteen are like foreigners.'[65] The notion of generational difference becomes prominent here. Like Jo in *The Taste of Honey*, who seems more responsible than her mother, the teenagers in 'The Danger Zone' as it turns out are seeking to protect their parents from another group of youngsters who live beyond the mountain side and who threaten to invade the valley where the parents reside to get at mineral water available there which appears to have particular, undefined properties. The play moves 'up' and 'down' across three locations: the valley, the mountain side, and the mountain top, where the two groups of youngsters negotiate. Whilst the language of the play remains realist, the content tends towards the absurd but suggests an engagement with the question of how one shares resources and what such sharing means. The end of the play sees the youngsters from beyond the mountain established in the valley and accepted as they join in the mineral-water drinking. The words of the parents: 'When you first came down here we couldn't decide what you were – Germans, Poles, Czech ... Chinese, Croats ... Serbs, Russians ...'[66] point to nationalities associated with being 'the enemy', instigators of war within Europe and beyond, but any 'threat' seems averted as the youngsters assimilate to the parents' habits.

Muriel Spark's 1962 stage play *Doctors of Philosophy*, in contrast, returns the audience to a London drawing-room where two women with PhDs, the unmarried Leonora, an academic who however longs for a child, and married mother Catherine who is a school teacher, are pitted against each other in a battle over intellectual competence.[67] The question of motherhood *versus* career is here raised in agonistic fashion, an issue that was to gain increasing prominence in feminist work throughout the 1970s and 1980s. Boringly, from a 2015 perspective, the married mother 'wins out' – she may not have a brilliant career, but, as the play suggests, she *can* play games.

Playing games became one of the common tropes of 1960s drama. The radio play 'Lovesick',[68] by Caryl Churchill (1927-)[69] explores notions of love as sickness and 'sick love' as the opening lines demonstrate: 'When Smith raped he didn't find what he was looking for ...'. Producing an alternation used in certain radio plays of 'being inside someone's head and out among extraordinary events'[70] the play, typical for the anti-psychiatry movement of the period and associated with Churchill's interest in R. D. Laing, a guru of that movement, engages with the manipulative power of Hodge, a psychiatrist who practises aversion therapy (a combination of emetics and images of what the aversion is supposed to be of), to explore how love can be conditioned by in/appropriate stimulants. Hodge is hoist by his own petard as his methods are used by another male character to re-engineer his patients' desires. Churchill's anti-institutionalism chimed with later feminist psychoanalytic writing which regarded psychiatry as a male-dominated domain designed to subjugate women and make them compliant with men's desires.

By 1969, in Maureen Duffy's stage play 'Rites',[71] women's desires as articulated *by* rather than *for* them, came to the fore. The women's movement, though not yet fully established in the UK, was gaining ground. Duffy describes her play as 'a version of *The Bacchae* set in a ladies' public lavatory'.[72] Two sets of women, lavatory cleaners and office girls, encounter one another in the loos in their common desire and disdain for men which they finally vent in an onslaught on a 'man' who enters the toilets but turns out, to the women's horror, to be a butch lesbian. In discussing this murder Duffy argues that 'All reductions of people to objects, all imposition of labels ... all segregation can lead only to destruction.'[73]

Where Duffy advised caution, the 1969 play *Vagina Rex and the Gas Oven*[74] by Jane Arden (1927-82)[75] threw caution to the wind in its unambivalent assertion of women's rage at their oppression. *Vagina Rex* was a first performance piece, as opposed to a conventional play, in which the stage directions not only describe the scenery but also detail the action on stage, much of which depends on projections, soundscapes, and non-verbal interaction. Significantly, in the text the stage directions are not set off from any direct speech by being in italics, thus collapsing the difference between the spoken and the unspoken. In its resistance to seeing women's experiences as 'private neurosis', the play argues that 'political and personal are beginning to cleave unto one another and yesterday's "deranged" females are emerging as today's formidable radical leaders.'[76] The play utilises archetypes such as 'FURIES' and 'WOMAN' to demand the end of women's oppression. In common with much feminist work from this period it makes the claim that 'We have no language. The words of women have yet to be written.'[77] The refusal to perform though conventional dialogue is here part of the message – the body, post-theatre-censorship, comes to stand for women's experiences that lack articulation. As the WOMAN'S VOICE says at the end: 'The rage is still impacted within us – I am frightened of the on-coming explosion.'[78]

The early 1970s

One might argue that that explosion occurred in 1970 when the Women's Movement was established and Gay Liberation Front was set up.[79] The early 1970s also saw a dramatic expansion of women's theatre, promoted by the post-censorship opportunities of the diversification of theatre venues (street theatre, the upstairs of pubs, fringe theatres, new arts venues), in the context of an increasingly turbulent public political sphere and the rise of alternative voices. The early 1970s, under a Conservative government, were characterized by mounting tensions in Northern Ireland, the 'Troubles', with the first British soldier killed in 1971 and 'Bloody Sunday' in Londonderry where British troops killed 14 people on 30 January 1972. The UK was experiencing increasing economic crises after a period of rising prosperity. Economic shifts included the UK's entry into the European Economic Union in 1973, strikes by miners and worsening industrial relations as the 'old' industries collapsed (that of Rolls Royce in 1971 was one of the first signs of this), and the oil crisis in 1973. Decolonization continued. In Uganda Idi Amin expelled the Indian community in 1972. The 1971 Immigration Act was but the most recent measure of the gradual tightening of immigration into the UK from the colonies. For women the most important legislation of the period was the 1970 Equal Pay Act which came into force in December 1975.

Caryl Churchill, at time of writing the *grande dame* of British feminist theatre, wrote mostly for radio in the early 1970s. 'The Ants' (1971), 'Abortive' (1971), 'Not Not Not Not Not Enough Oxygen' (1971), 'Henry's Past' (1972), 'Schreber's Nervous Illness' (1972), and 'Perfect Happiness' (1973) were concerned with power structures, in the family[80] as well as in institutions, particularly the mental hospital. These power structures were preoccupying the women's movement at the time. That movement, coming out of socialist alliances, was also concerned with wider social relations, with environmental issues, and with anti-capitalist politics. *Owners*,[81] Churchill's first professionally performed stage play, is about those politics and how they intersect with social relations. The staging of *Owners* inaugurated Churchill's life-long working relation with the Royal Court Theatre. However, that relation was somewhat atypical for the 1970s. Ann Jellicoe has maintained that at the time she 'didn't appreciate what tremendous disadvantages [she] was working under as a woman.' And that 'the men didn't really take a woman seriously, as a director, for instance ... the dice were loaded against women writers.'[82] However, in reaction against such conditions, and in response to the feminist politics of the early 1970s which favoured collectivism, feminist theatre companies operating outside conventional theatres began to form, inspired by the street-based protests that characterised the political scene of that period. Red Ladder Theatre, a mixed-sex socialist company formed in 1968, decided to put on a 'women's play' in 1972, conjoining issues of women's with workers' oppression. As they stated: 'Our view was summed up in two banners ... "Women will never be free while workers are in chains." And "Workers will never be free while women are in chains."'[83] The play addressed female and male workers' relations in the struggle for equality at work and in the home,[84] and it was intended to be performed at 'trade union meetings, weekend schools, tenants, [*sic*] associations, women's liberation meetings, women's groups, mothers' groups, in working mens' [*sic*] clubs, schools and colleges ...'[85] As such it was part of the emergence of the issue-based play, designed to be shown in non-theatre spaces and forming part of the tide of alternative theatre, experimental performance work and collective theatre making that swept Britain during the 1970s.

Red Ladder (1968) was one of the earliest mixed-sex companies with a socialist agenda; others such as the Women's Theatre Group (1973), Sadista Sisters (established 1974) and Monstrous Regiment (1975) with more sustainedly feminist agendas were to follow but the vast majority of these such as Les Oeufs Malades (1976), Clean Break (1977), Beryl and the Perils (1978), Mrs Worthington's Daughters (1978) and the Theatre of Black Women (1982) were set up only in the second half of the 1970s.[86] Like much early feminist theatre work in the UK, the productions of companies formed in the first half of the 1970s often started with a socialist agenda, workshopping issues around women and work into improvised performances and putting women centre-stage. From this they moved out to consider increasingly diverse women's issues.

Conclusion

Significant changes occurred in women's drama between 1945 and 1975. Fuelled by the political developments of the period and the proliferation of performance sites, women moved out of the home and domesticity, began to explore their sexuality and their bodies, and asserted women's autonomy, particularly for the younger generation. Formal experimentation emerged in the second half of that period as one means of expressing women's emerging cultural confidence and the demands to develop voices of their own, not always unproblematically. Caryl Churchill's Marion in 'Owners' tellingly says: 'We men of destiny get what we're after even if we are destroyed by it.'[87] In other words, 'getting what we're after' was, and is, not without its costs, and women, in various ways, found that the demands they made also had their costs, but it was not until the 1980s that these costs really began to be counted in women's theatre and performance.

Notes

1. Michelene Wandor, *Look Back in Gender: Sexuality and the Family in Post-war British Drama* (London: Methuen, 1987).
2. But see Dan Rebellato, *1956 and All That: The Making of Modern British Drama* (London: Routledge, 1999).
3. See Michelene Wandor, *Post-War British Drama: Looking Back in Gender* (London: Routledge, 2001).
4. Only brief general comments are made about that period.
5. Wandor, *Post-War British Drama*, p. 27.
6. See 'Bank, Coal, Aviation and Telecommunications', *National Archive* <http://www.nationalarchives.gov.uk/cabinetpapers/themes/bank-coal-aviation-telecommunications.htm> and 'Transport, Electricity, Gas, Iron and Steel', *National Archives*, <http://www.nationalarchives.gov.uk/cabinetpapers/themes/transport-electricity-gas-iron-steel.htm> [accessed 5 February 2015].
7. Clemence Dane, *Call Home the Heart: A Play in Two Acts* (London: Heinemann, 1947).
8. Clemence Dane, pseudonym for Winifred Ashton, was a highly successful though now largely forgotten novelist, playwright and artist who spent her life in London. Her novel *Regiment of Women* (1917) about a girls' school was 're-discovered' in the 1980s as part of the establishment of genealogies of lesbian writing and boarding-school novels dealing with romantic friendships between girls. Dane wrote numerous plays, both for stage and screen. She co-wrote the screenplay for *Anna Karenina* (1935), starring Greta Garbo. Her papers are held at the Victoria and Albert Museum Theatre and Performance Department.
9. See Maggie B. Gale, *West End Women: Women and the London Stage 1918–1962* (London: Routledge, 1996), p. 229.
10. Dane, 'St James's Theatre', *The Times* (London), 11 April 1947, p. 6. The Times Digital Archive,< http://gale.cengage.co.uk/times.aspx/> [accessed 27 May 2016]
11. Dane, *Call Home the Heart*, Act 1, p. 9.
12. Dane, *Call Home the Heart*, Act 1, pp. 25–6.
13. Dane, *Call Home the Heart*, Act 1, p. 35.
14. Dane, *Call Home the Heart*, Act 1, p. 20. On 15 April 1945 British troops liberated the Bergen-Belsen concentration camp. Films taken by the liberating troops of the horrors they witnessed on entering the camp were shown in many countries. They are now in the Imperial War Museum.
15. Dane, *Call Home the Heart*, Act 1, p. 38.
16. Dane, *Call Home the Heart*, Act 1, p. 44.
17. Dane, *Call Home the Heart*, Act 1, p. 46.
18. Dane, *Call Home the Heart*, Act 1, p. 11.
19. Dane, 'St James's Theatre'.
20. Dane, *Call Home the Heart*, Act 1, p. 11.

21. Dane, *Call Home the Heart*, Act 2, pp. 93–4.
22. Gale argues that there are 'very few unmarried stage mothers up until the early 1950s' (p. 128) and Hetty remains a secondary character in this play, featuring mainly in the second act. For a more sustained discussion of the representation of single mothers see Gale, *West End Women*, pp. 128–38.
23. Susan Bassnett, 'A Commercial Success: Women Playwrights in the 1950s' in *A Companion to Modern British and Irish Drama 1880–2005* ed. by Mary Luckhurst (Oxford: Blackwell, 2006), pp. 175–87.
24. Clare Hemmings, *Why Stories Matter: A Political Grammar of Feminist Theory* (Durham Duke University Press, 2011), p. 1.
25. Gale, *West End Women*, pp. 128–32.
26. Gale, *West End Women*, p. 232.
27. Stephen Brooke, 'Gender and Working Class Identity in Britain during the 1950s', *Journal of Social History*, 34:4 (2001), 773–95.
28. See 'A Short History of the BBC', *BBC* (2002) <http://news.bbc.co.uk/1/hi/entertainment/1231593.stm> [accessed 13 February 2015]
29. Muriel Spark, 'The Party Through the Wall', and 'The Interview' in *Voices at Play* (Harmondsworth: Penguin, 1961), pp. 175–188 and pp. 129–149 respectively. 'The Party Through the Wall' was first performed on the Third Programme in 1957, 'The Interview' in 1958. 'The Party Through the Wall' was revived for 30-Minute Theatre on BBC4 on 28 November 1989.
30. Spark, 'The Party Through the Wall', p. 177.
31. Spark, 'The Party Through the Wall', pp. 178, 179.
32. Spark, 'The Party Through the Wall', p. 180.
33. Spark, 'The Interview', p. 142.
34. It is worth noting that the lives of single women, women working as companions and female carers in the 1950s are utterly under-researched. Much of the literature looking at women during that period (e.g. J. Lewis, *Women in Britain Since 1945*, Oxford: Blackwell, 1992) focuses on married women's/mothers' employment, thus reinforcing the dominant heteronormative view of women's worlds of the period.
35. Spark, 'The Interview', p. 139.
36. The facts she rehearses interestingly require knowledge of other countries and the former colonies, and at time of writing the particular references the text makes to Lebanon, Afghanistan and Syria make fascinating reading as an index of how views of particular world regions change over time.
37. The reference to this quiz gestures towards the rise of popular culture in the 1950s.
38. Dane, *Call the Heart Home*, Act II, p. 107.
39. Shelagh Delaney was a playwright from a working-class background born in the north of England whose first play, *A Taste of Honey* (1958), became her most enduring work. Its film version, co-written with director Tony Richardson, won the BAFTA award for Best British Screenplay and the Writers' Guild of Great Britain Award in 1962. *A Taste of Honey*, featuring a single mother and her teenage daughter, is notable for its rejection of the notion of women as inherently nurturant and maternal, and its sympathetic treatment of the daughter's homosexual friend.
40. Ann Jellicoe, playwright and director, is best known for her two plays *The Sport of My Mad Mother* (1956), and *The Knack* (1962). Born in Yorkshire, she was educated at the Central School for Speech and Drama, London. She began experimenting

with theatre from early on, drawing on absurdist and physical theatre devices for her work. She was closely associated with the Royal Court Theatre, becoming its literary manager (1973–75) and championing, *inter alia,* the work of Caryl Churchill. In 1978 she established the Colway Theatre Trust, which later became the Claque Theatre, and developed the concept of community plays, focussing on local issues and involving local people.

41. A Correspondent, 'Stage Parents Come in for Punishment', *The Times* (London), 10 October 1958, p. 20.
42. The Royal Court Theatre opened in May 1956.
43. Littlewood was possibly the most prominent woman director, quite atypical for the period in this, in 1950s British theatre. See P. Rankin, *Joan Littlewood: Dreams and Reality – The Official Biography* (London: Oberon Books, 2014).
44. Gale, *West End Women,* p. 236.
45. 'Ann Jellicoe Talks to Sue Todd' in A. Jellicoe, *The Knack and The Sport of My Mad Mother* (London: Faber and Faber, 1985), p. 12.
46. Wandor, *Look Back in Gender,* p. 39.
47. Shelagh Delaney, *A Taste of Honey* [1959] (London: Methuen, 1982), Act II, Sc. I, p. 55.
48. Delaney, *A Taste of Honey,* Act II, Sc. I, p. 55.
49. This has to be seen in the context where 1958 saw the first race riots in Notting Hill and the Midlands.
50. Aleks Sierz, *In-Yer-Face Theatre* (London: Faber and Faber, 2001), p. 16.
51. Ann Jellicoe, *The Sport of My Mad Mother,* Act III, p. 168.
52. William Shakespeare, *King Lear,* Act IV, Sc. I, l. 36–7.
53. Doris Lessing, 'Each His Own Wilderness' in *New English Dramatists: 1* ed. by E.M Browne (Harmondsworth: Penguin Books, 1959), pp. 11–95.
54. A correspondent in *The Times,* fittingly, titled his review 'a year of short runs on the London stage', *The Times,* 15 January 1959, p. 15.
55. Lessing, 'Each His Own Wilderness', Act I, Sc. I, p. 13.
56. Lessing, 'Each His Own Wilderness', Act II, Sc. II, p. 94.
57. Lessing, 'Each His Own Wilderness', Act I, Sc. II, pp. 50–1.
58. Lessing, 'Each His Own Wilderness', Act II, Sc. II, p. 95.
59. In *Look Back in Gender,* set out by Wandor like a two-act play, the 'Interval' is devoted to Kenneth Tynan's famous 1965 diatribe against the theatre censor, titled 'The Royal Smut Hound', pp. 73–85.
60. 'Ann Jellicoe talks to Sue Todd', p. 13.
61. Ann Jellicoe, 'The Knack' in *The Knack and The Sport of My Mad Mother,* pp. 25–98 (p. 90).
62. 'The Knack', Act III, p. 84.
63. Spark, 'The Danger Zone' in *Voices at Play* (London: Macmillanm 1961), pp. 9–45.
64. Spark, 'The Danger Zone', p. 9.
65. Spark, 'The Danger Zone', p. 11.
66. Spark, 'The Danger Zone', p. 45.
67. Spark, *Doctors of Philosophy* (New York: Alfred A. Knopf, 1966).
68. Caryl Churchill, 'Lovesick' in *Caryl Churchill: Shorts* (London: Nick Hern Books, 1990), pp. 1–19. Churchill wrote a number of radio plays in the 1960s and 1970s, several of which are in this volume. See E. Aston, *Caryl Churchill* (Plymouth: Northcote House, 1997).
69. Caryl Churchill is Britain's foremost feminist playwright. After university, she began writing for radio but quickly moved to the stage. Her work always engages

with contemporary political issues, and is characterized by continuous high degrees of experimentalism, both theatrically and semantically. *Top Girls* (1982) made her a household name in feminist theatre. A commentary on Margaret Thatcher's Britain and the choices women felt forced to make between family and career, between submission and rebellion, *Top Girls* combines a first scene of various famous historical female figures talking about their histories of oppression with a second, contemporary half detailing the tensions between two sisters who made different life choices. Churchill's work has been staged predominantly by the Royal Court Theatre. She has written numerous, highly acclaimed plays, most recently *Here We Go* (2015) a play about old age and dying, and *Escaped Alone* (2016), featuring four older female actresses and juxtaposing their lives against the disasters of the wider world.

70. *Caryl Churchill: Shorts*, 'Introduction', n.p.
71. Maureen Duffy, 'Rites' in *Plays by Women, Vol 2* ed. by Michelene Wandor (London: Methuen, 1983), pp. 11–28.
72. 'Afterword: *Rites*' in *Plays for Women, Vol. 2*, p. 26.
73. 'Afterword: *Rites*' in *Plays for Women, Vol. 2*, p. 27.
74. Jane Arden, *Vagina Rex and the Gas Oven* (London: Calder and Boyars, 1971).
75. Jane Arden began her career as an actress in the 1940s but then became a playwright for stage and screen, appearing repeatedly in her own work. Through her interest in feminism and the anti-psychiatry movement Arden's work became increasingly radical and highly theatrically experimental. In 1970 she formed the radical feminist theatre group *Holocaust* for whom she wrote a play by the same title, about a woman's mental breakdown. It was adapted for the screen as *The Other Side of the Underneath* (1972). Arden continued to produce experimental work until her death by suicide.
76. Arden, 'Introduction', *Vagina Rex*, n.p.
77. *Vagina Rex*, p. 10.
78. *Vagina Rex*, p. 63.
79. See *Strike While the Iron Is Hot* ed. by M. Wandor (London: The Journeyman Press, 1980), p. 6.
80. Aston, *Caryl Churchill*, p. 5.
81. Caryl Churchill, 'Owners' in *Churchill: Plays 1* (London: Methuen, 1985), pp. 1–67.
82. 'Ann Jellicoe Talks to Sue Todd', p. 17.
83. Wandor, *Strike While the Iron is Hot*, p. 18.
84. It drew on experiences such as the 1968 Ford sewing machinists' strike at the Ford Dagenham plant, in 2010 nostalgically re-visioned in the film *Made in Dagenham* (Dir. Nigel Cole, Distr. Paramount Pictures).
85. Wandor, *Strike While the Iron is Hot*, p. 18.
86. See 'Companies', *Unfinished Histories*, <http://www.unfinishedhistories.com/history/companies/> [accessed 24/5/2016] for details of women's theatre companies.
87. Churchill, 'Owners', Act I, Sc. V, p. 31.

4
Journalism

Deborah Chambers

Introduction

The post-war period forms a decisive moment in the history of women's news writing when women engaged in cultural and political struggles to establish themselves in a male-defined profession and public sphere. Women journalists were marginalised in the profession by reporting about women's lives using techniques intended to appeal to a broader audience. This reinforced women's social subordination by trivializing women's issues. However, they developed strategies to challenge patriarchal discourses and address second wave feminism by politicising women's issues and perspectives within mainstream news. Through a study of the experiences and practices of women journalists in mainstream news between 1945 and 1975, this chapter charts transformations in women's coverage of news during this period. It explores the interconnections between women journalists, their audiences, the news media industry and the wider social and political culture of the period. Recognising news as a site of inequality and difference, it explains how women spearheaded the introduction of new topics and styles of reporting in print and broadcast news to attract women readers and audiences. I argue that through the women's pages and features, women introduced a new feminised public discourse which emerged as a 'counterpublic sphere' in the sense developed by Nancy Fraser in her critique of Jurgen Habermas's account of the public sphere. By these means, women journalists created a feminised counterpublic discourse.

The changing status of women reporters during and after World War II

Women's progression into journalism and broadcasting before World War II was hampered by rigid gender roles that defined women's place in the home after marriage. However, the commercial need to attract women readers

© The Author(s) 2017
C. Hanson and S. Watkins, *The History of British Women's Writing, 1945–1975*,
History of British Women's Writing, DOI: 10.1057/978–1–137–47736–1_5

formed a key strategy for expanding newspapers' readership and ensured women's access to the newsroom, albeit in a limited way. Women journalists were expected to develop and work within a distinctive style of news restricted to reports and reviews on fashion, society news and domesticity. Moreover, women's feature writing was separated from the front page reports on politics and foreign news written by men, leading to a division between 'hard' and 'soft' news. 'Hard news' was associated with business, politics and conflict while 'soft news' stories were defined as having a 'woman's angle' and regarded as 'fluff'.[1] Male journalists' refusal to cover the soft news corresponded with a feminization of human interest stories. Women's writing was segregated from other areas of news, conceived of as frivolous and apolitical reportage. Yet the women's pages comprised 'the one place where they had the power to define news'.[2]

The BBC, formed in 1922, followed other public sector institutions by introducing a marriage bar in 1932.[3] However, at the onset of war, these restrictions were lifted to allow women to be conscripted into wartime jobs. In journalism, the impact was dramatic. Women moved rapidly into newsrooms vacated by men who enlisted in the armed forces. In radio, several women announcers and news readers served on domestic and overseas services, with seven female presenters on the Forces Radio.[4] Yet women were barred from reporting from the war front.[5]

A memorable exception was Clare Hollingworth (1911–). In August 1939 aged 27, when she had been working as a journalist for less than a week, Hollingworth was sent by the *Daily Telegraph* to Poland to report on rising tensions in Europe. She came across a massive build-up of Nazi troops, tanks and armoured cars facing Poland during a journey across the border to Germany. The next morning she contacted the British embassy in Warsaw to report the German invasion of Poland. This eyewitness account turned out to be the scoop of the century. It was the first report received by the British Foreign Office about the Nazi invasion of Poland. During the following decades, she reported on conflicts in Palestine, Algeria, China, Vietnam and Aden.[6] Despite Hollingworth's remarkable revelation, not a single woman was among the 558 writers, radio journalists or photographers accredited by the British government to cover the D-day landings in June 1944. British women war correspondents were refused formal accreditation until later that year, when most of the action was over.[7] Raised in Leicester, Hollingworth went to the School of Slavonic Studies, London, after attending grammar school. She joined the staff of the League of Nations 1935–38, and then worked in Poland for the Lord Mayor's Fund for Refugees from Czechoslovakia before becoming a journalist with the *Daily Telegraph*. One of her scoops concerned the defection of Kim Philby, the "third man" in the Cambridge spy ring, to the USSR in 1963. In 2016, Hollingworth celebrated her 104th birthday in Hong Kong where she retired during the 1980s.

Having played a central role in newsrooms during the war, women were either dismissed from newsrooms in the immediate post-war period to make way for the return of male colleagues who had served in the forces, or were obliged to work in sections previously reserved for women. For example, Mary Stott (1907–2002), who famously edited the women's pages of the *Guardian*, began her career as a 'temporary' copyholder at the *Leicester Mail* because women were barred from membership of the Typographical Association or the Correctors of the Press Association. Stott then moved into a sub-editing post at the prestigious *Manchester Evening News* where she felt like a 'real journalist'.[8] She was sacked in 1950 when men were discharged from the war, to make way for a male progression from Deputy Sub-editor to Chief Sub-editor post. The only daughter of two journalists, Robert and Amalie Waddington (née Bates), Stott was also born and raised in Leicester.

These barriers and constraints were experienced by women right across the social and political spectrum. Although gaining the full franchise by 1928, women remained under-represented in parliament in 1945 with only 24 women MPs, at just 3.8 per cent.[9] Given this systematic exclusion, journalism formed a vital route into public and political life for women after World War II. Following the suffrage movement, women were sustaining a counter-civil community of alternative woman-only feminist press and voluntary associations.[10] In the case of *mainstream* news media, a vital plank of publicity, women re-entered post-war newsrooms on men's terms.

In his account of the public sphere, Jürgen Habermas claimed that the rise of a distinctive culture of "civil society" and an associated public sphere coincided with the rise of a bourgeoisie, as a marker of a liberal public sphere.[11] However, it was not accessible to all, as Fraser reminds us: 'On the contrary, it was the arena, the training ground, and eventually the power base of a stratum of bourgeois men, who were coming to see themselves as a "universal class" and preparing to assert their fitness to govern'.[12] Paradoxically, Habermas's explanation of the decline of the public sphere is premised on a *discourse of publicity* that promotes accessibility, rationality and equality yet functions as a strategy of distinction by distinguishing middle class men from the rest. Women's exclusion from the official public sphere therefore rested on class- and gender-biased notions of 'publicity'.

The ideological alignment of women with privacy, family and domesticity in post-war Britain fundamentally contradicted the codes of a public sphere as a discursive site representing all citizens' experiences, lives and aspirations. In mainstream news, professional women were therefore compelled to redefine the idea of the 'public' – as a realm that combined politics and popular culture – by creating a subaltern counterpublic. Drawn from Antonio Gramsci's concept of cultural hegemony which pinpoints social groups excluded from political representation, the term 'subaltern' is adopted in critical theory and postcolonialism to describe social groups excluded by the power structure of the colony and colonial homeland. In the context of the bourgeois public sphere, Fraser conceptualises "subaltern counterpublics" as responses to the discrimination and exclusion of women.

She argues that repressed groups such as women form subaltern counterpublics, "parallel discursive arenas where members of subordinated social groups invent and circulate counter-discourses to formulate oppositional interpretations of their identities, interests, and needs"[13]. For women journalists, creating a subaltern counterpublic was no easy task given that the media were and remain largely privately owned and operated for profit in Western societies. Women lacked equal access to the material means of participation. Fraser explains that subaltern counterpublics have a dual character:

> On the one hand, they function as spaces of withdrawal and regroupment; on the other hand, they also function as bases and training grounds for agitational activities directed toward wider publics. It is precisely in the dialectic between these two functions that their emancipatory potential resides. This dialectic enables subaltern counterpublics partially to offset, although not wholly to eradicate, the unjust participatory privileges enjoyed by members of dominant social groups in stratified societies.[14]

In the case of mainstream news, a feminised counterpublic was consolidated through a withdrawal and gradual politicisation of women's news in areas such as women's pages. This marginalised feminised space generated a vital training ground for women journalists, a stepping stone towards mainstreaming women's issues as public issues. The evidence outlined below indicates that, despite operating within commercial news frameworks that relied on advertising, women's efforts in mainstream newsrooms made a significant contribution to the publicising of women's discourses *as* popular public discourses.

The post-war growth in news media and increased competition among newspapers for advertising increased the demand for women readers. After driving women out of the newsroom, newspapers were obliged to recall them to attract women as consumers. Women's pages were viewed as a winning formula for the purpose. By the 1950s, women's pages were commonplace in the tabloid popular press, comprising a diet of society news, recipes, and advice columns and extended to broadsheets for commercial purposes.[15] These pages featured complex journalism agendas. Although garden parties, fashion and household tips comprised much of the earlier content in women's sections of papers, by the late 1960s and early 1970s the content broadened to include serious news about women's lives. Women were almost invariably required to write on topics or in styles that distinguished them from their male counterparts. Yet via column and feature writing, the impact of women's journalism extended way beyond the women's pages by the 1970s and came to redefine political debate. Women created a more informal, 'human interest' style that paved the way for an exploration of the relationship between the personal and the political. The post-war segregation of women's news acted as a springboard for the politicization of women's issues through the rise of feminist campaign journalism.

The rise of the women's pages

Mary Stott's biography exemplified this process of politicising women's issues. Stott became the longest serving editor of the *Guardian*'s women's page and one of the most notable campaigning journalists of the twentieth century. Between 1957 and 1972, she created a space for women's interests and issues on these pages under the title, 'Mainly for Women'. Stott campaigned for gender equality, focusing on the themes of poverty, unemployment and disability. In 1969, the page was changed to 'Woman's Guardian'. When asked to edit the *Guardian*'s women's page in 1957, Stott had to think carefully about taking it on. She recalls: 'It nearly broke my heart – I thought my chance of becoming a real journalist was finished.'[16] This fear of being typecast reveals the lowly status of news for and by women at the time. However, Stott set out to change the whole women's page concept. Katharine Whitehorn recalls: 'She dealt with personal relationships, education, medical matters, divorce – one forgets that such subjects, now found routinely in every paper's feature pages, once didn't figure in serious papers at all.'[17]

Stott cultivated an affinity with her readers by creating a platform on which women could share their experiences about their struggles in balancing family and professional life and form supportive networks. Although known for her skills as a columnist, Stott's approach was to evoke the authenticity of *amateur* writers. She received more than 50 volunteered manuscripts a week.[18] This strategy underpinned a news genre of human interest stories focusing on and framed by women's experiences. Stott also generated a core of regular and talented contributors in the 1960s to the *Guardian*'s weekly 'Women Talking' feature including key figures such as Shirley Williams, Margaret Drabble, Lena Jeger, Marghanita Laski, Taya Zinkin, and Gillian Tindall. These names ensured the *Guardian* women's page became one of the most widely debated newspaper features of the time. Contributors were invited to write about their personal relationships, sexual morals, education, the quality of social services and weaknesses in the welfare state. Publicising a social problem often prompted direct action. For example, the Housewives' Register was formed in 1961 after a letter described the social and intellectual isolation of so many 'housebound housewives with liberal interests and a desire to remain individuals'.[19] Similarly, the Pre-school Playgroups Association was established when the shortage of nursery education was reported.

Kira Cochrane, Guardian Woman's editor from 2006 to 2010, reminds us how constrained women's lives were from the late 1950s right up to the 'swinging sixties':

Women unable to get a mortgage in their own name; banished from the table at the end of dinner parties; having no access to safe, legal abortion; being told that their career options were nursing, secretarial work or, at a push, teaching; being sacked, quite legally, if they became pregnant; being paid – again, quite legally – less than a man in the same job. Treated like children. Or worse.[20]

Katherine Whitehorn states that 'Mary Stott's women's pages became almost a political force, with the very name "Guardian woman" purred or spat at.'[21] By the end of the 1960s, the term 'Guardian women' had entered public consciousness.

The scorn and derision coming from the 'men's press' drew attention to this new woman-centred set of discourses. Answering the question, 'how did the *Guardian* women's page become so influential?', Polly Toynbee (1946–) – the women's editor from 1977 to 1988 – states 'It helped that as the feminist movement of the 1960s and 1970s got under way, *Private Eye* [a British satirical and current affairs magazine] regularly sneered at the page, with male newspaper columnists writing biliously about hairy, dungaree-wearing, lentil-eating, man-hating Guardian wimmin. There were reams of articles in the tabloids and rightwing broadsheets back then about why men should now slam doors in women's faces to prove that women couldn't have it both ways – not chivalry AND equality. And that vitriolic backlash proved the making of the women's pages'.[22]

Toynbee was brought up in London and is the daughter of the literary critic Philip Toynbee and granddaughter of the historian, Arnold J. Toynbee. Although she won a scholarship to St. Anne's College Oxford from a comprehensive school background, Toynbee dropped out 18 months later. She took jobs in a factory and burger bar before working for Amnesty International in newly independent Rhodesia. Toynbee has written several books based on her own experiences of working on the minimum wage including *Hard Work: Life in Low-pay Britain* (2003)[23]. Described as the "queen of leftist journalism", she headed the poll of 100 "opinion makers" in 2008.[24]

Another key reason for the success of the *Guardian* women's page, in spite of the vitriol, was the skill with which Mary Stott and fellow journalists mainstreamed second wave feminist ideas. While radicalism was an approach adopted in the alternative women's press, Stott's success was said to be underpinned by her sense of moderation and cooperation. She forged solidarities among diverse women readerships but was reluctant to align herself with what she regarded as extremist views or the assertiveness of Betty Friedan's *The Feminine Mystique*.[25] Nonetheless, by focusing on human interest stories and evoking emotional responses to those stories, women were identifying new themes and advancing new techniques of personalised yet political writing in the mainstream. In these ways, they were developing a new public discourse: a discourse aimed at publicising and, in Fraser's words, 'universalising'[26], women's experiences and feminist politics. Mary Stott's news concept in the *Guardian* women's pages of the 1950s was extended to the *Observer* pages in the 1960s, thereby generating all those 'women's pages that aren't women's pages'.[27] Importantly, then, women's pages formed a precursor to now familiar section titles such as 'Currents', 'Style' and 'Outlook'. They reshaped the conception and meaning of 'news' by setting the style, tone and range of themes now commonplace in news. However, tensions were observable by the 1970s among participating women writers concerned about whether the views and standpoints of women were devalued and marginalised by their confinement to particular pages. Linda Christmas, who followed Stott as editor of the Women's page in 1972, expressed this dilemma stating:

> We wanted to get out of the ghetto. We didn't see the need for pages allocated to women ... These would be covered but not to the exclusion of subjects of interest to men and women ... Yet heads of circulation and advertising were fearful that circulation figures would plummet.[28]

Such was the power of the women's pages in attracting women readers to the paper that those in charge of circulation and advertising were reluctant to ditch the formula.

Christmas had to persuade the dedicated women freelancers, who contributed to the page on a daily basis, of the benefits of losing the woman's page. Resisting the transformation, they invited Christmas to discuss the issue at a soirée that Linda referred to as a 'wine and whinge event and, at worst, a Kangaroo Court'. She was accused of being a misogynist. 'Then they sold a vamped up version of the evening to *Private Eye!*'[29] Divisions arose about the appropriate strategy for mainstreaming women's issues and experiences and reshaping what was called 'news' through feminist ideas. Although there was strong resistance, the 'Women's Page' was renamed 'Guardian Miscellany' in 1973. When Suzanne Lowry replaced Christmas as woman's editor in 1975, the name 'Guardian Women' was reinstated. As Kira Cochrane muses, '... what they now provide is simply a guaranteed space, a space that persists and provides at least some balance on those days when every single major news story pivots around a bloke.'[30]

Despite the advances in promoting women's issues, women writers were ambivalent about taking on the women's pages as the 'women's editor'. The 1970s remained a time of widespread inequalities in the workplace exemplified by low pay, barriers to promotion, and sexual harassment. As well as the *Guardian's* women's pages, Christmas has worked for the *Swindon Evening Advertiser*, *Times Educational Supplement* and BBC *Newsnight* and is now Emeritus Fellow in Journalism at City University.

Demanding to be treated as equals by male colleagues, women journalists were compelled to promote and universalise women's rights in order to democratise gendered newsroom practices. Lowry confirms that while the newspaper's editor, Peter Preston, was hoping for something less feminist and more moderate and 'womansy' in style, it failed to reflect the 'fierce new mood' among women at this juncture.[31] 'Guardian women' evoked the boldness and confidence of feminism in the mid-1970s with, as Lowry recalls, a 'stunning kaleidoscope of women, men and ideas whirling around a special time and place'[32] such as Jill Tweedie, Posy Simmonds, Janet Watts. Posy Simmonds (1945–) is well known for her cartoon series for the *Guardian*, 'Gemma Bovery' (2000) and 'Tamara Drewe' (2005–06), in which the literary oriented English middle classes are parodied. Feminist writer and broadcaster, Jill Tweedy (1936–1993) succeeded Mary Stott as principal columnist on the *Guardian's* Women's Page. She was one of the first to write in the *Guardian* Women's Page about important and gritty feminist issues such as rape in marriage, the ways women were treated during childbirth, female circumcision and bride burning in India. Tweedie was educated at independent Croydon High School, South London and twice voted "Woman Journalist of the Year". She was known for her 'letters from a faint-hearted feminist'[33] and her autobiography, *Eating Children* (1994)[34]. Liz Forgan states, 'Her weekly column became an icon of all that was hairy and terrifying to men who found the women's movement a threat to their security. She was parodied, ridiculed and attacked.'[35]

While women were hesitant about editing the women's pages, given their marginal status and concerns about hostile reactions, it was recognised that a momentous change was occurring across the political landscape. Women's news was gradually forging a subaltern space, uneasily wedged within the pages of mainstream news. Through such attempts to universalise women's counterdiscourses as feminised discourses of publicity, traditional notions of the 'public' were challenged and gradually eroded. Campaigning women journalists publicly contested the privatisation of gender politics and women's exclusion from the official public sphere in the 1970s, corresponding with the government enforcement of the 1970 Equal Pay Act and implementation of the Sex Discrimination Act in 1975.

The multiple trajectories of women's campaign journalism

Women entered campaigning news through various routes. Historic changes in the style and content of news were occurring in the tabloid newspapers, beyond the *Guardian*. Marjorie Proops (1911–1996) made her name as an agony aunt on the *Daily Mirror* and became known as 'the nation's confidante'.[36] Yet she was also an accomplished writer and, driven by her socialist principles, a campaigning journalist and social commentator. Daughter of a publican, Proops was born in Woking, Surrey. She started her media career in 1939 through the familiar trajectory of fashion pages, but as a fashion illustrator for a women's magazine, *Good Taste*. She then moved to the *Daily Herald* as a fashion editor and became women's editor in 1950. Proops joined the *Daily Mirror* in 1954 as a columnist, woman's editor and then general features writer and took over the advice column as agony aunt in 1959. In those days, 'agony aunts were answering questions like whether the presents should be returned after a broken engagement.'[37]

As the 'problem page' editor, for over 30 years, Proops received millions of letters that began 'dear Marje', from people who saw her as a friend.[38] Editor Hugh Cudlipp, described her as 'the first British journalist to attain the Instant Recognition status previously enjoyed by film stars.'[39] Yet the style of her page steadily changed towards the end of the 1960s. Steered by the themes of her readers' letters, she used her column to champion women's causes such as sex education, contraception, the abortion law, help for rape victims and tolerance towards homosexuality. She often framed a whole feature around one letter.[40] By the 1970s, Proops had become an establishment figure. She was awarded an OBE in 1969. She was directly involved in government policy issues by serving on a government committee for One-Parent Families appointed by Richard Crossman and the gambling commission chaired by Lord Rothschild. Her range was impressive. Proops was a committed member of the National Union of Journalists, was quoted regularly in the broadsheet press, involved in children's rights and in Leo Abses's campaign to decriminalise homosexuality yet was also granted an exclusive interview with Princess Anne since royalty guaranteed popular readership appeal. Feminist issues were introduced, sometimes easily and sometimes uneasily, into popular discourses to gradually redefine mainstream news.

Author and columnist Katharine Whitehorn (1928–) took her first step on the journalism ladder in 1956 as sub-editor for a woman's magazine. Born in Hendon, and educated at private schools, Roedean then Glasgow High School, Whitehorn went on to Newnham College Cambridge. Her renowned Fleet Street career started when *Picture Post* photographer, Bert Hardy, asked her to model for him. The photograph of Whitehorn sitting in front of a bedsit room gas fire with a cigarette, called 'Lonely in London',[41] not only helped her to secure a job with *Picture Post* but also became an advertisement for the energy drink Lucazade. Whitehorn then moved to the *Spectator* and in 1960 she was taken on as fashion editor at the *Observer* where she was the first woman to have her own column. As a women's-feature writer, Whitethorn was known as a keen observer of the changing status of women. She developed a distinctive approach that would breach the condescending style adopted by existing women-targeted news and magazine columns. Rather than encouraging women to be perfect wives in post-War Britain, Whitehorn developed a more down-to-earth style liberally peppered with humour. She addressed major feminist issues associated with the everyday lives of real women and was quickly celebrated for her wit and perceptive observations about the shifting roles and treatment of women.

In her landmark 'slut column', Whitehorn revealed an impatience for the prissy and delicate conduct demanded of women by 1960s etiquette.[42] Whitehorn is immortalised by a column she wrote in 1963, called 'Sisters under the Coat'. This 'celebrating sluts' column was dedicated to 'all those who have ever changed their stockings in a taxi, brushed their hair with someone else's nailbrush or safety pinned a hem' and anyone who had 'taken anything back out of the dirty-clothes basket because it had become, relatively, the cleaner thing'.[43] Whitehorn's book, *Kitchen in the Corner: A Complete Guide to Bedsitter Cookery* published in 1961, became a classic. It was republished with the title *Cooking in a Bedsitter*, remaining in print for 35 years. Yet, as Rachel Cooke comments, 'it seems rather ironic that, of all the many words she has written, the book of Whitehorn's that is now being republished is about cookery.'[44] Nevertheless her recent autobiography, *Selective Memory* comprises a significant record of life as a woman journalist during this critical period of change. She served on several government committees and won a CBE for services to journalism in 2013 and, in her mid 80s, continues to write a column in the *Observer*.

Even beyond the campaign writing of the women's pages, women journalists suffered regular insults associated with their gender. This is illustrated by public reactions to successful women such as Jean Rook, Anne Leslie, and Janet Street-Porter who crossed over into broadcasting. These forthright women succeeded in forging a career in male-dominated media worlds but, in the process, were vilified and pilloried for being outspoken in much the same way as the feminist campaigning women. Jean Rook (1931–1991) was born in Hull, daughter of an engineer and usherette, and then raised in the East Riding of Yorkshire where she attended grammar school. After graduating from Bedford College, University of London she was the first woman to edit the Sunday newspaper, the *Sennet*. Rook wrote an opinion column in the *Daily Express* through which she cultivated an entertaining confrontational style. Acclaimed as 'The First Lady of Fleet Street', Rook was also known as the 'Bitch of Fleet Street'[45] and found that a *Private Eye* female columnist, caricatured as a brassy-styled 'scurrilous hackett' called 'Glenda Slagg', was modelled on her.

Following the conventional career path of women at the time, Rook worked as woman's editor at the *Yorkshire Post* and later moved to fashion magazine, *Flair*. She was the first woman to edit the Sunday newspaper, *Sennet*, and became fashion editor for the *Sun* in 1964. Rook explained in an interview, how she had 'clawed and scrambled' her way to become 'the First Lady of Fleet Street ... Britain's bitchiest, best known, loved and loathed woman journalist'.[46] In the 1970s, at the peak of her career, Rook was celebrated for her outrageous opinions on a range of subjects including those normally considered vulgar and taboo. She led a distinctive, right-wing style of column writing for women that male editors relished. Rook mocked members of the Royal family as well as celebrities, referring to

Prince Philip as a 'sponger',[47] and was contemptuous of what she called 'hairy-legged feminism'. Her writing in papers such as the *Sun* was characterised by disdain for female public figures to reflect 'the prejudice of their women readers'.[48] However, Rook also wrote about highly personal women's issues in her columns such as her own suffering with breast cancer and experience of widowhood. Rook summarised her work by stating: 'My readers look for the worst in me. They love me to sink my teeth and typewriter keys into some public figure they're dying to have a go at themselves'.[49]

In a different sphere, Anne Leslie (1941–) who was acclaimed for reporting on wars and conflicts across the globe, worked for the *Express* in the 1960s but left in 1967 in exasperation at the attitudes of male colleagues who thought women were incapable of foreign reporting. Leslie was born in Rawalpindi, Pakistan, and then sent to a convent boarding school in England in 1950 before attending Lady Margaret Hall, Oxford. She has won several British Press awards, two Lifetime Achievement Awards and an OBE in 2006 for "services to journalism". While never claiming to be a feminist, Leslie's style of reporting shared the personal angle adopted by the campaign styles of writing in the woman's pages of the *Guardian*. Addressing the differences between male and female war correspondents, Leslie states:

I've specialised in foreign politics and that quite often involves wars, obviously ... Men have much more of a Top Gear Clarkson-like concern with hardware. Women are more interested in the human stories. Some of the older foreign correspondents, some of them deceased, said to me they hated the feminisation of war coverage. One old crusty gent said to me: 'You women feminised all the news'.[50]

Throughout the post-war period, women journalists regularly faced this dismissal of women's news as inferior and even tainted.

Women and news in broadcasting

In newspaper journalism before the mid-1970s, women were typecast as undeserving of mentoring or training since they were expected to quit on marriage or after having children. In broadcasting, women faced additional challenges. Radio was a rigidly controlled public service broadcasting monopoly run by the BBC. In the UK, commercial radio did not arrive until 1973. Women's advancement in the medium was curtailed by the moral code of the BBC's first Director General Sir John Reith (later Lord Reith). Although he had left by 1937, Reith's patriarchal principles and strict moral standards continued for decades. Married and divorced women were barred from working for the BBC between 1932 and 1944, and women were banned from reading the news on radio and TV until as recently as 1974 and 1975 respectively. Women's voices were considered to be too high pitched and lacking in legitimacy when speaking about serious political or economic issues.

Within this patriarchal context, the creation of the BBC programme *Woman's Hour* in 1923 performed a role that was as ground breaking for radio as the women's pages were for newspapers. It became the BBC's longest running and most iconic radio programme. Ironically, it was initially cancelled after nine months because the National Federation of Women's Institutes objected to the way women were marked out and categorised, in the same manner as children, who also had their own special hour.[51] In 1946, *Woman's Hour* was re-launched in a magazine format to help demobbed women rebuild home life during peacetime. With rationing continuing until 1954, sober advice on domestic subjects ranged from how to save soap to ways of cleaning stair carpets.[52] However, the programme also covered other issues of relevance to women including the 1946 Royal Commission on Equal Pay and the 1947 campaign for better wages for home workers. In the early 1950s the programme was presented by women such as Olive Shapley who addressed health, human relationships and sexual issues, but without stereotyping women in the process.[53] Indeed at the time, these were topics scarcely mentioned in private conversations, never mind in public.

The programme had a magazine and human interest format blended with a journalistic and 'newsy' style which meant also addressing topical issues.[54] Wyn Knowles (1923–2010), sixth editor of *Woman's Hour* from 1971, was proud that the programme aired issues such as frigidity or venereal disease yet played down its 'campaigning' elements to ensure acceptance. 'It isn't a programme that campaigns, rather one that keeps up with changing tastes, reflecting women of today. I don't think we have ever been consciously controversial, although it has happened from time to time.'[55] Once again, the voice of moderation comes through and yet *Woman's Hour* is recognised, with hindsight, as pioneering. The men in power at the BBC paid little attention to the programme and failed to realise 'how "modern" it was becoming'. Dennis Barker explains, in his record of an interview with Knowles:

> The programme in those earlier days was a lunchtime one, starting at 2pm. By the time the power-broking men had come back from long lunches, the programme was over, so they never heard it. If they were ignorant enough to regard the programme as the harmless witterings of "the fair sex", so much the worse for them and the better for the programme.[56]

However, a discussion about menopause in 1948 caused such embarrassment among male colleagues that one Assistant Controller made a complaint about having to hear about hot flushes and damaged ovaries.[57]

Raised in Hampshire, Knowles went to finishing school in Switzerland before working as a cipher clerk in MI5 in the Second World War. She then became a secretary in the Talks department typing pool of the BBC in 1951 but then switched to Laurence Gilliam's features department which provided the opportunities for Knowles to write and record documentary programmes[58]. As editor, Knowles changed the style of *Woman's Hour* by shelving the formal rehearsals and adopting a looser and more flexible framework for the programme. The topics were discussed and selected democratically by its contributors according to Sue MacGregor (1941–) who was host from 1972 to 1987. Topics followed the news agenda by identifying a woman's angle. These included the battle for equal pay and the burgeoning women's liberation movement which was generally avoided by other current affairs radio programmes as mystifying or too risky. *Woman's Hour* began consistently featuring issues broached by feminists such as women's wages, contraception and legalised abortion.

Ironically, MacGregor was initially turned down as continuity announcer on the Home Service after reaching the last three finalists in an audition, aged 26. MacGregor's voice is now hailed as one of the most respected and well-modulated voices on radio. As Brenda Maddox puts it, 'At that time, a woman newsreader was as unthinkable as a woman priest'.[59] MacGregor was brought up in Cape Town South Africa where she went to a private boarding school. She moved to London to work as a typist at Australia House, and then at the BBC as a junior secretary but returned to South Africa to embark on her broadcasting career on SABC's English language radio service. However, in the late 1960s McGregor was offered work as a reporter on the BBC's *The World at One*. Then, hosting *Woman's Hour* from 1972, she interviewed famous figures such as Julie Andrews, Bette Davies, and Margaret Thatcher with enough airtime to explore gender-related topics with them.

In 1971 the professional group, Women in Media, campaigned for women to be employed as news announcers and on current affairs programmes.[60] A 1971 academic report on *Women in Top Jobs* prompted the BBC management to formally enquire into the obstacles facing women.[61] In 1973, a BBC internal report confirmed women's exclusion on air on radio and television as well as in managerial and production roles. Enquiring into the constraints facing women within the institution, the report recorded a 41-page list of difficulties, plus appendices, with several pages of hostile quotes exposing the prejudice of senior managers towards women throughout radio and television. These ranged from women's physical factors, their indifference to electronics, many references to the inferior nature of women's voices and even women's prejudices against men.[62]

The Editor of Radio News was quoted as saying: 'women are simply not able to do hard news stories as they 'see themselves as experts on women's features'.[63] Having been confined to women's features, women writers were deemed to be incapable of working in other areas such as broadcast news.

He went on to say that he would wish to limit the proportion of women journalists regardless, since 'Those who are dedicated ... are not really women with valuable instincts but become like men.' Women were either condemned for being too different from or too similar to men and therefore deemed unfit for news. As Suzanne Franks states, 'It is interesting to contrast all the prejudice in the 1970s to the realities of wartime in the 1940s when many women announcers and news readers served on domestic and overseas services ...' In the post-war period, it was not until 1974 that a woman, Gillian Reynolds, was allowed to present the news on Radio 4. The arrival of Angela Rippon as the first woman to read the main evening TV news bulletin on BBC 1 in April 1975 was also a dramatic historical moment. Later, commenting on Rippon's appointment, Director of Television said: 'Barriers crashed, taboos lay shattered and Lord Reith probably stirred and muttered in his private Valhalla.'[64]

Conclusion

Women's styles of news writing between 1945 and 1975 were shaped by a series of wider social dynamics that transformed the face of news. Despite the dramatic post-war constraints experienced by women who sought to build a career in mainstream journalism, women's pages in broadsheet and tabloid newspapers carved out a space for pioneering and campaigning women supported by the privileges of middle class backgrounds and a university education. These pages formed a counterpublic sphere to counteract the male- defined public discourses of news by reporting on women's issues of the time. Yet journalists such as Mary Stott and Marjorie Proops also became national figures, mainstreaming a new kind of news. They confirmed yet also subverted gendered distinctions between 'hard' and 'soft' news by promoting a style of human interest news reporting that was gradually adopted across broadsheets and tabloids alike. Propelled by the dictum that 'the personal is political',[65] this pioneering mode of campaign writing promoted the second wave women's movement by highlighting the impact of sex discrimination and gender inequality in all dimensions of women's lives.

In her critique of Habermas's public sphere and account of the ways members of subordinated groups invent and circulate counterdiscourses, Fraser explains that, as subaltern counterpublics, women construct counterdiscourses which provide them with the tools to formulate oppositional interpretations of their identities, interests and needs.[66] Women journalists of the post-war period played a central role in this endeavour. To bypass and critique patriarchal professional codes, certain media women were building a counter-civil society of alternative women-only writings, voluntary associations and publications such as *Spare Rib* in the 1970s. But in the case of mainstream news, women were compelled to work through masculine professional codes. Women journalists sought to broaden 'news' as a concept, process and set of practices in order to address gender inequality and women's issues as central economic, political and social themes. Working within the 'realm of the popular', women created a feminised public discourse that contested the privatisation of gender politics. This counterpublic discourse was a necessary precondition for entering a redefined public sphere by promoting women's issues as central features of 'news'. Through human interest news genres, they re-centred women's issues and popularised feminism. By these means, mainstream journalism formed a vital channel of entry into public political life for women – the public mainstream – at a time when women were otherwise systematically marginalised from the official public sphere.

Notes

1. John Hartley, *Understanding News* (London: Methuen, 1982), p. 38.
2. Dustin Harp, 'Newspapers' Transition from Women's to Style Pages: What Were They Thinking?', *Journalism*, 7:2 (2006), 197–216, 213.
3. Catherine Murphy, 'The BBC Marriage Bar: A Reflection of Inter-War Attitudes to Women?', *Thinking with History Workshop*, Goldsmiths, London, 30 November 2007; Suzanne Franks, 'Attitudes to Women in the BBC in the 1970s: Not So Much a Glass Ceiling as One of Reinforced Concrete', *Westminster Papers*, 8:3 (2011), <https://www.westminster.ac.uk/__data/assets/pdf_file/0005/124880/008Attitudes-to-women-in-the-BBC-in-the-1970s-Suzanne-Franks.pdf> [accessed 10 November 2015].
4. Franks, 'Attitudes to Women'.
5. Deborah Chambers, Linda Steiner, and Carole Fleming, *Women and Journalism* (London: Routledge, 2004); Franks 'Attitudes to women'.
6. Sarah Blake, 'Women War Correspondents', *Telegraph*, 12 July 2010, <http://www.telegraph.co.uk/culture/7872900/Women-war-correspondents.html> [accessed 10 November 2015]; E. Addley, 'A Foreign Affair', Profile, *Guardian*, Saturday 17 January 2004, <http://www.theguardian.com/books/2004/jan/17/featuresreviews.guardianreview13> [accessed 10 November 2015].
7. Blake, 'Women War Correspondents', and Addley, 'A Foreign Affair', also see A. Sebba, 'Media: The Story They Didn't Want Women to Tell: Britain Refused to Send Female Journalists to Cover D-Day', *Independent*, 23 October 1994, <http://www.independent.co.uk/news/media/media-the-story-they-didnt-want-women-to-tell-britain-refused-to-send-female-journalists-to-cover-dday-but-that-didnt-stop-the-intrepid-barbara-wace-as-she-told-anne-sebba-1419696.html> [accessed 10 November 2015] and A. Sebba, *Battling for News: The Rise of the Woman Reporter* (London: Hodder and Stoughton, 1994).
8. Mary Stott, *Forgetting's No Excuse* [1973] (London: Virago, 1989); Linda Steiner 'Newsroom Accounts of Power at Work' in *News, Gender and Power* ed. by Cynthia Carter, Jill Branston and Stuart Allan (London: Routledge, 1998) pp. 145–59.
9. 'The History and Geography of Women MPs since 1918 in Numbers', House of Commons Library (2013) <http://commonslibraryblog.com/2013/11/18/the-history-and-geography-of-women-mps-since-1918-in-numbers/> [accessed 10 November 2015].

10. Nancy Fraser, 'Rethinking the Public Sphere: A Contribution to the Critique of Actually Existing Democracy', *Social Text*, 25/26 (1990), 56–80, <http://my.ilstu.edu/~jkshapi/Fraser_Rethinking%20the%20Public%20Sphere.pdf> [accessed 10 November 2015]; M. Dicenzo, 'Militant distribution: Votes for women and the public sphere', *Media History*, 6:2 (2010), 115–128; Chambers et al, *Women and Journalism*.

11. Jurgen Habermas, *The Structural Transformation of the Public Sphere* (Cambridge, Massachusetts: MIT, 1989).

12. Nancy Fraser, 'Rethinking the Public Sphere', p. 60.

13. Fraser, Rethinking the Public Sphere', p. 67.

14. Fraser, 'Rethinking the Public Sphere', p. 68.

15. Chambers et al, *Women and Journalism*.

16. Lena Jeger, 'Mary Stott', *Guardian*, 18 September 2002, <http://www.theguardian.com/news/2002/sep/18/guardianobituaries.gender> [accessed 10 November 2015].

17. Katherine Whitehorn, 'A Hopeful 1929 Headline Reads: Snobbery – A Thing of the Past?', *Guardian*, 3 November 2007, <http://www.theguardian.com/news/2007/nov/03/digitalarchive.digitalarchivefeatures4> [accessed 12 March 2015].

18. Stott, *Forgetting's No Excuse*.

19. Mary Stott, 'Women Talking: Mary Stott, Women's Editor 1957–1972' (a piece that Stott wrote in 1962), 'Gender: 50 Years of the Womens' Pages', 18 July 2007, *Guardian*, <http://www.theguardian.com/world/2007/jul/18/gender.uk5> [accessed 10 November 2015].

20. Kira Cochrane, 'Still So Much to Do', *Guardian*, 18 July 2007, <http://www.theguardian.com/world/2007/jul/18/gender.uk16> [accessed 20 February 2015].

21. Whitehorn, 2007, 'A Hopeful 1929 Headline'.

22. Polly Toynbee, 'Why Does The Guardian Still Need a Women's Page? Because the Feminist Revolution is Only Half Made', *Guardian*, 18 July 2007, <http://www.theguardian.com/commentisfree/2007/jul/18/gender.pressandpublishing> [accessed 10 November 2015].

23. Polly Toynbee, *Hard Work: Life in Low-pay Britain*, (London: Bloomsbury Publishing, 2003).

24. Andy Mcsmith, 'Polly Toynbee, Reborn as a Lady of the Right', *Independent*, 26 November 2006, < http://www.independent.co.uk/news/people/profiles/polly-toynbee-reborn-as-a-lady-of-the-right-425833.html> [accessed 16 June 2016].

25. Betty Friedan, *The Feminine Mystique* [1963] (London: Penguin, 2010).

26. Fraser, 'Rethinking the Public Sphere'.

27. Whitehorn, 'A Hopeful 1929 Headline'.

28. Linda Christmas, 'Afraid to Be Frivolous', *Guardian*, 18 July 2007, <http://www.theguardian.com/world/2007/jul/18/gender.uk6> [accessed 10 November 2015].

29. Christmas, 'Afraid to be frivolous'.

30. Quoted in Jess McCabe, '50 Years of The Guardian's Women's Pages', *the F word blog: Contemporary UK Feminism*, 18 July 2007 <http://www.thefword.org.uk/blog/2007/07/50_years_of_the> [accessed 10 November 2015].

31. Suzanne Lowry, 'The Heady Days of Women's Lib', *Guardian*, 18 July 2007, <http://www.theguardian.com/world/2007/jul/18/gender.uk7> [accessed 10 November 2015].

32. Lowry, 'The Heady Days'.

33. Liz Forgan, 'For the Love of a Faint-Hearted Feminist', *Guardian*, 18 April 2000, <http://www.theguardian.com/world/2000/apr/18/gender.uk> [accessed 10 March 2015].
34. Jill Tweedy, *Eating Children: Young Dreams and Early Nightmares* (London: Penguin, 1994).
35. Forgan, 2000, 'For the Love of a Faint-Hearted Feminist'.
36. Penny Vincenzi, 'Obituary: Marjorie Proops', *Independent*, 12 November 1996, <http://www.independent.co.uk/news/people/obituary-marjorie-proops-1351984.html> [accessed 14 march 2015].
37. Linda Grant, 'Profile: Marjorie Proops', *Independent*, 3 January 1993, <http://www.independent.co.uk/voices/profile-marjorie-proops-marjes-mirror-image-britains-most-famous-agony-aunt-has-been-as-unhappy-as-her-readers-linda-grant-explores-a-pretence-that-deceived-millions-1476382.html> [accessed 14 March 2015].
38. Grant, 'Profile: Marjorie Proops'.
39. Vincenzi, 'Obituary: Marjorie Proops'.
40. Vincenzi, 'Obituary: Marjorie Proops'.
41. Whitehorn, *Selective Memory: An Autobiography* (London: Virago Press, 2007).
42. Sophie Heawood, 'Sisters Under the Coat: Katherine Whitehorn's Landmark Slut Column', *Guardian*, 9 Oct 2013, <http://www.theguardian.com/theguardian/from-the-archive-blog/2013/oct/09/katharine-whitehorn-sluts-observer-1963> [accessed 25 March 2015].
43. Katherine Whitehorn (1963) 'Sisters Under the Coat', *Observer*, 29 December 2013, <http://static.guim.co.uk/sys-images/Guardian/Pix/pictures/2013/10/9/1381318000770/Whitehorn29dec63-001.jpg?guni=Article:in body link> [accessed 25 March 2015].
44. Rachel Cooke, 'The Domestic Goddess Who Couldn't Cook', *Guardian*, 17 August 2008, <http://www.theguardian.com/lifeandstyle/2008/aug/17/british.vegetablesrecipes> [accessed 16th June 2016].
45. Carol Sarler, 'Unleashed and Unrepentant: Fleet Street's Bitch Goddesses', *Independent*, 13 July 2008, <http://www.independent.co.uk/news/media/unleashed-and-unrepentant-fleet-streets-bitch-goddesses-866278.html> [accessed 26 April 2013].
46. Hugh Massingberd, *The Daily Telegraph Third Book of Obituaries: Entertainers* (London: Macmillan, 1997), p. 203.
47. J. Booth, 'The British Don't Like Too Many Changes: They Like To Be Left Alone'', *Sunday Telegraph*, 31 March 2002, p. 5; Chambers et al, *Women and Journalism*.
48. See Joan Smith, 'What's My Line', *Guardian*, 15 September 1994, p. 13.
49. Jean Rook, *Rook's Eye View* (Worthing: Littlehampton Books Services, 1979).
50. Ann Leslie, 'If You Ask Me', *Press Gazette: Journalism Today*, 3 December 2007, <http://www.pressgazette.co.uk/node/39606> [accessed 22 April 2013].
51. Maggie Andrews, 'Domesticating the Airwaves', Interview, *Woman's Hour*, 11 September 2002, BBC Radio 4.
52. Sally Feldman, 'Twin Peaks: The Staying Power of BBC Radio's *Woman's Hour*' in *Women and Radio: Airing Differences* ed. by C. Mitchell (London: Routledge, 2002), pp. 64–72.
53. See Chambers et al, *Women and Journalism*.
54. Danica Minic, 'What Makes an Issue a Woman's Hour Issue?', *Feminist Media Studies*, 8:3 (2008), 301–15.

55. Dennis Barker, 'Wyn Knowles Obituary', *Guardian*, 23 July 2010, <http://www.theguardian.com/media/2010/jul/23/wyn-knowles-obituary> [accessed 10 November 2015].
56. Barker, 'Wyn Knowles Obituary'.
57. Feldman, 'Twin Peaks', p. 67.
58. Wyn Knowles Obituary, *Telegraph*, 22nd July 2010, <http://www.telegraph.co.uk/news/obituaries/culture-obituaries/tv-radio-obituaries/7905301/Wyn-Knowles.html> [accessed 16th June 2016].
59. Brenda Maddox, 'The Woman Who Cracked the BBC's Glass Ceiling', *British Journalism Review*, 13: 2 (2002), 69–72, 69.
60. Sebba, *Battling for News*, p. 205.
61. M. Fogarty, A. J. Allen, Isobel Allen, and Patricia Walters, *Women in Top Jobs* (London: PEP, 1971).
62. BBC (1973) *Limitations to the Recruitment and Advancement of Women in the BBC*, Report to Board of Management BM (73) 31.
63. BBC, *Limitations*.
64. Franks, 'Attitudes to Women', p. 135.
65. A phrase popularised by the second wave women's movement, originally developed by Carol Hanisch in 1969 and first published in 1970 as 'The personal is political' in Shulamith Firestone and Anne Koedt (eds) *Notes from the Second Year: Women's Liberation* (New York: Radical Feminism, 1970), <http://www.roehampton.ac.uk/uploadedFiles/Pages_Assets/PDFs_and_Word_Docs/Courses/Drama_Theatre_and_Performance/PersonalisPol[1].pdf> [accessed 10 November 2015].
66. Fraser, 'Rethinking the Public Sphere'.

Part II
Reconstructing Gender

5
Angry Young Women: Education, Class, and Politics

Mary Eagleton

The so-called 'Angry Young Men' who were prominent in drama and fiction in the 1950s and 1960s were an amorphous group, yoked together around protest at establishment orthodoxies and a loosely left-leaning politics.[1] Members of the group have walk-on parts in the work of several women novelists. Margaret Drabble (1939–) makes passing reference to Kingsley Amis in *A Summer Bird-Cage* (1963) and an aspiring actor, Simon, is reported to have 'a reasonably-sized working-class part in a working-class play at the Royal Court', where John Osborne's *Look Back in Anger* premiered in 1956.[2] Lynne Reid Banks (1929–) mentions 'a publishing house specializing in novels by Angry Young Men' in *The L-Shaped Room* (1960), and the eponymous William in *Sweet William* (1975) by Beryl Bainbridge (1932–2010) talks about 'that *Look Back in Anger* stuff' on a TV programme.[3] Amis plays a more significant role in the writing of A. S. Byatt (1936–). There is a scene in *Still Life*, published in 1985 but set in the 1950s, where Frederica, like Byatt a student at Cambridge University during that time, goes to the Literary Society to hear Amis talk about *Lucky Jim* (1954). Frederica feels 'a very simple sexual distaste for *Lucky Jim*' and its cruel misogyny and is suspicious about the claims for Amis's 'honest stand' and his 'decency' and 'scrupulousness'.[4] In 2001, Byatt returned to this scene in an interview with Philip Hensher. She recalls how, when she started publishing in the 1960s, she was met with 'all this sort of post-war nonsense, angry young men, nobody has ever reported the English provinces ... and the journalists just fell for it. As they fell for it with *Look Back In Anger* – as though nobody had ever reported lower-middle-class anger before'.[5] Byatt's objections are, at once, ones of sensibility – the sneering, the lack of tolerance she sees in Amis – and political – the sexism and the sudden 'discovery' of the lower middle class. Banks expresses a similar distance; she

© The Author(s) 2017
C. Hanson and S. Watkins, *The History of British Women's Writing, 1945–1975*,
History of British Women's Writing, DOI: 10.1057/978-1-137-47736-1_6

knew many of the group but felt no affinity.[6] The closest a woman author might get is in Drabble's 'Introduction' to the Virago edition of *Poor Cow* (1967) where she humorously describes Nell Dunn (1936–) as 'an affiliated member of the non-existent school of Angry Young Men'.[7]

Equally, women writers tended not to be grouped as 'Angry Young Women' though Shelagh Delaney *was* so named by the *Daily Mail*'s anonymous theatre critic when *A Taste of Honey* premiered in 1958, and the description resurfaced at the play's revival in 2014.[8] Penelope Mortimer (1918–1999) too got a belated inclusion. In 2015, on the re-issue of *The Pumpkin Eater* (1962) as a Penguin Classic, Rachel Cooke called her 'the original Angry Young Woman'.[9] When Methuen published the student edition of *A Taste of Honey* in 1982, however, the 'Suggestions for Further Reading' included Amis, John Braine, Osborne, Harold Pinter, and Arnold Wesker, but no women. Yet, even if there was no group, the frequency with which women's fiction from this period was adapted for film and television gives some sense of how these authors captured the cultural *Zeitgeist*. Dunn co-operated with Ken Loach on the television adaptation of *Up the Junction* (TV 1965) and the film script for *Poor Cow* (film 1967); Delaney wrote screenplays, including one for *A Taste of Honey* (film 1961), with director, Tony Richardson, and Bainbridge wrote the screenplay of *Sweet William* (film 1982); both Banks's *The L-Shaped Room* and Mortimer's *The Pumpkin Eater* became films, in 1962 and 1964 respectively. The script for *The Pumpkin Eater* was by Pinter who was to some another Angry Young Man.

Still, in the period of post-war austerity, the 'never had it so good' 1950s, and the 'swinging sixties', there was much for women to be angry about and it was uncertain if women could reconcile new aspirations with established expectations about their traditional roles.[10] Moreover, as we can see in the work of Dunn, Delaney, Maureen Duffy, and other women's theatre of the period, for the working-class woman there was little sign of the affluence and consumerist delights the country was being promised. In slum housing and grubby, rented rooms, they encountered their own version of the 'kitchen-sink', that symbol of confining domesticity against which the Angry Young Men railed.[11] This chapter discusses the position of the Angry Young Women in three ways. First, I consider representations of the middle-class woman, often well educated but chaffing against normative expectations. She is divided within herself and, frequently, at odds with other women. In the second section, we see the interest in working-class voices, and how the critique of the Angry Young Woman extends into problems of class difference, race, and sexuality. Maternity, in particular, is an issue of anguish for all our authors. The final section is concerned with place – the significance of particular locations, the hope of finding a place where fulfillment is possible, and the fear that you will never really escape your place of origin. The Angry Young Women feel the weight of their past and, just occasionally, the promise of a different future.

Forms of anger

Byatt and Drabble began publishing in the early 1960s. For the clever women who people their novels a corrosive sense of frustration is one of the dominant emotions. Their protagonists pre-date the expansion of UK Higher Education; they usually attend Oxford or Cambridge where the practice of quotas limited the number of female students; they do not have the benefit of student grants which were not introduced until 1962.[12] They do profit, however, from a developing ethic of meritocracy and fiercely play meritocracy's competitive games.[13] As the fiction explores, there is a conflict between the academic and professional aspirations of the educated woman, and a life of the domestic and the maternal, possibly alleviated by romance or maternal love. The intellectual woman is one who 'has no place, but must shift from one place to another, who is forever "out of category"'.[14] The lives of these protagonists are close to those of Byatt and Drabble themselves and, interestingly, in later essays and interviews, both return to their early fiction to highlight their personal predicament at that time, living a dilemma and unable to see any solution.[15]

Byatt and Drabble have a troubled history as sisters and strained relationships between women feature frequently in their texts. In Byatt's *The Game* (1967), the opposition between the academic and the domestic is expressed through the lives of two sisters, Cassandra, who leads an almost monastic life as an Oxford don, and Julia who is married and a mother (though happy in neither role). The opposition extends into their writing: Cassandra, a mediaevalist, is focused on the private writing of a journal and has been working for a long time on an unpublished critical edition of *Morte d'Arthur*; Julia is a best-selling novelist who appears on television arts programmes and gets reviewed in the *Guardian*. Women generally are at odds. Not only sisters but cousins (Drabble's *The Waterfall*, 1969) are in competitive or antagonistic relation; the mother has to be defeated; and female friendship groups are notably absent. A sense of what in the 1970s became known as 'sisterhood' is rare. Indeed, Deborah Philips points out how the focus in the fiction of the 1960s is on the rather isolated individual in comparison with the group focus of 1970's 'college fiction', particularly in the US.[16] For Rosamund in Drabble's *The Millstone* (1965), an identification with other women after the birth of her daughter comes as a surprising, new experience. This is not a problem only for high-achieving, intellectual women. The novels of Fay Weldon (1931–) – *The Fat Woman's Joke* (1967), *Down Among the Women* (1971), *Female Friends* (1975) – reveal relations between women that are, often, anything but friendly.

Opposition and conflict is present also *within* the individual. The title and epigraph of Drabble's *A Summer Bird-Cage* are from John Webster's *The White Devil* (1612). The dilemma he poses of the birds outside the cage who are desperate to get in while those who are in the cage are desperate to get out is used by Drabble to explore the contradictory and constrained position of her recent female graduates. Their ambition opens up the world. Clara in

Jerusalem the Golden (1967) believes, momentarily, that '[t]here seemed to be
no end to the possibilities of mad aspiration'.[17] But, then, that aspiration
is curtailed with an intense force. As Drabble's heroine, Jane Gray, says in
The Waterfall: 'I felt split between the anxious intelligent woman and the
healthy and efficient mother – or perhaps less split than divided', or, as Byatt
remembers: 'I see now, as I didn't dare to then, that the mind/body problem
of an intellectual woman in the 1950s was also one of rigorous conflict ...
the body required sex and childbearing, and quite likely the death of the
mind alongside'.[18] The need, which Clare Hanson illustrates in her discussion of Drabble and natality, is to ensure that the move from one role to
another is not an exchange but 'cumulative and inclusive'.[19] This is not easy.
At different stages in their careers, both Drabble and Byatt have scenes where
their heroine sits in an antenatal clinic and tries to read an academic text,
an emblematic expression of the irreconcilable.[20] The fiction reveals that the
women's hopes have little credibility or cultural support. Though Cassandra
in Byatt's *The Game* and Rosamund in Drabble's *The Millstone* do become university lecturers, most of the women know that they are treading water until
marriage. Occasionally there is mention of a secretarial course, in Drabble's
A Summer Bird-Cage and Andrea Newman's *A Share of the World* (1964), for
example, but this is clearly just a time-filler. The fiction marks a proto-
feminist moment: the need is there, the critical questioning is beginning,
but what is not in place is an elaborated discourse or any supportive group.

Anger is revealed not only in frustration. Even in Barbara Pym's (1913–80)
decorous world of the 1950s, where disagreements might focus on whether
marrows at a garden fête should be wrapped in copies of the *Times* or blue
tissue paper (*Some Tame Gazelle*, 1950), much darker currents flow beneath
the comedy of manners. Byatt, in a largely negative review of Pym's work,
nevertheless recognizes the intertwining of comedy and anger. She sees the
major characteristics of Pym's writing as 'malice and a kind of narcissistic
self-pity'; she notes moments that are both 'comic and appalling'; and she
sees characters 'cut down to size, no less ruthlessly because she (Pym) is so
deceptively mild'.[21] Weldon explores her own modes of anger in biting satire, the comic grotesque, and savage aphorisms; as Jocelyn tells us in *Down
Among the Women*: 'The cleaner the house, the angrier the lady'.[22] Weldon's
early job as a copywriter in advertising served her well as an apprenticeship
in the pithy phrase and the striking image. The problem, though, is always
how this anger can be expressed and to what effect. In the upper-middle-
class world of Penelope Mortimer's novels, for instance, fury is present but
stifled. Valerie Grove argues that Mortimer 'was voicing the kind of helpless
dissatisfaction that was to animate the feminist rebellion', again a proto-
feminist position, but that rebellion seems far away.[23] Like Mortimer herself,
her protagonists marry young, have lots of children, suffer their husbands'
many affairs, and experience great psychological distress. The status-quo can
be maintained only by a strenuous performance of normality. Women are
'little icebergs' with 'a bright and shining face above water' while beneath

'each keeps her own isolated personality'.[24] Trapped in domestic spaces, they are too restrained by propriety, too distraught and self-doubting to find a way out and, like Ann in Bainbridge's *Sweet William*, they can neither live with their partners nor live without them. They are the protagonists of what Gayle Greene terms 'mad housewife novels'.[25]

Mrs. Armitage in *The Pumpkin Eater*, a semi-autobiographical novel, is the quintessential example. In the nursery rhyme that gives Mortimer her title, Peter, the pumpkin eater, keeps his wife in a pumpkin shell. Mrs. Armitage – she is given no other name – is thirty-one, on her fourth marriage, with numberless children, and has no identity independent of her husband, Jake. In the course of the novel, she becomes pregnant, has an abortion, and a sterilization to save the marriage, but the discovery that Jake's lover is pregnant precipitates a breakdown. In the daughters there are tentative signs that they might not follow their mothers' routes and a more autonomous life beckons. In *The Pumpkin Eater*, Dinah makes occasional comments about gender inequality; in *Daddy's Gone A-Hunting* (1958), Angela is studying at Oxford; in *The Home* (1971), Eleanor sees in her daughter, Daphne, 'a kind of swagger, a rebellion against prettiness and niceness and ladylike subterfuge'.[26] But then convention, the confused psycho-dynamics of the family, or an identification of femininity with maternity drive the daughters as well to marriage and motherhood. Both Angela and Daphne become involved with men just like their fathers while Cressida, another daughter of Eleanor's, feels her body is 'paralysed' unless she has a child.[27] The narrator's bleak conclusion in *The Home* is that the daughters lived 'secretly, storing up unhappiness until they were old enough to feel it'.[28] When interventions do come they are always from outside the closed unit of the upper-middle-class family and social circle. In *The Pumpkin Eater*, a woman with a pram appears at Dinah's netball match – 'I was irrationally convinced she had come to give me some message from the outside world' – and a desperate letter arrives from a 'Mrs. Evans'. The letter contains 'the only evidence I had in the world that I was not alone'.[29] At the end of *The Home*, a woman in a PVC coat, referred to as one of the '[d]ykey ladies', takes Eleanor home with her.[30] These interventions hint of the surreal as if, whatever they represent, they will never break through into the lives of daily desperation.

A widening focus

Byatt is, rightly, suspicious of the status given to the Angry Young Men's focus on the lower middle class but one can still appreciate how significantly writing in this period extends its boundaries across class divisions, and shows a willingness to explore contentious subjects relating to sexuality and race. An aspect of the historical context here is the trend in the 1950s and 60s to teenage pregnancy and early marriage. Carol Dyhouse indicates how '[i]n each year of the 1950s around 27 per cent of all teenage brides were pregnant at their weddings' while, by 1960, 26.4% of girls under 20 were married.[31] In one respect, the writing constitutes a response to the post-war moral panic about women's sexuality and the importance of the mother-child dyad. It also responds to fears about immigration and miscegenation, and about homosexuality. A more liberal culture is on the verge of being created but not yet in existence. Homosexuality was not decriminalized in England and Wales until 1967 and, even then, only for men over 21 who were not in the armed forces; the Abortion Act did not come into effect until 1968; and it was not until 1970 that Family Planning Associations were obliged to make contraceptive provision for unmarried women.

One important shift lies in the representation of working-class women as having problems but not as intrinsically problematic. The writing expresses a growing discontent with women's maternal and domestic roles and frankness about women's sexual desire. Maroula Joannou refers to Dunn's characters as offering 'new models of subjectivity, in which propriety plays no part, and the quest for individual pleasure is seen as potentially liberating'.[32] The stories in Dunn's *Up the Junction* (1963) are brief and episodic – in the factory, at the wash-house, at the clipjoint, down the pub – and carried by the elliptical, overlapping, largely unattributed dialogue, full of bawdy quips. The tenor of the voices is non-reflective and eager for sensation. In *Poor Cow*, Joy, with a young baby and both her violent husband and her kind lover in prison, makes her way the best she can by 'modeling'. She is 'Joy' and 'joyous'; she has vitality, determination, and a deep maternal love for Jonny. But she is also a 'poor cow', impoverished, used, with no future. The comment in *Up the Junction* – 'Why should we think ahead? What is there to think ahead to but growing old?'– represents not fecklessness or fatalism but a clear-eyed recognition of the material circumstances.[33] With so few prospects you find excitement where you can and, as Joy makes clear to her friend, Beryl, sex is 'all I've got; you lose the pleasure of it if you turn professional'.[34]

But sex has its, sometimes troublesome, consequences and the literature is dominated by the figure of the unmarried mother. As Drabble's *The Millstone*, Banks's *The L-Shaped Room*, Bainbridge's *Sweet William*, Mortimer's *Daddy's Gone A-Hunting*, and Byatt's *The Shadow of the Sun* (1964) indicate, the unwanted pregnancy is as much a middle-class problem as working-class but the solution is rigidly class divided. In *Daddy's Gone A-Hunting*, the professional resources of the middle class are activated to ensure an abortion in a private London clinic; in *Up the Junction* and *Poor Cow*, an aborted foetus is thrown down the toilet. Kathleen Kiernan, Hilary Land, and Jane Lewis illustrate how, in the twentieth century, discussion of 'lone motherhood' was disproportionately focused on mothers who had never married rather than women who were widowed or co-habiting. The unmarried mother was pathologized. For some, she constituted a moral problem and voluntary organizations employed 'moral welfare workers' to deal with her. Across the period, unmarried mothers moved in public discourse from 'abnormal and victims' in the 1950s and early 1960s to 'normal but unfortunate' in the late 1960s and 1970s.[35] In literary representations of the working-class, unmarried mother, she is 'normal', 'unfortunate' in that she is battling a range of social and economic problems, but she is also often perceptively resentful at the limitations on her life.

This is the case in Delaney's *A Taste of Honey* where the 'problem' of the unmarried mother meets the 'problem' of the inadequate mother, emphatically undercutting any notions of 'good mothering' or 'natural motherhood'. The action follows a short period in the life of Jo from when she is about to leave school, to her meeting with her first boyfriend and the resulting unwanted pregnancy, to the time just before the birth. The most vivid relationship is that with her mother, Helen, who, in her headlong pursuit of any gratification, delivers, at best, indifferent mothering. Three of the play's four scenes end with Helen leaving. Her many affairs and flittings constitute an exuberant retreat from the quotidian. She would be an example of what was called the 'good-time girl'. Jo is aggressively negative about the forthcoming baby. Breastfeeding is 'cannibalistic'; she declares: 'I hate motherhood'; 'I'll bash its brains out. I'll kill it'; 'I don't want to be a mother. I don't want to be a woman'.[36] At the end of the play, Helen returns from her latest disastrous relationship. One is unsure whether her return signifies any maternal feeling or simply the need for a roof over her head. Certainly, the discovery that Jo's baby has been fathered by a black sailor doing his National Service precipitates a rapid retreat to the pub.

Michelene Wandor comments on the 'Lady Macbeth Syndrome' in the plays of male authors in the 1950s and 1960s. Male identity, she believes, 'is predicated on the imaginative annihilation of motherhood'.[37] As a woman dramatist, raising issues of relevance to women, Delaney is going against the grain but she was not completely alone. Doris Lessing and Ann Jellicoe are further examples of playwrights, if not actively feminist, then open to the concerns and aspirations of women. Lessing's *Each His Own Wilderness* and Jellicoe's *The Sport of My Mad Mother* were both first staged at the Royal Court, London in 1958, two years after Osborne's *Look Back in Anger*. Lib Taylor sees these three women dramatists as marking 'the beginning of a search for a theatrical form appropriate for the representation of women'.[38] Indeed, Lessing makes clear in her 'Author's Notes' to *Play with a Tiger* (premiered at the Comedy Theatre, London in 1962) that her interest is in 'rootless, declassed people who live in bed-sitting rooms or small flats or the cheaper hotel rooms' but, importantly, that this new material demands a new form. With kitchen-sink drama in mind, she rejects the 'detailed squalor of realism'; her play has a sparsely furnished set, dissolving walls, and shifts back and forth in time.[39]

In the explicitly political theatre of the 1960s and moving into the 1970s, an educative and provocative function is to the fore. Developments in radical politics during this time – the Campaign for Nuclear Disarmament, the anti-Vietnam protests, trades' union activity, *les événements* in Paris in 1968 and, not least, the development of the Women's Liberation Movement – brought fresh subject matter into the theatre, and the abolition of the censorship powers of the Lord Chamberlain in 1968 facilitated this. Change was also evident in production practices. Delaney's play was produced by Joan Littlewood at her Theatre Workshop, Stratford East and subsequently moved to the West End and New York. Littlewood's collaborative mode of working, involving the cast in research and improvisation and including music and movement in the drama, was an important model for future feminist work. Like Littlewood, other radical theatre companies – for example, Red Ladder (1968), the Women's Theatre Group (1970) and Monstrous Regiment (1975) – drew on ideas from Brechtian and agit-prop theatre. Furthermore, theatre moved out of traditional locations. Plays might be performed at trades union meetings, youth clubs, women's groups, tenants' associations, lunchtime theatres in pubs etc. 'Performance' could be at once theatre and protest. Just as the groups themselves were involved in consciousness raising, so audiences would be engaged in after-play discussions, or theatre might take place alongside demonstrations.

The Red Ladder Theatre's production of *Strike While the Iron is Hot* (premiered 1974) illustrates this interest in radical subject matter and new forms. It considers the problems working-class women face with respect to domesticity, employment, equal pay, abortion rights, and traces the growing consciousness of Helen who, across nine scenes, moves from romantic newly-wed to addressing union meetings on matters of equal pay. Thus, problems of sexual politics and labour politics are intertwined. In the Women's Theatre Group's production of *My Mother Says I Never Should* (premiered 1974), the focus is the common adolescent predicament of first sex, suspected pregnancy, and contraception planning. Even more emphatically than in Lessing's *Play with a Tiger*, these plays, in Wandor's words, 'break through the boundaries of naturalistic story telling'.[40] In *Strike While the Iron is Hot*, dialogue is interspersed with songs, direct comment to the audience, and the verbal links to the visual through stage props such as a red ladder, an umbrella, placards and banners. Indeed, the two banners that are presented to the audience towards the end of the play read: 'Workers will never be free while women are in chains' and 'Women will never be free while workers are in chains'.[41] Laudable though this sentiment is, it does not quite recognize that women are also workers.

In drama not so directly political, stylistic and formal inventiveness is still important. Maureen Duffy's *Rites* (premiered 1969) is a re-working of Euripides's *The Bacchae* set in a women's public convenience. The shocking events of the play – an attempted suicide and a murder, with the body casually disposed of in the incinerator – happen alongside the women's ribald conversation about men and the commercial benefits of prostitution, revelations about poverty, dead-end jobs, and domestic subservience.

In Duffy's words, the play should be performed not as social realism but as 'black farce', a style that is 'between fantasy and naturalism', while the stage directions evoke classical theatre in their formal ritual.[42] In fiction too, there is a line of dark, subversive comedy from Muriel Spark, through Bainbridge, to Angela Carter, Weldon, and on to Hilary Mantel. As Bainbridge explores the eruptions of violence into suburban, domestic life, the border between farce and horror becomes uncertain. In *The Bottle Factory Outing* (1974), for instance, a dead body is driven round and round Windsor Great Park, then squeezed into an empty hogshead of sherry to be dumped at sea. Though *A Taste of Honey* is closer to social realism, the pacey dialogue that marks the conversations between Jo and her mother, full of acerbic jibes and jokey banter, deliberately suggests a music-hall double act.

Texts might widen their focus but there can be an unfortunate schematic quality to the representations. The characters in *The L-Shaped Room* comprise of one unmarried mother-to-be (Jane), one Jewish man (Toby), one white gay man (Malcolm), one black gay man (John), two prostitutes (Sonia and, significantly named, Jane). In addition, widening representation does not necessarily mean a radical questioning of norms. In *Up the Junction*, gays are for jokes or feature as a drag act at the local pub; Geof in *A Taste of Honey* is maternal; Malcolm in *The L-Shaped Room* is bitchy and hysterical while John likes cooking and needlework; Marcus in Mortimer's *The Home* dresses in pastels and carries a poodle. The political position is particularly problematic when the narrative is told through a voice with which the reader is supposed to identify. Jane, in *The L-Shaped Room*, denies to herself the impending consequences of her pregnancy, is self-punishing, and takes on society's negative attitudes towards the unmarried mother. The plot follows her move towards a hesitant questioning of male authority and traditional views on femininity. However, the racism, anti-Semitism, and homophobia of characters, including the narrative voice of Jane, though exposed, are largely uninterrogated. At the start of the book, Jane is overwhelmed by John's 'animal smell' and his 'powerful negro odour'; at the end, she *laughingly* counters her father's comment that John smells 'like a polecat'.[43] Again, at the start, she describes 'a queer called Malcolm' as 'disgusting'; at the end, when realizing that John is gay, she does not feel 'the faint revulsion I had felt for Malcolm and others like him in the past'.[44] If this is the development of a more general political consciousness, extending from her questioning of gender norms, it is very limited.

There are similar problems when one looks at the authorial position and the slippages between authorial and narrative voices. In her Preface to the 2013 edition of *Up the Junction*, Dunn describes going to live in Battersea in 1959. From a wealthy, upper-middle-class background (her father was Sir Philip Dunn) she was obviously an outsider but she mixed easily with her neighbours, who knew she was writing stories about them, and she worked in a local sweet factory. The voice closest to Dunn's in the text is that of the narrator, Lily, described as 'an heiress from Chelsea'.[45] It is an uncritical, non-interventionist voice. The racist, anti-Semitic, and homophobic comments, the cruelty towards 'bent Sheil', a disabled woman, are left to stand. Just occasionally, a wry tone is heard. The episode set in the clipjoint ends with Rena's comment: 'The great thing in this life is you can choose – to do or not to do – if you get my meaning – at least we're free!'[46] One can sense the author's raised eyebrow.

For both authors and characters, political questions are stimulated by encounters across difference. Joannou thinks Dunn's position could be interpreted as an example of 'slumming' in the tradition of George Orwell; Drabble wonders if there is 'a little idealisation' in Dunn's representation of the working class; Dominic Head recalls Raymond Williams's phrase 'the orthography of the uneducated'.[47] As Williams explains, it has been 'one of the principal amusements of the English middle class to record the hideousness of people who say *orf*, or *wot*'.[48] Dunn is not laughing at her subjects; rather, there is a genuine sympathy and no sense of superiority. But Philips's suggestion that she acts as 'a participant observer of working-class women's lives' has credibility and it carries a sense of Dunn as involved in a kind of ethnographic exploration of other, very different, cultures.[49] Pym's perspective is similar. In her case, she is describing a world she knows well, that of fading gentlewomen on limited means and the tight communities around the local church. But she views them with an astute, assessing eye like that of the anthropologists she encountered in her work at the International African Institute and who feature so frequently as characters in her novels. Moreover, some of the sharpness of Bainbridge (in her perception of social relations and troubled psychologies, and linguistically) comes from her own experience of class difference in a downwardly mobile family. Characters too – Rosamond in *The Millstone* or Jane in *The L-Shaped Room* – nudge towards a new consciousness when removed from their known environments. Yet it is hard to say that the experience of class difference is prime. For Rosamond and Jane, as for Jo in *A Taste of Honey*, gender difference, particularly recognizing the vulnerabilities of women's bodies and the constraints on women's roles, also leads to a wider questioning.

Finding your place:

In an interview with Shusha Guppy, Bainbridge dismisses as 'rubbish' writing about 'girls having abortions and single mothers living in Hampstead and having a dreadful time'.[50] This she describes as the dominant mode when she started writing in the 1960s and the remark is a lead-in to a further response where she stresses her anti-feminist views. The comment is not quite true. Alex Clark indicates that Bainbridge does cover some of this material in *Sweet William*.[51] In fact, in many of her novels – *Harriet Said* (1972), *The Bottle Factory Outing*, *The Dressmaker* (1973) – the sexual exploitation of girls and women is acknowledged. The reference to 'Hampstead' has its own history and what was called 'the Hampstead novel' was particularly prominent in reviews in the 1960s and 1970s. The term was used as a gibe against fiction that was deemed middle class, white, self-regarding and, predominantly, the focus was *women's* fiction, dismissed for its concern with small-scale social relations, with culture, and moral scruples. Penelope Lively, Weldon, Margaret Forster and, particularly, Drabble featured in these attacks. For D. J. Taylor, Drabble offers 'the view from the Hampstead dinner table, sectional and stage managed', while *Private Eye's* anonymous reviewer finds ironic consolation in 'Maggi Drabble's moving studies in sexual frustration in Hampstead'.[52] But, as we have seen, women writers had another view of the metropolis. Not far from Hampstead lie the bug-infested bedsits of Fulham (*The L-Shaped Room*), or the streets of Battersea in the midst of slum clearance (*Poor Cow*) or, as Pym shows in *Excellent Women* (1952), the shared rooms 'so very much the "wrong" side of Victoria Station, so definitely *not* Belgravia' that her downwardly-mobile characters inhabit.[53] There is nothing glamorous about this London. Furthermore, despite her dismissiveness, Bainbridge fully appreciates these quirks of location. In *The Bottle Factory Outing*, Freda and Brenda live on the Finchley Road, another unfashionable London address, in a shared bed and with a broken lavatory. As Bainbridge remarks with characteristic sardonic humour about Brenda's restricted life: 'Existing as she did between the bedsitting room on the first floor and the bottle factory down the road, she mostly imagined herself as still living somewhere in the vicinity of Ramsbottom'.[54]

Drabble's pre-eminence as a Hampstead author is, in many ways, curious since, as Lorna Sage discusses, her heroines 'have their roots in the English provinces, like Drabble herself'.[55] To this extent, Drabble does link with the Angry Young Men who were seen as representing a change of focus from London and the Home Counties. Drabble's childhood home of Sheffield is reconfigured throughout her fiction as 'Northam'. It is the place that Clara leaves to go to university in *Jerusalem the Golden*, the childhood home of Liz Headleand who features in a trilogy of novels published between 1987 and 1991, and a number of characters in *The Peppered Moth* (2001) move between 'Breaseborough' and Northam.[56] Clara does 'look back in anger' at what she sees as a mean, suburban, petit-bourgeois upbringing but, as with other Northam characters, she is also haunted by her home town, and forced to re-evaluate it. For the working-class woman, though, there is little opportunity for a retrospective look; she is unlikely to change her place socially, economically, or geographically. For Jo in *A Taste of Honey*, the woman's place, in the home, is the location she fears most: 'I'm not frightened of the darkness outside. It's the darkness inside houses I don't like'.[57] The noises off – a siren, children's voices, a tugboat, fairground music – speak of a public world not that far removed from post-war rationing (rationing ended in 1952) but on the verge of a consumer boom. Though the average weekly wage almost doubled in the 1950s, there are few signs that Jo will profit. Her personal ambitions are restricted and the potential hinted at in Jo's artistic ability is leading nowhere.

Delaney felt strongly the absence of her experience from an established cultural world, but she is, in fact, part of a continuing multi-media interest in Salford life and it is characteristic of this period how certain locations are reconstructed in the public imagination. Salford was the source of much of Friedrich Engels's research in the mid-1840s for his study, *The Condition of the Working Class in England* (1845); it was the location for Ewan MacColl's folk-song, 'Dirty Old Town' (1949); and it was a major inspiration for the work of artist L. S. Lowry. Could Jo have become the female Lowry? Two years after the first production of *A Taste of Honey*, came the first broadcast of Granada Television's *Coronation Street* (1960), based on a Salford street. Intriguingly, Bainbridge, who worked as an actress before turning to writing, had a part in an early episode. In the same year, Albert Finney, born and educated in Salford, starred in the film version of Alan Sillitoe's *Saturday Night and Sunday Morning*, Sillitoe being another unwilling member of the Angry Young Men group. Some years later, Delaney wrote the screenplay for *Charlie Bubbles* (1968), again starring Finney. Salford featured as *The Classic Slum* (1971) in Robert Roberts's social history and, in recent years, it has been revived as both MediaCityUK, a media and digital hub, and, since the late 1990s, the location for a series of BBC Television's *Newsnight* programmes on poverty, the need for regeneration, social unrest, teenage pregnancy etc., all depressingly reminiscent of Delaney's world.

Liverpool is another provincial location that has a similarly rich cultural resonance. Just as the Angry Young Men were establishing their claim so too were the 'Liverpool Poets' and the 'Mersey Sound'; the area had its own soap-opera in the BBC's *Z-Cars* (1962) and its own sitcom in *The Liver Birds* (1969). It is the place that preoccupied Bainbridge, in both her fiction and travel writing, decades after she actually left.[58] Precise details locate the novels in the time and place of Bainbridge's childhood. In *Harriet Said*, for instance, the potholed beach, the old ARP uniform, the nearby POW camp tell us the war is still close while *The Dressmaker*, with its references to the munitions factory, strips of asbestos on windows, the GIs who are cutting a dash in the area, is situated after D-day but before the final defeat of Germany. Bainbridge imaginatively returns to Liverpool to recover her family (warring parents feature frequently and her aunts are the source of *The Dressmaker*) but also the landscape she knew (not a cityscape but the suburban location of Formby, close to woods, sand dunes, and the sea) and to hear again the conversational idiom which is the source of much of her humour. Her family, said Bainbridge, 'used words as though they were talking to save their lives'.[59]

In doing this, you might 'find your place' but, as with Drabble and Delaney, it also reminds you of the difficulty of ever really escaping your place. Bainbridge's plots during this period are frequently structured around twinned characters – parents, friends, siblings, aunts – fixed in relationships of dominance and subordination. The unnamed narrator in *Harriet Said* believes Harriet is 'like a colossus, carrying me with her', while Brenda in *The Bottle Factory Outing* feels 'she had escaped Stanley only to be dominated by Freda'.[60] The dominant girl or woman is always bigger, more vibrant and articulate, the subordinate constantly placating and/or admiring. The older characters re-enact years of festering resentment, abandoned hopes, and sour comments. In addition, Bainbridge often frames her narratives with a first chapter that only becomes explicable in the final one. In *The Dressmaker* she also begins with the word, 'Afterwards', inevitably raising the question, 'After what?' which the novel then goes on to answer. That first chapter provides in coded form the story's narrative. Sometimes, it is numbered '0'. Hence, in *The Dressmaker*, Chapter 0 mentions, with insouciance, sharp scissors, American cigarettes, a rosewood table, a missing curtain, and a broken figurine, all playing a part in the eventual murder of a GI. The seemingly inconsequential details become portents, reiterated and developed as the narrative progresses. On other occasions, as at the end of *The Bottle Factory Outing*, words from early in the novel are repeated as events come to pass with a terrible inevitability.

Though focused on a very different social world, Pym also pairs female characters: for example, Harriet and Belinda (sisters) in *Some Tame Gazelle*; Jane and Prudence (once tutor and student, now friends) in the novel of that name (1953); Dulcie and Viola (friends) in *No Fond Return of Love* (1961). She also explores a similar circular narrative structure. After temporary upsets or frissons of possibility, everything returns to how it was. Like Bainbridge too, Pym sometimes reinforces this with the repetition of phrases or events. For instance, at both the beginning and end of *Some Tame Gazelle*, the new young curate arrives, a meal of boiled chicken is offered, and jokes are made about Queen Victoria. These enmeshed relationships, the narrative framings, and, in Bainbridge's case, the figure '0' all suggest a sealed structure. Whatever is being worked out returns the reader to the beginning; you can never get away. Yet, equally, the play with narrative form, the interest, in both drama and fiction, in a mode which Duffy calls 'funny at the same time as fearful', the slightly bizarre intrusions in Mortimer's texts indicate a writing pushing at the boundaries of realism.[61] The 'shattering' of the social order that Hélène Cixous forecasts may still be a distance away but in the forms of these texts, as much as the questioning content, we see significant cracks in the edifice.[62] In the future, your place might be elsewhere.

Thinking of the early 1960s, Sheila Rowbotham comments: 'We appeared to have no history, no culture, certainly no movement, just snatches of suggestion to ponder'.[63] The coming of the feminist movement, from the late 1960s onwards, was not, of course, *the* answer to these problems. But it did provide women with a politics, a history, and a language through which they could begin to understand their situation. If the Mortimer protagonist felt that 'anger, unrighteous and irrational indignation, was not available to her', feminists increasingly believed that their anger was legitimate and, if focused into political and cultural activity, potentially productive.[64] They might even be able to re-write the kitchen sink. As the feminist slogan of the 1970s attests: 'It starts when you sink in his arms and ends with your arms in his sink', a wonderfully caustic undermining of the ideology of romance. Emma Tennant, though, offers a wise caution. As women's writing became a marketing opportunity, she noticed how the kitchen table, as opposed to the kitchen sink, became the location for male literary editors and reviewers to position the woman author. Women's writing is 'something knocked off or whisked up in the proximity of the Magimix and the dishwasher. A homely dresser will, if possible, be included in the author's photo, complete with striped mugs and home-made bread'.[65] The kitchen is, certainly, no substitute for a genuinely Woolfian 'room of one's own' – private, economically secure, and redolent with possibilities.

Notes

1. Many members did not like the title and several – Kingsley Amis, John Braine, John Wain, John Osborne, for example – soon lost any radical pretensions. In later life, Amis accepted a knighthood and Wain a CBE.
2. Margaret Drabble, *A Summer Bird-Cage* [1963] (Harmondsworth: Penguin Books Ltd, 1967), p. 76.
3. Lynne Reid Banks,*The L-Shaped Room* [1960] (London: Vintage Books, 2004), p. 125; Beryl Bainbridge, *Sweet William* (London: Gerald Duckworth & Co. Ltd, 1975), p. 21.
4. A. S. Byatt, *Still Life* [1985] (London: Vintage, 1995), pp. 148, 149.
5. Phillip Hensher, 'A. S. Byatt 'The Art of Fiction No. 168', *The Paris Review*, No. 159 (2001), p. 5.
6. Jonathan Derbyshire, 'The Books Interview: Lynne Reid Banks', *New Statesman*, 10 September 2010, <http://www.newstatesman.com/books/2010/09/interview-israel-writing-write> [accessed 14 September 2014].
7. Nell Dunn, *Poor Cow* [1967] (London: Virago Press, 1988), p. ix.
8. Kate Dorney and Francis Gray, *Played in Britain: Modern Theatre in 100 Plays* (London: Methuen, 2013), p. 46; Rachel Cooke, 'Shelagh Delaney: the Return of Britain's Angry Young Woman', *The Observer*, 25 January 2014, <http://www.the-guardian.com/stage/2014/jan/25/shelagh-delaney-angry-young-woman-a-taste-of-honey> [accessed 21 October 2014].
9. Rachel Cooke, 'Penelope Mortimer – Return of the Original Angry Young Woman', *The Observer*, 28 June 2015, <http://www.theguardian.com/books/2015/jun/28/penelope-mortimer-the-pumpkin-eater-angry-young-woman> [accessed 23 May 2016].
10. 'Never had it so good' was the claim of Prime Minister Harold Macmillan when speaking at a Tory Party rally in 1957.
11. The phrase 'kitchen sink realism' or 'kitchen sink drama' was commonly attributed to the Angry Young Men. It suggested a gritty, realistic mode and a concern with disenfranchised groups.

12. For a fuller discussion of women's university novels in the context of the social history of the period, see Mary Eagleton, 'The Anxious Lives of Clever Girls: the University Novels of Margaret Drabble, A. S. Byatt, and Hilary Mantel', *Tulsa Studies in Women's Literature*, 33:2 (2014), 103–21.

13. On the history of meritocracy, see *The Rise and Rise of the Meritocracy* ed. by Geoff Dench (Oxford: Blackwell Publishing, 2006) and Jo Littler, 'Meritocracy as Plutocracy: The Marketising of "Equality" under Neoliberalism', *New Formations*, 80/81(2013), 52–72.

14. Hilary Radner, *Shopping Around: Feminine Culture and the Pursuit of Pleasure* (Abingdon: Routledge, 1995), p. 105.

15. Byatt interviewed by Juliet Dusinberre in *Women Writers Talking* ed. by Janet Todd (New York: Holmes & Meier, 1983), pp. 181–95; Byatt's Introduction to *The Shadow of the Son* (London: Vintage, 1991); Nicolas Tredell, 'A. S. Byatt in Conversation', *P. N. Review*, 17: 3 (1991), 24–8; A. S. Byatt, 'Soul Searching', *Guardian*, 14 February 2004, <http://www.guardian.co.uk/books/2004/aug/15/summerreading2004.summerreading3> [accessed 20 August 2014]; Drabble, 'Women Writers as an Unprotected Species' in *Writing: A Woman's Business* ed. by Judy Simons and Kate Fullbrook (Manchester: Manchester University Press, 1998), pp. 163–71; Drabble interviewed by Gillian Parker and Janet Todd in Todd, *Women Writers Talking*, pp. 161–78.

16. Deborah Philips, *Women's Fiction From 1945 to Today* (London: Bloomsbury, 2014), p. 64.

17. Margaret Drabble, *Jerusalem the Golden* [1967] (Harmondsworth: Penguin Books, 1969), p. 159.

18. Margaret Drabble, *The Waterfall* [1969] (Harmondsworth: Penguin Books, 1986), pp. 103–4; A. S. Byatt, 'Soul Searching', *The Guardian*, 14 February 2004, <http://www.guardian.co.uk/books/2004/aug/15/summerreading2004.summerreading3> [accessed 20 August 2014].

19. Clare Hanson, *Hysterical Fictions* (Basingstoke: Macmillan Press Ltd, 2000), p. 99. See also Hanson, *Eugenics, Literature, and Culture in Post-War Britain* (Abingdon: Routledge, 2013), Chapter 1.

20. In Drabble's *The Millstone*, Rosamund is reading Rosemond Tuve's work on George Herbert; in Byatt's *Still Life*, Stephanie reads Wordsworth.

21. A. S. Byatt, 'Review', *Times Literary Supplement* (August, 1986). Included in Byatt, *Passions of The Mind: Selected Writings* (London: Chatto & Windus, 1991), pp. 242 and 244.

22. Fay Weldon, *Down Among the Women* (Harmondsworth: Penguin Books Ltd, 1973), p. 83.

23. Valerie Grove, Introduction to Penelope Mortimer, *Daddy's Gone A-Hunting* (London: Persephone Books, 2008), p. vi.

24. Mortimer, *Daddy's Gone A-Hunting*, pp. 33–4.

25. Gayle Greene, *Changing the Story: Feminist Fiction and the Tradition* (Bloomington: Indiana University Press, 1991), Ch. III. Two of Greene's examples are Mortimer, *The Pumpkin Eater* and Weldon, *The Fat Woman's Joke*.

26. Penelope Mortimer, *The Home* (Harmondsworth: Penguin Books Ltd, 1973), p. 41.

27. Mortimer, *The Home*, p. 58.

28. Mortimer, *The Home*, p. 20.

29. Mortimer, *The Pumpkin Eater* (London: Bloomsbury Publishing, 1995), pp. 23, 124.

30. Mortimer, *The Home*, p. 148.

31. Carol Dyhouse, *Students: A Gendered History* (Abingdon: Routledge, 2006), p. 92. Note that the description 'girls' is technically correct; until 1970 the age of majority in the UK was 21.
32. Maroula Joannou, *Contemporary Women's Writing: From* The Golden Notebook *to* The Color Purple (Manchester: Manchester University Press, 2000), p. 70.
33. Nell Dunn, *Up the Junction* [1963] (London: Virago Press, 2013), p. 91.
34. Dunn, *Up the Junction*, p. 60.
35. Kathleen Kiernan, Hilary Land, and Jane Lewis, *Lone Motherhood in Twentieth-Century Britain: From Footnote to Front Page* (Oxford: Oxford University Press, 1998), pp. 102, 110.
36. Shelagh Delaney, *A Taste of Honey* (London: Methuen, 1982), pp. 56, 75.
37. Michelene Wandor, *Post-War British Drama: Looking Back in Anger* (London: Routledge, 2001), p. 96.
38. Lib Taylor, 'Early Stages: Women Dramatists 1958–68' in *British and Irish Women Dramatists since 1958: A Critical Handbook* ed. by Trevor R. Griffiths and Margaret Llewellyn-Jones (Buckingham: Open University Press, 1993) p. 11.
39. Doris Lessing, *Play with a Tiger* in *Plays By and About Women* ed. by Victoria Sullivan and James Hatch [1958] (New York: Vintage Books, 1974), p. 204. Lessing wrote the play at the same time as she was writing *The Golden Notebook* (1962) and there are similarities of character and theme between the two.
40. *Strike While the Iron is Hot: Three Plays on Sexual Politics* ed. by Michelene Wandor (London: The Journeyman Press, 1980), p. 11.
41. Red Ladder Theatre, *Strike While the Iron is Hot*, p. 60.
42. Maureen Duffy, *Rites* in *Plays By and About Women* ed. by Victoria Sullivan and James Hatch [1969] (New York: Vintage Books, 1974), p. 350.
43. Banks, *The L-Shaped Room*, pp. 51, 65, 247.
44. Banks, *The L-Shaped Room*, pp. 12, 263.
45. Dunn, *Up the Junction*, p. 2.
46. Dunn, *Up the Junction*, p. 67.
47. Joannou, *Contemporary Women's Writing*, p. 67; Drabble, Introduction, *Poor Cow*, p. xv; Dominic Head, *The Cambridge Introduction to Modern British Fiction, 1950–2000* (Cambridge: Cambridge University Press, 2002), p. 91.
48. Raymond Williams, *The Long Revolution* (Harmondsworth: Pelican Books, 1965), p. 245.
49. Philips, *Women's Fiction From 1945 to Today*, p. 57.
50. Shusha Guppy, 'Beryl Bainbridge, The Art of Fiction No. 164', *The Paris Review*, No. 157 (2000),< http://www.theparisreview.org/interviews/561/the-art-of-fiction-no-164-beryl-bainbridge> [accessed 14 October 2014].
51. Alex Clark, Introduction to Beryl Bainbridge, *A Quiet Life* [1976] (London: Virago Press, 2013), pp. ix–x.
52. D. J. Taylor, *After the War: the Novel and English Society since 1945* (London: Chatto & Windus, 1993), p. 286; *Lord Gnome's Literary Companions* ed. by Francis Wheen (London: Verso, 1994), p. 112.
53. Barbara Pym, *Excellent Women* [1952] (Harmondsworth: Penguin Books, 1983), p. 9.
54. Beryl Bainbridge, *The Bottle Factory Outing* (London: Abacus, 2011), p. 83.
55. Lorna Sage, *Women in the House of Fiction: Post-War Women Novelists* (Basingstoke: Macmillan Press Ltd, 1992), p. 90.
56. The Liz Headleand trilogy consists of *The Radiant Way* (1987), *A Natural Curiosity* (1989), and *The Gates of Ivory* (1991).

57. Delaney, *A Taste of Honey*, p. 22.
58. Bainbridge's travel writing includes *English Journey or The Road to Milton Keynes* (London: BBC and Gerald Duckworth & Co. Ltd, 1984), a revisiting of J. B. Priestley's (1934) *English Journey*, and *Forever England: North and South* (London: BBC Books, 1987).
59. Bainbridge, *English Journey*, p. 100.
60. Beryl Bainbridge, *Harriet Said* [1972] (Harmondsworth: Penguin Books, 1992), p. 83; *The Bottle Factory Outing*, p. 121.
61. Duffy, *Rites*, p. 350.
62. See, for example, Hélène Cixous, 'The Laugh of the Medusa', trans. Keith Cohen and Paula Cohen, *Signs*, 1:4 (1976), 875–93.
63. Sheila Rowbotham, *Promise of a Dream: Remembering the Sixties* (London: Allen Lane: Penguin Press, 2000), p. 10.
64. Mortimer, *The Home*, p. 87.
65. Emma Tennant, *The ABC of Writing* (London: Faber and Faber Ltd), 1992, p. 83.

6
Sex, Censorship and Identity

Kerry Myler

This chapter examines the gradual liberalisation of sex censorship in the post-war period and considers how this affected women's ability to write about sex, desire and reproduction. The period begins with sex taking a prominent but safely enclosed position in women's writing. It is, as Nancy Mitford's Fanny comments in *The Pursuit of Love* (1945), 'our great obsession',[1] but it is an obsession which remains couched in metaphor and humour. In the 1960s, after the watershed events of the *Lady Chatterley's Lover* trial and the advent of the contraceptive pill, the sexual experiences of women begin to be fully and explicitly represented in women's fiction. It is at this point that the literary landscape alters significantly not only in terms of *what* experiences women can represent but *how* they represent those experiences. Here the politics of sex and the politics of representation meet in a conscious and critical examination of the 'nature' of female sexuality and its place in print. Towards the end of the post-war period, from 1969 onwards, the focus shifts again and sex, desire and reproduction become differently implicated in a more comprehensive and nuanced representation of female experience in the late twentieth century.

Sex, censorship and shame

In the Obscene Publications case against gynaecologist Eustace Chessler's sex manual, *Love without Fear: A plain guide to sex technique for every married adult*, the defence argued that 'in the year 1942, it is ridiculous and absurd to suggest that the discussion of sex and sex relationships in a book is obscene'.[2] The jury seemingly agreed and returned a Not Guilty verdict. Nevertheless, almost 20 years later, D. H. Lawrence's *Lady Chatterley's Lover* faced the same charge. When Radclyffe Hall's *The Well of Loneliness* (1928) was banned under the Obscenity Publications Act of 1857, the prosecution

© The Author(s) 2017
C. Hanson and S. Watkins, *The History of British Women's Writing, 1945–1975*,
History of British Women's Writing, DOI: 10.1057/978–1–137–47736–1_7

argued that its literary merit only made it more likely to 'deprave and corrupt'.[3] In the wake of the revised Obscene Publications Act of 1959 – which allowed the defence of 'as being for the public good'[4] – the Chatterley trial successfully used literary merit as a point of defence. In doing so the trial linked the legitimacy of sexual content to the highly subjective notion of a text's literary value – a trait 'women's books' have historically been denied. The post-war period saw a loosening of sex censorship and a testing of newly adjusted boundaries but, inevitably, this also raised the question of the double standard. For female authors there had to be a careful negotiation of this new territory of representation – their own sex and bodies – not only in terms of what could be written but also what could be written about women *by* women. To write explicitly of women's sexual experience was to write of something that had hitherto been alluded to in only the most general, elusive and inexplicit of ways, as in Radclyffe Hall's famously discreet representation of lesbian sex in *The Well of Loneliness*: 'and that night they were not divided'.[5]

Literary sex censorship is amusingly sent up in Elizabeth Taylor's early post-war novel *A View of the Harbour* (1947). The harbour's old librarian, armed with ink pad and oval stamp, conducts 'a passionate, erratic campaign against slack morals' in the library's collection: 'murder he allowed: but not fornication. Childbirth (especially if the character died of it), but not pregnancy. Love might be supposed to be consummated as long as no one had any pleasure out of it'.[6] Hera Cook argues that 'extensive sexual experience' was not 'usual or acceptable to conventional respectable people before the 1950s' and that the community, here represented by the local librarian, 'supported and maintained sexual norms'.[7] Luckily the librarian sees 'no need to be prejudiced against lady novelists' who have 'their own contribution to make. A nice domestic romance. Why ape men?'[8] The women novelists of this period do not 'ape men' but nor do they write 'nice domestic romances' – there is romance and these romances do largely occur in domestic spaces, but they are rarely 'nice'. Indeed, sexual desire is seldom found in its 'proper place' – the marriage bed. The novels generally feature women engaging in illicit affairs, either pre-marital or extra-marital; the women are usually past the first flush of youth, already married, widowed or resigned to spinsterhood; they are generally upper-middle to upper-class and despite post-war austerity still enjoy the privileges of that class position, including to some extent a license to transgress the contemporary codes of moral behaviour – which they do. Sex is often central to the plots of these novels but the textual presence of the female sexual body remains elusive – as if subject to the author's own self-censoring 'oval stamp'. So Tory and Robert, the adulterous lovers in Taylor's *A View of the Harbour*, do fornicate – and this is not merely supposed but narrated – but the descriptions of the act are suitably framed within a romantic rhetoric: 'their fingers gripped desperately together and in the thickening silences oceans roared in their ears and the room was full of the sound of their hearts beating'.[9] There are body parts – fingers and even a 'throbbing wrist' – but the description of the lovers' union is brief – less than half a dozen lines – and the materiality of sex is evaded by way of metaphor. Similarly, *The Pursuit of Love*, by Nancy Mitford (1904–1973) begins with two girls 'obsessed with sex', childbirth and abortions[10] but any 'wickedness' that occurs in the text – including Linda's passionate love affair with a French aristocrat and Fanny's mother's romantic exploits with a 'ruffianly-looking Spaniard'[11] – is duly judged as scandalous and any discussions of sex are brief, inexplicit and humorously philosophical as opposed to material. Furthermore, Taylor's librarian might find pregnant bodies in these novels – including Mitford's 'great figures of fertility, heaving tremendous sighs'[12] – but he would be gratified to discover that, in the Victorian manner, the adulterous female is still punished for her sins through maternal death or stillbirth.

The older generation's censure is compounded by the current generation's own ambivalence about how love, sex and desire are to be understood and performed in this new post-war world. What becomes clear in the women's novels of the period is that in the aftermath of war – during which moral and sexual boundaries were to some extent blurred – sex again becomes heavily invested with shame. As Cook writes, 'women's guilt regarding their fall from grace [during the war] would not necessarily translate into future liberality'.[13] In *The North Face* (1949), by Mary Renault (1905–1983) Ellen's frigidity is not the consequence of any kind of moral stand on pre-marital sex but rather a post-traumatic reaction to a (failed) incestuous sexual encounter during the war. For these lovers there is a happy ending – Ellen overcomes her past demons and she and her lover still wagging tongues by marrying – but most of the love affairs in these novels simply end. In *A View of the Harbour* the lovers cannot overcome their 'sensations of shame and horror';[14] Robert returns to his wife and Tory marries the much older Bertram. In Taylor's 1951 novel, *A Game of Hide and Seek*, the would-be lovers Harriet and Vesey make it to the guesthouse but cannot go through with the act: 'we can't not be sordid' says Vesey, the double negative emphasising the impossibility of their union.[15] When Harriet attempts to find comfort in numbers she confronts an anachronistic vision of 'women who, in the name of love, brought down great harm on others and died in poverty and solitude or even – such was her anxiety – on the gallows'.[16] Despite the prevalence of female sexual desire, the love affairs in these novels are generally sad, abortive affairs.

1950s: 'All this so-called biology'

Sex and childbearing became topics for open discussion in the 1950s with an emphasis on medicine, biology and education. The end of austerity and better standards of health 'reduced the age of sexual maturity and thus of readiness for marriage. [There was] increasing expert advice to women in books, women's magazines, and radio broadcasts on childbearing and rearing [and] a mutually satisfying sex life was increasingly seen as an essential element within marriage'.[17] In Taylor's *A View of the Harbour* – as early as 1947 – Mrs Bracey bemoans her daughters' early knowledge of the 'facts of life' and 'all this so-called biology'.[18] In Rosamond Lehmann's *The Echoing Grove* (1953), Madeleine expresses a similar sentiment when she finds the next generation 'bent, all of them, on fulfilling themselves with the aid of textbooks'.[19] These novels register a disjuncture between the way sex was understood – as something private, unspoken, and supposedly instinctive – and how it is now being learnt, discussed and practiced by a new generation of women. This is a world which, as Lehmann's Dinah explains, is 'in flux'[20] and the women in the 1950s novels often find themselves struggling against the values and practices of the past in order to welcome in a more transparent and scientific sexual era.

In the early 1950s, after the success of her first novel, *The Grass is Singing* (1950), Doris Lessing (1919–2013) published the first two instalments of her *Children of Violence* series; her heroine, Martha, is caught in this 'flux'. Martha despises her mother's acquiescence to social norms and rebels against all of her principles – including her aversion to sex and female sexuality – but she must still negotiate a social world which is caught between old values and new practices. Martha's knowledge of sex is influenced by the literary but also the sex 'textbooks' that Madeleine finds so 'deplorable'.[21] At the beginning of *A Proper Marriage* (1954) the newly wed Martha is sent to visit Dr Stern to discuss contraception and it soon becomes clear that Martha, thanks to her books, is far more knowledgeable than the weary practitioner. When she returns home her husband asks if she remembered to mention her periods: 'Well, you did say they were a bit irregular'.[22] Hera Cook explains that 'expanding sales meant sex manuals and other similar sources were providing a new respectable, medicalized language that men and women could share'.[23] The doctor's appointment and her husband's interest in her menstrual cycle emphasise firstly the general transition from sex-and-shame to sex-and-science and secondly the advent of the female sexual and reproductive body as *an object* for both scientific and general enquiry. As Clare Hanson writes, Lessing 'conveys the sense of hostility between pregnant women and the medical establishment that was developing in the 1950s and 1960s ... Who had the right to speak of pregnancy? And how was it best known – through the pregnant woman's perceptions or the medical practitioner's gaze?'[24] Lessing writes frankly and explicitly about sex, contraception, gynaecology, abortion, childbirth – Martha's labour extends across a dozen pages – and breastfeeding; but this textual freedom is coupled with a sense of the female body as bound by discourses that are outside of women's control (including the writer's) and which thus separate women from their bodies. The 'map of her flesh' provided by 'the book' means that Martha regards her body – and 'every part of it' – as a 'disconnected partner'.[25] New medical discourses about female sexuality might allow women writers to depict sex and reproduction without risk of censure, but Lessing's novel suggests that the uncoupling of gynaecological 'knowledge' and female experience might be just as damaging and alienating as the shame and silence that came before.

1960s: Sex and the single girl

If the early post-war women's novel took adultery as its theme and examined the sexual, psychological and social effects of this particular female transgression, the later texts – from 1960s onwards – generally took a different theme: sex and the single girl. Lynne Reid Banks' *The L-Shaped Room* (1960) and Margaret Drabble's *The Millstone* (1965), 'iconic "women's" novels' of the period,[26] both begin in much the same way as Lessing's *A Proper Marriage* – with an unplanned pregnancy, doctor's appointments, and abortion attempts – only here there is no marriage, proper or otherwise. This is an altered post-war landscape and the rules regarding pre-marital sex are now meant to be broken. In *The Millstone*, Rosamund's 'brand new, twentieth-century crime' is not adultery but frigidity: in the swinging sixties 'the scarlet letter' remains but now the 'A stood for Abstinence, not for Adultery'.[27] So when Rosamund discovers her pregnancy she reasons that her 'crime' is not the single act with George, but rather the years of abstinence that went before; unfortunately, the punishment remains the same: 'being at heart a Victorian, I paid the Victorian penalty'.[28]

Set before the 1967 Abortion Act and before unmarried women could legally obtain the contraceptive pill, stories like *The Millstone* and *The L-Shaped Room* narrate the prejudices and difficulties of unwed motherhood in 1960s Britain as well as concerns about bastard children and eugenics – both women fear they will give birth to 'freak' children because of their indiscretions.[29] These are tales of lost virginity, sexual disenchantment, pregnancy outside of wedlock, eviction from the family home, reduced circumstances, botched abortion attempts, National Health Service clinics, and – eventually – childbirth and unwed motherhood. Melissa Benn, in her 2010 review of *The L-Shaped Room*, writes that 'it is still depressing to contemplate the prejudice that women "in trouble" faced in this gloomy, class-bound post-war world. The novel illustrates beautifully the tortured interplay between internal shame and external strictures'.[30] Jane is abandoned by her father, forced to leave her job and her doctor tries to 'sell' her an abortion, warning her not to 'make the mistake of imagining the word bastard doesn't carry a sting anymore'.[31] Rosamund, like Harriet in Taylor's *A Game of Hide and Seek*, cannot help but imagine the anachronistic but pervasive images of sin and sordidness associated with sexual transgression: 'Gin, psychiatrists, hospitals, accidents, village maidens drowned in duck ponds, tears, pain, humiliations'.[32] The novels do feature gin, hospitals and accidents but there are no duck ponds and there is certainly no eighteenth-century narrative of girlhood innocence, unscrupulous seduction and callous abandonment.

These are not innocent, 'bad' or even ignorant girls – they are educated women in their mid-to-late twenties who come from respectable homes and have been exposed to a culturally advanced and diverse social scene. Both women make the conscious decision to engage in sexual intercourse. Rosamund recognises that 'I myself had made the decisive move'[33] and Jane carefully plans the circumstances of her first sexual union: 'I was ripe for an affair and I thought with him I could have one and enjoy it and still feel like the nice clean girl-next-door afterwards'.[34] They don't want marriage but they do want sex. Unfortunately, though these girls are very different to the heroines of the past, literary tradition demands the inevitable: pregnancy.

Deborah Philips argues that neither heroine 'has any understanding of birth control, a situation that is borne out in Geoffrey Gorer's 1969 study *Sex and Marriage in England Today*, in which he found that the majority of sexually active unmarried couples did not use any form of contraception'.[35] However, when Rosamund's lover asks '"Is this all right?" she understands that he is asking her whether or not she is taking the contraceptive pill.[36] This indicates knowledge but not practice – and indeed the pill would not have been widely available to unmarried mothers before 1974.[37] More likely solutions would have been abortion or adoption but, as Jane's doctor points out, she is 'old enough to appreciate it'.[38] Indeed, abortion and adoption – though considered, even attempted – are ultimately disregarded and each woman resolves to have her child and raise it on her own. Rosamund 'simply did not believe that the handicap of one small illegitimate baby would make a scrap of difference to [her] career'[39] and though Jane is forced to 'suspend' her employment she is invited back after the baby's birth. Being a single mother even seems to chime with the times: in opposition to Jane's doctor's warning, Rosamund's friend Lydia tells her that 'ordinary babies aren't much of a status symbol, but illegitimate ones are just about the last word'.[40] There is still scandal but it is associated less with shame and more with the kind of delicious notoriety Nancy Mitford's young Fanny and Linda so coveted; indeed, Lydia even writes a (bad) novel about Rosamund and her 'scandalous' pregnancy. The texts present a still troubled but ultimately optimistic portrait of a changed landscape in terms of social values and tolerance. These are essentially heart-warming stories in which women demonstrate their strength and endurance, friends prove their worth, and – significantly – in which old stigmas are exposed as new falsehoods.

Experimental sex

With the passing of the Obscene Publications Act of 1959 and the *Lady Chatterley's Lover* trial victory in 1960, texts might still attract scandal but they were much less likely to be censored. In *The Magic Toyshop* (1967), by Angela Carter (1940–1992), Lawrence's infamous novel is used to indicate the sexual awakening of the fifteen-year old, upper middle-class heroine,

Melanie: 'After she read *Lady Chatterley's Lover*, she secretly picked forget-me-nots and stuck them in her pubic hair'.[41] Melanie's discovery that she is 'made of flesh and blood'[42] is celebrated rather than censored in the romantic, innocent play of the opening chapter: she poses naked in front of the mirror in the style of famous artists' models as she fantasises about her wedding night with a 'phantom bridegroom'.[43] Melanie's courtship with the working-class, artist-boy Finn (her own Oliver Mellors) repeatedly fails to live up to her romantic fantasies or Lawrence's novel; indeed, when Finn uses the word 'fuck' she thinks: 'her phantom bridegroom would never have fucked her. They would have made love'.[44] Towards the end of the novel, the opening scenes are replayed as she prepares for her role as Leda in her Uncle Philip's puppet show; Melanie hopes that she will 'be a nymph crowned with daisies once again; he saw her as once she had seen herself'[45] but when she presents herself to him he tells her '"Your tits are too big"'.[46] The final remnants of Melanie's romantic vision are stripped away when she is raped by the Swan and Finn tells her '"The play is over"'.[47] Melanie's fantasy of autonomous female sexuality is over: it has been exposed as a performance, a fantasy, a fairy-tale – and thus revealed as always and only controlled by the puppet strings of the male gaze and Law. The novel ends optimistically with the burning down of the house of the Father and with it, the novel suggests, his Laws. With their old world burning around them, Melanie and Finn are left facing one another 'in a wild surmise'.[48]

What is only surmised in *The Magic Toyshop* – a sexuality conceived outside of Patriarchal Law – finds its wildest expressions in Nell Dunn's novels. Margaret Drabble, in her introduction to the 1987 edition of Dunn's *Poor Cow* (1967), writes that 'this was one of the first post-Chatterley books to speak out, to treat women's sexuality as though it were entirely natural, as natural as man's'.[49] Likewise, in Adrian Henri's introduction to the 1988 edition of *Up the Junction* (1963), he explains that part of the 'scandal attendant on … publication (now needing a little historical imagination to conceive) was that we are almost eavesdropping on women talking as uninhibitedly about their sex lives as men would in similar circumstances'.[50] These working-class Battersea girls are certainly not the privileged 'nice clean girl[s]-next-door' of Drabble, Banks and Carter's novels. As Cook explains, 'by the early 1960s accepted standards of sexual behaviour differed widely between classes, by age, and amongst various groups',[51] and Dunn's novels clearly articulate this difference. Post-Chatterley and post-pill, Dunn's characters desire sex for sex's sake and suffer little of the 'internal shame and external strictures'[52] of Drabble and Banks's heroines. With the freedom to write without fear of censorship, however scandalous, the problem of *what* one can write about is replaced with *how* one should write about topics previously considered taboo. Freedom from sex censorship encouraged women writers to free themselves from the traditions of the male pen, to experiment, and to seek out an authentic female voice through which to articulate female experience.

Up the Junction is constructed from a series of brief, loosely related 'apparently artless'[53] sketches narrated by the 'heiress from Chelsea'.[54] Dunn, like Drabble and Banks, uses an upper class narrator but this character is essentially a vehicle (a Nell Dunn avatar) through which to deliver the 'real' voices of the working-class girls (voices with which she was intimately familiar). With such little narrative interference, the novel consists almost entirely of dialogue in a working-class London vernacular; we are, in effect, privy to the unfiltered personal conversations and goings-on of a group of 'real' working-class girls, including Sylvie who 'pisses in the road' and 'don't wear no drawers Friday nights – it's 'andy ...'[55] and Rube who visits the local abortionist seven times before her supposedly three month old baby is finally delivered, breathing, and, once cold, 'wrapped in the *Daily Mirror*, and thr[own] down the toilet'.[56] Dunn's next novel, *Poor Cow*, has a more familiar, linear structure but combines impersonal and personal narratives in order to emphasise the disjuncture between the seemingly dreadful 'facts' of Joy's life (single mother, husband in jail, promiscuous, whore) and her actual experience which is largely positive – she has a wonderful zest for life, loves her son, is a good mother, and provides for him by doing something she (mostly) enjoys.

Another experimental text of the 1960s also alternates between personal and impersonal narrative voices, this time in order to provide a comprehensive view of the complexities of female experience. Doris Lessing's *The Golden Notebook* (1962) is renowned for its frank depictions of sex and the female body (it is often noted that this novel 'contains the first tampon in English Literature'[57]). The early post-war novels avoided the material body, using metaphor and the rhetoric of romance to describe sex and sexual desire. In response to this literary history, Lessing, through her writer-protagonist Anna Wulf, explicitly challenges herself to write about the female body and to confront the difficulties associated with finding an appropriate and truthful way in which to describe female bodily processes and experiences. Anna makes a promise to 'write down, as truthfully as I can, every stage of a day' only to find that the day she chooses happens to be the day she begins to menstruate.[58] To write honestly Anna must put aside the 'instinctive feeling of shame and modesty' and in a defiant gesture – as much Lessing's as Anna's – she writes 'I stuff my vagina with the tampon of cotton wool'.[59] Over the course of the novel, as Anna struggles to imprint the page with her material body, she exposes the ways in which women's bodily and sexual experiences have been, and continue to be, ignored and denied: 'I am thinking, I realize, about a major problem of literary style, of tact'.[60] Like Dunn's, Lessing's experiments in narrative prose and voice are used to examine and condemn the gendered politics of sexual agency and pleasure.

Pleasure and politics

Lessing wrote freely about sex and reproduction in *Martha Quest* and *A Proper Marriage* but she, like many of contemporaries, still adhered to

Taylor's old Librarian's rule: sex is ok so long as no one gets any pleasure out of it. When Martha loses her virginity and fails to 'explode suddenly in a drenching, saturating moment of illumination' she consoles herself with the belief that 'everything still awaited her'.[61] This might be a metaphor for the transition from the 1950s novel to the 1960s, and indeed, by the fourth instalment of Lessing's series, *Landlocked* (1965), Martha's body, once so thoroughly colonised by medical discourses, has become a 'newly discovered country with laws of its own' and 'every other experience with a man had become the stuff of childhood'.[62] Martha has fallen in love and, for the first time, experiences sexual pleasure. Of course, one of the most infamous assertions in *The Golden Notebook* is that women's ability to feel sexual pleasure is dependent on being in love. According to Anna's alter ego, Ella, 'the truth is they get erections when they're with a woman they don't give a damn about, but we don't have an orgasm unless we love him'.[63] Ella also makes a marked distinction between the vaginal and clitoral orgasm, maintaining that the vaginal orgasm is the 'real female orgasm'.[64] Lessing is engaging with contemporary medical and feminist debates in the post-war period about female sexual pleasure, the validity of female orgasm,[65] and whether the 'female vagina is an active organ'.[66] Advances in contraception, the increasing dissociation of sex and reproduction, and the 'ongoing relaxation of sexual mores', were aiding the long-awaited acknowledgement of women's sexual pleasure but, as indicated in Lessing's novel, that pleasure continued to exist within a framework of 'heterosexual male dominance of sexual activity'.[67] Once Ella's relationship ends she can find no pleasure in other men (whom she does not love) nor through masturbation which results in only 'a sharp violence';[68] eventually she 'becomes completely sexless'.[69] Ella's sexual pleasure is wholly constructed out of 'male words' and experience.[70] Ella is, of course, doubly removed from Lessing, via Anna, and we should not make the mistake of thinking the text as a whole endorses Ella's point of view; her experience needn't be 'true' for all women – rather her experience is emphasising the importance of sex in debates on gender inequality as well as the difficulties of reconciling women's experiences of sex with an emerging feminist politics.

Sex *is* political in the 1960s, but this is in no sense straightforward for women. Thus we find towards the end of *The Golden Notebook* a naked postcoital Anna oscillating between luxuriating in her sexual body and finding it repulsive. The text does not settle on either of these positions but rather presents the difficulty of inhabiting a female body that has been historically constructed as both desirable and disgusting and which continues to be caught in the 'flux' between conflicting cultural and political positions. Sex, pleasure and the materiality of the body were clearly no longer taboo subjects in 1960s post-Chatterley women's writing but, rather than occasioning an uncomplicated celebration of female sexuality, women writers were engaged in a conscious and critical examination of women's experience, how that experience can be represented in writing, and how that experience is engaged in the cultural and political shifts of the 1960s.

Love of 'the other sort'

If heterosexual sex remained bound by Victorian sensibilities and censorship in the early post-war period then homosexual unions were all but eclipsed by them. Mary Renault's overlooked contemporary romances *Return to Night* (1947) and *The North Face* (1949) have very little of the homosexual intrigue which is more safely packaged in the later Greek histories (1956–1981) which made her career. There is only one explicit reference to homosexuality in *The North Face* when Ellen says to her would-be lover: 'They say some women are queer and don't want to know about it. I thought perhaps I was, only one day a woman got sentimental about me, and that was no good. So I must be frigid, I thought'.[71] This casual dismissal of same-sex desire between women sits in stark contrast with the representations of *male* same-sex desire in Renault's and Mitford's next novels. Sarah Dunant writes that 'freed from the grey British skies of post-war austerity and culture, in 1951 [Renault] wrote *The Charioteer*, an explicit portrait of homosexuality during the war'.[72] Male homosexuality has a long literary and artistic history but to represent male same-sex desire in the near-contemporary period, as Renault does in *The Charioteer*, was – as Durant writes – 'a cultural thunderbolt (in America it took another six years to find a publisher)'.[73] Mary Ellen Snodgrass writes that it was Renault's ability to 'distanc[e] herself through an impersonal academic pose' that allowed her to 'idealize the carnal relationships of men as lyrically as standard romances of her day exalted heterosexual love'.[74] If Renault escapes censorship through academic prose, Mitford does so through humour. The success of *The Pursuit of Love* was repeated with her follow-up novel, *Love in a Cold Climate* (1949); together the texts secured Mitford's reputation as a bold, witty and provocative post-war woman writer. The novel is again narrated by Fanny Wincham and this time focused on her cousin Polly. When Polly is disinherited, the 'tremendous vacuum created by her departure' is filled with Cedric, a 'glitter of blue and gold ... a human dragonfly' and, in the words of the Boreleys, one of 'those awful effeminate creatures – pansies'.[75] Cedric's proclivities are made palatable to a late 1940s audience through Mitford's humorous light touch where everyone and everything – including the personal narrator – are ripe for ridicule. Sexual transgression is also safely encased in a world of wealth, aristocracy and European sensibilities, particularly the Parisian. At the same time, any censorship of Cedric comes from the worst of the British: the 'balanced Boreleys'.[76] When the novel was nevertheless 'condemned ... for immorality and decadence',[77] Mitford responded characteristically: 'I shall never write about normal love again as I see there is a far larger and more enthusiastic public for the *other sort*'.[78]

Despite Mitford's endorsement, love of 'the other sort' remains on the fringes of post-war women's writing and where it does appear it generally concerns itself with male same-sex desire. In *The Echoing Grove* Rickie and his university chum Jack are 'tight as ticks,' wrestling 'without so much as a stitch of underwear' between them, but later he explains 'I'm not a pansy – did you realize? – never felt even a touch of queerness since I left school – well, Oxford to be strictly truthful';[79] in *The Millstone* Rosamund suspects the 'kind and camp' father of her child is 'queer' and always 'on the verge of some confession';[80] in *The L-Shaped Room* there is the affectionate but savage 'queer called Malcolm'[81] and where homosexuality is sympathetically found – in Jane's neighbour John – it is coupled with racial difference and mental retardation. Even Lessing – usually so forward thinking – reveals a marked distaste for homosexuality. On the one hand these novels demonstrate the pervasiveness of male same-sex desire and on the other they keep it firmly at bay – it quite evidently exists but it remains on the periphery, suggested but not examined.

Male homosexuality was decriminalised in Britain in 1967 but lesbian sexual relations have never been subject to the same legal restrictions. Despite the legal anomaly – and the overturning of the ban on Radclyffe Hall's *The Well of Loneliness* in 1959 – lesbian desire is even less visible in post-war women's literature than male homosexual desire. Bryan Magee stated in 1966, it 'is still a fact ... that society does not acknowledge the existence of lesbianism'.[82] Hera Cook, on the other hand, makes the case for the emergence – and consequent fear – of lesbianism in the mid twentieth century and attributes this to a number of interrelated factors, including the popularization of Freudian thought and fears connected to female empowerment, particularly sexual empowerment, as encouraged by a growing knowledge of contraceptive methods and female sexuality. The 'rejection of lesbianism,' she writes, 'rose in parallel with the tentative emergence of positive attitudes to heterosexual female physical sexual desires and pleasure'.[83] The few references to lesbianism – in Lehmann and Lessing – are categorically negative representations. Female same-sex desire remained taboo – or, as Elizabeth Wilson puts it, 'simply ... not fashionable'.[84]

Risking the 'unfashionable', Maureen Duffy (1933–) published her first overtly lesbian novel, *The Microcosm*, in 1966. After several years writing for theatre and television, Duffy had already established a reputation for engaging with contemporary attitudes towards race, class and, less explicitly, homosexuality. In this third novel, Duffy's representation of lesbian desire *is* explicit; it is not consigned to the margins of the text nor is it safely encased in a historical moment or hidden within a safe and recognisable mainstream heterosexual culture. Duffy situates her novel *in* the margins – in the lesbian 'scene' occurring in the dark spaces of 1960s London nightclubs and house parties. In 1988 Duffy wrote the novel's 'Afterword', stating that the novel was originally conceived as a non-fiction book consisting of recordings of lesbian women's experiences. However, such a 'risky subject' could not find a 'reputable' publisher because the author 'had no academic qualifications in the sociology or psychology of sex' and Duffy was advised to rewrite the book as fiction.[85] This allowed her to experiment with the realist novel form, much as Nell Dunn did with *Up the Junction* three years before; as in Dunn's novel, it is the voices of the women that are central to this experimental writing. The novel opens in the famous lesbian Gateways club and introduces a whole host of characters with male names who are 'butch or femme or just a little old inbetween'.[86] Like Dunn's Battersea, this is a world within a world, the characters tightly enclosed in a 'microcosm' of British life, except that the heterosexual norm is replaced with the homosexual one. However, the message of the book – clearly articulated by the main protagonist in the closing pages of the book – is that this microcosm should not exist, and indeed does not exist: 'it's a fallacy':

> We're part of society, part of the world whether we or society like it or not, and we have to learn to live in the world and the world has to live with us and make use of us ... just as in the long run it'll have to do with all the other bits and pieces of humanity that go to make up the whole human picture.[87]

Duffy is looking ahead to a moment in which homosexuality – indeed, all sexualities and all differences – will be accepted in one integrated social context. *The Microcosm* thus heralds in a final shift in the representation of sex in post-war women's writing – a shift that seeks to situate sex within a wider 'human picture'.

1969: Sex and 'other things'

Two years after *The Microcosm* and in the aftermath of the political and cultural shifts of 1968, Maureen Duffy published her highly explicit heterosexual novel *Wounds* (1969); in the same year Doris Lessing published the final instalment of her *Children of Violence* series, *The Four-Gated City* (1969). Both novels are set in a grim post-war London and seek to encompass a wide-range of characters and social contexts; both are also interested in how sex and love might feature in the healing of post-war psychological and social wounds. The novels move far beyond the early 1960s critical and political examination of the 'nature' of female sexuality to consider the potential of sex to bridge gender inequalities and bring about a better world.

Wounds begins with sex, and not the metaphorical kind: 'Gently this time he came into her from behind, climbing up through the yielding reaches of soft flesh that drew him in until he lay full length over the undulations of buttock'.[88] The demure 'fingers' and 'throbbing wrists' of the early post-war novels are here replaced with explicit descriptions of foreplay, penetration, fellatio and cunnilingus. However, it is not the explicitness of the acts of lovemaking that is surprising; rather it is the way in which gender inequalities are resolved in the couple's union and attendant discussions. Although the first passage has the female lover in a position of 'quiescen[ce]', apparently enjoying the pain of penetration with her 'arms bent under the head reminding him of crucifixion',[89] the subsequent passages reveal a much more nuanced power-play at work. This is a representation of a mutual, nurturing, and erotic love and it is inclusive, recognising homosexual desire as well as interracial desire and miscegenation. Sex presents itself as an escape from the grim realities of post-war Britain but more importantly as an answer – a way to resolve the inequalities and prejudices of modern existence. Just as Duffy's earlier novel, *The Microcosm*, ends with the main protagonist declaring 'I know it'll be alright',[90] this novel ends with the male lover asking '"Is it truly all right, for you?" … "Oh my dear," she said, "it is *so* all right"'.[91] As 1970 dawns, Duffy tells us that sex is 'all right' for women and – however wounded we might have been – love and sex have the power to heal.

Lessing's *The Four-Gated City* also examines the spiritual decay of a modern post-war world and begins with a heterosexual couple in bed. In the second chapter, Martha engages in sexual intercourse with her friend Jack, a war hero. Here sex is about finding solace and experiencing human connection – love, or even a monogamous relationship, is not a necessary requirement (a very different perspective on sex and love to that so controversially mapped out in *The Golden Notebook*). Through the careful execution of the stages of foreplay and intercourse, Martha is able to rediscover her past self and access her psychic potential. Lessing reimagines sex as a gateway to higher consciousness – a way of accessing latent, extrasensory abilities. As in *Wounds*, sex seems to be an answer – a way to heal and move forwards. However, by the end of *The Four-Gated City*, sex has almost entirely given way to more advanced methods of psychic connection and to far more pressing issues – not least the end of the world. Indeed, in order to focus her energies on fully realising her psychic potential, Martha completely renounces sex, desire and reproduction. If *Wounds* ends with the suggestion that sex might be the answer to post-war anxiety, loneliness and spiritual decay, *The Four-Gated City* ends by reminding us that sex isn't everything – and that most of the time it just gets in the way. For Lessing, sex continues to be too burdened with a history of inequality to be the 'answer' to anything.

In *The Microcosm* we are reminded that '"when we're not all obsessed by sex … There are other things"'.[92] As the 1960s comes to a close, women's obsession with sex – first articulated by Fanny in Mitford's *The Pursuit of Love* – reaches its peak and, eventually, gives way to 'other things'. As Lessing writes in her 1971 preface to *The Golden Notebook*, 'we should all go to bed, shut up about sexual liberation, and go on with important matters'.[93] The political, cultural and personal battles for women (and for humanity), as

Lessing makes clear, are also located elsewhere. And so too were the literary battles of the post-war period. John Sutherland marks 1976 as the year that 'it seems tacitly to have been agreed that nothing printed could be obscene'[94] and even the necessity for the 'literary merit' defence was becoming redundant.[95] The late 1960s and onwards saw modern literary theories radically change the way we think about text and, indeed, sex; the subject of women's writing and sex remains a part of that field – particularly in terms of Feminist, Psychoanalytical and Queer theories – but sex censorship is no longer an agenda. The gradual liberalisation of sex censorship has shifted the representation of sex in women's writing significantly: from self-censorship and shame, to a conscious and critical examination of female sexuality, to a women's writing free of sex censorship and thus finally free to take the battle out of the bedroom.

Notes

1. Nancy Mitford, *Love in a Cold Climate and Other Novels* [1949] (London: Penguin, 2000), p. 18.
2. Lesley A. Hall, *Sex, Gender and Social Change in Britain since 1980* (Basingstoke: Macmillan, 2000), pp. 136–7.
3. Esther Saxey, 'Introduction', in Radclyffe Hall, *The Well of Loneliness* [1928] (Ware: Wordsworth, 2014), p. xix.
4. *Obscene Publications Act, 1959* (London: Her Majesty's Stationery Office), p. 4. <http://www.legislation.gov.uk/ukpga/1959/66/pdfs/ukpga_19590066_en.pdf,> [accessed 22 September 2015].
5. Radclyffe Hall, *The Well of Loneliness*, p. 284.
6. Elizabeth Taylor, *A View of the Harbour* [1947] (London: Virago, 2013), pp. 37–8.
7. Hera Cook, *The Long Sexual Revolution: English Women, Sex, & Contraception 1800–1975* (Oxford: Oxford University Press, 2007), p. 179.
8. Cook, *The Long Sexual Revolution*, p. 38.
9. Taylor, *A View of the Harbour*, p. 164.
10. Mitford, *The Pursuit of Love*, in *Love in a Cold Climate and Other Novels*, pp. 18–19.
11. Mitford, *The Pursuit of Love*, p. 193.
12. Mitford, *The Pursuit of Love*, p. 150.
13. Cook, *The Long Sexual Revolution*, p. 184.
14. Taylor, *A View of the Harbour*, p. 219.
15. Elizabeth Taylor, *A Game of Hide and Seek* [1951] (London: Virago, 2009), p. 173.
16. Taylor, *A Game of Hide and Seek*, p. 262.
17. Hall, *Sex, Gender and Social Change in Britain since 1980*, p. 152.
18. Taylor, *A View of the Harbour*, p. 17.
19. Rosamond Lehmann, *The Echoing Grove* [1953] (Glasgow: William Collins Sons & Co, 1984), p. 155.
20. Lehmann, *The Echoing Grove*, p. 311.
21. Lehmann, *The Echoing Grove*, p. 155.
22. Doris Lessing, *A Proper Marriage* [1954] (London: Flamingo, 2002), p. 43.
23. Cook, *The Long Sexual Revolution*, p. 182.
24. Clare Hanson, *A Cultural History of Pregnancy: Pregnancy, Medicine and Culture, 1750–2000* (Basingstoke, Hampshire: Palgrave Macmillan, 2004), p. 141.

25. Lessing, *A Proper Marriage*, p. 86.
26. Deborah Philips, *Women's Fiction: 1945–2005* (London & New York: Continuum, 2006), p. 38.
27. Margaret Drabble, *The Millstone* [1965] (London: Weidenfeld and Nicolson, 1981), p. 20.
28. Drabble, *The Millstone*, p. 21.
29. See Deborah Philips and Ian Haywood's discussion of the novels in *Brave New Causes: Women in British Postwar Fictions* (London: Continuum, 1998), pp. 36–7.
30. Melissa Benn, 'Middle-Class Mores', *New Statesman*, 139.5020, 81–3 (2010), 81, *Humanities International Complete*, <http://search.ebscohost.com/login.aspx?direct=true&AuthType=athens&db=buh&AN=53875732&site=eds-live&authtype=ip,athens> [accessed 10 June 2015].
31. Lynne Reid Banks, *The L-Shaped Room* [1960] (London: Vintage, 2004), pp. 32–3.
32. Drabble, *The Millstone*, p. 39.
33. Drabble, *The Millstone*, p. 37.
34. Banks, *The L-Shaped Room*, p. 132.
35. Philips, *Women's Fiction*, p. 44.
36. Drabble, *The Millstone*, p. 34.
37. Andrew Rosen, *The Transformation of British Life 1950–2000* (Manchester: Manchester University Press, 2003), p. 54.
38. Banks, *The L-Shaped Room*, p. 33.
39. Drabble, *The Millstone*, p. 129.
40. Drabble, *The Millstone*, p. 86.
41. Angela Carter, *The Magic Toyshop* [1967] (London: Virago, 2003), p. 2.
42. Carter, *The Magic Toyshop*, p. 1.
43. Carter, *The Magic Toyshop*, p. 2.
44. Carter, *The Magic Toyshop*, pp. 151–152.
45. Carter, *The Magic Toyshop*, p. 141.
46. Carter, *The Magic Toyshop*, p. 143.
47. Carter, *The Magic Toyshop*, p. 167.
48. Carter, *The Magic Toyshop*, p. 200.
49. Margaret Drabble, 'Introduction', Nell Dunn, *Poor Cow* [1967] (London: Virago, 1988), p. xii.
50. Adrian Henri, 'Introduction', Nell Dunn, *Up the Junction* [1963] (London: Virago, 1988), p. xiii.
51. Cook, *The Long Sexual Revolution*, p. 186.
52. Benn, 'Middle-Class Mores', p. 81.
53. Drabble, 'Introduction', *Poor Cow*, p. ix.
54. Nell Dunn, *Up the Junction*, p. 13.
55. Dunn, *Up the Junction*, p. 97.
56. Dunn, *Up the Junction*, p. 66.
57. Heather Walton, *Literature, Theology and Feminism* (Manchester & New York: Manchester University Press, 2007), p. 42.
58. Doris Lessing, *The Golden Notebook* [1962] (London: Paladin, 1989), p. 297.
59. Lessing, *The Golden Notebook*, p. 303.
60. Lessing, *The Golden Notebook*, p. 304.
61. Lessing, *Martha Quest* [1952] (London: Flamingo, 1993), p. 249.
62. Lessing, *Landlocked* [1958] (St Albans, Herts: Panther, 1976), pp. 104–5.
63. Lessing, *The Golden Notebook*, p. 404.
64. Lessing, *The Golden Notebook*, p. 200.

65. The novel also includes a discussion about a lecture in which a 'male professor,' based on the study of swans, claims 'women have no physical basis for vaginal orgasm' (*The Golden Notebook*, p. 200).
66. Cook, *The Long Sexual Revolution*, p. 245.
67. Cook, *The Long Sexual Revolution*, p. 184.
68. Lessing, *The Golden Notebook*, p. 277.
69. Lessing, *The Golden Notebook*, p. 404.
70. Lessing, *The Golden Notebook*, p. 200.
71. Mary Renault, *The North Face* [1948] (London: Virago, 2014), p. 286.
72. Sarah Dunant, 'Introduction', *Return to Night* (London: Virago, 2014), p. xii.
73. Dunant, 'Introduction', p. xxi.
74. Mary E. Snodgrass, *Encyclopaedia of Feminist Literature* (New York: Facts on File, 2006), p. 445.
75. Mitford, *Love in a Cold Climate*, pp. 280, 247, 287.
76. Mitford, *Love in a Cold Climate*, p. 287.
77. Allan Hepburn, 'The Fate Of The Modern Mistress: Nancy Mitford And The Comedy Of Marriage', *Modern Fiction Studies*, 45: 2 (1999), 340–68, 362.
78. Quoted in Hepburn, 'The Fate Of the Modern Mistress', p. 362.
79. Lehmann, *The Echoing Grove*, pp. 54, 262.
80. Drabble, *The Millstone*, pp. 24, 33, 196.
81. Banks, *The L-Shaped Room*, p. 12.
82. Brian Magee quoted in Gabriele Griffin, *Heavenly Love? Lesbian Images in Twentieth-Century Women's Writing* (Manchester: Manchester University Press, 1993), p. 41.
83. Cook, *The Long Sexual Revolution*, p. 176.
84. Elizabeth Wilson, *Only Halfway to Paradise: Women in Postwar Britain: 1945–1968* (London & New York: Tavistock, 1980), p. 158.
85. Maureen Duffy, 'Afterword', *The Microcosm* [1966] (London: Virago, 1989), p. 289.
86. Duffy, *The Microcosm*, p. 17.
87. Duffy, *The Microcosm*, p. 287.
88. Maureen Duffy, *Wounds* [1969] (London: Methuen, 1984), p. 11.
89. Duffy, *Wounds*, p. 11.
90. Duffy, *The Microcosm*, p. 288.
91. Duffy, *Wounds*, p. 156.
92. Duffy, *The Microcosm*, p. 10.
93. Doris Lessing, 'Preface' in *The Golden Notebook*, p. 9.
94. John J. Sutherland, *Offensive Literature: Decensorship in Britain, 1960–1982* (Totowa, New Jersey: Barnes and Noble, 1983), p. 3.
95. In 1969 C. H. Rolf published *Books in the Dock* (London: Andre Deutsch, 1969) in whose Foreword John Mortimer demands that 'we should not only be able to defend to the death other people's right to say things with which we disagree; we must also allow them to do it in abominable prose' (p. 10).

7
The Second Wave

Leanne Bibby

Introduction

The 'second wave' in western feminism is the name given to the period of organised feminist activism in the second half of the twentieth century, conventionally dated from the early 1960s in the United States. Several writers locate the origins of the British Women's Liberation Movement in the publication of American liberal feminist texts including Betty Friedan's *The Feminine Mystique* in 1963.[1] Historians of this period have also, however, identified important roots of the second wave in earlier, global, anti-colonial liberation movements: for instance, Judith Evans refers to 'those who fought for socialism in the 1960s Left in the US, Germany, and the UK; women who denounced their male comrades for preaching liberation for all the peoples of the world: all except women.'[2] 'The second wave' also designates a period of significant intersections between feminist activism, in the sense of practical organisation, and women's writing, with literary roots that pre-dated the organised movement. This chapter examines some of the references in women's writing from the 1950s to the 1970s to debates emerging in anticipation of or alongside the British Women's Liberation Movement, and argues that these prefigure the imaginative dimensions of feminist activism. From the postwar period onward, writers from Stevie Smith to Penelope Mortimer contemplated women's changing consciousness of their situation in illuminating ways. While these authors may not have identified themselves with the imminent women's movement in Britain, they nevertheless laid crucial literary groundwork for that movement, and for later feminist polemics including those in which Juliet Mitchell (1940-), Germaine Greer (1939-), and Sheila Rowbotham (1943-) confronted both the cultural and material factors of women's oppression within patriarchal

© The Author(s) 2017
C. Hanson and S. Watkins, *The History of British Women's Writing, 1945–1975*,
History of British Women's Writing, DOI: 10.1057/978–1–137–47736–1_8

society. This chapter is divided into sections examining some of the major ways in which what I term proto-second-wave literature explored debates connected to the second wave in Britain. My selection of texts is not intended to be representative, but rather to assist readers in 'looking again' at celebrated texts and the persistently powerful and relevant forms of feminist expression they helped to establish.

The second wave in Britain: Breaking for freedom

Second wave feminists built on the achievements of the 'first wave' earlier in the twentieth century, which was concerned with women's rights in the public sphere, to own property and to vote. The second wave focussed on a wider set of issues concerned at their core with the politics of 'reproduction' – meaning, in a Marxist sense, both the oppressive co-opting of women's bodies for heteronormative sexuality and childbearing, and women's 'reproduction' of political ideas,[3] meanings echoed in the writings of Sheila Rowbotham and Juliet Mitchell. The writers of the second wave played with these ideas, (re)producing ideas in imaginative, exploratory ways and speaking into and alongside conventional manifestos. The British Women's Liberation Movement, with writing a core form of activism, drove real social changes, including refuges for battered women and rape crisis centres, and held their first conference in Oxford in 1970, the same year as the publication in London of *The Female Eunuch* by Australian-born academic Germaine Greer. *Spare Rib*, the feminist magazine launched at this time, reviewed and recommended women's novels, and Mary Eagleton highlights the often concurrent publication of feminist manifestos and pioneering works of feminist literary criticism, including Kate Millett's *Sexual Politics*, first published in the UK in 1971, and by Virago Press in 1977. Eagleton also emphasises Millett's stylistic 'energy and sense of urgency' – 'the audacity and élan of Millett's writing testifies to the excitement of that juncture'.[4] Recently, Catherine Riley has examined the intersections between feminist literary criticism and polemic in an illuminating study of these two pioneering works by Millett and Greer.[5] Literature and literary criticism are central to the history of second-wave feminist activism, because, I would stress, literature is a crucial part of that activism's 'pre-history' prior to the foundation of the movement proper. I therefore build on Eagleton's and Riley's acknowledgement of this aspect of second wave history to contend that the examples of pre-1970 literature discussed in this chapter are the 'prototypes' of later, avowedly feminist writing.

Although the popular image of the second wave is still of campaigning on issues fundamental to women's equality, the period is also one of important developments in the history of ideas. Second-wave feminism is certainly tied intellectually to other global movements at this time: in America, to the New Left and the Civil Rights and anti-psychiatry movements, and in the UK, to the 'organised Left', a tradition of socialist thinking, anti-Vietnam campaigns and the Campaign for Nuclear Disarmament (CND). Furthermore, women's employment and entry into higher education had increased, and divorce rates had risen.[6] Marxist concepts, in particular, allowed authors to scrutinise the making of social structures and the gendered subjects within them, even before the women's movement was fully formed. Mitchell's essay 'Women: the Longest Revolution', for example, discusses the period 'before there was a women's movement in Britain' although its cultural origins were indeed present.[7] Meanwhile, in 1973's *Woman's Consciousness, Man's World*, Rowbotham engages with Friedan's *The Feminine Mystique* but criticises the book for neglecting 'the manifestations of women's oppression through to the material structure of society', and describes the new movement Friedan called for evocatively as 'shuffling about within capitalism'[8] instead of pushing for structural change. The British movement thus grew out of critical and imaginative thinking and writing about its counterparts, focusing afresh on issues of social organisation and cultural representation. Feminists in the UK were well aware that the image of the emotionally and psychologically struggling housewife, familiar from *The Feminine Mystique*, was of one who was suffering from the 'false consciousness' of patriarchy (to borrow Engels' ideas, as Marxist feminists have).[9]

Mitchell is one key author of the British second wave to locate her work in precisely these worldwide contexts, for example by noting her early 'indignation' at Frantz Fanon's argument that women should only be emancipated after a revolution for Algerian independence.[10] Cora Kaplan also underlines resistance to racist and imperialist ideologies as a driving force behind second wave feminist thinking – thinking grounded in critical readings of male-authored theory and literature.[11] Women in Britain had been part of campaigns for social reform since long before the 1960s and 70s, the 1960s especially having seen unprecedented advances in women's rights including the introduction of the contraceptive pill and the Abortion Act (1967).[12] Marxist, socialist, psychoanalytic, and other bodies of theory provided feminists with new methods and frameworks for rethinking the relation between the public and the private. This theoretically-informed thinking was rooted in literature; critical works such as Ellen Moers's *Literary Women* (1963) and Millett's *Sexual Politics*, indeed, are as strongly associated with Women's Liberation as other polemics, and the polemics themselves, Friedan's and Greer's included, refer frequently to literature to support their claims. Greer and Millett critique male-authored literature, primarily. Among many examples, Greer memorably traces modern terms of misogynistic abuse back to Shakespeare, including 'flibbertigibbet', used to describe both a 'foul fiend from hell' in *King Lear* and an alleged victim of rape in the twentieth century;[13] and Millett reads Lawrence's *Lady Chatterley's Lover* as a dismaying 'program for social and sexual redemption' for men and women based on a reversion to Freudian active and passive sexual roles, respectively. While male literature came under scrutiny in the service of Women's Liberation, the first dedicated feminist publishers, including Virago (founded in 1973), contributed to a new sense of the role of women's literary writing as canon-changing activism also: as Catherine Riley says about Virago, the press's early lists demonstrate a decisive 'intention to change the constructions of gender through literature'.[14]

The first issue of *Spare Rib* magazine, published in 1972, reveals interests in the same breaking-points of patriarchal culture as other forms of writing, and its hopes to empower its readers and subjects through imaginative and polemical writing of many kinds. While inviting contributions by new and established writers, the issue features articles (most presented in brash visual styles) on cultural and social issues, history, the activities of women's liberation groups, DIY how-to guides, education campaigns, an article on beauty 'behind the dirt', advertisements for a novel by Margaret Drabble and a women's legal support group, and recipes 'for people who don't want to spend much time in the kitchen'.[15] The precise relationship between British second-wave feminism and British women's writing is ambivalent, but looking at writing that pre-dates the Women's Liberation movement of the 1970s is instructive. Although most of the authors I will refer to here did not ally themselves with Women's Liberation, there is an observable sense of proto-second-wave exchange between feminist ideas and literary forms of expression. I will explore this exchange now through literary work from the 1950s onward whose written forms broke free from conventional expectations, suggesting ways in which changed consciousness could lead to changed realities.

In the second half of the twentieth century, images of women in psychological distress figure in many British literary texts, their distress positioned in terms of resistance to the structural and ideological limitations on their lives. In Doris Lessing's *The Golden Notebook* (1962), protagonist Anna Wulf's narrative is dispersed among fragments from her five notebooks and a novel-in-progress, suggesting not only multiple forms of 'breakdown' but also determined literary (re)production. Lessing's 1971 introduction to the novel expresses a prickly, unsure kind of feminism – she strives to 'get the subject of Women's Liberation over with'[16] – but the text's discursive interventions remain. In a moving example, Anna is canvassing for votes for the Communist Party when she observes 'Five lonely women going mad quietly by themselves'.[17] As Maroula Joannou has noted in relation to *The Golden Notebook* and another classic British-published text of female breakdown, Sylvia Plath's *The Bell Jar* (1963), these fictions highlight 'the metonymic links between mental illness and the post-war feminine mystique', disturbing historical notions of 'madness' as a 'purely individual phenomenon',[18] and a feminised one into the bargain. It is worth noting that Plath's novel became associated with second-wave feminism retrospectively, rather than as a consequence of any explicit authorial identification with the movement.

Furthermore, these novels' depictions of breakdown challenge social and cultural structures in ways that call to mind, thematically and stylistically, psychiatrist R. D. Laing's near-contemporary suggestion in *The Politics of Experience* (1967) that medical practices of diagnosing/labelling mental illness fail to recognise the 'ill' person as potentially experiencing valuable 'other' types of consciousness. For Laing, the schizophrenic is capable of forming a particular 'inner life' in response to inadequate social conditions:

> We are socially conditioned to regard total immersion in outer space and time as normal and healthy. Immersion in inner space and time tends to be regarded as anti-social withdrawal, a deviancy, invalid, pathological *per se*, in some sense discreditable.[19]

The Bell Jar's Esther Greenwood's experience of 'inner space and time' is one of anguish at the features of her environment as much as at her mental condition; her disappointments in education, work, and relationships combine with the damaging impact of food poisoning and other physical pains. She reflects, with disarming insight (and recognition of the value of writing in all this), that 'People were made of nothing so much as dust, and I couldn't see that doctoring all that dust was a bit better than writing poems people would remember'.[20] Writing and narrative go on during and despite breakdown, and provide a certain, useful version of reality, as they do for Mrs Armitage in Penelope Mortimer's *The Pumpkin Eater* (1962), who narrates her experiences to the reader and her doctor, and concludes her interior narrative thus: 'Some of these things happened, and some were dreams. They are all true, as I understand truth. They are all real, as I understand reality'.[21] Along with Lessing's text, these proto-second-wave novels assert the capacity of 'mad' women to critique their surroundings incisively – a paradoxical kind of power, from within positions of ostensible weakness.

By way of writing about, around, and beyond entrenched ways of thinking, speaking and participating in society, conventions could be rendered strange, patriarchy itself defamiliarised, and female breakdown seen as a form of resistance to oppression. In addition, much women's writing of the British second wave challenged anew the idea that there should or could be a clear distinction between literary and polemical writing. Women's writing of this time, whether feminist in its declared aims or not, participates in often unexpected ways in representing and examining the 'social training' that allows patriarchy to subjugate women.[22] In A. S. Byatt's *The Shadow of the Sun* (1964), for example, teenage Anna Severell, the daughter of an eminent novelist, works to develop her own identity as an intellectual, but in seeking a wider range of knowledge about life, becomes pregnant during an affair with her tutor. Byatt's novel is one of the clearest examples of a woman-centred narrative to link the act of writing directly to a woman protagonist's changed consciousness, before organised Women's Liberation. Anna's story concludes with her abandoning a convenient marriage and choosing an uncertain future that will, however, include writing and self-determination: 'I've never tried yet,' she thinks, 'I've never put pen to paper.'[23] Her conventional destiny broken down, there is nothing yet to replace it, but this uncertainty allows for the interlinked possibilities of exploration, art, and autonomy. Mortimer's Mrs Armitage in *The Pumpkin Eater* takes similar control of her own narrative and vision, although she is classed as unbalanced within the culture Laing criticised. For her, like Anna, uncertainty creates crucial possibility: 'Most people, I know, have this fantasy. One day they'll walk out of the door, through the garden gate, and ... then? Then what? ... you need a state of mind to think all of these things, and that state of mind is the one that keeps you at home'.[24] Conventional 'states of mind' are all that is sanctioned – all others produce only 'fantasy', which feminist art must then re-characterise as a serious engagement with ideas.

The subversive states of mind represented in the postwar period's proto-second-wave fiction exploited the manifold possible breaking-points of patriarchal culture and society mentioned earlier, and fed into later, polemical writing that sought to convey ideas in subversive, imaginative form. Maroula Joannou stresses the well-known idea that the 1970s were a turning point in organised British feminism – 'the decade of women' where the 1960s had been 'the decade of youth'.[25] Compelling manifestos and polemics were required to establish this movement and to 'centre' women culturally as subjects and agents – although, contrastingly, provocative 'decentring' was also part of the era's feminisms. Polemics and manifestos, therefore, sharpened certain styles and strategies already present in women's writing, whether by declared feminists, or not: texts like those by Lessing, Plath, Byatt, and Mortimer centre women, while also resisting and interrogating boundaries or borders, and find distinctive ways to represent women's experiences in their bodies, homes and wider environments, particularly where these experiences are troubling to patriarchal order. In terms of centring, Joannou's notion of 'woman-centred fictions', or fictions that 'address women about issues of primary concern to women',[26] illuminates various writings' participation in the second wave. Patricia Duncker also emphasises the role of fiction in activism and argues for a clear interplay between the discourses of imaginative writing, academic feminism, and activism. With vivid details of her own involvement in the British women's movement, she argues that 'the radical basis of feminism is storytelling',[27] and in addition, that writing is 'an act of transgression, an articulation of all the things we should not *feel or think*' [emphasis added].[28] For Duncker, moreover, all feminist writing is 'necessarily confrontational, in opposition. We will always write polemic'.[29] On the broken-down borders between fiction and polemic, it seems, British second-wave feminism began.

Appearing in 1970, the start of Joannou's 'decade of women', Germaine Greer's *The Female Eunuch* was a bestseller, setting it apart from academic and 'underground' feminist publications, while all nevertheless participated in the same project. In 2006, novelist Fay Weldon recalled that 'In the 1970s everyone was reading this'; as she worked as the sole female television writer in 'an entirely male world', Greer's book 'gave shape to what [she] was already doing'.[30] The expression 'gave shape' is very apt, as the book takes clear inspiration from the feminist 'classics' before it and makes use of their forms and polemical styles, resulting in an approach both erudite and confrontational. *The Female Eunuch* borrows aspects from, for example, Simone de Beauvoir's analysis of the situation and history of the category of 'woman' in *The Second Sex* (1949), Betty Friedan's critique of the American cult of 'the happy housewife heroine' in *The Feminine Mystique* (1963), and the anarchic (and satirical and performative) call for the elimination of the male sex in Valerie Solanas's *SCUM Manifesto* (1967).[31] In an importantly British-based instance of feminist polemic, *The Female Eunuch* gave a provocative and accessible new shape to feminist writing.

Reading *The Female Eunuch* is still a jolt for audiences familiar with its overall message (transmitted in a muted manner by subsequent academic texts and word of mouth) but not with its acidly confrontational style. Women's subjugation is explained with an energising conciseness as the 'castration of women', which 'has been carried out in terms of a masculine-feminine polarity, in which men have commandeered all the energy'.[32] Greer expounds this argument across themed sections on 'Body', 'Soul', 'Love', and 'Hate', moving between disciplines including science, anthropology, history, literature, and mythology, to assert both the problem's severity and the necessity of solutions that will break down inadequate versions of reality. Visually and formally, the text announces its close relationship to magazines and polemics published as periodicals, such as *Spare Rib*: its short sections are not exactly chapters but rather quasi-journalistic pieces, written with a brevity and directness that would attract a wide readership of forms besides books. The border-defying discursive project of second-wave feminism in Britain seems to crystallise in Greer's polemic, and the literature analysed in the following sections demonstrates that project's much earlier beginnings.

Women as subjects

The diverse body of second-wave feminist writing in Britain sought to establish women as autonomous subjects with the ability to change society and culture, rather than as the 'Others' of man that Simone de Beauvoir described in her critique of patriarchy, *The Second Sex*. This autonomous subjectivity is the discursive basis of the notion of 'rights' within organised feminism (the term 'subject' also implies, at the same time but in very different ways, the concept of interior, subjective experience so crucial to feminist writing). Fiona A. Montgomery surveys how legal reforms in British women's favour after the Second World War dramatically illustrate their changing position in society. Laws including the 1945 Family Allowances Act, the 1967 Medical Termination of Pregnancy Act (often simply called the Abortion

Act) and the Family Planning Act of the same year, the 1970 Equal Pay Act and the 1975 Sex Discrimination Act suggest the shifting ways in which the law 'created the legal category "woman"'.[33] Although women gained agency later in the twentieth century, they were initially constructed in legal discourse and granted rights only in relation to men, their children and other dependents within the family. Basic patriarchal structures, such as the conventional family, persisted as norms. The effect of giving women some legal autonomy and rights was thus, paradoxically, to emphasise discursively their central place within patriarchal structures such as the bourgeois family, a place which their own written interventions could then disturb and resist. British authors including Mortimer and Byatt, and poets Stevie Smith and Elizabeth Jennings (1926-2001) wrote within, but also against these rigidly patriarchal systems. With the blurring of boundaries between writing and activism, and between literature and polemic, then, women became more prominent subjects in many accounts of social and public life in ways that questioned and compromised the status quo.

One of the most useful critical frameworks for examining this process retrospectively is Maggie Humm's notion of 'border crossings' in feminist writing. She defines 'borders' as more than 'simply discontinuities, temporary barriers to women's drive for knowledge'; rather, they are the transitional spaces between cultures and identities, and between self and other: spaces in which British women authors of the twentieth century could 'problematise narrative forms and question the limits of representation and of consciousness'.[34] Doris Lessing, for example, has Anna Wulf write about the language of supposedly 'fixed' feminine subjectivities even within the fictional fabric of *The Golden Notebook,* by attempting to record the minutiae of female perceptions.[35] In view of this, we can regard an episode in Anna's blue notebook as one such test of 'the limits of representation' in its inclusion of Anna's experience of menstruation: this stimulates her intention to be 'conscious of everything so as to write it down', although she records mainly her worry of 'a bad smell, emanating from me', which she feels as 'an imposition from outside.' Writing her physical self extends her consciousness beyond taboos regarding women's bodies. Still, even as she evokes several times the sensory realities of smells, for instance, she paradoxically resists this heightened consciousness, pushing her period 'out of her mind'[36] behind the excuse of cleanliness. This emotional and physical minutiae remains inscribed in the notebook, meanwhile; the experience both voiced and unvoiced at the same time

Proto-second-wave literary authors, including Doris Lessing, Sylvia Plath, and Fay Weldon, exploited paradoxical, both/and relationships between forms and genres to represent women's social, psychological, emotional, and physical experiences more closely, directly, and therefore inherently more challengingly. Elizabeth Jennings and Stevie Smith are two poets whose work explores women's subjectivity and its productively uneasy relationship to patriarchal forms of culture, in ways clearly anticipating the writing of the later second wave. This work lays the type of formal and thematic groundwork for Women's Liberation discussed earlier. Jennings is an often overlooked example of a mid-twentieth-century poet carrying out this groundwork: a devout Catholic with no declared feminist allegiance, nonetheless her work and its concern with women, writing, and border crossings has been seen as challenging conventional oppositions between tradition and progressiveness.[37] The poetry is often read in terms of female mysticism, with Amanda G. Michaels arguing that mysticism is 'a border subject, existing both within and without religious tradition'.[38] Formally and thematically, Jennings's work anticipates many key motifs of second wave literature. The 'border' condition of being both within and outside the 'symbolic boundaries' Humm describes[39] is a disarming dimension of Jennings's treatment of, in particular, memory, relationships, art, religion, death, and the simple act of narration from within and outside domains of experience. In 'Telling Stories' (1958), 'stories' are defined as 'large things' beyond the rigorous control of 'A verb, an adjective, a happy end'. The speaker defends an unruly but powerful form of storytelling:

> The stories that we tell, we tell against
> Ourselves then at the last
> Since all the worlds we make we stand outside

The unidentified controller of language may 'stand firm within the fragile plot'.[40] The domineering 'you' of the poem guards the centres and forms of narratives, while the speaker gives an exhilarating sense of possibilities around and beyond these discursive boundaries. 1953's 'Identity' dramatises a thinking subject's perception of a relationship, and awareness of her (her gender can be assumed) definition in relation to the loved and loving other:

> So then assemble me,
> Your exact picture firm and credible,
> Though as I think myself I may be free
> And accurate enough.[41]

The focus on the female subject here is enough to set aside, for a time, the power of outside institutions to define and limit the subject, her thoughts, emotions and decisions.

For Jennings, the possibility of transcendence in religious thought and experience is a way of querying patriarchal borders. Further to this, 1958's 'The Annunciation' takes an icon of maternity and feminine submission, the Virgin Mary, and makes her experience immediate, sensory, and ambivalent. She is both powerless and powerful, refusing stasis: aware of 'the pain to come' but nonetheless 'in ecstasy'. The visiting angel has 'terrified her', but she speaks and reasons her way through uncertainty about the 'god before' to the 'god' that now 'grows'. One halting thought follows another towards her focus on the 'human child she loves', the one she nurtures and *knows*, beside the vast idea of the 'god' that 'stirs beneath her breast'.[42] Immediate, physical, feminine experiences both within and outside the cult of maternity Mary represents take precedence over religious revelation, giving her a powerfully liminal new subject position between body and spirit. In 1966's 'Caravaggio's "Narcissus" in Rome', the speaking subject is also one with the ability not only 'Simply to see this picture' as do 'many', but also to 'stare' reflectively at the art that supports culture and knowledge. The myth of Narcissus looking at himself and the artist painting the mythic scene to gain 'self-knowledge' becomes an opportunity for the subject to do the same – though not without risk: 'Look at yourself, the shine, the sheer / Embodiment thrown back in some / Medium like wood or glass'. Thinking and meaning-making continue; when the making of art stops, meanings that the artist 'could not find' become apparent.[43] Staring, not just looking, becomes an imaginative, productive act, again tantalisingly so in relation to an apparently female speaking subject akin to the activist or polemicist looking back forcibly at culture.

Stevie Smith's poetry intervenes in familiar narratives at the level of conversation, gossip, letters, and well-known cultural images: in other words, in the narratives produced by and supporting the forms of social life that define and confine the genders. Mark Halliday describes Smith, a prolific writer of fiction and poetry concerned with middle-class experience, as 'a deeply original and serious poet who masqueraded as a poet of eccentric light verse', and 'a radical objector to the frustrations and limitations of reality' in England.[44] Smith and her work are not associated explicitly with the British women's movement, but the poetry's style and investment in transgression nonetheless make it a contribution to literary proto-feminism. The poems' edge of knowing humour is reminiscent of the spiky, sardonic tones of a great deal of *Spare Rib*'s journalism and Greer's *The Female Eunuch*. Her poetry is a satire on conventions that is ferociously knowledgeable about and exasperated with them. Much of Smith's poetry of the 1960s, reprinted in the *Collected Poems* of 1975, uses dry humour, a vocal and irreverent form of subjectivity from within established forms of speech and behaviour, to assert those forms' absurd limitations.[45] 'Was He Married?' poses a series of questions beyond its titular enquiry, on the identity and status associated with marriage, to notions of love and death, strength and weakness, so that the comic 'masquerade' Halliday notes gives way to the telling question:

> Do only human beings suffer from the irritation
> I have mentioned? learn too that being comical
> Does not ameliorate the desperation?[46]

The short verse 'Poor Soul, poor Girl!' gives a darkly humorous voice to the debutante depicted in one of Smith's pen drawings accompanying the poem, a seated woman in evening gown and small shoes, with a pointy tiara, imagining being 'struck by lightning and killed suddenly'.[47] Smith thus breaks the debutante's decorous, prescribed, and seemingly natural silence, exposing the disruptive experiences therein. Like Jennings, Smith exploits these feminine silences by populating them with voices. 'Everything is Swimming' is another verse in the deceptive form of gossip, the subject of which is a supposedly 'Silly ass' and 'silly woman', maybe drunk or on the hallucinogen 'mescalin [sic]', whose almost mystical perspective is nevertheless given in the poem's first line and repeated in its second – 'Everything is swimming in a wonderful wisdom'.[48] Both conventional and marginal discourses of feminine life are also imagined in 'Emily writes such a good letter', in which 'Emily's' trite comments on marriages, homes, and visits sit beside moments of high emotion, such as terror of illness – 'It was cancer' – and spite – 'In my opinion Maud / Is an evil woman'.[49] The work of Jennings and Smith constructs a provocative dissonance between patriarchal forces of family, religion, subdued forms of speech and thought (sober, proper), and a sense of the speaking and thinking subject's actual experience and consciousness. That consciousness is in flux, unpredictable, and liable to cross the borders of which British culture during the second wave was so strongly aware: borders between bodies and spirits or intellects, maternal and intellectual (re)production, interpretation and critique, and between patriarchal institutions and possible experiences beyond them.

Women's bodies

Across the history (in the broadest sense) of writing about women, their bodies have been represented frequently as sites of instability and madness (again, crossing acceptable borders), and as objects of distrust and fear. They are policed by the institutional and cultural forces of patriarchy, notably medicine, the relationships sanctioned in marriage and the family, and the more or less obvious cultural codes, scrutinised in feminist theory, that define women as either (as Montgomery summarises) 'potential mothers, actual mothers or retired mothers'.[50] In other words, historically, discourses of female embodiment have discouraged women from taking action on desires other than those for nurturing family life and domesticity. The question of women's (re)productive capacities, a driving concern of second wave feminism, has proved especially problematic for the status quo when deployed for feminist purposes. The female body is, after all, both a material fact and a symbol of its own very long history as the other of the male body.

Later feminist philosophy, including the work of Luce Irigaray and Hélène Cixous, would consider women's bodies as systems of linguistic meanings and their 'otherness' as potentially productive, but bodies have long been often unstable literary tropes of women's experiences and desires. Fay Weldon's first two novels, *The Fat Woman's Joke* (1967) and *Down Among the Women* (1971) are sharply knowing with regard to the tradition of patriarchal philosophy which designates the female body as unruly, messy, threatening, and voracious. Weldon engages in the same debates as Greer, who argues that at the moment of the second wave, 'Women's sexual organs are shrouded in mystery' and that most women's 'knowledge of the womb is academic' in an educational milieu characterised by misogynistic myths, fantasies, and taboos. Greer observes that if the female body is represented in discourse at all, it is distorted to unnatural proportions to emphasise its 'curves'.[51] With a formally simple but uncompromisingly direct language, comparable to Greer's, Weldon's writing walks the fine line between fiction and polemic. It depicts physical acts of excess by means of food and sex and (often temporary) rejections of the institutions of marriage and the family. The women and men in Weldon's *The Fat Woman's Joke* are hungry, for one form of sustenance or another: food, sex, career success, or a sense of the identity they feel should be theirs. Their sense of, or lack of sense of, their own bodies is paramount in every case.

Esther Sussman, separated from her husband, eats excessively; food has replaced sex in her life as an object of desire and source of pleasure: 'When you eat, you get fat, and that's all. There are no complications'.[52] Her weight gain and transgression of socially acceptable behaviour (she is associated with slovenliness, mess, and outspokenness) are stripped of their restrictive, middle-class social implications because for her, 'love and motherhood and romance' are 'no more than dreams remembered'.[53] She is no longer socially (or biologically) 'visible' or 'necessary', and so she enjoys a type of freedom in which her body's sexual significance is beside the point, as she exists outside the 'buyers' market' of women Greer describes.[54] Susan is in her early twenties, and the secretary and (for most of the novel, aspiring) mistress of Esther's husband Alan who, ironically, desires food more than he does Susan, who is spitefully described by another woman as 'Plump, biteable and ripe'.[55] Alan himself expresses a wish to 'eat' part of her leg,[56] but while Susan constructs herself as a liberated artist and mistress on her own terms, she experiences a sensation of phantom pregnancy as a result of another boyfriend describing his wife's pregnancy to her.[57] Esther's friend Phyllis, ordinarily a devoted wife to her own cheating husband, succeeds in having an impulsive affair with Alan, who calls her 'a proper feminine woman' with 'pretty little eyes that never see more than they should'.[58] Her lack of awareness extends to the absence of her body from the text: like the idealised, 1960s romance heroines Greer describes,[59] she is 'overwhelmed' during an oddly bodiless paragraph of sex with Alan, which she tries to excuse by saying 'It's me. I'm frigid, you see. I was only trying to help you'.[60]

When Alan describes Phyllis, he echoes patriarchal narratives of women in relation to which acts of bodily excess and desire are defined as deviant.

Both *The Fat Woman's Joke* and *Down Among the Women* are reminiscent, formally, of feminist stage plays (for instance by Caryl Churchill), often taking the form of conversations between women continually 'speaking' into and against scenarios. The novels' speakers, therefore, never quite 'settle' into their predicaments, although those predicaments remain: as Wanda in *Down Among the Women* says, knowingly, 'down here among the women we have no option but to stay'.[61] Unmarried, wily Scarlet has a baby daughter, Byzantia, plans to become a professional mistress, and eventually marries for 'security'. Her contemporary Jocelyn achieves a convenient middle-class marriage, for status. Both women's unions are emotionally and sexually unhappy, a state linked to their shifting sense of control of their respective situations. Marriage is 'necessary' to them both, for different reasons, although as Greer has it, in a cruel paradox, 'Loveless marriage is anathema' in their time and place.[62] The novel looks back retrospectively at three generations of working- and middle-class women as they negotiate relationships and sex, marriages and motherhood, with contradictory and confrontational bluntness and humour (reminiscent of Stevie Smith) overlaying moments of anger, violence, and sadness. The text is, as Margaret Chessnut suggests, important for 'its presentation of female case-histories and the consciousness of middle-class women',[63] and along with *The Fat Woman's Joke*, it is an uncompromising representation of the conditions which Women's Liberation would imminently address, while cultural and legal changes responded to the realities of female embodiment.

Women, home and family

Second-wave feminism's critical confrontation with women's subjectivities and experiences, within and in spite of the patriarchal discourses (such as popular culture, history, and law) that sought to describe them, meant that the private and traditionally 'feminine' spheres of home and middle-class models of the family would be scrutinised in writing as never before. To paraphrase the second wave's definitive slogan, these aspects of the 'personal' would ever after be 'political' and become objects of suspicion, even while conventional social models remained largely in place. Juliet Mitchell, whose background, like that of many other feminist authors of the second wave, is in both Marxist and feminist politics, broke crucial feminist ground in considering the family as a focus for feminist analysis in the 1966 essay 'Feminism and the Question of Women'. She scrutinises in detail 'the gap between reality and ideology' in bourgeois society's valorisation of the family, and proposes instead to look at the 'separate structures' of 'women's condition' – production, reproduction, sexuality, and the socialisation of children – 'which together form a complex – not a simple – unity'.[64]

Mitchell's understanding of the complexity of women's problems can be read as a virtual co-text to Penelope Mortimer's novels *The Pumpkin Eater*

(1962) and *The Home* (1971) whose deceptively simple narrative constructions of middle-class family life accommodate a disturbing sense of the fragility of the ideologies on which they depend. Mitchell notes the 'sheer absurdities' observed in propaganda for 'mother-care as a social act'.[65] She argues that 'the problem of women has been submerged in an analysis of the family',[66] a discursive situation which Mortimer explores by way of specific aspects of family life which are then subtly undermined by their protagonists' uneasy relationship to the family, an officially non-negotiable institution. In Mitchell's analysis, women are culturally disassociated from 'production', or physical labour, because of the strong ideological link between what is seen as their role in bearing and raising children within a home they maintain, and the perceived structure of society. Mitchell argues that 'an advanced society not founded on the nuclear family is now inconceivable', ensuring the 'natural character' of the family and its oppression of women.[67] Linked to this are the requirements of sexual monogamy and the expectation that middle-class women will identify as the main 'socialisers' in their children's lives as part of a cult of 'motherliness'.[68] For Mitchell, these 'structures' should be 'transformed' by means of the structural and ideological changes proposed by second wave feminist writers and activists. Mortimer's novels supply provocative interventions in relation to these processes of change, with characters and forms of language alike challenging the repetitions, absurdities, and contradictions of women's position.

In *The Pumpkin Eater*, the character known only as 'Mrs Armitage' narrates her multiple marriages, other experiences, reactions, and desires, in a combination of supposed realities and remembered dreams. The observed disjunctions between ideology and reality result in a disjointed, dialogue-heavy first-person narration, and an accompanying, perilous sense of woman's identity as a vacuum, when it is not 'filled' with relationships, marriages, and childbearing. In a dreamlike discourse on shopping, Mrs Armitage asks herself 'What did I come here for? Why did I walk, in spring, along a mile of pavement? Do I want a bed rest, a barbecue, a clock like a plate or a satin stole or a pepper mill or a dozen Irish linen tea towels painted, most beautifully, with the months of the year?'[69] None of her movements and pursuits seem natural, a source of order and fulfilment – rather the opposite. They are symptoms of breakdown and the painful insights that go with this. The novel's formal reliance on interior monologue and dialogue maps Mrs Armitage's situation and family on to the factors Mitchell identifies, and shows their failure to produce a promised social order whose subjects have meaningful places in society. Housewife Mrs Armitage consumes, reproduces (her doctor comments that 'she drops those babies like a cat'),[70] and then she and other characters demonstrate the ill effects of social expectations regarding women's sexual behaviour and devotion to parenting. Her doctor accuses her of seeing 'sex without children' as 'unthinkable'; he seemingly misses the irony of the fact that bourgeois family ideology shares this view.[71] The narrative is not linear or chronological and is disrupted by her memories, insecurities and illnesses which all, paradoxically (and recalling R. D. Laing), expand her vision, albeit painfully. There do not seem to be any alternatives yet to the middle-class cult of intertwined sexuality, marriage, motherhood, and family noted by Mitchell, which represents a devastatingly narrow but dominant set of standards. Both Mitchell and Mortimer express this 'stationary' cultural condition.[72]

With similarly close attention to the elements of home and family life that are prone to failure and in need of transformation, Mortimer's *The Home* explores the ruined marriage of Eleanor and Graham Strathearn as a formerly 'cheerful fantasy'.[73] The middle-class formula of their past home and lifestyle is very easily undermined because it is based on a mystique of masculine and feminine roles whose 'naturalness' is inherently compromised, its key features doubted. A new suitor remarks to Eleanor 'Who ever heard of a happily married couple in 1971?'[74] The end of her marriage and home, furthermore, produces possibility but also fearful uncertainty – Eleanor begins 'slipping, losing faith'.[75] There is an accompanying edge of unreality to Eleanor's new house: 'It was a woman's house and the colours were those of fruit' and its pretensions are 'a private joke',[76] a cover for indistinct realities and as yet unrealised freedoms. Her former home and family are one in her imagination, symbols of broader ideals of heteronormative, conjugal life. Eleanor has a recurring nightmare, 'of being in the old, the original, house, which was decomposing' and where her ex-husband is a terrifying 'absence'.[77] The novel uses haunting interior episodes such as these to suggest the need for action and imagination in response to the absences, wreckages, and times of stasis left after the failure of, or escape from, feminine domesticity. A deep-seated and imaginative questioning and rejection of bourgeois ideology is necessary, for Eleanor and for the feminists of the second wave. Existing on the cusp of nearly-defined alternatives results in breakdown of many kinds but an expanded feminist vision need only be distressing as long as it is not pursued further, into art and polemic. These novels, like Weldon's, point as strongly as does second-wave polemic to the need for imaginative discourse to underpin ideological and structural change.

Conclusion

In the chapter of *The Female Eunuch* titled 'Rebellion', Greer calls for a society pivotally altered at the level of women's imagination, speech, and consciousness, to enable change at a practical level. Quoting from activist Beverly Jones's 'nine point policy' for women's liberation, Greer reasserts the centrality of narrative to activism itself. Point four demands, simply but compellingly, that

Women should share their experiences with each other until they understand, identify, and explicitly state the many psychological techniques
of domination in and out of the home. These should be published and
distributed widely until they are common knowledge.[78]

The second wave of feminism in Britain engineered a decisively imaginative
set of confrontations with patriarchy, in which literature is deeply embedded, even if much of this literature lies outside the conventional, historical
boundaries of the organised Women's Liberation Movement. The period's
feminist polemic can be read productively alongside a broader range of
women's writing than is often assumed, in groupings that give heightened
discursive force to stories of women's oppression, and which in turn suggest new forms for culture and society. Women's Liberation's consciousness
was generated before its organised beginnings, in a restless literature with
a sharpened sense of the interior, subjective experiences of living within
patriarchy. This literature is often preoccupied with themes of psychological distress and breakdown, the subversive significance of women's bodies,
and the changing meanings of home and family life, because these are sites
of the private, interior, and often publicly silenced female experiences with
which second-wave feminism was so much concerned.

Notes

1. See, for example, Maggie Humm, *Feminisms: A Reader* (Harlow: Harvester
   Wheatsheaf, 1992), and Ian Buchanan, 'Second Wave Feminism', *A Dictionary
   of Critical Theory* (Oxford: Oxford University Press, 2010), p. 426. They see the
   publication of Betty Friedan's *The Feminine Mystique* as a USA-based landmark and
   shift towards second-wave thinking and activism.
2. Judith Evans, *Feminist Theory Today: An Introduction to Second-Wave Feminism*
   (London: Sage, 1995), p. 1.
3. Humm, *Feminisms: A Reader*, pp. 53–4.
4. Mary Eagleton, *Feminist Literary Criticism* (New York: Longman, 1991), p. 2.
5. Catherine Riley, 'The Intersections Between Early Feminist Polemic and
   Publishing: How Books Changed Lives in the Second Wave', *Women: A Cultural
   Review*, 26: 4 (2016), 384–401.
6. Humm, *Feminisms: A Reader*, pp. 54–5.
7. Juliet Mitchell, *Women: The Longest Revolution: Essays in Feminism, Literature and
   Psychoanalysis* (London: Virago, 1984), p. 17.
8. Sheila Rowbotham, *Woman's Consciousness, Man's World* (London: Penguin,
   1973), pp. 5–6.
9. Friedrich Engels uses the phrase 'false consciousness', meaning the manner
   in which ideology deceives members of a society, in his 14 July 1893 letter
   to Franz Mehring, online, https://www.marxists.org/archive/marx/works/1893/
   letters/93_07_14.htm, accessed 28 June 2016.
10. Mitchell, *Women: The Longest Revolution*, p. 17.
11. Cora Kaplan, *Sea Changes* (London: Verso, 1986), p. 18.

12. See the British Library's timeline of British Women's Liberation, online, http://www.bl.uk/sisterhood/timeline accessed 28 June 2016.
13. Germaine Greer, *The Female Eunuch* (London: Paladin, 1971), p. 294.
14. Catherine Riley, '"The Message is in the Book": What Virago's Sale in 1995 Means for Feminist Publishing', *Women: A Cultural Review*, 25: 3 (2014), pp. 235–255, p. 240.
15. *Spare Rib*, 1:1 (1972), p. 35.
16. Doris Lessing, *The Golden Notebook* [1962] (London: Harper Perennial, 2007), p. 9.
17. Lessing, *The Golden Notebook*, p. 161.
18. Maroula Joannou, *Contemporary Women's Writing: From* The Golden Notebook *to* The Color Purple (Manchester: Manchester University Press, 2000), p. 16.
19. R. D. Laing, *The Politics of Experience and The Bird of Paradise* (London: Penguin, 1967), p. 103.
20. Sylvia Plath, *The Bell Jar* (London: Faber and Faber, 1963), p. 53.
21. Penelope Mortimer, *The Pumpkin Eater* (London: Hutchinson and Co., 1962), p. 222.
22. Jennifer Breen, *In Her Own Write: Twentieth Century Women's Fiction* (Basingstoke: Macmillan Education, 1990), p. 123.
23. A. S. Byatt, *The Shadow of the Sun* (London: Vintage, 1964), p. 297.
24. Mortimer, *The Pumpkin Eater*, p. 215.
25. Joannou, *Contemporary Women's Writing*, p. 6.
26. Joannou, *Contemporary Women's Writing*, p. 11.
27. Patricia Duncker, *Sisters and Strangers: An Introduction to Contemporary Feminist Fiction* (Oxford: Blackwell, 1991), p. 7.
28. Duncker, *Sisters and Strangers*, p. 15.
29. Duncker, *Sisters and Strangers*, p. 33.
30. Fay Weldon, 'The Books that Changed Me...', *The Sun Herald* (Sydney, Australia), 8 January 2006, Late Edition, p. 65.
31. Several writers have analysed the theatrical and imaginative features of Solanas's provocative *SCUM Manifesto* and her 1966 play *Up Your Ass*, including Mavis Haut, 'A Salty Tongue: At the Margins of Satire, Comedy and Polemic in the Writing of Valerie Solanas', *Feminist Theory*, 8:1 (2007), 27–41. She argues that the *SCUM Manifesto* satirises and critiques masculine stand-up comedy. Breanne Fahs, 'The Radical Possibilities of Valerie Solanas', *Feminist Studies*, 34:3 (2008), 591–617 highlights the radical ironies in Solanas's writing and 'character' that are much less (in)famous than her shooting of Andy Warhol in 1968.
32. Greer, *The Female Eunuch*, p. 16.
33. Fiona A. Montgomery, *Women's Rights: Struggles and Feminism in Britain c. 1770–1970* (Manchester: Manchester University Press, 2006), p. 7.
34. Maggie Humm, *Border Traffic: Strategies of Contemporary Women Writers* (Manchester: Manchester University Press, 1991), pp. 6–7.
35. Humm, *Border Traffic*, p. 51.
36. Lessing, *The Golden Notebook*, pp. 304, 305.
37. J. R. Teller, '"The Misrule of our Dust": Psychoanalysis, Sacrament, and the Subject in Elizabeth Jennings's Poetry of Incarnation', *Christianity and Literature*, 57: 4 (2008), 531–557, (p. 532).
38. Amanda G. Michaels, 'The Mystic and the Poet: Identity Formation, Deformation, and Reformation in Elizabeth Jennings' "Teresa of Avila" and Kathleen Jamie's "Julian of Norwich"', *Christianity and Literature*, 59: 4 (2010), 665–681 (p. 665). The notion of female mysticism, and its significance for feminist writing, also

calls to mind Byatt's discussion of women's difficulty in identifying as artists in the preface of *The Shadow of the Sun*: 'Female visionaries are poor mad exploited sibyls and pythonesses. Male ones are prophets and poets. Or so I thought. There was a feminine mystique but no tradition of female mysticism that wasn't hopelessly self-abnegating' (Byatt, *The Shadow of the Sun*, p. x).

39. Humm, *Border Traffic*, p. 20.
40. Elizabeth Jennings, *New Collected Poems* (Manchester: Carcanet, 2002), pp. 24–35.
41. Jennings, *New Collected Poems*, p. 3.
42. Jennings, *New Collected Poems*, p. 32.
43. Jennings, *New Collected Poems*, p. 79.
44. Mark Halliday, 'Stevie Smith's Serious Comedy', *Humor*, 22:3 (2009), 295–315 (p. 296).
45. A new edition of Smith's work, titled *The Collected Poems and Drawings of Stevie Smith*, edited by William May, was published by Faber in September 2015.
46. Stevie Smith, *The Collected Poems of Stevie Smith* (London: Allen Lane, 1975), p. 390.
47. Smith, *Collected Poems*, p. 396.
48. Smith, *Collected Poems*, p. 429.
49. Smith, *Collected Poems*, p. 431.
50. Montgomery, *Women's Rights*, p. 194.
51. Greer, *The Female Eunuch*, pp. 39, 47, 34.
52. Fay Weldon, *The Fat Woman's Joke* [1967] (London: Flamingo, 2012), p. 5.
53. Weldon, *The Fat Woman's Joke*, p. 8.
54. Greer, *The Female Eunuch*, p. 35.
55. Weldon, *The Fat Woman's Joke*, p. 23.
56. Weldon, *The Fat Woman's Joke*, p. 86.
57. Weldon, *The Fat Woman's Joke*, p. 120.
58. Weldon, *The Fat Woman's Joke*, p. 134.
59. Greer, *The Female Eunuch*, p. 45.
60. Weldon, *The Fat Woman's Joke*, p. 136.
61. Fay Weldon, *Down Among the Women* (London: Heinemann, 1971), p. 1.
62. Greer, *The Female Eunuch*, p. 198.
63. Margaret Chessnut, 'Feminist Criticism and Feminist Consciousness: A Reading of a Novel by Fay Weldon', *Moderna Språk*, 73 (1979), pp. 3–18 (p. 18).
64. Mitchell, *Women: The Longest Revolution*, pp. 42, 26.
65. Mitchell, *Women: The Longest Revolution*, p. 42.
66. Mitchell, *Women: The Longest Revolution*, p. 22.
67. Mitchell, *Women: The Longest Revolution*, pp. 31–2.
68. Mitchell, *Women: The Longest Revolution*, pp. 37–8, 39–42.
69. Mortimer, *The Pumpkin Eater*, p. 47.
70. Mortimer, *The Pumpkin Eater*, p. 51.
71. Mortimer, *The Pumpkin Eater*, p. 64.
72. Mitchell, *Women: The Longest Revolution*, p. 48.
73. Penelope Mortimer, *The Home* (London: Hutchinson, 1971), p. 11.
74. Mortimer, *The Home*, p. 120.
75. Mortimer, *The Home*, p. 22.
76. Mortimer, *The Home*, p. 63.
77. Mortimer, *The Home*, p. 125.
78. Greer, *The Female Eunuch*, p. 304.

8

The Aftermath of War

Kristin Bluemel

> And he went on to say that there was a lot of the war left
> over from the fighting time, I do not know, he said, that
> we can bear not to be at war.
> I agree; always there is some more war to be written about.
> Stevie Smith, *The Holiday*[1]

The speakers in the epigraph are characters in Stevie Smith's 1949 novel, *The Holiday*. *The Holiday* is a war book in the sense that it was written by Stevie Smith during World War II, while she worked, year after weary year, as the personal secretary to the London publisher Sir Neville Pearson. It is also a war book in the sense that initially it was set during the war. When Smith returned to the manuscript in the late 1940s, she transformed it into a post-war book, a book of aftermaths, through fairly simple alterations, including insertions of hand written post's above typed iterations of 'war' in the manuscript.[2] Thus this third of Smith's three war novels became her only post-war novel through a trick of type and prefix. The author's experience of rescuing a manuscript lost amid the violence of war, and the manuscript itself, with its inked post-war revisions, stand as metaphors for British women's writing in the aftermath of war. This chapter is devoted to understanding this women's writing as part of a distinct literary period, one that is defined by the ambiguous intimacy of peacetime to wartime; it is a literature written in and written over war and the literature of war.

In *The Holiday* the feelings and actions of Smith's first person narrator, Celia Phoze, mean very different things within the post-war social and political landscape than they would have in the wartime conditions assumed by the earlier manuscript. The tears that saturate *The Holiday* – the tears of Celia who is hopelessly in love with her cousin Caz, Caz's tears,

© The Author(s) 2017
C. Hanson and S. Watkins, *The History of British Women's Writing, 1945–1975*,
History of British Women's Writing, DOI: 10.1057/978–1–137–47736–1_9

Celia's friend Tiny's tears – all these tears, in their seemingly endless excess, acknowledge the complexity of mourning that had to take place after the shock of active war. Celia, overwhelmed by sadness, seeks to drown herself in tears or more threatening waters. Suicide becomes a last act of resistance to the wan, dispiriting aftermath of war:

> I leant over the palings of the little bridge, my eyes close upon the dark water. An army, I said, in victory, full tongue across the desert 'For pleasure and profit together allow me the hunting of men'. It is exciting, is it not? And it is masculine. I sighed again. But here we are, caught in the bewilderment of a post-war consequence, the trivial, the boring, the necessary, the inescapable; what is one's duty.[3]

Caz pulls Celia back from the rotting handrail. Are we left then with a representative woman's text in the aftermath of masculine war that achieves its highest aims, its clearest vision of an implicitly feminine post-war, when it dwells on 'the trivial, the boring, the necessary, the inescapable; what is one's duty'? In Smith's narrative world of 1949, the answer is 'yes'.

Smith herself tried to commit suicide on 1 July 1953, and never went back to work for Sir Neville Pearson at Newnes Publishing Company. Nor did she ever write another novel. However, she began in this despairing moment to concentrate more fully on the poetry and doodles on which her posthumous literary reputation rests. This work, undertaken not in her employer's central London office, but in her aunt's house in the north London suburb of Palmer's Green, would bring her the Queen's Gold Medal for Poetry in 1969. What might seem from the perspective of the 1950s a work of withdrawal, of private quest and public failure, appears from the critical perspective of the twenty-first century to be work of cultural significance. Underestimated, misunderstood, and overlooked, this work and the alternative web of relationships that sustained it has waited decades for attention from scholars. Situated in the ambiguous, awkward space between active war and active recovery, between economies of wartime production and peacetime demobilization, between a concern with survival amid violence to concern with development amid peace, Smith's poetry, like much of the women's work discussed in this chapter, challenged as it tried to accommodate mainstream literary institutions and cultures. As we shall see, it is in the gap between Smith's life as a novelist and poet, city girl and suburban spinster, that we can find the literary alliances and rivalries – at the level of theme, of form, and at the level of professional experience – that represent more generally a British women's literature written in the aftermath of war.

Love in houses

To understand how women's fiction written in the aftermath of war contributes to our understanding of the years 1945–1975 as a literary period, readers must seek out texts by Betty Miller, Elizabeth Bowen, Elizabeth Taylor, and Rosamond Lehmann. It was not until the late twentieth century that feminist scholars Gill Plain, Jenny Hartley, Karen Schneider, and Phyllis Lassner published studies that began the process of theorising a women's literary tradition in relation to the imperatives of history and politics of World War II.[4] These studies prepared the way for twenty-first century accounts by Nicola Humble, Jane Dowson, Victoria Stewart, Marina MacKay, Kristine Miller, and Eve Patton that have brought greater visibility to this body of writing, in part by locating it within gendered cultural hierarchies.[5] The labels highbrow, middlebrow, and lowbrow designated critics' judgments of the women novelists' relation to the literary establishment. For example, Bowen and Lehmann, with connections to Bloomsbury, were more likely to be regarded as 'highbrows' than 'middlebrows' Smith and Miller, who were connected to London suburbs. Correspondingly, Bowen and Lehmann enjoyed an earlier and more robust critical treatment in the early years of feminist recovery work.[6]

For all these women, writing in the aftermath of war meant confronting contradictions imposed by disruptions in national and global politics; they found themselves living in a nation that was victorious but impoverished, in communities where women were empowered by war work but increasingly found in the home, in a culture emboldened by democratic ideals but hostile to activist feminism. In the face of such confusion, they tended to write narratives focused on the place they were told they belonged: home. Once there, however, they did not adopt a compliant attitude toward dominant ideas for feminine behaviour or thought. Rather, they contested at close range, from the inside, easy assumptions made about home life, about the meaning of family, children, marriage, celibacy, sex, love, work, and politics for women and the people who wanted to read women's stories.

On the Side of the Angels (1945), by Betty Miller (1910–1965), published in the last year of the war, exemplifies this kind of quiet resistance to gendered plots.[7] Miller, who had been born in Ireland to Jewish parents, typed her novels in her Hampstead home which she shared with her two children and her husband, the prominent psychiatrist Emanuel Miller. There she welcomed Smith and other young women writers such as Inez Holden, Cecily Mackworth, Naomi Lewis, Kay Dick, and Marghanita Laski[8] who, during the interwar years, aspired to literary fame as they published with so called middlebrow houses like John Lane, the Bodley Head, Jonathan Cape, Heinemann, Cresset Press, or Chapman and Hall rather than the more elite houses such as Virginia Woolf's Hogarth Press or T. S. Eliot's Faber and Faber. Miller was regarded as a rising star among this group of literary women. She had been the protégée of the Anglo-Jewish publisher Victor Gollancz, who brought out her first novel in 1933 when she was only 22. In a marketplace where women could write novels but men acquired, edited, and published them, Miller's despair over Gollancz's rejection of her fourth novel about English antisemitism, *Next Year in Jerusalem*, assumes a symbolic weight.

Women were outsiders in literary London, and the careers of women writers depended on their ability to navigate within that often blatantly sexist culture. Only with the support of another male publisher, Robert Hale, who in 1941 brought out *Next Year in Jerusalem* as *Farewell Leicester Square*, did Miller regain her confidence and return to writing.[9]

In its exploration of the gendered politics of war, with its special betrayals of women and children, *On the Side of the Angels* is typical of novels by women written in the aftermath of war. The protagonist of Miller's tale is a young mother, Honor Carmichael, the wife of Captain Colin Carmichael, a doctor working at a military hospital where the CO, Colonel Mayne, enjoys dictatorial powers through the exercise of his charismatic personality. Set in the country, far away from the Blitz, the novel focuses on the impact the homosocial institutions of war have on the most tender of domestic relations. Honor reflects on the early days of her marriage, when Colin was 'another Colin' and asks: 'What had happened since then?'

> She looked at him standing there in his khaki tunic, neatly belted and buttoned. It was the uniform, she felt suddenly, that had changed him. It was as if the anonymity conferred on him by uniform gave him a new sense of freedom and irresponsibility.[10]

Honor observes how men who remain attached to a 'normal way of life', who do not fall under the influence of the uniform and the power of 'imposed discipline', earn nothing but contempt from Mayne and his acolytes. The Scottish Major Smith, who is 'secretly elated' at the news the fascistic Mayne is leaving England, earns Colin's scarcely disguised contempt: 'Always on the side of the angels, eh, Smith?'[11] The side of the angels is a feminised side, the side of the women and children who represent for Colin 'the destroying intimacy of private life'.[12] Colin, once a gentle healer, is depressed only by 'the fact that war could not last for ever', that 'this state of affairs, the soldiering, the freedom, the new uninhibited life must come to an end' and men like himself return to 'the greyness and uneventfulness of every-day life'.[13]

Everyday life for Honor means managing family affairs inside her rented Victorian house. Descriptions of this house, explicitly gendered feminine, frame the novel which begins with these sentences: 'At that hour of the afternoon the house, it seemed, was empty. Nothing stirred: the long windows yawned, creeper was motionless on the walls'.[14] The primary architectural details that Miller inserts into her text are doors and windows – often open, sometimes swinging, inviting exit, entry, eavesdropping, transformation. There is 'the front door, standing open, reveal[ing] a bright greenish oblong of the outside world'.[15] Later, Miller describes the transformative effects of moving during blackout through the external glass-panelled door of the hospital.[16] Such scenes are repeated again and again, highlighting the possibility of passage and growth within Honor's seemingly static plot and isolation within maternal spaces.

We see a similar attention to windows and doors in *The Heat of the Day* (1949), widely regarded by critics as the best novel to emerge from the Blitz, by Anglo-Irish writer Elizabeth Bowen (1899-1973).[17] Windows in Bowen's novel more obviously than in Miller's symbolise the dangers of movement over thresholds, of the possibility of deathly transformation in combinations of light, glass, and bombs. Bowen's heroine, Stella Rodney, when faced with an impossible choice of sleeping with a man she despises in order to save the man she loves, maps her emotional turmoil upon the terrain of her rented flat, the meaning of her dilemma and the meaning of war measured in relation to windows and doors. Waiting in her flat for the arrival of Harrison, the man who, it turns out, knows her lover Robert is a spy, Stella has deliberately, defiantly, left the street door unlatched and the door of her flat ajar. Meanwhile, she 'stood at a window of her flat, play-ing with the blind-cord'. Coiling and uncoiling the cord, tapping its acorn on the pane, 'She mimed by this idiotic play at the window the disarray into which the prospect of Harrison had thrown her'.[18] Stella's emotional disarray is both a consequence and reflection of the disarray of a war that subjects even the most intimate relations between lovers to examination by the state. Everyone is co-opted by the national imperative to become a watcher. And in Bowen's world, skilled watchers measure motive in relation to place. When Robert confesses to Stella that he is spying, Stella, in grief and wonder, asks '[W]hy are you against this country?' Robert, puzzled, asks 'Country?' and she clarifies, 'This, where we are'.[19] Where they are is Stella's flat. A bedroom – 'where we are' – is also a country.

Bowen, enjoying renewed attention in studies of late modernism, should lead critics to other women writers, all of whom joined Bowen in look-ing back at the war to find not just bombs and blackouts, but women stretched emotionally by domestic displacements. Stella Rodney is kin to Julia Davenant, the young wife of an RAF officer who is the protagonist of Elizabeth Taylor's first novel *At Mrs. Lippincote's*.[20] Written and published in 1945 while Taylor's husband was in the Royal Air Force and Taylor was involved in an affair with the painter Raymond Russell, the novel begins with Julia's question, 'Did the old man die here? What do you think?' Julia's husband Roddy can't think what old man she is referring to, upon which Julia clarifies, 'The husband. Mr. Lippincote. Oh, how I wish we needn't live in other people's houses!'.[21] If death is the first association we have with Mrs. Lippincote's borrowed house, the second is its suffocating corners and contents. 'The room itself was filled with mahogany – wardrobe, chest, tall-boy, medicine cupboard ... The window was in one corner and was semi-circular. For it formed, as one saw from the outside, a little turret with a gilt weather-vane upon it'.[22] Anticipating Bowen's narrative strategies in *The Heat of the Day*, Julia's alienation from the things and spaces of Mrs.

Lippincote's mirrors her increasing alienation from the man in her life, her two-timing officer husband. Like Rapunzel in her tower, Julia cannot view herself or her dissolving marriage from the outside. She is caught within the metaphorical turrets of convention, propriety, and habit, in part as a function of being caught in the gendered ideologies of war.

War and its long shadow function similarly as backdrop for the actions and emotions of Madeleine Masters, her husband Rickie, and her sister and Rickie's lover, Dinah in *The Echoing Grove* by Rosamond Lehmann (1901–1990).[23] Published in 1953, the novel builds its story out of flashbacks and shifting narrative perspectives which contribute to its relentless feeling of claustrophobic melancholy. Houses, again, structure and predict human relations as Lehmann's fragmented narrative plays out betrayal of marriage and sisterhood against remembered scenes of war when Rickie was alive and of attempted reconciliation between the sisters after Rickie's death, in the aftermath of war:

> They were meeting to be reconciled after fifteen years. This present mood in which they sat relaxed was nothing more than the relief of two people coming back to a bombed building once familiar, shared as a dwelling, and finding all over the smashed foundations a rose-ash haze or willow herb. No more, no less. It is a ruin.[24]

Sisterhood as 'a ruin', a 'bombed building once familiar', is a powerful image of human relations that, from the perspective of the aftermath of war, is a source of pain as well as calm or 'relief'. Lehmann is explicit about the emotional meaning ruins must carry in her narrative. Yet even as ruins symbolise disarray in human affairs, they also gesture towards the possibility of human adaptation and survival, their wild gardens of rose-ash and willow herb quietly imposing a pastoral aesthetic on the engineered geometry of memory.

Life in ruins

Silent, imposing, and abandoned, ruins characterised the urban landscape of Britain's cities for decades after the end of war. Like food rations, which extended until 1954, bombsites endured long after the end of hostilities. They were occasions for nostalgia and mourning, reminding survivors of a distant human past once performed amid the surreal scenes of broken buildings, as well as a recent past of wartime violence, bombs, destruction, and noise. In *The World My Wilderness* (1950) by Rose Macaulay (1881–1958) and Muriel Spark's *The Girls of Slender Means* (1963), ruins draw their metaphorical potency from these ambivalent gestures to interrupted human stories.[25] In contrast, the broken buildings in immigrant writer Doris Lessing's book-length essay *In Pursuit of the English* (1960) are mundane, everyday. They do not signify surreal jokes of an ironic history, but appeals for political action directed at Britain's working class women as they adjust to the new economic realities of Clement Attlee's post-war welfare state.[26] With a Labour government dedicated to building a more democratic Britain, the political demand for restructuring society took strength from the material demands posed by miles of bombsites. What might the future look like? Where would women find themselves? How could they feel at home?

Women writers and working class women do not get much attention in a recent critical study titled *Reading the Ruins*, but author Leo Mellor does argue convincingly that ruins were a dominant theme in books and media that satisfied diverse tastes and genres within post-war cultural hierarchies.[27] One of the most memorable literary works about London's ruins, Rose Macaulay's *The World My Wilderness* (1950), was promoted by dust jacket copy that read, '"a good read for all brows"'.[28] Macaulay's 'good read' takes readers into the abandoned acres of the ruins around St. Paul's Cathedral with Barbary, a seventeen year old girl raised by her divorced mother in the south of France. Barbary spent the war years running with the *maquis*, the French resistance. 'Maquis' means wilderness or bush, and Barbary interprets the London ruins as her new maquis, her new wilderness. She finds familiar and somehow necessary the lawless terrain of ruins where trust is nonexistent, moral codes are upended, theft, gain, and survival the only ends. Dancing on top of a ruined house to the bells of St. Paul's, Barbary and her step-brother Raoul suddenly 'stood still, gazing down on a wilderness of little streets, caves and cellars, the foundations of a wrecked merchant city, grown over by green and golden nettles, among which rabbits burrowed and wild cats crept and hens laid eggs'.[29] For a girl whose aid to the *maquis* led to the death of her mother's second husband, such disorder feels safe. All signs of English law and authority, on the other hand, bespeak danger. When Barbary falls from a wall during a chase with a policeman, her resulting illness brings her French mother, then gambling at Monte Carlo, back to her. Reversing the classic narrative romance plot of male homosocial bonding, of one man giving his daughter into the hands of another man, we see the figuratively prostrate figure of Sir Gully, the father, lawyer, and rejected husband, serving as conduit for the mother-daughter union, an achievement – fragile, vulnerable, imperfect but for Barbary life-sustaining – out of war and the ruin of her parents' love.

Another novel organised around the idea of ruins, Scottish writer Muriel Spark's *The Girls of Slender Means*, begins with the memorable sentence, 'Long ago in 1945, all the nice people in England were poor, allowing for exceptions'.[30] Its next sentence links poverty and niceness to ruins, the shabby buildings surrounding and including the May of Teck Club where the girls of slender means reside. The Club has removed the most obvious signs of Blitz defense and damage from its surface, its bituminous black-out paint gone, its shattered windows replaced with new glass. We're told by the narrator

Windows were important in that year of final reckoning: they told at a glance whether a house was inhabited or not; and in the course of the past years they had accumulated much meaning having been the main danger-zone between domestic life and the war going on outside: everyone had said, when the sirens sounded, 'Mind the windows. Keep away from the windows. Watch out for the glass'.[31]

After a hidden bomb explodes in the back garden and the Club catches fire, it is a missing window, a skylight blocked with bricks, that proves fatal, preventing the quick escape of the girls from the collapsing building. In Spark's brief novel of feminine life in post-war London, it is not only people who are displaced, but also wartime violence. The late-exploding bomb does not clear the way for precarious beginnings and post-war renewal. Instead, it signifies the capacity of the War to linger in the material and metaphorical dark spaces of Britain, sabotaging the future. Making a ruin of the May of Teck Club, the bomb blast, suspended for years, indiscriminately kills off one of the nicest poor girls in London.

'Poor girls' in Spark's novel are genteel poor. Poor girls in Lessing's documentary essay, *In Pursuit of the English*, are working-class poor. Lessing's book documents in spare prose the author's journey from Rhodesia to South Africa to England with her two year old son. In her description of her arrival in an overcrowded Cape Town, where 'no one but a lunatic would arrive without arranging accommodation',[32] it is not houses but housing that overshadows all else. Later, in pursuit of housing in London, the writer-narrator meets the most memorable character of this memorable book: Rose, who is both English and working class. Having survived the Blitz, Rose finds little emotional sustenance outside of nostalgia for her childhood slum and the war. While she can't bring back the war, which from the perspective of 1950 has acquired for her meanings of 'warmth, comradeship, a feeling of belonging and being wanted' rather than death, fear, or danger, she can go back to the neighbourhood where she spent her childhood.[33] Seated on 'a low wall that enclosed a brownish space of soil where a bomb had burst', the narrator describes Rose's slum as a waste land:

> There was a tree, paralysed down one side, and a board leaning in a heap of rubble that said: "Tea and Bun-One Penny" ...
> 'Who sold the tea?' I asked
> 'Oh, that? He got hit. That was before the war.' [Rose] spoke as if it was a different century. 'You don't get tea and a bun for a penny now.' She looked lovingly around her.[34]

Bombsites, ruins, abandoned signs of slum commerce: Lessing's narrator dispassionately describes them all but equally dispassionately insists that we hear the meaning of this place for her working-class companion. While it seems likely that Rose and her neighbours will squander their potential for realising a collective political voice, their wartime community and energy dissipating in the face of a new t.v. culture, to the extent that this development strikes readers as a social tragedy, a loss of what was best about living amid the ruins, Lessing has herself made a significant political intervention in post-war British culture. Loss, mourning, and nostalgia are only part of the story of the aftermath of war. Lessing makes us attend equally to the signs of renewed hope for working class women's claims to greater sexual autonomy, economic parity, and political agency.

Britain and global war

In 'Legacies of the Past: Post-war Women Looking Forward and Back', feminist scholar Elizabeth Maslen insists that 'the late 1940s and the 1950s [were] as complex and complicated as any previous decades in which to attempt to formulate definitive accounts of where women were feeling impelled to go'.[35] Reading women's writing in the context of 'the H bomb ... the end of empire, the debacle of Suez, the Russian invasion of Hungary',[36] she reminds us of the pressure of post-war global politics upon post-war novels that look most intently at the war. Maslen's curious and exact phrase, 'Where women were feeling impelled to go', joins the characteristic literary patterns discussed above – of reading love in houses, life in ruins – to global politics and locations. Shifting her attention to novels set overseas, Maslen emphasises the role of European place in the political imaginations of British women. Her vision of an activist, feminist post-war literary tradition contradicts accounts of women writers happy in retreat to the home. This outward looking British women's literature is best characterised in Maslen's account by Storm Jameson's novels *The Other Side* (1946), *The Black Laurel* (1947), and *The Hidden River* (1955), all of which pursue plots of love, vengeance, and betrayal in France or Germany during the war or during Allied Occupation.[37]

More famous than Jameson's novels are the five books that make up Doris Lessing's epic post-war novel, *The Children of Violence* series (1952–1969), partly set in Zambesia, a fictionalised colony modelled on Lessing's childhood home, the British colony of Southern Rhodesia.[38] Lessing's protagonist, Martha Quest, comes of political age during the War. As a member of the Communist Party, which she calls with reverence 'the group', Martha naively imagines with her fellow socialists that after the war all Europe will be Communist. But this vision of a political future as 'a release into freedom, a sudden flowering into goodness and justice'[39] is betrayed by history and Martha must reinvent herself again. This time, having tried marriage, motherhood, and political activism, she seeks a sense of home and belonging in a 'pale, misted, flat' country even as she wonders '[H]ow can I be an exile from England when it has nothing to do with me?'.[40] Martha fiercely pursues her quest of female fulfilment into the heart of post-war Britain in

The Four Gated City (1969). There, in London five years after the end of the war, still dodging bomb craters, surrounded by signs of blackout, decay, and damp, Martha is the delighted vagrant, the anonymous, unnoticed wanderer recording the ambivalent possibilities of her new home: 'Never before in her life had she known this freedom!'[41]

Martha Quest is the most fiercely visionary of post-war British heroines discussed in this chapter. But she is not necessarily the most important for understanding British women writers' negotiations with global politics in the aftermath of war. That role falls to Harriet Pringle, the heroine of the six novels that comprise *The Balkan Trilogy* and *The Levant Trilogy*, by Olivia Manning (1908–1980). Harriet is at the centre of one of the century's most wide-ranging fictional inquiries into the British experience of war.[42] Harriet begins her journey with her husband Guy on the Orient Express heading East towards Bucharest. Guy, like Manning's husband Reggie Smith, works for the British Council and also like Reggie, has to flee Bucharest for Athens and then Cairo and Jerusalem before the Nazis' advance across Europe and the Middle East.

Eve Patton's critical biography of Manning begins by admitting 'Olivia Manning's reputation as a difficult personality often threatens to obscure her reputation as a writer'.[43] Much maligned for her spiteful, backbiting comments in private and print about the works of literary friends, Manning's bitterness distinguishes the political force of her fiction, contributing to its status as 'an extended post-war narrative of reproach'.[44] Her bitterness also distinguishes her relation to the central institutions of British literary culture. Despairing over the lack of sufficient critical appreciation of her work, Manning raged against what she regarded as Bloomsbury coterie publication and promotion.[45] Impolitic in her criticism of powerful Bloomsbury figures, Manning helps readers identify the contours of the cultural divide between highbrow and middlebrow. In her terms, books like her own that were labelled middlebrow were actually more original and significant than books that were labelled highbrow. But perversely, she wasn't happy with her position in the very hierarchy she helped sustain through her critical essays and reviews; she wanted the 'insider' voices of literary London – including those of John Lehmann and his sister Rosamond – to agree that her outsider work was not just different, but better than their own or that of their friends.

An expert at diagnosing and representing displacement, Manning's novels are peopled with innumerable refugees, the dispossessed of Europe. These refugees are represented sympathetically against a background of hopeless British officialdom accelerating political disorder and misunderstanding in the last days of a crumbling empire. At the end of *Friends and Heroes*, the last volume in *The Balkan Trilogy*, the Pringles are evacuated out of Athens. Nearly refugees themselves, they leave for Cairo by rusting boat, bringing one suitcase and a rucksack of books. An acquaintance, Mrs. Brett, also escaping under the authority of the British Legation, explains to Harriet the reason for her enthusiasm amid the crisis of Nazi invasion: 'it's exciting to see the world. And we're going to Egypt where the news is good. We keep capturing places in Egypt'[46]. Readers have learned with Harriet to see such naiveté as a sign of British corruption and both political and moral failure.

Manning's very different novel *The School for Love* (1951) adopts a lost child, a naïve orphaned boy named Felix Latimer, as her means of conveying the ordinary human tragedies of wartime displacement.[47] Other lost children do similar work in women's novels written in the aftermath of war. What is Barbary if not Macaulay's lost child? The sensitive, thin, five year old orphan Jean in Marghanita Laski's *Little Boy Lost* (1949), is one of the most endearing of children lost in the maelstrom of global war.[48] *Little Boy Lost* brings readers to the provincial "town of A_____" fifty miles outside Paris (790), where the moral vacuum set up by occupation and collaboration impacts every human relationship. And it is here that the English poet Hilary Wainwright has come to determine whether Jean might be his son. Hilary's son was lost after Hilary left Paris for the front lines in 1940 and after his beloved wife Lisa had been betrayed and then captured, tortured, and killed by the Gestapo for her activities on behalf of the French resistance. This father knows nothing about his child and has only the slimmest of evidence from underground channels that Jean is actually his. Jean is no Barbary, too young to have taken any position or decision in the conflicts of adults, and his utter helplessness in the face of history comes to stand for the lost lives of Europe's youngest wartime generations. Laski, the child of English Jews, shifts our focus from female to male perspective in this novel's exploration of the possibilities of parenthood, family, and love, thus challenging the notion that domestic spaces and themes belong exclusively to women or that novels probing implications of global politics belong to men. *Little Boy Lost*, like *School for Love*, insists that we move across the globe if we hope to make sense of the emotional and moral legacy of war. There, out in the world, as Hilary debates whether to accept Jean as his own, it is not rescue of soldiers at war, but the rescue of a child in war's aftermath that tests the moral calibre of a continent.

Epic and lyric

Grappling with epic loss at home and abroad, women were rewarded by male editors when they submitted novels, series novels, short stories, or prose nonfiction, the latter including Rebecca West's account of the Nuremberg Trials, *A Train of Power* (1946), and Storm Jameson's two volume autobiography, *Journey from the North* (1969–1970).[49] Poetry was another matter. The only woman poet to achieve critical recognition approaching that accorded Britain's prewar male poets was the American immigrant and one-time protégée of Ezra Pound, H.D. (1886–1961). Her *Trilogy* (1946) and *Helen in Egypt* (1961), are the exceptional poems about war that prove the rule of women's sequestration within narrative literary traditions.[50] The first volume of *Trilogy*, *The Walls Do Not Fall*, begins with lines that seem to situate us in contemporary England or Europe: 'An incident here and there / And rails gone (for guns) / from your (and my) old town square'.[51] The next stanza uses H.D.'s fabled palimpsestic allusion to collapse boundaries between present and past, modern and ancient wars, human and animal industry. Now in ancient Egypt, we encounter 'the Luxor bee, chick and hare / ... in green, rose-red, lapis', who 'continue to prophesy from the stone papyrus'.[52] The power of ancient prophesy of war and ruin is challenged by the authoritative speaker who bids 'us' not 'listen if they shout out, / Your beauty, Isis, Aset or Astarte, / is a harlot'.[53] The complexity of H.D.'s response to war, inherited classical traditions, sexism, and Pound's modernism is extended in *Helen in Egypt*. This poem takes as its origin the little known myth recorded by the poet Stesichorus of Sicily that 'Helena, Helen hated of all Greece',[54] 'had been transposed or translated from Greece into Egypt' by Zeus and that the Trojan War was fought for an illusion, a female phantom installed by jealous deities.[55] H.D., writing in the aftermath of World War II, offers a unique solution to the problem of our inheritance of war stories indebted to the sexual blame motivating Homer's Trojan War: the feminist modernist epic.

Stevie Smith, working in the late 1940s and early 1950s in her preferred genre, poetry, struggled to find a publisher who would bring out her substantial volumes. In no way modernist, in no way epic, rarely autobiographical, not obviously about war, her poems, accompanied by doodles, confused editors, publishers, and the public, who didn't know how to place them. This didn't stop Smith from writing them, but she was all too aware of their unpopularity, writing to a friend in February 1950 that her publisher, Chapman and Hall, was 'coming up to the point of being about to be prepared in a frame of mind resolute sober and quite without enthusiasm to bring out another book of poems and drawings'.[56] Nineteen years and five volumes of poetry later, Smith had become a literary celebrity, influencing a younger generation of poets who could look beyond her fey appearance to a rebellion against social and ideological norms, including norms of gender, that resonated with their own demands for cultural revolution.

Smith's gendered rebellion is wickedly evident in any number of the poems in *Harold's Leap* (1950), published in that immediately post-war decade known for feminine domestic retrenchment.[57] Only occasionally and obliquely about violence or global political strife, the poems in *Harold's Leap* more frequently challenge readers to understand everyday conditions for women living in post-war Britain. For example, 'Deeply Morbid' is an ekphrastic poem about a seemingly ordinary office girl named Joan who escapes into a Turner painting during one of her many lunchtime visits to the National Gallery where 'She would go and watch the pictures ... / All alone all alone'.[58] Slyly perverse, 'Deeply Morbid' finds in art a basis for gendered rebellion against social norms upheld by 'Lady Mary, Lady Kitty / The Honourable Featherstonehaugh'. Joan's is not a feminist rebellion, since she is acutely solitary and silent, but Smith uses rhythms of poetry to translate a typist into an otherworldly, idealised figure, content 'To walk forever in that sun'.[59]

A very different kind of gendered rebellion is found in 'Lightly Bound':

> You beastly child, I wish you had miscarried.
> You beastly husband, I wish I had never married.
> You hear the north wind riding fast past the window? He calls me.
> Do you suppose I shall stay when I can go so easily?[60]

This poem speaks the unspeakable. Utterly detached from H.D.'s rewriting of Helen of Troy's ancient, tragic suffering or Lessing's depiction of contemporary communities of working class women, its speaker seems to defy community with other post-war women encountered in this chapter. The venom driving the first two lines of Smith's monologue is balanced by the hope and daring of the last two. Who is the north wind? What does his call promise? Where will the defiant speaker go 'so easily'? Smith's lightly bound woman is existentially alone in her home, a home whose window promises a way out of gendered social scripts.

Like so many of the texts by women writers discussed in this chapter, Smith's 'Lightly Bound' insists that a woman's story ends with a question, specifically a question of place. Just as importantly, it also insists that a woman's life is a quest to know why and how to seek that place. Read in the context of other works by women written in the aftermath of war, Smith's poetry challenges readers to imagine what startling, unsettling, maybe horrifying truths they might find if they looked through windows into the hidden interiors of women's literary houses. Having examined women writers in relation to the gendered conditions of post-war literary life, this chapter argues against judging them as failed feminists or modernists. Rather, we can regard them as intermodernists, artists whose work bridges periods of war and peace, imperial past and postcolonial present, domestic and global places, modernist and middlebrow aesthetics, conservative and Communist politics.[61] Reading their novels, stories, documentaries, memoirs, and poetry as testimonies to historical conditions and moral imperatives imposed by the experience of war, we can witness and affirm their efforts to write their way into a new landscape, to construct a place for themselves and for us in a Britain that had yet to be imagined.

Notes

1. Stevie Smith, *The Holiday* [1949] (London: Virago, 1979), p. 8

2. Gill Plain, *Literature of the 1940s: War, Post-war, and Peace* (Edinburgh: Edinburgh University Press, 2013), p.185. Thank you to William May, author of *Stevie Smith and Authorship* (Oxford: Oxford University Press, 2010), for help with this citation.
3. Smith, *The Holiday*, p. 184.
4. Gill Plain, *Women's Fiction of the Second World War: Gender, Power and Resistance* (New York: St. Martin's Press, 1996); Jenny Hartley, *Millions Like Us: British Women's Fiction of the Second World War* (London: Virago, 1997); Karen Schneider, *Loving Arms: British Women Writing the Second World War* (Lexington: University Press of Kentucky, 1997) and Phyllis Lassner, *British Women Writers of World War II: Battlegrounds of Their Own* (New York: St. Martin's Press, 1998).
5. Jane Dowson, *Women's Writing, 1945–1960: After the Deluge* (Basingstoke: Palgrave Macmillan, 2003); Victoria Stewart, *Narratives of Memory: British Writing of the 1940s* (Basingstoke: Palgrave Macmillan, 2006); Marina MacKay, *Modernism and World War II* (Cambridge: Cambridge University Press, 2007); Kristine A. Miller, *British Literature of the Blitz: Fighting the People's War* (Basingstoke: Palgrave Macmillan, 2009); Eve Patton, *Imperial Refugee: Olivia Manning's Fictions of War* (Cork: Cork University Press, 2011).
6. The earliest of these studies are Diana LeStourgeon, *Rosamond Lehmann* (New York: Twayne Publishers, 1965), Victoria Glendinning, *Elizabeth Bowen: Portrait of a Writer* (London: Weidenfeld & Nicolson, 1977), and Hermione Lee, *Elizabeth Bowen: An Estimation* (London: Vision Press; Totowa, NJ: Barnes and Noble, 1981).
7. Betty Miller, *On the Side of the Angels* [1945] (London: Virago, 1985).
8. *Stevie: A Biography of Stevie Smith* ed. by Jack Barbera and William McBrien (London: Heinemann, 1985), p. 156.
9. Betty Miller, *Farewell Leicester Square* [1941] (London: Persephone Books, 2000)
10. Miller, *On the Side of the Angels*, p. 104.
11. Miller, *On the Side of the Angels*, p. 112.
12. Miller, *On the Side of the Angels*, p. 124.
13. Miller, *On the Side of the Angels*, p. 127.
14. Miller, *On the Side of the Angels*, p. 7.
15. Miller, *On the Side of the Angels*, p. 13.
16. Miller, *On the Side of the Angels*, p. 157.
17. Elizabeth Bowen, *The Heat of the Day* [1948] (New York: Anchor Books, 2002). I want to thank Hannah Tichansky of Monmouth University for sharing with me her writing on Bowen's treatment of material spaces, in particular liminal spaces of windows, thresholds, and doors.
18. Bowen, *The Heat of the Day* p. 20.
19. Bowen, *The Heat of the Day* p. 301.
20. Elizabeth Taylor, *At Mrs. Lippincote's* [1945] (London: Virago, 2006)
21. Taylor, *At Mrs. Lippincote's*, p. 1.
22. Taylor, *At Mrs. Lippincote's*, p. 1.
23. Rosamond Lehmann, *The Echoing Grove* [1953] (London: Flamingo, 1996).
24. Lehmann, *The Echoing Grove*, p. 13.
25. Rose Macaulay, *The World My Wilderness* [1950] (London: Virago, 1983) and Muriel Spark *The Girls of Slender Means* (New York: New Direction, 1963).
26. Doris Lessing, *In Pursuit of the English* [1960] (New York: Harper Perennial, 1996).
27. Leo Mellor, *Reading the Ruins: Modernism, Bombsites and British Culture* (Cambridge: Cambridge University Press, 2011).

156   *Kristin Bluemel*

28. Mellor, *Reading the Ruins*, p. 123.
29. Macaulay, *The World My Wilderness*, p. 53.
30. Spark, *The Girls of Slender Means*, p. 7.
31. Spark, *The Girls of Slender Means*, p. 8.
32. Lessing, *In Pursuit of the English*, 12.
33. Lessing, *In Pursuit of the English*, p. 113.
34. Lessing, *In Pursuit of the English*, p. 68.
35. Elizabeth Maslen, 'Legacies of the Past: Post-war Women Looking Forward and Back' in *Women's Writing, 1945–1960: After the Deluge* ed. by Jane Dowson, (Basingstoke: Palgrave Macmillan, 2003), pp. 17–28 (p. 19).
36. Maslen, 'Legacies of the Past', p. 19.
37. Maslen, 'Legacies of the Past', p. 18.
38. Doris Lessing, *The Children of Violence* series: *Martha* Quest (1952), *A Proper Marriage* (1954), *A Ripple from the Storm* (1958), *Landlocked* (1965), *The Four-Gated City* (1969), reprinted in Harper Perennial editions (New York: Harper Perennial, 1995).
39. Lessing, *Ripple from the Storm*, p. 200.
40. Lessing, *Ripple from the Storm*, p. 113.
41. Lessing, *The Four-Gated City*, p. 12.
42. Together, these trilogies are known as *Fortunes of War*. *The Balkan Trilogy* is made up of *The Great Fortune* (1960), *The Spoilt City* (1962) and *Friends and Heroes* (1965), all reprinted in a single volume (Harmondsworth: Penguin, 1981). *The Levant Trilogy* is made up of *The Danger Tree* (1977), *The Battle Lost and Won* (1978), and *The Sum of Things* (1980), all reprinted in a single volume (Harmondsworth: Penguin, 1982).
43. Patton, *Imperial Refugee*, p. 1.
44. Patton, *Imperial Refugee*, p. 3.
45. Patton, *Imperial Refugee*, p. 3.
46. Manning, *The Balkan Trilogy*, p. 912.
47. Olivia Manning, *The School for Love* ([1951] (London: Arrow, 2004).
48. Marghanita Laski, *Little Boy Lost* [1949] (London: Persephone Books, 2001).
49. Rebecca West, *A Train of Powder* (New York: Viking, 1955) and Storm Jameson, *Journey from the North*, 2 Vols. (London: Collins and Harvill Press, 1969, 1970).
50. H.D. *Trilogy* [1946] (New York: New Directions, 1998) and *Helen in Egypt* (New York: New Directions, 1961).
51. H.D., *Trilogy*, p. 3.
52. H.D., *Trilogy*, p. 3.
53. H.D., *Trilogy*, p. 5.
54. H.D., *Helen*, p. 2.
55. H.D., *Helen*, p. 1.
56. Barbera and McBrien, *Stevie*, p. 176.
57. Stevie Smith, *Harold's Leap* in *Stevie Smith: Collected Poems* (New York: New Directions, 1976), pp. 225–99.
58. Smith, *Harold's Leap*, p. 296.
59. Smith, *Harold's Leap*, p. 298.
60. Smith, *Harold's Leap*, p. 266.
61. Kristin Bluemel, 'Introduction: What is Intermodernism?' in Kristin Bluemel, *Intermodernism: Literary Culture in Mid-Twentieth-Century Britain* (Edinburgh University Press: Edinburgh, 2009), pp. 1–18.

Part III
Global Politics

9
Responding to the Holocaust

Sue Vice

Holocaust literary consciousness is often described as coming into its own from the 1970s onwards, and especially so after 1993, described in hindsight as 'the year of the Holocaust'.[1] These dates have particular significance in a North American context, since they take for granted the importance of such events as the broadcast of the 1978 television miniseries *Holocaust* (Marvin J. Chomsky) and the release of Steven Spielberg's *Schindler's List* (1993). In Britain, while these texts were undoubtedly important, other dates also take on significance in the immediate post-war decades. These include the liberation of camps undertaken by British troops in 1945, most notably Bergen-Belsen and Neuengamme; such post-war trials as the Nuremberg Trials of 1945–46, the Eichmann Trial of 1961 and the Frankfurt Auschwitz Trial of 1967, represented in non-fiction accounts as well as such novels as Muriel Spark's *The Mandelbaum Gate* (1965); and the real or fictionalised experiences of first-generation refugees, including those who came to Britain before the outbreak of war, as well as survivors of the camps who arrived after the war's end.

The period under discussion here pre-dates what Annette Wieviorka has called 'the era of the witness',[2] characterised by survivors' accounts, and the term 'Holocaust' itself was not yet in widespread use. Although the word was employed during the war and in its immediate aftermath to refer to mass murder, its appearance in common currency without a qualifying term, such as 'Nazi' or 'Jewish', occurred only after the mid-1970s, encouraged by the eponymous television series. However, although they are not by survivors, most of the texts analysed here are by eyewitnesses: those who attended trials or visited refugee camps, or were themselves refugees. The texts' concerns are those which remain significant in British Holocaust writing. These include Britain's wartime record; the pre- and post-war

© The Author(s) 2017
C. Hanson and S. Watkins, *The History of British Women's Writing, 1945–1975*,
History of British Women's Writing, DOI: 10.1057/978–1–137–47736–1_10

reception of refugees and the implications for constructions of Britishness itself; diasporic writing; and second- and third-generation memory. Indeed, in these examples of women writers' work up to 1975, it is possible to trace the earliest development of Holocaust consciousness in an era which has since been subsumed by that of the witness. Thus the concern with the Nazis and efforts to imagine their subjectivity in Rebecca West's trial commentaries is succeeded by a post-Eichmann awareness of Jewish victims as well as perpetrators in those of Sybille Bedford, and then by a varied range of writings on the experience of refugees in Britain. The focus of responses to the Holocaust in women's writing of this era moves gradually inwards, from that of external observation to the depiction of survivors' subjectivity.

The nature of a gendered critique of Holocaust literature has been the subject of debate in relation to women's survivor writing and its representation of the different ways in which persecution was undergone, yet this is not the particular experience or concern of the journalists and novelists considered here.[3] While the nature of gender division, and, as we will see, gender performance, is an element in the writing of each, it appears in a variety of ways that are implicit. For the reporters Rebecca West and Sybille Bedford, the spectacle of the Nazis on trial takes over from any consistent self-reflexiveness of this kind on their part. By contrast, the unusual and difficult path to becoming a female writer in the immediate post-war era is an element in the story of the Judith Kerr's fictional alter ego Anna in *When Hitler Stole Pink Rabbit* (1971), and the latter's decision to make her refugee experience the subject of that writing becomes more overt in the two later volumes of fictionalized autobiography (1975, 1978). In her novel *The Nice and the Good*, Iris Murdoch's character Willy Kost is a former prisoner of Dachau whose inability to testify to his experiences is conveyed in relation to his having to renounce intimacy with women. In Elaine Feinstein's novel *Children of the Rose* (1975), the legacy of the Holocaust is equally played out in the terms of gender relations, since we learn that the protagonist Lalka did not have the chance to take part in armed resistance against the Nazis, by contrast to the experience of her husband Alex. However, the trajectory traced by the present writers, as one that increasingly emphasizes subjective, survivor-focused experiences, follows the history of Holocaust representation itself as much as that of a consistently gendered viewpoint or discourse.

War crimes trials

British women writers' accounts of Nuremberg include, for instance, that of the national war artist at the trial, Dame Laura Knight, who painted the defendants from a vantage-point just above their heads in the press box, and kept a diary of her impressions of each day's testimony as well as her plans for the courtroom paintings, later dramatised for radio by Amanda Whittington (2014). The journalist and novelist Rebecca West (1892–1983) had written about the effects of war in her 1918 novel about a shell-shocked veteran, *The Return of the Soldier,* and in works of political reportage, for instance *Black Lamb and Grey Falcon* (1941), her two-volume study of pre-war Yugoslavia, when she was commissioned to cover the Nuremberg Trials for the *New Yorker* in the aftermath of the Second World War. West's pieces on the trial of senior Nazis were originally published in 1946 and appeared in revised shape in the volume *A Train of Powder* in 1955, entitled in their later form 'Greenhouse with Cyclamens I', along with two further articles, 'Greenhouse with Cyclamens' II and III. As Lyndsey Stonebridge points out, the almost decade-long gap between West's original articles and their appearance in book form meant that her anti-communist sentiments became increasingly evident in her estimates of the Nazis.[4] The latter two 'Cyclamens' essays were written, respectively, as a reconsideration of the German situation at the time of the Berlin blockade of 1948–49, during which all transport access to the Western sectors was blocked by the Soviets; and as a look back at the Nuremberg Trial on the publication of Hans Fritzsche's *Sword in the Scales* in 1954, a critical account of the trial by Goebbels' director of radio propaganda, who had been acquitted by the International Tribunal: a minor and 'negative matter', as West puts it in 'Cyclamens I'.[5]

West's essays on Nuremberg are not explicitly concerned with the genocide of the Jews. Neither the trial itself, nor its commentators, made a direct link between crimes against humanity and the Nazis' antisemitism, as Margaret Stetz argues.[6] West's focus is, rather, on the architects and the architectonics of the Third Reich, as these are revealed in court. Her account begins with the defendants, who included such figures as Hermann Göring, Rudolf Hess and Alfred Rosenberg, and attempts to decipher connections between the individuals on the benches and the detail of their crimes as these emerged during the trial. Among the ways in which West conveys what she sees as the 'diminution' of the defendants' personalities, and the eerie ordinariness by means of which 'none of them looked as if he could ever have exercised any valid authority',[7] is her description of them, perhaps unexpectedly, in feminised terms. Thus Baldur von Schirach, who had been the director of the Hitler Youth, resembles a 'neat and mousy governess ... as it might be Jane Eyre', while Göring, whether clad in his loose-fitting German Airforce uniform or 'a light beach suit in the worst of playful taste', has 'an air of pregnancy'.[8] Such apparent domestication, and a gendered sense of absent authority, conveys the almost bathetic aftermath of horror.

By contrast, the murdered Jews themselves are mentioned infrequently by West, identified for the most part in quoted utterances by unrepentant locals in the trial's present. Only once is the experience of a Jewish victim cited, as might be expected in the context of a trial which was not centred on testimony from survivors. West observes that the defendants 'wriggled on their seats' when Sir Hartley Shawcross, the leading British prosecutor, quoted a witness describing 'a Jewish father who, standing with his little son in front of a firing squad, "pointed to the sky, stroked his head, and seemed to explain something to him"'. West's analysis of the defendants' reaction to this description of a mass shooting is that they were acting like 'children rated by a schoolmaster'. But whereas the father in Shawcross's account takes the most adult role possible towards his son, by comforting him in the face of violent death, the accused seem to regress to the level of boys themselves, as if in denial of the gravity of their misdeeds. As West puts it, 'There was a mystery there: that Mr Prunes and Prisms should have committed such a huge, cold crime'.[9] In this evocation of Oscar Wilde's comically pedantic governess Miss Prism from *The Importance of Being Earnest* (1895) a further instance of gender reversal is apparent, implying that the defendants view their own deeds as if they were simply social *faux pas*.

It is West's interest in the 'mystery' of motivation and subjectivity, one that runs throughout her 'Greenhouse with Cyclamens' essays, which makes them into meditations on what we now call the Holocaust, even though the genocide is not explicitly reflected upon. Such a concern equally underlies the essays' deceptively painterly-sounding title, since, in West's phrasing, 'flowers were the visible sign of that mystery'.[10] The one-legged gardener who has set up a flourishing pot-plant business selling giant cyclamens in trial-era Nuremberg is at once a symbol of post-war German regeneration and, for West, of a kind of moral tunnel-vision, as she outlines in 'Cyclamens II': 'He was as indifferent to all but his own industry as if it were a stupefying drug, and his fellows knew the same obsession'.[11] By the time of 'Cyclamens III', West's view has sharpened further, and she describes how the gardener's 'absorption in industry left a vacuum in his mind which sooner or later would be filled', perhaps by the kind of deathly 'fantasy' that had afflicted the Third Reich.[12] All of this is implied by West's observation that, in order to ensure a plentiful supply of international customers at the trial's end, the gardener wants to know 'how many trials were likely to be held in Nuremberg now that this one was finished'.[13] It is as if the gardener is indifferent to the crimes that would have to be committed for there to be more trials, since justice is seen simply as the occasion for business.

By contrast to the 'lavishness' of West's style,[14] and her use of concrete detail as moral symbolism, the report by Sybille Bedford (1911–2006) on the 1963–65 Frankfurt Auschwitz Trial is written with what Elaine Ho calls 'noticeable reticence', alongside, at least at first, an absence of narratorial commentary.[15] Bedford's account, written just a few years after the watershed event of the Eichmann Trial of 1961, addresses the Jewish genocide more directly than that of West. Bedford was born in Germany, but left in the 1920s and spent the rest of her life abroad, subsequently returning only 'as a reporter', as she put it in an interview.[16] She covered the trial of 22 former SS guards for the *Observer* and the *Saturday Evening Post*, and it is the material from the latter, published in 1966, that was reprinted in the early editions of a collection of her writings, *As It Was* (1990).[17]

In contrast to Nuremberg, the Auschwitz Trial included testimony from more than 300 eyewitness survivors alongside defendant statements, but it is speculation about the latter that once more preoccupies Bedford. As does Rebecca West, Bedford attempts to divine a sense of intention and responsibility from the defendants' appearance, by noting the gulf between surface and action. Of Robert Mulka, who was Rudolf Höss's adjutant at Auschwitz for nine months in mid-1942, she writes that he resembled 'a not undistinguished clergyman in mild distress'.[18] As Bedford leads us to see, by citing Mulka's own words, such 'distress' was solely on his own account. An exchange between Mulka and the judge is set out as dramatic dialogue with Bedford's commentary taking the form of stage directions, as if anticipating the playwright Peter Weiss's use of the Frankfurt trial transcripts for his 1965 'verbatim' play *The Investigation*. As in West's accounts, it seems that it is gender ambiguity which most aptly encodes the surprising and 'inscrutably ordinary' demeanour of men charged with, as in Mulka's case, 'complicity in mass murder'. Bedford reports the defendant's response to the judge's query about whether the Auschwitz inmates had sufficient food and water, following his claim never to have set foot in the camp itself:

> *Mulka* (Compressing his lips spinsterishly): I never heard of any complaints.[19]

Bedford's subsequent emphasis on the 68-year-old man's advanced years performs a similar function of registering the ordinariness of his blameless appearance, as a clergyman or spinster, in the midst of atrocity recalled. This time such everydayness works in juxtaposition with overt ideological horror, when the judge follows Mulka's admission to knowledge of the gas chambers with a question about his thoughts on the arrival of thousands of people at the camp:

> *Mulka* (Weakly, an old man not sure of his ground): One wanted to liberate the Reich from the Jews.[20]

In lieu of any comment on this, Bedford places after Mulka's avowal that of another defendant, Karl Höcker, a 'middleman of death' who had worked as adjutant to Richard Baer, the commandant of Auschwitz towards the war's end. The judge asks whether Höcker believed that the children in the camp had to be killed because they were a 'public danger', and receives the response:

> *Höcker*: Well, they were Jews.[21]

Elaine Ho writes of Bedford's awareness of an 'alternative temporality' in her courtroom account, by means of which she registers the uncanny persistence of the Nazi past in the very effort to make its agents accountable in the present.[22] These utterances by Mulka and Höcker, in which it is hard to distinguish current from past reasoning, constitute just such moments.

Both West and Bedford see the legal process in symbolic as well as restitu-
tional terms. For West, despite the anomalies she identifies in 'Cyclamens III',
the Nuremberg Trials were essential for the sake of 'civilization' itself, in
order to bring to account those Nazis who had 'done their best to murder
justice'.[23] Such an observation bears similarities to Jean-François Lyotard's
argument that the Holocaust was like an earthquake which destroyed not
only buildings and lives but also 'the instruments used to measure earth-
quakes'.[24] West invokes the necessity of attempting to account for this
'seismic force' in relation to such individuals as Hans Frank, the Governor-
General of occupied Poland, whose punishment for 'breaking Polish laws'
was needed precisely because he had 'murdered Poland and the corpse was
incapable of prosecuting him'.[25] Yet she does not mention the fate of the
Polish Jews directly. Bedford likewise questions the detail of the trial process
at Frankfurt, including the fact that the defendants could only be charged
as accomplices to those murders ordered by their superiors, but she sees
great significance in the Frankfurt setting itself. As she argues, the Auschwitz
Trial took place 'not in Jerusalem, not in Nuremberg under an alien code,
but under the German criminal code established nearly a century ago', its
meticulous adherence to protocol constituting 'a tiny triumph over that vast
injustice of the past'.[26]

Bedford attempts to make sense of the 'civic savagery' revealed by the
Auschwitz trial, and she ascribes its appearance to the reversal of customary
morality under the Nazis, in such a way that violence was used for ideological, political and economic ends.[27] She addresses the danger of racial thinking directly, answering back to Margaret Setz's concern about its absence
from Nuremberg. As Bedford puts it, 'The belief in race as the determining
factor of human quality' is not just 'false and wicked', but a 'hopeless and
defeatist creed' constructed on the principle of 'damnation by birth'.[28]
Bedford's final call to the reader, 'Beware of being sheep',[29] is an expression
of what Carl Rollyson claims of Nuremberg, that, 'It was not only a trial of
the accused but of those who witnessed it'.[30] That is, the trial's observers are
thrown into anguished self-reflection by the spectacle of ordinary but geno-
cidal humanity on trial. Further than this, it is tempting to hear in Bedford's
phrase 'Beware of being sheep' a reversal of its usual reference to the Jews'
alleged failure to resist:[31] here, the sheep are, rather, those enablers whose
weakness might result in the deaths of others.

Among the British journalists who were sent to report on the Eichmann
Trial of 1961 was the novelist Muriel Spark, whose accounts for the *Observer*
never appeared in print but whose subsequent fiction is concerned with
both fascism and the racial ideology of Nazism.[32] *The Prime of Miss Jean
Brodie* (1961), published the year of the trial and centring on the career of
the eponymous Edinburgh schoolteacher, relies on a structure of flashfor-
wards, with the effect that – although some significant narrative surprises
are withheld – the reader knows from early on that in adulthood the novel's

focaliser Sandy Stranger will enter a nunnery and that her schoolmate Mary Macgregor will die in a hotel fire. Judy Suh argues that prolepsis here is a narrative figure for the novel's antipathy to fascism's radical certainties, prompting as it does in the reader a desire instead for 'unpredictability'.[33] Yet the dangers of fascism appear equally strikingly in relation to the opposite temporal formation, the novel's look backwards at the 1930s. This retrospection ironises Jean Brodie's enthusiasm not only for Mussolini's *fascisti*, as she refers to them, but also for Franco and Hitler. Such identification on Miss Brodie's part with charismatic totalitarian leaders is defamiliarised as well as ironised. This is accomplished by means of the reader's likely sympathy with this teacher who is herself charismatic yet absolutist, and whose dour antagonist, the headmistress Miss Mackay, uses Miss Brodie's politics simply as an 'excuse', as both Sandy and Miss Brodie herself put it,[34] to get rid of a troublesome colleague when other misdemeanours cannot be proved.

Spark's *The Mandelbaum Gate* (1965) likewise represents Nazism in a variety of fictional ways. The novel's protagonist, Barbara Vaughan, undertakes a pilgrimage to Israel and Jordan in 1961 at the time of the Eichmann Trial in Jerusalem, which she briefly attends. Barbara's personal circumstances echo those of Spark herself, since she is a Catholic convert with a Jewish father, making *The Mandelbaum Gate*, as Bryan Cheyette puts it, the only one of Spark's novels to explore 'in depth her Gentile-Jewish background'.[35] Barbara experiences ways in which individuals are defined by external strictures based on descent, as she is by the Jewish and non-Jewish members of her family, as well as by the interest-groups of English expatriates, Jews and Muslims whom she encounters in Israel. Such strictures have their most horrifying apotheosis in the 'hundreds of thousands of dead' and the racially motivated crimes for which Eichmann, who was responsible for the mass deportation of Jews to the ghettos and camps of Eastern Europe, is on trial.[36]

As several critics have pointed out, there is some irony in Barbara's considering those parts of Eichmann's obfuscatory trial testimony which she hears firsthand in the terms of the French *nouveau roman*, whose techniques Spark herself often used. The reader learns that, for Barbara, Eichmann, 'a character from the pages of a long *anti-roman*, went on repeating his lines which were punctuated only by the refrain *Bureau IV-B-4*'.[37] Barbara's sense that Eichmann's testimony is 'part of a conspiracy to stop her brain from functioning' is the result of his arid 'monologues': as she perceives it, 'the lips in the glass-bound dock continued to move'[38] even if the words thus produced make little sense. The narrator of Spark's later novel *The Driver's Seat* describes its mysterious protagonist Lise, a woman who seeks her own death, using analagous phrasing. There is a repeated focus on the detail of Lise's 'slightly parted lips',[39] behind which her inner life is inaccessible. The narrator asks rhetorically, 'Who knows her thoughts? Who can tell?',[40] as if Lise's interiority is denied both by the form of the novel and by the heartless violence of the contemporary – and post-Eichmann – world.

Indeed, a different aesthetic to the *nouveau roman*, one more akin to that of objectivist or concrete poetry, is evident in *The Mandelbaum Gate*'s representation of the Eichmann Trial. In Spark's novel, the snatches of Eichmann's verbatim testimony as filtered through Barbara's consciousness resemble such poetic refashionings of Nazi war-crimes trial testimony as Charles Reznikoff's long prose-poem *Holocaust* and Heimrad Bäcker's *Transcript*:[41]

> *Bureau IV-B-4. Four B-four.*
> I was not in charge of the operation itself, only with transportation ...
> Strictly with timetables and technical transport problems.
> I was concerned strictly with timetables and technical transport problems.
> *Bureau IV-B-4. Four B-four-IV-b-4.*[42]

The simple act of editing serves in Spark's novel, as it does in the case of Reznikoff's and Bäcker's poetry, to bring out the horror of the documentary material. It does so by revealing a self-justifying rhetorical form, as we see in the quotation above, in the almost elegantly repetitive patterning and alliteration of these utterances on the subject of genocide. Thus rhetoric replaces the inner life, in Spark's fictive realisation of Arendt's perception about Eichmann that, 'clichés, stock phrases, adherence to conventional, standardized codes of ... conduct have the socially recognized function of protecting us against reality',[43] to murderous effect in his case.

Refugees

British Holocaust writing is particularly characterised by its focus on the refugee experience, in contrast to the canon of Holocaust writing in those European nations which were occupied by the Nazis. The latter centres rather on experiences of deportation, ghettoization, life in hiding or in the camps, while British refugee writing includes work by or about those who arrived from Germany and occupied Europe before the war, notably but not exclusively as children on the Kindertransport trains or as adult domestic workers, as well as camp survivors who arrived after the war's end. It is the former category of pre-war arrival that is especially distinctive in relation to Britain's wartime role, and writing of this kind published up to 1975 includes such work as the Berlin-born Eva Figes's experimental fiction about exiled and alienated individuals, for instance *Equinox* (1966); Karen Gershon's varied output of poetry and memoir, based on her own and others' Kindertransport experience and their adult life in Britain; and some of the first poetry by Gerda Mayer (1927–), who arrived in Britain as part of the Kindertransport initiative from Czechoslovakia on on 14 March 1939, the day before the Nazi invasion of Prague. Neither of her parents survived, and

Mayer settled in Britain, where she continued the practice of writing poetry that she had started as a very young child in her native German.

Mayer is, like Gershon, unusual in having written 'extensively but not exclusively', as she puts it,[44] about the detail of her exile and loss starting as early as the mid-1960s, whereas other Kindertransport poets, including Lotte Kramer, did not publish until a decade later, while Alice Beer did not begin to write until the 1980s.[45] Mayer's poem 'Babes in the Woods' is an advance example of the fairytale being adopted as a vehicle by which to express the atavism of Nazism with surprising directness (more recent examples are Figes's *Tales of Innocence and Experience*, 2003, and Eliza Granville's *Gretel and the Dark*, 2014). The poem's subtitle, 'I.M. Hans and Susi Kraus', hints at the historical foundation for this disquieting revisioning of the Grimms' tale of 'Hansel and Gretel', 'the well known story' in which 'two little children who crossed / A dark and dangerous forest were lost'. The first name of Hans, Mayer's cousin who was murdered with his sister Susi at Auschwitz, partially echoes that of his fairytale namesake. The ambiguity of 'lost' here, suggesting both that the children lost their way and that they perished, is clarified in the poem's final stanza, where the nursery-rhyme rhythm and couplets bluntly emphasise the finality of their fate:

> Alas for the Happy Ending
> Of how the tables were turned;
> There was no reversal of fortune –
> It was Hansel and Gretel who burned.[46]

The children's fate makes horrifyingly real the conceit of the Grimms' story, which concludes with Hansel and Gretel pushing the witch into her own oven, while the capitalizing of 'Happy Ending' reveals its stock fictive role, of no help to Hans and Susi. Mayer's poetic representations of post-Holocaust life take up a variety of subject-positions, including that of the distanced speaker or onlooker in 'Babes in the Woods', which contrasts with the first-person narrator in her other poems. In 'Fragment' (1971), the opening stanza's personal recall, 'My father lifted / a mouthorgan up / to the wind on a hill', is succeeded in the final stanza by a shift to third-person utterance, conveying the difficulty of remembering not just this hillside scene, but a past that has been obliterated: 'man and child / in a harebell light / frail ghosts ... faint tune'.[47]

The figure of the refugee is represented from the outside by a third-person narrator in fiction of the period. Examples include Judith Kerr's 1971 novel *When Hitler Stole Pink Rabbit*, based on her own experiences as the child of an exiled German family, Iris Murdoch's *The Nice and the Good* of 1968, in which the role of the survivor is symbolically secondary, and Elaine Feinstein's 1975 *Children of the Rose*, where the experience of Jewish refugees

168   *Sue Vice*

is central to the novel's concerns. In the novels by Murdoch and Feinstein, the encounter between British interlocutors and European exiles is crucial to the plot. Although Willy Kost is described in Murdoch's *The Nice and the Good* as a 'refugee scholar',[48] and Stonebridge repeats this in her apt characterization of him as 'one of Murdoch's melancholic refugees',[49] he is what we would now call a Holocaust survivor. Yet his presence acts for the most part as an adjunct to the other characters' stories. Willy's tangential relation to the plot is signalled by his location, living in a cottage set at a distance from the home of his benefactors, Kate and Octavian Gray, while his willingness to teach the children of the house Greek but not German conveys his allegiance to a classical past in the face of contemporary atrocities. As is the case in more recent fiction, including Alison MacLeod's *Unexploded* (2013) in which romantic attachments develop between a male Jewish refugee and a British woman, the relationship between Willy and his suitor Mary Clothier is transitional and unconsummated. His turning down Mary's offer of marriage is followed by her realizing that her true feelings are for John Ducane, the novel's protagonist. It is as if such a pairing of Jewish refugee and gentile British subject cannot be encompassed in the novel's world.

The members of Kate and Octavian's household are unsure if Willy is from Vienna or Prague, but they are aware of the fact that he 'spent the war in Dachau'. Willy's implied trauma makes him into all the characters' confidant, and his repeated German-accented question, '"What ees eet?"' is an exilic prelude to his insights, but the specificity of what he has undergone is never fully revealed. The everyday nature of a British attitude towards such experience is dramatised in the novel in the form of the other characters' response to Willy's silence. Kate believes that '"it would do Willy good if he were just forced to tell somebody what it was like in that camp"' since '"one must be reconciled to the past"'.[50] Her words, like those of Ducane, who envies the 'power' that accompanies 'an understanding of suffering and pain',[51] reveal the fact that Willy's acquaintances view historical in terms of personal trauma. Indeed, this slippage is one that is also supported by the plot. Willy's delayed and partial confiding of his experiences reveals his burden to be one of what he too sees as personal failure in extreme historical circumstances. As he puts it to his friend Theo: '"It's not what [Hitler did]. It's what I did"'. Willy vouchsafes the nature of this particular act – '"I betrayed two people because I was afraid, and they died ... They were gassed, Theo"' – but not '"the whole thing"', in Theo's words.[52] When Willy starts at last to relate his experiences, Theo decides not to listen: thus for both him and for the reader, 'Willy's voice murmured on' but his words are inaudible.[53] Like the romantic relationship between Willy and Mary, the camp experience lies outside the conceptual field of *The Nice and the Good*. As its title suggests, the novel's concern is rather with personal ethics. Indeed, its focus on matters other than the Holocaust is emphasised by the fictional contradictions in the detail of where Willy 'spent the war' and what he did there: although such long-term incarceration is less unlikely in a concentration camp such as Dachau than in an extermination camp, no gassings took place in the former.[54] Specificity thus exists not for the sake of accuracy but to construct a notional grey zone for Willy, in which he constantly considers suicide.

Thus Willy's ethical life contrasts with that of the novel's aspirant to evil, Joseph Radeechy, who kills himself before its opening. Radeechy's practice of black magic in the basements of Whitehall, where he works as a civil servant, is a gothic performance in which even he seems not to have believed. Ducane pronounces it a 'dreary' evil, characterised by 'the grotesque and the childish ... something small'.[55] In this kind of language, and even more so in another character's declaration that '"there's no more to [the Radeechy business] than meets the eye"', there resounds an echo of Arendt's analysis of Eichmann, of whom she says, 'The deeds were monstrous, but the doer ... was quite ordinary, commonplace, and neither demonic nor monstrous', and possessed of 'extraordinary shallowness'.[56] As West and Bedford were also at pains to convey in relation even to those accused of crimes against humanity, surface and essence are uncannily hard to separate. Arendt's phrasing is invoked in Ducane's conclusion about Radeechy: 'The great evil, the dreadful evil, that which made war and slavery and man's inhumanity to man lay in the cool self-justifying ruthless selfishness of quite ordinary people'.[57] It seems that in *The Nice and the Good*, Murdoch drew on different kinds of sources for these two characters, Willy the tainted Holocaust survivor and Radeechy the would-be perpetrator, perhaps revealing why the former is more directly embodied in historical terms than the latter, whose black magic strikes a fanciful note. While critics suggest that Murdoch's friendship and tentative romance with the Czech exile Franz Baermann Steiner underlie her portrayal of such figures as Willy Kost in the present novel and Peter Saward in *The Flight from the Enchanter* of 1970,[58] the political philosophy of Arendt more obliquely infuses the character of Radeechy, the mystery of whose death and deeds haunts the novel.

Although we do not hear them, Willy claims that his memories are '"all just there ... Every hour, every minute"',[59] but it is, rather, the inaccessibility of the past that afflicts the protagonists Alex and Lalka Mendez in Elaine Feinstein's novel *Children of the Rose*. Feinstein, who grew up to be a poet and translator as well as a novelist, was born in 1930 in Liverpool and describes the shock of learning about the Nazis' genocide immediately after the war, her sense of it as a 'terrible abyss I might have been caught up in' one she has never been able to 'shake ... completely away'.[60] As in *The Nice and the Good*, the proximity of the Second World War is evident throughout *Children of the Rose*, but set in Feinstein's narrative against other characters' concern with contemporary conflicts including the war in Vietnam and the Troubles in Ireland. Once more, the response of the British host nation to refugee suffering is dramatised, in the form here of Alex's lawyer Tobias

Ansel who 'felt nothing but disgust' for the 'horrors' of Poland's 'landscape of the dead'.[61] When confronted on the Channel ferry taking her and her journalist friend Katie on a visit to Poland, by an 'impudent, good-looking young Irishman' who is angry about the presence of British troops in his country, Lalka's riposte refers to the Polish past and not her British present: 'Don't talk to me about occupations ... I'm *not* English'.[62] Lalka's return to Poland results in her becoming almost literally ill with history, and she is confined to a Krakow hospital after an undiagnosable collapse. The novel's narrative construction, with its Sebaldian absence of quotation marks and blurring between uttered and reported speech, represents memory's confusions. Katie reads from a guidebook about Warsaw's layering of history: 'They've completely rebuilt it ... As it was in the 1800s. Can you remember at all how it was before the war?', prompting Lalka's imagistic and even linguistic recall of her childhood:

> She was walking across streets of droskies and push-carts, a child, holding someone's soft hand ... She could taste and smell. Honeycake. Cherry. Aniseed.[63]

Katie responds as if this interior monologue, expressed in free indirect discourse, has been partially uttered: 'What did you say? repeated Katie impatiently', yet the reader hears neither Lalka's words nor Katie's first question, in a manner that allies us with the former's confusion. Lalka's childhood memories provoke a 'queasiness' that cannot be cured by Katie's offer of a Kwell seasickness pill.

The occupation of Poland and the war appear in even more disturbing form in Feinstein's novel as a bodily 'memory of violence',[64] and the fragmentary nature of her memories seems to be to blame for Lalka's illness. As in the case of the reconstructed Warsaw, covering over the past is not wholly successful. The visit to Poland is not just geographical but temporal, and conjures up for Lalka a subjective, sensory recall of hiding with her mother and baby sister in a Polish village that is given historical meaning only in retrospect, apparent in her confused flashback to a moment of danger: 'But who was the figure then who found them in their outhouse? Black, lean, with frightened eyes? Moving them on. She could smell a baby's wet knickers. She must have been carrying Clara, she thought'.[65] Lalka's estranged husband Alex has similarly oneiric memories of the war, although his are not of chaotic flight but of resistance and 'hiding in a forest': 'The voices about him were unbroken, childish voices. He was with his brothers. Among the partisans. Unafraid. Blessed. Euphoric with the desire for resistance'.[66] Yet Alex's brothers perished while Lalka and her sister Clara survived.

It is Clara who warns Lalka against a return to the past that visiting Poland entails, and sums up its implications: 'None of us really escaped'.[67] Thus the novel is embedded in its historical moment just a quarter-century after the war's end, in which the 'children' of its title, those whom Susan Suleiman has called 'the 1.5 generation',[68] are perilously close to the source of an imperfectly recalled trauma. Although the memory of the war and what we now call the Holocaust is threaded throughout both *The Nice and the Good* and *Children of the Rose*, its aftermath constitutes the central concern of the latter alone, as its ironic title reveals. Lalka sees a rose growing in the Jewish cemetery in Krakow and envies the 'peaceful' resting-place of those buried there, until told by the guide that it is a mass grave for those shot during the war. Thus she realises that 'There was blood in the grass. The weeds, the grass, and the rose all grew from that blood. It was horrible'.[69] The imagery echoes that of the survivor-poet Paul Celan, for whom John Felstiner claims that the rose similarly conveys both 'vulnerability [and] beauty',[70] as it does in his poem 'Psalm', composed in 1961. As in the title of Feinstein's novel, the speaker in Celan's poem protests against being 'the No-One's-Rose',[71] a member of a forsaken people, by means of an image that paradoxically implies new life.

Judith Kerr's novel *When Hitler Stole Pink Rabbit* represents, as its title suggests, an intertwining of historical with domestic experience in a way that befits its crossover status. The novel is based on Kerr's own experiences, as a Jewish refugee from Germany who arrived with her parents and brother in Britain in 1933 at the age of ten, and who has become a celebrated writer and illustrator of children's books. It is suited to both a young and an adult readership in reproducing the viewpoint 'from below' of Anna, who is thirteen by the novel's conclusion in 1936 when her family arrives in Britain. Indeed, it is hard not to see the influence of the conceit of Kerr's novel on another crossover work set in Nazi Germany, John Boyne's *The Boy in the Striped Pyjamas* (2006). Both novels open with a child's struggle to understand the political reasons for having to leave the familiarity of a house and friends in Berlin, and to negotiate family relations in a new environment. However, the title of Boyne's novel reveals a much more exaggerated confusion between historical and domestic realms, since its child focaliser Bruno is the son of the Commandant of Auschwitz. The discord in his family relations, in contrast to the redemptive solidarity Anna experiences, is in part responsible for Bruno's belief that the camp uniforms are the eponymous pyjamas of the novel's title, and for his misrecognizing the suffering of his Jewish friend Shmuel to the extent that he accidentally dies alongside him.

In *When Hitler Stole Pink Rabbit*, by contrast, the bathetic reactions of Anna and her German friends to circumstances in Berlin in 1933 convey pragmatism rather than the almost wilful blindness evident in Bruno's responses. Anna worries about the burden of not being allowed to tell anyone, including her schoolfriend Elsbeth, about her father's fleeing Germany, but the reader learns that 'Elsbeth's mind was on more important matters': the purchase of a yo-yo.[72] This is not the extremity of Bruno's failure to understand, but, it is implied, a focus on the children's shared everyday concerns which reassures Anna. Indeed, Anna gauges events by just such means. The significance of her mother's absence from the dinner-table where the family is eating dessert, after what turns out to be a warning telephone-call, is understood by her as 'odd' because 'Mama was particularly fond of apple strudel'.[73] Both Anna and the implied reader are left to work out what this failure to return to the table means within the context of the story.

Yet horror also irrupts explicitly within the narrative, in relation to the kinds of atrocities that affected Anna and which also act as knowing flash-forwards to the Holocaust. The account of a 'famous professor' who was 'chained to a dog kennel' in a concentration camp is mediated by Anna's responses: her initial sense that this is a 'silly' thing for the Nazis to have done is replaced by a 'black wall' of horror on hearing that the man was driven mad by this mistreatment: 'She could not breathe [and wanted] to be rid of it, to be sick'.[74] The fate of the animal-loving Onkel Julius, a family friend who remains in Germany, acts as a synecdoche for what the fate of Anna's father might have been, and, by extension, that of thousands of others. Under the Nuremberg Laws, having a Jewish grandmother means that his rights are progressively removed, and Julius commits suicide after receiving 'an official letter revoking his pass to the Zoo'.[75] Not only are the Nazis' atrocities in both cases, as they are in the novel's title, represented in the terms of animals that are suited to a child reader, but an alternative animal-based ethics is hinted at. We learn that Onkel Julius sent Anna's family a picture-postcard of bears carrying the message, '"The more I see of men, the more I love animals"', and that the monkeys at the Zoo seemed to recognise '"a sort of gentleness in him"'.[76] Thus being denied entry to the Zoo is a historical affront as well as a psychic symbol.

Conclusion

The period between 1945 and 1975 consists largely of Holocaust-related writing by witnesses: those like Rebecca West, Sybille Bedford and Muriel Spark who had observed war-crimes trials; writers who had worked in refugee camps and encountered exiled scholars, as in the case of Iris Murdoch; individuals who were themselves refugees or survivors, such as Gerda Mayer and Judith Kerr; or writers like Elaine Feinstein, whose engagement with British-Jewish life necessarily included the post-war refugee experience. The writing of this transitional era reveals an indebtedness to 'intermodern' British women writers' fiction about Nazism and persecution from the pre-war era, as well as to wartime poetry and prose about the experiences of refugees, for example the internment of 'enemy aliens'. The period also lays the foundations for later and more specifically Holocaust-centred work by British women writers. This later material includes testimonies and memoirs, by such camp survivors now living in Britain as Anita Lasker-Wallfisch-Lasker (1996). Other recent work concerns the transmission and inheritance of wartime experience for subsequent generations; and, following the early writings of West and Bedford, a return to interest in the subjectivity of perpetrators, as evidenced by Rachel Seiffert's *The Dark Room* (2001). This neglected era is significant due to its proximity to the events of the war and its uncanonised responses, as well as its influence on post-1975 Holocaust literature.

Notes

1. Peter Novick, *The Holocaust in American Life* (Boston: Houghton Mifflin, 1999), p. 1.
2. Annette Wieviorka, *The Era of the Witness* (Ithaca: Cornell University Press, 2006).
3. See Pascale R. Bos, 'Women and the Holocaust: Analyzing Gender Difference', in *Experience and Expression: Women, the Nazis, and the Holocaust* ed. by Elizabeth R. Baer and Myrna Goldenberg (Detroit: Wayne State University Press, 2003) for a discussion of gender difference in Holocaust writing.
4. Lyndsey Stonebridge, *The Judicial Imagination: Writing After Nuremberg* (Edinburgh: Edinburgh University Press, 2011), p. 36.
5. Rebecca West, *A Train of Powder: Six Reports on the Problem of Guilt and Punishment in Our Time* (Chicago: Ivan R. Dee, 1955), p. 56.
6. Margaret Stetz, 'Rebecca West, Aestheticism, and the Legacy of Oscar Wilde', in *Rebecca West Today: Contemporary Critical Approaches* ed. by Bernard Schweizer (Cranbury, NJ: Associated University Presses, 2006), pp. 157–69 (p. 62).
7. West, *A Train of Powder*, p. 5.
8. West, *A Train of Powder*, p. 6.
9. West, *A Train of Powder*, p. 20.
10. West, *A Train of Powder*, p. 21.
11. West, *A Train of Powder*, p. 139.
12. West, *A Train of Powder*, p. 248.
13. West, *A Train of Powder*, p. 30.
14. Stonebridge, *The Judicial Imagination*, p. 41.
15. Eyl Ho, 'Everyday Law in the Court Writing of Sybille Beford' in *Reading the Legal Case: Cross-currents Between Law and the Humanities* ed. by Marcus Wan (New York: Routledge, 2012), pp. 61–79 (p. 76).
16. Shusha Guppy, 'Interview with Sybille Bedford', *Paris Review*, 126 (1993), 230–49 (239).
17. Sybille Bedford, *As It Was* (London: Picador, 1990).
18. Bedford, *As It Was*, p. 219.
19. Bedford, *As It Was*, p. 220.
20. Bedford, *As It Was*, p. 221.
21. Bedford, *As It Was*, p. 223.
22. Ho, 'Everyday Law in the Court Writing of Sybille Bedford', p. 76.
23. West, *Train of Powder*, pp. 242, 245.
24. Jean-François Lyotard, *The Differend: Phrases in Dispute*, trans. George Van Den Abbeele [1983] (Minneapolis: University of Minnesota Press, 1988), p. 56.
25. West, *A Train of Powder*, p. 245.
26. Bedford, *As It Was*, pp. 232, 238.
27. Bedford, *As It Was*, pp. 245, 250.
28. Bedford, *As It Was*, p. 249.

29. Bedford, *As It Was*, p. 260.
30. Carl Rollyson, *Rebecca West and the God That Failed: Essays* (New York: Universal, 2005), p. 85.
31. Despite this customary usage, the phrase originates in a context of the opposite kind, that is, the poet and partisan Abba Kovner's wartime call for armed resistance in the Vilna Ghetto – 'We shall not stretch our necks like sheep for the slaughter! Jews! Defend yourself with arms!', quoted in Yitzhak Arad, *Ghetto in Flames: The Struggle and Destruction of the Jews in Vilna in the Holocaust* (Jerusalem: Yad Vashem, 1980), p. 412.
32. Stonebridge, *The Judicial Imagination*, p. 73; Bryan Cheyette, *Muriel Spark* (London: Northcote House, 2000), p. 53.
33. Judy Suh, 'The Familiar Attractions of Fascism in Muriel Spark's *The Prime of Miss Jean Brodie*', *Journal of Modern Literature*, 30: 2 (2007), 86–102, 99.
34. Muriel Spark, *The Prime of Miss Jean Brodie* [1961] (London: Penguin, 1965), pp. 121, 125.
35. Cheyette, *Muriel Spark*, p. 27.
36. Muriel Spark, *The Mandelbaum Gate* [1965] (London: Penguin, 1967), p. 178.
37. Spark, *The Mandelbaum Gate*, p. 179. On Spark's links to the 'anti-roman', see for instance Cheyette, *Muriel Spark*, p. 70, and James Bailey, '"Repetition, boredom, despair": Muriel Spark and the Eichmann Trial', in *Representing Perpetrators in Holocaust Literature and Film* ed. by J. Adams and S. Vice (London: Vallentine Mitchell, 2013).
38. Spark, *The Mandelbaum Gate*, p. 179.
39. Muriel Spark, *The Driver's Seat* [1970] (London: Penguin, 1974), p. 9. The description of Lise's lips being 'slightly parted' occurs thirteen times in the novel, as Jonathan Kemp points out in his article '"Her Lips Are Slightly Parted": The Ineffability of Erotic Sociality in Muriel Spark's *The Driver's Seat*', *Modern Fiction Studies*, 54: 3 (2008), 545–57, 554.
40. Spark, *The Driver's Seat*, p. 50.
41. Charles Reznikoff, *Holocaust* (Los Angeles: Black Sparrow Press, 1975); Heimrad Bäcker, *Transcript*, trans. Patrick Greaney [1986] (Champaign: Dalkey Archive Press, 2010). While Reznikoff, like Spark, uses material from the Eichmann Trial, Bäcker draws, among other sources, on the Nuremberg Trial transcripts.
42. Spark, *The Mandelbaum Gate*, p. 178.
43. Hannah Arendt, *The Life of the Mind* [1978] (New York: Harcourt Brace, 1981), p. 4.
44. Gerda Mayer, *Prague Winter* (London: Hearing Eye, 2005), p. 17.
45. Dilys Wood, 'Pain into Poetry', *Artemis*, 2 (2009), <http://www.poetrymagazines. org.uk/magazine/print.asp?id=25605> [accessed 20 April 2017].
46. Mayer, *Prague Winter*, p. 56.
47. Mayer 'Fragment', *Ariel*, 2: 1 (1971).
48. Iris Murdoch, *The Nice and the Good* [1968] (London: Vintage, 2000), p. 17.
49. Stonebridge, *The Judicial Imagination*, p. 164.
50. Murdoch, *The Nice and the Good*, p. 47.
51. Murdoch, *The Nice and the Good*, p. 54.
52. Murdoch, *The Nice and the Good*, p. 342.
53. Murdoch, *The Nice and the Good*, p. 343.
54. Although a gas chamber was present at Dachau, there is no evidence that anyone was killed in it; victims of 'selections' were sent to the 'euthanasia' centre at Schloss Hartheim in Austria.

55. Murdoch, *The Nice and the Good*, pp. 214, 320.
56. Murdoch, *The Nice and the Good*, p. 235; Arendt, *The Life of the Mind*, p. 4; Arendt, 'Thinking and Moral Considerations: A Lecture', *Social Research*, 38: 3 (1970), 417–46, 417.
57. Murdoch, *The Nice and the Good*, p. 320.
58. Stonebridge, *The Judicial Imagination*, p. 144.
59. Murdoch, *The Nice and the Good*, p. 343.
60. Belinda McKeon, 'Interview with Elaine Feinstein', *Irish Times*, 10 May, 2005, n.p.
61. Elaine Feinstein, *Children of the Rose* (Harmondsworth: Penguin, 1975), p. 9.
62. Feinstein, *Children of the Rose*, pp. 96, 98–9.
63. Feinstein, *Children of the Rose*, p. 101.
64. Feinstein, *Children of the Rose*, p. 43.
65. Feinstein, *Children of the Rose*, p. 102.
66. Feinstein *Children of the Rose*, p. 63.
67. Feinstein *Children of the Rose*, p. 170.
68. Susan R. Suleiman, 'The 1.5 Generation: Thinking about Child Survivors and the Holocaust', *American Imago*, 59: 3 (2002), 277–95.
69. Feinstein, *Children of the Rose*, p. 125.
70. John Felstiner, *Paul Celan: Poet, Survivor, Jew* (New Haven: Yale University Press, 1995), p. 61.
71. Paul Celan, *Selected Poems and Prose of Paul Celan*, ed. John Felstiner (New York: W. W. Norton, 2001).
72. Judith Kerr, *When Hitler Stole Pink Rabbit* [1971] (London: Collins, 1974), p. 5.
73. Kerr, *When Hitler Stole Pink Rabbit*, p. 16.
74. Kerr, *When Hitler Stole Pink Rabbit*, p. 113.
75. Kerr, *When Hitler Stole Pink Rabbit*, p. 260.
76. Kerr, *When Hitler Stole Pink Rabbit*, pp. 222, 260.

10
Internal Empire

Katie Gramich

Nostalgic feelings about the British Empire die hard, as the British refer-
endum vote to leave the European Union in June 2016, so-called 'Brexit',
has clearly demonstrated. Equally clearly delineated have been the stark
divisions among the four constituent parts of this disunited kingdom, with
the majority in Scotland and Northern Ireland voting for remaining in the
European Union; England, with the notable exceptions of some large cities
including London, for leaving; and Wales split between the 'remain' votes
of the Welsh-speaking west and the capital, Cardiff, and the 'leave' votes
of the rest of the country. Looking back on the period 1945–75 from this
momentous present, we can see how our current divisions, conflicts, and
differences were already being foreseen, anatomised, satirised, and lamented
by the prescient women writers of the period who, moreover, reflected the
instability of their times in their stylistic innovations and in their willingness to experiment with hybrid literary forms.

In 1975 the American sociologist, Michael Hechter, published an influential book entitled *Internal Colonialism: The Celtic Fringe in British National
Development 1536–1966*, in which he argued that the 'peripheral' nations
of the British Isles, namely Ireland, Wales, and Scotland, had functioned as
internal colonies within the British Empire.[1] Hechter's theory foregrounds
the analogy between what he calls the 'Celtic fringe' and the overseas
colonies of the Empire, arguing that the 'internal colonies' had suffered
from similar, Anglocentric cultural and economic exploitation. He sees the
burgeoning nationalist movements in Scotland and Wales, foreshadowed
by the nationalist struggle in Ireland earlier in the century, as signalling
the beginning of the end of this imperial system. 1966, the date chosen by
Hechter as the end point of his study, coincides with the date of the election
of Gwynfor Evans as the first Plaid Cymru (Welsh Nationalist) MP; he was

© The Author(s) 2017
C. Hanson and S. Watkins, *The History of British Women's Writing, 1945–1975*,
History of British Women's Writing, DOI: 10.1057/978–1–137–47736–1_11

soon joined in Westminster by Winifred Ewing, the first Scottish Nationalist MP. These parties had been established in the mid-1920s but events in the 1950s and 1960s suddenly boosted their popular support.[2] The '60s was also the period when many erstwhile British colonies were achieving independence, often in the wake of successful nationalist campaigns, for example Jamaica in 1962, and Botswana in 1966. The 'melancholy, long, withdrawing roar'[3] of the British empire had, of course, been heard for many decades but it was undoubtedly intensified in the post-war period, especially after the independence and partition of India and Pakistan in 1948. Hechter's thesis has been disputed by many historians, notably Tom Nairn and Neil Evans, primarily because it ignores important differences among the countries it discusses.[4] Nevertheless, the analogy between the three 'internal colonies' and the overseas empire was undoubtedly a potent element of the imagined nation, however historically inaccurate it may have been, and the post-imperial themes and concerns are particularly evident in the work of the British creative writers of the time, not least women novelists. In recent years, moreover, postcolonial approaches to the literatures of Ireland, Wales, and Scotland have borne fruit, indicating that literary scholars are more receptive than historians to the colonial analogy proposed by Hechter.[5]

If the so-called 'Celtic fringe' was affected by and responding to the decline of empire, arguably England itself was plunged into an existential crisis of its own. Certainly, this was a period when Englishness was being redefined through complex negotiations between the present and the past, and women writers such as the Anglo-Irish Elizabeth Bowen and the English Elizabeth Taylor played their part in charting shifts in the psychic geography of a country accommodating itself to economic and political decline. In the 1960s Enoch Powell attempted to rouse a new English nationalism not only with the infamous 'rivers of blood' speech of 1968 where he warned of a racial apocalypse on the streets of England,[6] but also in less well known pastoral poetry yearning for a lost English idyll. In the poem sequence *Dancer's End*, for instance, Powell's speaker has a vision of the ghosts of the 'old English ... hovering in the fields that once they tilled' which makes the speaker '[b]rood ... on England's destiny.'[7] Deliberately echoing Gray's 'Elegy in a Country Churchyard', Powell's verse is simultaneously nostalgic and hopeful about a new national resurgence of the 'old English', who will presumably fulfil their destiny by displacing contemporary England's hybrid, postcolonial population. Though Powell's political demagoguery elsewhere is extreme, his chauvinism and anxieties about the present are not uncharacteristic of many English writers' work in this period.[8] Women writers of the time tend to use the changing English landscape as a metaphor for the changing nation, while their use of 'private' domestic space charts the post-war shifts in gender roles and expectations.

In Elizabeth Bowen's *The Heat of the Day* (1948), set in London and Ireland during the Second World War, the protagonist, Stella Rodney, discovers that her lover, Robert Kelway, is a Fascist spy. When she asks him why he is against 'this country', he replies, angrily, '"what *do* you mean? Country? – there are no more countries left; nothing but names"'.[9] Stella herself drifts from one rented flat to another, rather like a patrician version of a Jean Rhys heroine, feeling 'the anxieties, the uncertainties of the hybrid. She ... had come loose from her moorings ... Her own extraction was from a class that ha[d] taken an unexpected number of generations to die out ...'[10] The tense atmosphere of wartime London and the disorientating timelessness of the great house in rural Ireland create a fictional world in which nothing is safe or certain, a world characteristically described in terms of a shifting landscape: 'There can occur in lives a subsidence of the under soil – so that, without the surface having been visibly broken, gradients alter, uprights cant a little out of the straight.'[11]

Already in the 1970s, English women writers were beginning to chart the post-imperial demographic shifts which were transforming England. In the title story of Elizabeth Taylor's *The Devastating Boys* (1972), for instance, Harold, an Archaeology professor and his timid wife, Laura, have two 'coloured' immigrant children from the city to stay with them for a country holiday, as an act of charity. The two boys, Septimus Smith and Benny Reece, turn out to be difficult and funny characters who dominate and exhaust poor Laura. It is Laura's friend, Helena, a writer of 'clever-clever little novels', according to Harold, who exclaims that the boys are 'simply devastating!'[12] The adjective 'devastating', meaning astonishing or stunning, points to Helena's hyperbolic and trivial use of language, and yet there is perhaps a hint here of the etymological meaning of 'devastating', namely laying waste to a territory. The boys unconsciously present a threat to the 'old English' society praised by Enoch Powell. In the story they respond to their encounter with this world by accurately mimicking Helena's affected speech and manner. The boys object when Laura plays 'God Save the Queen' on the piano and are not impressed with the local Anglican church service either; Septimus observes "I prefer my own country. I prefer Christians". "Me, too", Benny said. "Give me Christians any day."[13] In this story, Taylor holds English attitudes and mores up to ridicule, and places two black characters at the centre of rural England, inviting the reader to judge 'traditional' Englishness through their eyes. Taylor's stories engage directly and sensitively with the changing landscape, population, and class structure of post-imperial England, in a disarmingly gentle and yet acerbic mode of social comedy.

Like Bowen and Taylor, the Welsh writer, Kate Roberts (1891–1985), was a gifted short story writer. Born to a poor family in the slate-quarrying area of Caernarfonshire in north-west Wales, she was a scholarship girl who was one of the first female students at the newly-established University College of North Wales in Bangor. She began writing in her native language, Welsh, in the late 1920s, and by 1945 she was an established author, having published six volumes of creative prose, but there had been a hiatus in her creative work for some years, largely because she had thrown her energies into running a successful publishing house. But after the war, and the sudden death of her husband, Roberts gradually began to publish her own work once more. In 1946 there appeared the first selection of English translations of Roberts's short stories, in the volume, *A summer day and other stories*, which had an enthusiastic introduction by the prolific English writer, Storm Jameson. The latter praises what she sees as Wales's 'living culture which is not that of the elsewhere triumphant machine age.' Comparing Wales to Slovakia, for both are small countries with 'a native culture which has so much energy left,' Jameson implicitly suggests a contrast with the exhaustion of English culture. Indeed, she finds Roberts's work 'enriched and steadied by her deep sense of continuity with the past ... [and an] active sense ... of a complex tradition'.[14] Interestingly, then, from the perspective of English writers, both Wales and Ireland seem to retain a sense of stability which is absent from England; as Elizabeth Bowen's character, Stella, perceives when she visits Ireland during the war: 'she could have imagined this was another time, rather than another country, that she had come to.'[15]

Yet, seen from within, the view is different. Welsh and Irish writers often engage with the changes that have overcome their allegedly static nations. In the post-war period Kate Roberts, for example, creates psychological narratives exploring women's position in a changing world, using private, domestic spaces as metaphors for the restriction of Welsh women's opportunities. Her 1956 novel *The Living Sleep* concerns a woman, Laura Ffennig, suddenly abandoned by her husband and attempting to come to terms with her new, unfixed life. Its form is different from Roberts's earlier, realist mode, containing lengthy passages of dream narrative and interior monologue, as well as pages from the protagonist's journal.[16] While the novel tackles contemporary concerns about marital and social breakdown, it also engages with Laura's internal battles with her conservative, Welsh identity and explores her attempts to gain autonomy through a therapeutic act of writing. Another Roberts novel of this period, *Fairness of Morning* (1957–58) is partly autobiographical and set in the pre-World War One era, evoking nostalgically a lost age of innocence.[17] One of Roberts's best-known works, *Tea in the Heather*, a humorous collection of stories about childhood and adolescence in rural Wales, also belongs to this period.[18] Roberts's recurring interest in *looking back* and *looking inward* in this fiction and in chronicling and recording what has been irrevocably lost chimes with the concerns of other British and Irish women writers of the time, though its implicit attitudes towards notions of Britishness and of empire are invariably negative.

The novella *Gossip Row* (1949) represents Roberts's generically experimental work at this time. It takes the form of a diary written by the disabled protagonist, Phoebe. This is a highly inward-looking narrative, focussing exclusively on Phoebe's thoughts, feelings, and observations. Her invalid status means that she is unable to move from her bed, unless she is physically carried outside. Her paralysis has lasted three years and it is clear that Roberts is using her condition as a metaphor for the stagnant, monotonous and incestuous condition of the society of this small-minded, north Welsh town. The narrative offers an unflattering portrait of Welsh life, centred on chapel and shop, with the main concern of its inhabitants seemingly being to gossip and make snide remarks about their neighbours. Families are seen as restrictive and warping, not unlike the depiction found in the northern Irish writer, Janet McNeill's, *Tea at Four O'Clock* (1956), discussed below. Like that text, Roberts's begins with a death, which is one of the mainsprings of the plot.

And yet there are positive aspects to this society, too – there is lifelong friendship here, considerable kindness, and a real bond between sisters. The narrative is full of satire at the expense of a hypocritical chapel-going society, a picture not unlike Muriel Spark's satire of Scottish Presbyterianism in *The Prime of Miss Jean Brodie*. By the end of the narrative Phoebe feels remorse for her feelings of hatred and jealousy, which have been fostered by 'Gossip Row', and has an epiphany in which she is able to acknowledge her own selfishness and self-deception. The diary ends with a quotation from a fifteenth-century Welsh poem by Siôn Cent: 'My hope lies in what is to come'.[19] The poem refers to the future of Wales and wishes for a '*mab darogan*' [son of prophecy] who will save the country, but Phoebe hopes for a personal, spiritual and perhaps even physical resurrection. This allusion is the only veiled reference to the contemporary nationalist politics of Wales, in which Kate Roberts was centrally involved, but which she chose to keep as separate as possible from her creative work.

In *Fairness of Morning*, another novel from the late 1950s, Roberts's protagonist, Ann Owen, a schoolteacher, feels a similar growing discontentment with the narrow-minded milieu of small town Welsh society. She describes the place as 'like some mask over one's face; the world moves on but Blaen Ddôl stays the same'.[20] In the second half of the novel, Ann's life is shadowed by the First World War in which her beloved younger brother is killed (echoing events in the author's own life). Looking back, Ann sees her life as a meadow, one half bathed in the 'fair' light of 'morning', separated from the other half by a deep trench, which represents the war. The deployment of landscape as metaphor both for the nation and the individual is once again clear.

If the general tenor of Kate Roberts's fiction in this period is one of sad reflection upon losses, the work of her younger Welsh contemporary, Menna Gallie (1920–1990), is characterised by subversive humour and exuberant energy, though certainly with dark undertones. Gallie was from industrial South Wales and in her two novels, *Strike for a Kingdom* (1959) and *The Small Mine* (1962) she can be credited with a bold re-framing of the male-dominated Welsh industrial novel which had its heyday in the 1930s from a different gender perspective. Surprisingly, too, Gallie was one of the first writers to register in fictional form the Troubles in Northern Ireland in her 1970 novel, *You're Welcome to Ulster*. The earlier novels are based on her own background growing up in Ystradgynlais in the Swansea Valley, given the fictional name Cilhendre in the novels, while *You're Welcome to Ulster* speaks of Gallie's experience of living near Belfast between 1954 and 1967. Although Gallie was a Welsh speaker, her politics were very different from those of Kate Roberts. Gallie's early novels *Strike for a Kingdom* (1959) and *The Small Mine* (1962) reflect a very South Walian socialist worldview, implicitly rejecting nationalist aspirations and yet charting carefully the ways in which Welsh workers and Welsh speakers had been systematically disempowered by an Anglocentric capitalist system. If that description sounds excessively dogmatic, the good news is that Gallie leavens her politics with large doses of humour and irony. Her style is striking – a racy, recognizably Welsh idiolect, not unlike some of the prose of Dylan Thomas or Gwyn Thomas. She is an irreverent novelist who does not shy away from satirizing some of the foundational institutions of Welsh society, such as the chapel. In *Strike for a Kingdom*, for example, one of the workers complains that his wife has become obsessed with religion: '"she goes down that chapel they have in Clydach and comes home with diarrhoea and messages."'[21] Similarly, she mocks those with social pretensions who feign an inability to speak Welsh, such as Evans the police inspector, who 'spoke Welsh but preferred not to let it be known that he suffered from this disability.'[22] Gender roles are also explored in a largely comic mode, with male pretensions being deflated and middle-class women's notions of propriety being openly mocked: at Mr Nixon, the mine manager's funeral, a sister-in-law of the deceased is described as: '[s]o corseted ... and firm that she felt to the touch like a dead crusader on his tomb.'[23]

The plot of *Strike for a Kingdom* is set against the background of the miners' Lock-Out which took place after the 1926 General Strike. Interwoven with the men's labour disputes is a personal drama involving surreptitious love affairs and exploitation of women by the odious Mr Nixon, the mine manager, who is found murdered. The investigation of his murder constitutes the plot, but Gallie's novel is hardly a conventional whodunit. On the contrary, the text – her first published work – is much more concerned with the vivid evocation of a place, a time and a community. This convergence of potentially tragic subject-matter with a robust comic style is highly characteristic of Gallie's work and contributes to making her novels slightly uneasy reading – there can be a modulation from the humorous to the heart-rending within the space of one paragraph.

Gallie's 1962 novel, *The Small Mine*, is set some decades later, after the Second World War and the nationalisation of the coal mines. The main concern here is with social change in the valley community, though again this is animated by a kind of detective plot. Structurally, the novel is daring in that the character whom we might identify as the 'hero', Joe, is killed in the mine halfway through the text. Social change is represented in this novel with the final emblematic closure of the 'small mine', a throwback to earlier industrial practices which have been superseded by the highly mechanised new coal industry run by the National Coal Board. Another emblematic scene of social change is the burning of the old bardic chair on the children's bonfire on November 5th. Nevertheless, this society is still strongly connected to the Welsh language and culture, a fact indicated in the texture of the narrative itself, where there are frequent literal translations of Welsh idioms and a suggestion from the syntax and rhythms that the direct speech of the characters has been translated from the Welsh.

Both of Gallie's Welsh-set novels engage with gender issues in a Welsh cultural context. In *The Small Mine*, Flossie Jenkins is of the older generation of women who willingly perform their domestic duties and whose role in the novel is defined as that of the archetypal Welsh Mam. Once her son, Joe, is killed, she loses her vitality and her voice in the novel. Up until the accident, though, she is a formidable presence, ruling her household with energetic glee. She adheres to a rigid domestic system of labour which is described as analogous to the shift system operated in the coal mines; all through the working day she wears curlers in her hair as an emblem of being 'on duty' and only takes them out last thing at night when her work is done: 'combing out her sausage curls was Flossie's clocking-off signal.'[24] If Gallie uses terms usually associated with the male world of work in describing Flossie's working day, she reverses the process in her description of Dai Dialectic and Jim Kremlin's labour in the mine: 'They were both good colliers, taking pride in their roofing and in the proper organization of their stall, as a housewife is proud of a well-organized, uncluttered kitchen.'[25] The effect of these unexpected transpositions is to assign equal weight and importance to the work of both genders. Gallie may have been reluctant to accept the label 'feminist' but her literary practice certainly suggests a belief in gender equality.[26]

Gallie is a fascinating figure not least because she seems to embody the 'Four Nations' of the British Isles in both her life and work. Welsh-born and Welsh-speaking, she married a Scottish academic, Bryce Gallie, and moved with him to live in Northern Ireland and England for extended periods of her adult life. The complicated relations and interactions among the Four Nations are reflected in her works, especially in her pioneering 1970 novel, *You're Welcome to Ulster*, which focuses particularly on relations between Northern Ireland and Wales.

But in order to approach that text, it is necessary to take a few steps back to understand the history of activism in Wales in the 1960s. In 1962, Saunders Lewis made a ground-breaking broadcast on the BBC entitled 'Tynged yr Iaith' (The Fate of the Language) in which he argued that: 'Welsh will end as a living language, should the present trend continue, about the beginning of the twenty-first century ... Thus the policy laid down as the aim of the English Government in Wales in the measure called the Act of Union of England and Wales in 1536 will at last have succeeded.'[27] He went on to issue a call to arms, or at least to the barricades: 'this is the only political matter which it is worth a Welshman's while to trouble himself about today ... It will be nothing less than a revolution to restore the Welsh language in Wales. Success is only possible through revolutionary methods.'[28] As a direct result of that broadcast, the Welsh Language Society or Cymdeithas yr Iaith Gymraeg was established in August 1962 and has spent the last half-century often successfully campaigning for language rights for Welsh speakers. In the 1970s, Cymdeithas yr Iaith mounted a direct action campaign against Anglicised road signs in Wales, either taking down or defacing English-language signs for Welsh places. As is so often the case, names are politically powerful. Cymdeithas yr Iaith saw the symbolic power of changing the way a country is named, rejecting the imposed Anglicised names and reverting to the original Welsh ones. Women were prominent in these campaigns during the 1970s, some being incarcerated for their 'revolutionary methods', and this experience begins to be registered in fiction during the period, notably in Meg Elis's autobiographical novel, *I'r Gad* (*To battle*, 1975).

Members of Cymdeithas yr Iaith did not hesitate to destroy property and to disobey the law, but they were never a paramilitary organization. In the 1960s and 1970s there were, however, a number of such organizations operating in Wales, such as the Free Wales Army and the Mudiad Amddiffyn Cymru (Wales Defence League). In 1969, in the period leading up to the Investiture of Prince Charles as the 'Prince of Wales', there was considerable protest against this very public ritual which appeared to some to be celebrating and consolidating Wales's continuing colonised status. On the morning of the Investiture two members of the 'Mudiad Amddiffyn Cymru' were killed when the bomb they were carrying exploded prematurely. Later that same summer, Northern Ireland witnessed the worst flare-up of sectarian violence for many decades, and historians now tend to date the beginnings of the Troubles back to 1969. These events in Wales and Ireland are explicitly linked up by Menna Gallie in her daring 1970 novel, *You're Welcome to Ulster*. In the novel a Welsh woman, Sarah Thomas, travels to visit friends in Northern Ireland and becomes embroiled in the violence which has flared up there. The novel focuses both on Sarah's body and her desire, reflecting a new atmosphere of sexual freedom typical of the late 1960s and upon the new political activism which is bubbling over into violence in both Northern Ireland and Wales. Indeed, in an explanatory Prelude to the novel added to the US edition in 1971, Gallie makes explicit the links between the IRA and a group of Welsh paramilitaries, who are expecting a delivery of arms from their Irish 'brethren'. One of the young Welsh extremists in the novel is called Mab, in a clear echo of the 'mab darogan' of Welsh mythology, but his attempts at violent action fizzle out into failure. In contrast, events in Northern Ireland take a literally fatal turn. One young Irish Civil Rights activist, called Una, appears to be a fictional representation of Bernadette Devlin, who in 1969 'became the youngest woman elected to

Westminster.'[29] Gallie's novel can be seen as a warning to Wales about the dangers of following in Irish footsteps, but the novel is by no means wholly negative about the new political activism of the period, showing how the liberation movements of the time broaden the possibilities and sphere of women in both Wales and Ireland in a hitherto unprecedented way.

Gallie's Welsh view of Irish politics received mixed reviews. It actually took Irish women writers themselves a few more years to write directly of the violence overtaking the North. *Shadows on our Skin*, the novel in which Jennifer Johnston engages directly with Northern Ireland's Troubles, for instance, was not published until 1977. Johnston, born in Dublin in 1930 but for many years resident in Derry, is one of Northern Ireland's most distinguished contemporary writers. Her first novel, *The Captains and the Kings* (1972) is set in a dilapidated Irish great house and revolves around the relationship that develops between an elderly widower, Charles Prendergast, the owner of the great house and a veteran of the First World War, and a local lad, Diarmid Toorish. The book shows how the recluse, Charles, has had his whole life blighted by the experience of war, which has left him incapable of love and human communication, until the impertinent young truant, Diarmid, trespasses on his life and a doomed attachment for the boy develops in Charles's soul: 'The child had, somehow, halted for a while the inevitable, dreary process of dying.'[30] The novel is firmly in the tradition of the Irish great house novel but it also brings that genre into the modern world, showing how the past is never dead and buried but always a ghostly inhabitant of the present. Charles's long-dead brother, Alexander, killed in the war, becomes a palpable presence in the house as Charles and Diarmid play complex games with toy soldiers and reality and memory become blurred in Charles's disordered mind. He reflects: 'So much debris ... Useless debris ... If only there was some way of disposing of the debris, leaving the mind neat and ordered, but more and more now the mess, the past, kept breaking through the barriers.'[31] The novel begins and ends with the local gardai going to arrest Charles for his paedophiliac designs on the boy.

The colonial themes of the novel are implied in the title, taken from a song by Brendan Behan which satirises the British imperial past and its ideologies, as in the third stanza:

Far away in dear old Cyprus, or in Kenya's dusty land,
We all bear the white man's burden in many a strange land.
As we look across our shoulder, in West Belfast the school bell rings,
And we sigh for dear old England, and the Captains and the Kings.
And we sigh for dear old England, and the Captains and the Kings.[32]

Janet McNeill's 1956 Belfast-set novel, *Tea at Four O-Clock*, also examines what Seamus Deane has called the 'plight of a lost Protestant gentility which looks back'.[33] McNeill (1907–1994) is almost an embodiment of three of the 'Four Nations', having been born in Dublin, educated in England and Scotland, returning to live in Belfast from the 1920s to the 1960s, and spending the last years of her life in Bristol. Beginning to write creatively in the mid-1950s, McNeill immediately established herself as an astute commentator on women's lives in the complex and shifting religious and political terrain of Northern Ireland at the time. The focus in *Tea at Four O'Clock* is on the family as a repressive and restrictive structure, and on women's complicity in upholding the very structures which incarcerate them. Again, the setting is a great house, but one built on the commercial gains of the linen industry rather than the seat of ancestral landed gentry. The novel charts the decline of the Percival family, focusing on Laura Percival, a spinster who has sacrificed her own happiness to care for her tyrannical older sister, who has just died. The possibility of freedom is now there for Laura, but she fails to take it, relapsing instead into the empty and rigid rituals of family life, as encapsulated in the novel's title, *Tea at Four O'Clock*. The freedom which Laura refuses also has a political dimension, as indicated by the name of the house, Marathon, situated 'between the Castlereagh Hills and the Belfast Lough' but recalling Byron's poem about Marathon in which the speaker 'dreamed that Greece might still be free'.[34] When the house is built, Aunt Augusta disapproves of the house's name, keeping 'a careful eye on her nephew for any deplorable Home Rule tendencies, and was relieved that she was able to detect none'.[35] As Laura sadly watches a train departing for Cork, carrying emigrants bound for the United States, she realises that she will never escape like them. She says, fatalistically, to her brother, George: '[Mildred's] dead ... but the poison is living in us now.'[36]

If the events of the 1960s in Scotland and Wales led to an increased nationalism and to some direct action and protest, in Northern Ireland some of the same drivers led to more catastrophic consequences. Northern Ireland had been partitioned by act of parliament in 1921 but in 1948 the Irish Free State officially became a Republic and in the following year Ulster's partitioned status became enshrined, controversially, in the Ireland Act. Then, in the late 1960s, the Northern Irish Troubles began, lasting until the Good Friday Agreement of 1998 and leading to the deaths of more than 3,500 people in total. The early seventies saw the worst death toll in the province. Clearly, nothing analogous to this came to pass in Wales, Scotland, or England, although some of the terrorist acts spread to English cities in the 1980s. The political comparison among the three 'internal colonies' in the period are invidious, showing up the weaknesses of Michael Hechter's theory, and yet the underlying connections and similarities are often perceived by the writers of the time, notably Menna Gallie, whose life placed her in a uniquely panoptic position.

In Scotland, Naomi Mitchison was already a well-established and acclaimed novelist by the post-war period. From a landed and scholarly family, Mitchison quickly established her reputation as a brilliant and daring historical novelist in the 1930s. Her novel *The Bull Calves* (1947) is typical of her command of the genre of the historical novel, and deals centrally with issues of Scottish identity relevant to the twentieth century, though the work is set in the eighteenth. However, like her contemporaries Kate Roberts and Doris Lessing, this period saw her experiment with new genres and modes of writing, including science fiction, fantasy, and writing for children. Rooted in Scotland and active in socialist politics there, by sheer accident while travelling she developed an extraordinary relationship with the Bakgatla people of Botswana, eventually having the title of 'Mmamarona' (mother) bestowed upon her. This African link affected her politics and writing, making her acutely aware of the Scottish contribution to British imperialism. As she put it in one of her autobiographical works, 'I was so filled with horror and guilt at the thought of what might have been done to my people here, by my people there.'[37] This is reflected in a curious 1975 story, entitled 'The Hill Modipe', in which Kenneth, a Scottish botanist, takes a plant-collecting trip into the interior of Bechuanaland with two gold-prospecting Boers. It is the early twentieth century and the Boers, Jan and Hendrik, treat the local people with contempt and are single-mindedly bent on making their fortunes through exploitation of the African land. Kenneth, meanwhile, is mild-mannered and bewitched by the beauty of the unfamiliar flora. The hill Modipe is regarded with awe and fear by the local people and Kenneth feels its hostility. Nevertheless, Jan and Hendrik charge in and proceed to desecrate the place. The story is full of analogies between Scotland and Africa, partly because Kenneth's grandfather has been a missionary there. As Kenneth sleeps and dreams of the Scottish Highlands he is miraculously transported to safety by a mysterious snake-like creature. Half-asleep, Kenneth mutters 'You'll know Loch Ness?'[38] When he wakes, he finds himself with friendly native people miles from the hill Modipe; the fate of his Boer companions remains uncertain, but the implication is that they have succumbed to the hill's malevolence, while Kenneth has been saved. The ending is open; Kenneth reassures himself: 'I am on a visit. A good visit. And it will work out fine.'[39] Arguably, this ending reflects Mitchison's own feelings about the Scottish participation in the colonial exploitation of Africa: like Kenneth, she wants the Scottish 'visit' to the colonies to have been a positive one – she seeks to redeem the past and reconcile 'her people there' with 'her people here'.

Mitchison's science fiction is also concerned with colonialism. In *Memoirs of a Spacewoman* (1962), for example, the telepathic protagonist, Mary, is a mother and a space explorer who comes across many different worlds and societies. One particular world is populated by butterflies and caterpillars, the latter oppressed and made to feel inferior by the former, in a clear metaphor for imperialism. Mitchison's venture into the new genre is also not uncharacteristic of the post-war period when science fiction and fantasy, erstwhile a male-dominated form was beginning to attract the pens of a range of supremely talented women writers, notably Ursula LeGuin in America and Doris Lessing in England, as explored elsewhere in this volume.[40]

Muriel Spark, like Naomi Mitchison born in Edinburgh, also had unexpected African connections and interests, which found their way into her fiction. During the Second World War Spark lived in Southern Rhodesia (now Zimbabwe) and her experiences there influenced some of the stories in *The Go-Away Bird and Other Stories* (1958) which deal with race relations and conflicts. In the title story, Daisy, an orphan, is brought up by her uncle Chahata Patterson on his tobacco farm in an unnamed African Colony. The story provides an acid analysis of race relations and divisions; Daisy is eventually murdered by Tuys, her uncle's Afrikaaner farm manager. Race is also addressed in 'The Black Madonna' in which a Catholic couple from Liverpool pray to a black Madonna for a child. They also befriend two lonely Jamaican men. Their prayers are answered but the baby turns out to be black, a fact which immediately shows their 'enlightened' attitudes to race to have been completely false. Some of these stories bear comparison with those of Elizabeth Taylor, discussed above, though Spark's style is more experimental and her authorial positioning more distant, colder. Nevertheless, Spark is also capable of some delicious social comedy à la Elizabeth Taylor, as she would prove a few years later, in *The Prime of Miss Jean Brodie* and, here, in a story such as 'You should have seen the mess'. In the latter, the first-person narrator, Lorna Merrifield, obsessed with propriety and cleanliness, is gleefully ironised through her non-sequiturs; Laura reflects: 'Mavis did not go away to have her baby, but would have it at home, in their double bed, as they did not have twin beds, although he was a doctor.'[41]

This deadpan irony is developed to brilliant effect in *The Prime of Miss Jean Brodie* (1961), which is still Spark's best known novel and one of the few of her works firmly set in Scotland and engaging directly with Scottish identity and mores. Set in Edinburgh during the 1930s, it revolves around the eponymous Miss Brodie, an eccentric schoolmistress who cultivates a privileged 'set' of girls in the Marcia Blaine Academy where she teaches. The novel is scathing in its satire of the hypocrisy of Scottish Presbyterianism as embodied in the ostensibly upright spinster Miss Brodie, who flouts the church's teachings on sexual behaviour, fails to teach her girls the school curriculum, and is a devoted follower of the Fascists in Italy and Germany. Though Miss Brodie is a striking individual, Spark's narrator makes the point that 'there were legions of her kind during the nineteen-thirties, women from the age of thirty and upward, who crowded their war-bereaved spinsterhood with voyages of discovery into new ideas and energetic practices in art or social welfare, education or religion ... Some assisted in the

Scottish Nationalist Movement; others, like Miss Brodie, called themselves Europeans and Edinburgh a European capital ...'[42] Miss Brodie is, finally, a manipulative and dangerous woman; Sandy Stranger, the girl in her set who betrays her, perceives that 'She thinks she ... is the God of Calvin, she sees the beginning and the end.'[43] Both inveterate storytellers, Jean Brodie and Sandy Stranger can be seen as versions of the author; the former thinks that she has, godlike, created her story from beginning to end but Sandy usurps her role and changes the story's conclusion. This self-referentiality, along with the disorientating prolepses and analepses that punctuate the text, are typical of the strange and discomfiting world of Spark's fiction. Yet it is a world connected at a slant to the real one, reflecting some of the political, religious, and social concerns of contemporary Britain.

Spark is a writer who is also discomfiting for some Scottish critics and literary historians, largely because she was for many years the most internationally renowned living Scottish writer and yet she did not invariably signal her Scottishness in her writing. Even in the twenty-first century, she remains for some a 'cosmopolitan misfit who does not ... have an insistent enough agenda of being Scottish', as Gerard Carruthers puts it.[44] In the later twentieth century the Scottish writer and critic, Christopher Whyte, encapsulated the pressure placed upon Scottish writers to focus on Scottish subjects as the enjoinder 'Don't imagine Ethiopia!'[45] Spark had, of course, boldly 'imagined Ethiopia' for decades, ignoring the prescriptions of nationalism and expressing her characteristic 'systemic doubleness' which, ironically enough, turns out to be characteristically Scottish.[46] This doubleness is perhaps best expressed in her autobiographical short story, 'The Gentile Jewesses', in which she explores her 'mixed inheritance' in a characteristically playful and unusually positive way.[47] The central figure in this story is the narrator's grandmother, a small, ugly, clever woman and former suffragette, who keeps a shop in Watford, and it is she who, in answer to the question, 'Are you a Gentile, Grandmother, or are you a Jewess?' gives the answer 'I am a gentile Jewess.'[48] Grandmother is also a formidable storyteller and the narrator clearly has in mind not only her cultural and religious affiliations when she affirms 'I was a Gentile Jewess like my Grandmother.'[49] When Grandmother dies she is 'buried as a Jewess since she died in my father's house [in Edinburgh] ... Simultaneously my great-aunts announced in the Watford papers that she fell asleep in Jesus.'[50] Here, systemic doubleness is embodied in the figure of Grandmother and perpetuated through the generations in a line of female inheritance which recalls not just Jewish custom but also the nature of literary genealogy for women writers who, as Woolf asserted, 'think back through' their 'mothers.'[51]

At a time when writers from Britain's erstwhile overseas colonies, such as the West Indies, were beginning to make their mark on English letters, then, we can see that women writers from the so-called 'internal empire' were also engaging with the decline of empire and its consequences, especially for women.[52] Women writers were also alert to the shifting political landscape of the Four Nations and the ways in which new opportunities were opening up for women outside the domestic sphere and the confines of the family. There is a strong element of satire or at the very least sharp social comedy in many women writers' engagement with family life and rituals in this period. While an elegiac note can be heard in the writing of many women, who express disquiet at the post-war transformation of urban and rural landscapes, others appear to welcome the new freedoms, not least sexual, promised by the loosening of traditional ties and bonds, and the new mobility which allowed some to travel and to adopt an increasingly international perspective. Above all, women writers of the 'internal empire' display a refreshing willingness to experiment with genre, perhaps mirroring the attempted reforging of national boundaries and gender identities in their reinvention of form, challenging imperial rhetoric with an imaginative, positive, and outward-looking creative prose.

Notes

1. Michael Hechter, *Internal Colonialism: The Celtic Fringe in British National Development, 1536–1966* (London: Routledge, 1975).
2. One of the most significant drivers in Wales was the public outrage over the building of the Tryweryn dam to provide water for the city of Liverpool. Despite universal opposition in Wales, the valley, including the village of Capel Celyn, was drowned. See R. S. Thomas's poem, 'Reservoirs', for a characteristic and poignant nationalist response: R. S. Thomas, *Selected Poems* (London: Penguin, 2003), p. 74.
3. Matthew Arnold, 'Dover Beach' in *Selected Poems of Matthew Arnold* [1867] (London: Macmillan, 1910), p. 165.
4. See Tom Nairn, *The Break-Up of Britain: Crisis and Neo-Nationalism*, 2nd expanded edition (London: Verso, 1981), and Neil Evans, 'Internal Colonialism? Colonization, Economic Development and Political Mobilization in Wales, Scotland and Ireland' in *Regions, Nations and European Integration: Remaking the Celtic Periphery* ed. by Graham Day and Gareth Rees (Cardiff: University of Wales Press, 1991), pp. 235 64.
5. Even earlier than Hechter, Ned Thomas in his seminal *The Welsh Extremist: Modern Welsh Politics, Literature and Society* (London: Gollancz, 1971) had argued for a postcolonial approach to Welsh writing; later examples include: Kirsti Bohata, *Postcolonialism Revisited* (Cardiff: University of Wales Press, 2004); Declan Kiberd, *Inventing Ireland: The Literature of the Modern Nation* (London: Jonathan Cape, 1995); *Scottish Literature and Postcolonial Literature: Comparative Texts and Critical Perspectives* ed. by Michael Gardiner, Graeme Macdonald, and Niall O'Gallagher, (Edinburgh: Edinburgh University Press, 2001).
6. Enoch Powell, speech given in Birmingham in April 1968, cited in Nairn, *The Break-Up of Britain*, p. 256.
7. Enoch Powell, 'Poem XXIV', *Dancer's End* (1951), cited in Nairn, *The Break-Up of Britain*, p. 258.
8. Evelyn Waugh's *Brideshead Revisited* (1945) may be said to have set the tone of English post-war, post-imperial disillusionment, captured also in the poignant

poems of Philip Larkin, such as 'MCMXIV' which, of course, harks back to the First World War.

9. Elizabeth Bowen, *The Heat of the Day* (London: Jonathan Cape, 1948), p. 258.
10. Bowen, *The Heat of the Day*, p. 109.
11. Bowen, *The Heat of the Day*, p. 291.
12. Elizabeth Taylor, 'The Devastating Boys' in *The Devastating Boys* [1972] (London: Virago, 1984), p. 26.
13. Taylor, 'The Devastating Boys', pp. 30–1.
14. Storm Jameson, Introduction, *A Summer Day and Other Stories* (Cardiff: Penmark Press, 1946), p. 14.
15. Bowen, *The Heat of the Day*, p. 156.
16. Kate Roberts, *Y Byw sy'n Cysgu* (*The Living Sleep*) (Denbigh: Gee, 1956).
17. Roberts, *Tegwch y bore* (*Fairness of Morning*) (Llandybïe: Christopher Davies, 1967).
18. Roberts, *Te yn y Grug* (*Tea in the Heather*) (Denbigh: Gee, 1959).
19. Roberts, *Te yn y Grug* (*Tea in the Heather*), p. 94. My translation.
20. Roberts, *Tegwch y Bore* (*Fairness of Morning*) (Llandybïe: Christopher Davies, 1967) p. 142. My translation.
21. Menna Gallie, *Strike for a Kingdom* [1959] (Dinas Powys: Honno, 2003), p. 56.
22. Gallie, *Strike for a Kingdom*, p. 87.
23. Gallie, *Strike for a Kingdom*, p. 138.
24. Gallie, *The Small Mine* [1962] (Dinas Powys: Honno, 2000), p. 3.
25. Gallie, *The Small Mine*, p. 28.
26. Claire Connolly and Angela John note Gallie's rejection of the label 'feminist' in their introduction to the Honno edition of her later novel, *You're Welcome to Ulster*, discussed above. They quote Gallie as saying 'I'm not much of an -ist except that I'm a socialist'. See C. Connolly and A. John, 'Introduction', *You're Welcome to Ulster* [1970] (Dinas Powys: Honno, 2010), p. xvii.
27. Saunders Lewis 'Tynged yr Iaith' (The Fate of the Language) translated from the Welsh by G. A. Williams in *Presenting Saunders Lewis* ed. by Alun R. Jones and Gwyn Thomas (Cardiff: University of Wales Press, 1973), pp. 127–41 (p. 127). Saunders Lewis was both one of the founders of Plaid Cymru in the 1920s and one of the most acclaimed Welsh poets and dramatists of the twentieth century. He was also a close friend of Kate Roberts.
28. Saunders Lewis, 'Tynged yr Iaith' in *Presenting Saunders Lewis*, p. 141.
29. Connolly and John, 'Introduction', *You're Welcome to Ulster*, p. xiii.
30. Jennifer Johnston, *The Captains and the Kings* [1972] (London: Coronet, 1979), p. 91.
31. Johnston, *The Captains and the Kings*, p. 103.
32. Brendan Behan, 'The Captains and the Kings', *Brendan Behan Sings Irish Folk Songs and Ballads* (Arran Records, 2008).
33. Seamus Deane, quoted in Janet Madden-Simpson, Introduction to Janet McNeill [1956] *Tea at Four O' Clock* (London: Virago, 1988), p. v.
34. McNeill, *Tea at Four*, p. 19.
35. McNeill, *Tea at Four*, p. 19.
36. McNeill, *Tea at Four*, p. 178.
37. Naomi Mitchison, *Return to the Fairy Hill* (London: Heinemann, 1966), pp. 111–12.
38. Mitchison, 'The Hill Modipe' in *Scottish Short Stories 1975* ed. by T. A. Dunn (London: Collins, 1975), p. 170.

39. Mitchison, 'The Hill Modipe', p. 175.
40. See, for example, Ursula K. Le Guin, *The Left Hand of Darkness* (New York: Ace Books, 1969) and Doris Lessing, *Memoirs of a Survivor* (London: Octagon, 1974).
41. Muriel Spark, 'You should have seen the mess', *The Go-Away Bird and Other Stories* [1958] (Harmondsworth: Penguin, 1963), p. 139.
42. Spark, *The Prime of Miss Jean Brodie* [1961] (London: Penguin, 2013), pp. 42–3.
43. Spark, *The Prime of Miss Jean Brodie*, p. 120.
44. Gerard Carruthers, '"Fully to Savour her Position": Muriel Spark and Scottish Identity', *Modern Fiction Studies*, 54: 3 (2008), 487–504, 488. Carruthers does not endorse this critical view.
45. Christopher Whyte, '"Don't imagine Ethiopia": Fiction and Poetics in Contemporary Scotland,' in *Nations and Relations* ed. by Tony Brown and Russell Stephens (Cardiff: New Welsh Review, 2000), pp. 56–70. Nevertheless, Whyte is hopeful that political devolution will help to avoid the necessity for such deadening prescription in future; as he puts it 'the setting-up of a Scottish parliament will at last allow Scottish literature to be literature first and foremost, rather than the expression of a nationalist movement.' Whyte, 'Masculinities in Contemporary Scottish Fiction', *Forum for Modern Language Studies*, 34: 2 (1998), 274–85, 284.
46. The term 'systemic doubleness' is Christopher Whyte's; see '"Don't imagine Ethiopia"', p. 62.
47. Spark herself referred to her 'mixed inheritance' but at the same time insisted that 'I am certainly a writer of Scottish formation and of course think of myself as such': see A. Bold, *Muriel Spark* (London: Methuen, 1986), p. 26. For the story 'The Gentile Jewesses', see Muriel Spark, *The Complete Short Stories* (London: Penguin, 2001), pp. 310–16.
48. Spark, 'The Gentile Jewesses', p. 312.
49. Spark, 'The Gentile Jewesses', p. 314.
50. Spark, 'The Gentile Jewesses', p. 316.
51. Virginia Woolf, *A Room of One's Own* (London: Hogarth, 1929), p. 114.
52. See for example: Phyllis S. Allfrey, *The Orchid House* (London: Constable, 1953), Sam Selvon, *The Lonely Londoners* (London: Wingate, 1956), and V. S. Naipaul, *The Mimic Men* (London: Andre Deutsch, 1967). Jean Rhys holds a particularly interesting position here in that she was a West Indian-born writer of Welsh and Scottish extraction, a fact which is addressed occasionally in her work. She even uses the Welsh word 'hiraeth' (longing, homesickness, looking back) in her autobiographical novel *Voyage in the Dark* [1934] (London: Penguin, 1969), p. 81.

11
The Transcultural Tryst in Migration, Exile and Diaspora

Sandra Courtman

> In another's country that is also your own, your person
> divides, and in following the forked path, you encounter
> yourself in a double movement ... once as stranger, and
> then as friend.[1]

Strictly speaking, the writers discussed below barely qualify for inclusion
in this volume of *The History of British Women's Writing*, since they were
neither born nor necessarily settled in the British Isles, but were from British
colonies and ex-colonies. Over time, they have been subsumed into our
shared literary histories, but their arrivals were subject to the paradoxes of
belonging and unbelonging that Homi Bhabha describes above. The very real
divisions between indigenous women writers and those of a different nation,
ethnicity, class, culture and linguistic tradition must be acknowledged, but as
this chapter will demonstrate, women writers born in faraway continents had
a transformative impact on the field of British literary studies. As we shall
see, the women discussed below resist being labelled as migrant, immigrant,
Diasporan or exiled; equally their work very often resists formal and genre
categorisation. Coming from Africa, India, China and the Caribbean, they
sought a space for creative development and an appropriate form to express
what often had gone unexpressed. They were also searching for a publisher
who would give their work a much wider audience. For many, their restless
journeys to and from Britain may have provided the stimulus to write, but
others were established authors anticipating contracts from British publishers
trawling for new subjects for a post-war readership.

The context for these non-British born women writers is multifaceted.
Each of them is part of a history involving economic migration flows, the
need to travel for educational, intellectual and creative opportunities in

© The Author(s) 2017
C. Hanson and S. Watkins, *The History of British Women's Writing, 1945–1975*,
History of British Women's Writing, DOI: 10.1057/978-1-137-47736-1_12

the metropole, a lack of publishing opportunities in the colonies, controversies surrounding their language choice for publication, the entrepreneurial imperative of the post imperial Diasporas and the nuanced and almost invisible practices of patriarchal gate-keeping. This disparate group were agents for change and are included here because of their importance to the period that this volume is mapping.

Introduction

Whilst the 1950s and 1960s are now recognised as periods of growth and opportunity for African and West Indian male authors, the situation was different for their female contemporaries, with women writers largely absent from an emerging black European canon. In the post-Second World War imperial centres of London and Paris, reputations were being built for future Nobel Prize winners and luminaries. For example, V. S. Naipaul came to Oxford University in 1950 and, nurtured by André Deutsch, began writing and publishing.[2] In Paris in 1952, Frantz Fanon published the influential *Peau Noire, Masques Blancs* (*Black Skin, White Masks*).[3] This kind of success was mocked at the time by Trinidadian author Sam Selvon. In his 1956 migration novel *The Lonely Londoners*, he parodies this turn of fate:

> Daniel was telling him how over in France all kinds of fellas writing books what turning out to be best-sellers. Taxi-driver, porter, road-sweeper – it didn't matter. One day you sweating in the factory and the next day all the newspapers have your name and photo, saying how you are the next literary giant.[4]

This essay explores some of the reasons why Selvon was able to make a joke of the fact that 'all kinds of fellas writing books ... [and becoming labelled as] the next literary giant' whilst their women contemporaries were struggling for patronage and recognition. There are, of course, exceptional women writing in exile who made it into the literary canon, the most notable of these being Doris Lessing (brought up in Southern Rhodesia) and Jean Rhys, the interwar, modernist writer who was born and brought up in Dominica. Doris Lessing arrived from colonial Southern Rhodesia via apartheid South Africa with her remarkable first novel *The Grass is Singing* (1950). Jean Rhys was thought to have died in obscurity until 1956 when the BBC found her living in Cornwall. She went on to regularly contribute short stories to *The London Magazine*, *The Times Literary Magazine* and *Art and Literature* throughout the 1960s. Rhys's postcolonial re-imagining of Charlotte Bronte's mad Creole first wife in *Jane Eyre* was finally published as *Wide Sargasso Sea* by André Deutsch in 1966.

There are many other 'women from elsewhere' who make contributions to British literature with novels, poems, short stories and autobiographies published in exile or Diaspora. These are crucial decades for these writers whose energies are absorbed by the challenge of a hegemonic double discourse of patriarchy and empire. Bhabha describes them as 'vernacular cosmopolitans' whose double vision enables them to translate between cultures in a way that transforms the understanding of the modern world. For them it is the only means by which they can negotiate their multilayered identities. Bhabha explains the genesis of their form of cosmopolitanism in this way: '[v]ernacular cosmopolitans are compelled to make a tryst with cultural translations as an act of survival. Their specific and local histories, often threatened and repressed, are inserted "between the lines" of dominant cultural practices'.[5]

This chapter will briefly trace some of the historical and political contexts for women from elsewhere publishing in Britain in the period 1945–1975. Throughout this period there were significant changes in the demographic flow of immigration from the British colonies, former colonies and the newly established post independent Commonwealth. This can be mainly attributed, amongst other push and pull factors, to changes in legislation which alternately enabled and restricted immigration. In the period immediately after 1948 and until the 1962 Immigration Act, by far the largest number of migrants was from the Anglophone West Indies. Many had served their mother country in two World Wars and they came in response to the call for labour to rebuild a bombed out Britain. After the Second World War, the literal and symbolic massacre arising from the partitioning of India and Pakistan in 1947 devastated and divided the South Asian subcontinent and its peoples. Those Indian writers with British passports could escape the violence of partitioning: Attia Hosain (1913–1998), for example, writes that in 1947 'We had a legal right to be British citizens, which I exercised'.[6] Anglophone West Indians also had British passports but this 'right' was withdrawn by 1962. Writers from the Caribbean and Africa were often perceived as working class 'poor immigrants' regardless of their educational or professional status back home. After this period, throughout the late 1960s and 1970s more people arrived from South Asia and Africa.

Single stories, multiple lives

There are significant differences between the reception of Indian and Chinese born women writers and those from the Caribbean and Africa. Far from being homogenised as ignorant natives, the former are seen as exotic beauties and negotiate the long-established stereotypes and fantasies associated with what we now term 'Orientalism'. Helen Kanitkar explains that Indian women writing in English might have to

> ... tread delicately in order to avoid mere fascination with the exoticisms of arranged marriage, fearsome mothers-in-law, the ghostly memories of *sati*, or the tensions of the joint family, and yet all these cannot be ignored, as they are part of the discourse of South Asian life.[7]

The publication in 1978 of Edward Said's seminal analysis of 'Orientalism', was apposite to the continued arrival of South Asian women writers who challenged the stereotypical images generated by centuries of European Orientalism. Multi-lingual Anita Desai (1937–) is an example of how Indian women writers complicate what Elleke Boehmer refers to as 'unitary or "one eyed" forms of consciousness'.[8]

Desai was born in Delhi in 1935 to a German mother and Bengali father and grew up speaking German, English and Hindi. She began her career in England and brought her work to London for publishing opportunities not available for writers in English in India. She published her first novel *Cry the Peacock* with Peter Owen in 1963 and became an award-winning and critically acclaimed writer of fiction and short stories.[9] Other Indian women writers published their work in the United States rather than Britain, hoping for a more hospitable reaction. Nayantara Sahgal published her memoir *Prison and Chocolate Cake* in New York. After a brief spell as a Professor at Girton College, Cambridge in England (1986–1987), Desai moved to America in 1987 and chose to settle there.[10]

Ranjana Ash explains that writers like Desai, Kamala Markandaya and Attia Hosain were educated, empowered and wealthy cosmopolitan travellers and therefore could not be treated as economic immigrants.[11] Hosain was born into a landed Muslim family and left Lucknow in 1946 when her husband was posted to England. She published her earliest fiction, *Phoenix Fled and Other Stories*, in London in 1953 and has written about language and its dichotomous role in the struggle for cultural sovereignty, explaining that '[i]n the struggle for freedom, English was both a weapon as well as the key to what I call the ideological arsenal'.[12] In 1961, she published *Sunlight on a Broken Column*, a novel narrated by a young woman who is growing up as India moves towards Independence. She is witness to the violent birth of a new nation: 'And in 1947 came the partition of the country, and the people of India and Pakistan celebrated Independence in the midst of bloody migrations from one to another'.[13] Laila is orphaned and lives in an extended Muslim taluqdari family whose support of British colonial rule historically allowed them privileges as land-owners. However, the family is in turmoil following the violence of Partition, when conflicting choices about where to live (Muslim Pakistan or Hindu dominated India) become personal and political. With various members of her family making different but equally difficult choices, Laila reflects on the cost of transition for her uncle Hamid, the man with 'such English ideas'.[14] In a retrospective narration, she is ambivalent about the journey Hamid has had to make from pro-British to reluctant participant in nationalist politics:

During the war Uncle Hamid had begun to listen to every news bulletin, read every paper he possibly could. The habit persisted. Through the years he passively allowed himself to be battered by the speeches and statements that poured from the legion of leaders and propagandists of every party as they bargained with the British and with each other, incited emotions and pleaded for peace, spoke for and to the people unscathed while blood flowed and hatred spawned. ... Death spared him the putrescent culmination, the violent orgasm of hate that followed independence. ... It was easy to be detached as I looked back; easier than when every thought and action has waited for the morrow.[15]

Given that Partition had effected a profound change in British imperial consciousness, this period saw several Asian novels published in England.[16] However, as illustrated through the characters in Hosain's *Sunlight*, the writers' nation/class/caste/linguistic affiliations were often complex. Ash claims that, for example, the work of Kamala Markandaya was considered too pro-British for Indian sensitivities.[17] Hugely popular at the time, arguably for their ability to cater to a taste for new Orientalism as the British Raj receded, many of these writers have fallen into obscurity.[18]

Chinese born women writers with an international audience are rare in this period but John Gittings has argued for the importance of the physician and author Han Suyin on the grounds that 'Half-Chinese, but striving to be whole Chinese, she was as full of contradictions as her motherland. When the epic of modern China is re-examined she and her works will provide important and readable evidence'.[19] Han Suyin (Elizabeth Comber) was born Elizabeth Kuanghu Chow in 1917 in the Henan province of China of a Chinese father and a Flemish mother. Writing her obituary in 2012, Gittings suggests that: 'The ambiguities of her identity, as the daughter of a Chinese engineer and his Belgian wife, were always close to the surface. Her writings offered more than one version of herself'.[20] Speaking both Chinese and French, living and working in several countries and writing in English, her most famous book is the autobiographical novel *A Many-Splendoured Thing* published in London by Jonathan Cape in 1952. The protagonist, who shares the author's name Han Suyin, has an affair with a married, English correspondent, Mark Elliot, who is fascinated by her Eurasian identity: 'The multiple you – I never know which you it is going to be next time I see you'.[21] It may be alluring but her conflicted identity has to be constantly negotiated:

It is rather frightening to be so many different people, with so many dissimilar and equally compelling emotions, affections, ideas, *élans*, apprehensions, aware of so many delicate differences in restraint, nuances of phraseology in the enunciation of a similar mood in three different languages, always so aware of shades of meaning that life becomes occasionally unbearable. ... I am usually torn between at least two worlds, involving different ways of existence.[22]

This interracial, extramarital love story with its historical and political backdrop was so compelling that it became the 1955 award winning film

'Love is a Many Splendored Thing'.[23] In her work Han Suyin explores the theme of cultural schizophrenia as a colonial legacy as did many of her contemporaries from India, Africa and the Caribbean. At the plenary lecture for a symposium of papers on Asian literature in English, she said

> We have to accept that we are divided, schizophrenic – but we are working schizophrenics ... and functioning precisely because of this dichotomy, which is a reflection of the world today. We live with half ourselves immersed in the past and other half striving toward the future.[24]

This comment resonates powerfully with Bhabha's assertion that these writers 'have to make a tryst with cultural translations as an act of survival'.[25]

Her work satisfies an emerging trend in the West to understand both its imperial connections and political alternatives. *A Many Splendoured Thing* is set in British Hong Kong and in its neighbouring Communist China. This taste for the exotic proves to be a critical factor in the publication of work by writers from Britain's colonies and ex-colonies. In the UK, the end to official paper rationing in June 1953 and a rapid turnover in books in general fuelled a production drive for publishers which continued until the mid 1960s. This included new ventures designed to cater to a niche domestic market which wanted to read about the subjects of former empires and a new export market focused on the provision of relevant educational material for former colonies.

In the case of African women writers, the publishing industry behaved consistently in diminishing or ignoring their contributions. In the early part of the period, the Heinemann Educational African Writers Series (AWS) nurtured male writers like Chinua Achebe and Ngũgĩ wa Thiong'o and made their work accessible, to Africa in the first instance and by 1969 to British bookshops.[26] Achebe's *Things Fall Apart* opened the series in 1962 and he continued as editor until 1972, exerting his influence beyond that point. The African Writers Series and its Caribbean equivalent, the Longman Caribbean Series, were entrepreneurial neo-colonial missions which aimed to address the Eurocentric bias in University literature teaching. The AWS claimed that it 'published work by all the major authors of this period, together with classic earlier texts and new writing, giving the series a unique importance in African cultural history'.[27] In its early years, James Currey claims that 'It was a series by Africans for Africa ... [with] about eighty percent of its sales ... in Africa'.[28] There was concern that having a separate African series would situate anti-colonial revisionist fiction in a neo-colonial publishing context. However, the series provided affordable paperbacks for the new postcolonial curricula and in so doing established a canon of African classics.

The whole series, which lasted until 2000, is male-dominated and in the first twenty years even work labelled as 'new writing' largely excluded women authors. Flora Nwapa, a student at Edinburgh University in 1958, was the only African woman writer to be published in the series with her first novel, *Efuru* (1966). In the revisionary period, writers were judged according to their supposed essentialism – the ability to 'fit' into an Africanist nationalism which initially was black and male (as represented by Achebe). This rubric discriminated against white African writers (and, at the time, equally against white West Indian writers in the Caribbean). So Doris Lessing's 1950s classic, *The Grass is Singing* had to wait until 1973 to be considered part of the AWS canon. It took until 1980 for the series to reprint Buchi Emecheta's *The Joys of Motherhood* which had been first published by Allison and Busby in 1979.[29] So whilst the series challenged the Eurocentric account of Africa, it compounded the gender bias and patriarchal gate-keeping that had always existed. Post the 1980s and under the growing influence of feminist scholarship, series editors would have to acknowledge this bias. Submissions editor Becky Clarke sought to redress the imbalance by:

> ... giving voice to an increasing number of women writers who were marginalized at the inception of the series ... The AWS has a flowering of female writing which started later than that of their male counterparts because of the predominantly patriarchal nature of African cultures and societies.[30]

The marginalisation of women writers in the early part of the period would have far reaching effects for many of them.

The BBC fraternity around the Caribbean Voices programmes was similarly effective as a 'literary club' which encouraged a group of new West Indian writers and increased opportunities for contact with the London literary intelligentsia and with publishers. But like the African Writers Series 'the club' was typically male-oriented, revolving around 'the separate anxieties of young or youngish *men*'.[31] The position of editor was held by a succession of men, in spite of the fact that the service had evolved as a direct result of Una Marson's pioneering war-time broadcasts to the Caribbean. A number of women (some now largely forgotten) contributed work to *Caribbean Voices*: Louise Bennett, Gloria Escoffery, Barbara Ferland, Vivette Hendriks, Constance Hollar, Mary Lockett, Una Marson, Stella Mead, Daisy Myrie, Dorothy Phillips.[32] Gloria Escoffery and Pauline Henriques broadcast in London, but the majority of women contributors were isolated, sending in work through Caribbean-based agents, and they had little experience of being part of a 'fellowship' of writers. In London, women also held a different position in the social and informal networks of publishers and agents. The pioneering writer Beryl Gilroy (1924–2001) came to further her education at London University from British Guiana in 1953 but struggled to get access to the publishing networks revolving around a 'pub culture' that benefitted her male contempories. However, Anne Walmsley was appointed as Longman's first Caribbean editor in 1966 and became Beryl Gilroy's first educational publisher. She was also a committed member of the Caribbean Artists Movement and remembers how certain networks excluded her:

> [They met] at parties, night-clubs and pubs. It was a male thing. Even in publishing the men would go off to the pub and if I went I didn't feel welcome. I was intruding in their world. ... Also the network of *Caribbean Voices* was where a lot of people met.[33]

Partly because of this social exclusion, literary success has been hard-won for writers like Buchi Emecheta who was born in Lagos, Nigeria in 1944. By the 1960s, Emecheta was living in London as a single mother of five and this gave her the material for her first novel *In the Ditch* (1972). Her autobiography, *Head Above Water* (1986), suggests it was something of a miracle that she was able to write, given her lack of qualifications, her poverty, her struggle with British racism and African patriarchy, multiple pregnancies and sole responsibility for her small children. In this scene depicting her abusive marriage in *Second Class Citizen* (1974), Adah's husband attempts to destroy her aspirations to become a writer:

> Now Francis had that sickly smile on his face, and Adah guessed that he was smug with some heroic deed. He picked up the last sheet, among the crumpled papers she saw the orange cover of one of the exercise books in which she had written her story. Then reality crashed into her mind. Francis was burning her story; he had burned it all. The story that she was basing her dream of her becoming a writer upon.[34]

Francis reasons that his 'family would never be happy if a wife of mine was permitted to write a book like that'. A violent row prompts a neighbour to call the police fearing for Adah's life and Francis is ordered to 'relinquish a box of clothes for the children'. On the street 'Adah walked to freedom, with nothing but four babies, her new job and a box of rags. Not to worry, she had not sustained many injuries apart from a broken finger and swollen lips'.[35] Despite the parallels between Adah's experience and her own, Emecheta's aspirations were realised when she finally had her work serialised in the *New Statesman*.

Emecheta found small independent publishers Barrie and Jenkins for *In the Ditch* and Allison and Busby for *Second Class Citizen*. This was part of a trend in publishing which, as Low writes, was an important if niche growth area:

> What is significant about this earlier period is the significant part that smaller and medium-sized independent publishers like Faber, André Deutsch, Michael Joseph, Martin Secker, Peter Owen and Hutchinson played in the dissemination of writers from, to use Lehmann's term, the 'Queen's Commonwealth'.[36]

André Deutsch was one of the publishers who catered for this niche market with Diana Athill working with him as one of the most influential commissioning editors of postcolonial fiction. During this period she nurtured the notoriously difficult writers Jean Rhys and V. S. Naipaul.[37] She explains that it was not just the domestic market that was expanding and that there was a commercial motivation for pursuing a new trade in African writers for Africa. There was a feeling that 'the market out there was certainly going to expand, however slowly … It would prove, in the long run, to be good business'.[38] Her editorship proved critical for the career of Jean Rhys. Margaret Busby (of Allison and Busby) and Anne Walmsley of Longman were equally important in bringing a female perspective to postcolonial ventures in the publishing industry.

Emecheta may have been one of the first African women writers to be published in England (she was awarded the OBE in 2005) but she is still bemused by attempts to 'contain' her:

> By now, I have become an established writer. *The Guardian* described me some time ago as a first-generation immigrant writing in London. And in America they say I am a Nigerian writer living in London. Nigerian papers still call me a Nigerian writer. I do not dispute all these categorizations, I do not even mind being called an African writer, even though many of my colleagues reject this because they claim it has a patronising ring. Well, maybe it has. All I know is that I am doing my work the best way I know how. But when people start disputing whether to regard me as an English writer writing about Africa, or to regard me as an African writing in English, I then know it is time to go home, or, if this is not possible, it is time to pay a long visit to Africa. Maybe my ideas are becoming too Europeanised.[39]

This sense of losing touch with Mother Africa, the Caribbean, India or China is part of the dichotomy of being a writer in exile. Writers struggle to resolve the separation anxiety which is elemental to the 'tryst' they make as cultural translators. Real creative development means being in a critical dialogue with a peer group which shares the same cultural shorthand. The group survives creatively, economically and professionally in a liminal space and few members manage a permanent residence in their birthplaces. They may fly back and forth in order to reconnect with the culture of their birth whilst knowing it is becoming increasingly estranged. Emecheta has exploited what Savory Fido has termed 'the resource of exile within the English-speaking, multi-national world'. This Western resource is 'often emotionally and physically cold, racist, excluding' but still nevertheless provides the condition for writing and international audiences for their work.[40]

West Indians reverse their colonisation

The 1950s saw large-scale migration from the West Indies. There had been black settlers in Britain since the Roman invasion and these included freed slaves, treasured servants, trades people, entertainers, and the merchant seamen of the seventeenth century. However, it is the sheer number of highly visible arrivals after the Second World War that disturbs British consciousness. In spite of their experience of racial discrimination during the War, patriotic service men and women went home to a quieter lifestyle and when Churchill visited the West Indies and encouraged former recruits to return to Britain, many did so willingly. They were persuaded to leave, as in the War years, by newspapers like *The Jamaica Gleaner*, this time to fill labour shortages. Migrants arrived to find a bombed out metropolis and an exhausted people, still subject to rationing and suffering from enormous losses in their male workforce. Britain needed to rebuild its cities but there was a labour deficit which is apparent in Ministry of Labour statements that, in 1956, job vacancies were running at 934,111, and that by 1960 there were still 848,542 unfilled jobs.[41] Thus began a systematic recruitment drive and the escalation of West Indian migration.

By 1961, amidst growing rumours of impending legislative restrictions, there were 48,850 arrivals.[42] There was a mass media response which imagines Britain being 'swamped' by black, initially male, West Indians. Anxieties were gendered and, by 1956, had shifted to questions about the morality of black women and the likelihood of their becoming prostitutes.[43] Mass migration from the West Indies forced Britain to confront its amnesiac historical relationship with its empire and contributed to the struggle for a new national identity after the Second World War. As a moment in history, this constituted a crisis in consciousness for British culture. Colonial subjects across the globe demanded political, intellectual, psychological and economic independence and Britain simply could no longer afford, financially or ideologically, either to resist these demands or maintain its colonies. As we have seen, a first generation of Caribbean male writers made a name for themselves 'in exile' usually in London or, in the case of the French Caribbean, Paris. The ability to profit from a self-constructed position of exile does not operate equally for men and women writers, however. Like their African counterparts, women from the West Indies who sought publication in the so-termed 'Windrush era' found it much more difficult to establish themselves as writers in a metropolitan patriarchal space.[44]

Some women would go on to produce important writing but in forms that would often struggle to be valued by a metropolitan literary audience. For example, the gifted Guyanese teacher, Beryl Gilroy, came over to study at the University of London in 1951. She successfully fought the education authority's refusal to employ her and went on to become the first black head teacher in London.[45] Having got there, she was appalled by the racist teaching materials she found in the cupboards of her multicultural school. She set to producing a series of *Blue Water Readers* in 1961 and *Green and Gold Readers* in 1967. Peter Fraser describes her as 'one of Britain's most significant post-war Caribbean migrants'.[46] Gilroy was a teacher, children's writer, counselling ethno-psychologist, autobiographer, novelist and poet. In the years when she was unable to get employment as a teacher, she worked in a series of low-paid jobs including a skilled performance as a ladies maid which gave her 'A good education in class language, class habits and in class behaviour and how they relate'.[47] Elsewhere I have written in more detail about her work and why she has received very little serious critical attention despite her considerable achievements.[48] She and her work were always an anomaly and often ahead of their time. She refused to conform to any political agendas (feminist, nationalist) and, in terms of form and content, her work consistently fell outside the expectations for West Indian literature.

When she presented publishers with her Guyanese reminiscences *Sunlight on Sweet Water*, they were misunderstood. She submitted the manuscript 'everywhere and nobody wanted it'. British publishers responded by asking her to fictionalise the account of her village life. In order to make it 'fit in with their list' it should be a novel or at least resemble the picaresque style of Sam Selvon's *The Lonely Londoners*.[49] She refused and it waited thirty years to be published by Peepal Tree.[50] In writing this book, which she said was important for her children growing up in the British Diaspora, she continued a strong African Caribbean oral tradition which had kept the rituals and memories of enslaved people alive for future generations. With chapter titles like 'Ochro – the Village Crier' and 'Mama Darlin' – Village Midwife', publishers failed to recognise the importance of her contribution to a history that had been by necessity held safe in an oral tradition. At the time, in choosing to turn the oral into the scribal she was, like Louise Bennett, unlikely to be taken seriously as a writer.

It was not just the issue of content that determined whether work was valued and understood. Language for Caribbean writers (as in Africa and Asia) became a political choice and issued a statement about whether they were writing for British literati or their own people who had been educationally disenfranchised by colonialism. During the 1960s, Louise Bennett, 'Miss Lou', chose to write in the Creole tongue of her fellow Jamaicans and her work was broadcast on the BBC and in Jamaica to a largely illiterate population. Louise Bennett Coverley (Jamaica 1919–2006), folklorist, poet and educator, is now regarded as a pioneering writer of 'nation language'. She was linguistically inventive and wonderfully satirical about the West Indian migration imperative. However, her choice to write in Jamaican Patois would mean that at the time she would be dismissed as a comic performer rather than a poet. She wrote the now famous poem 'Colonization in Reverse' and not only parodied the effects of mass migration for the British but also mocked the aspirations of numerous migrants.

Me say Jane will never fine work
At de rate how she look,
For all day she stay pon Aunt Fan couch
An read love-story book.[51]

Bennett was inventing a new scribal language out of an oral tradition but, at the time, critics separated language into a standard or Creole form of English. Kenneth Ramchand explains how these writers' choices actually represented a development towards a richer and more nuanced language continuum:

> In the twentieth century, we have to give up the notion of separate languages (Creole English and Standard English) and we have to envision a scale ... The emergent levels of dialect can be ranged on a continuous scale from Standard English and residual hard-core Creole or Black English. At opposite ends we seem to have two different languages but they move towards each other by mutually intelligible means.[52]

Bennett is now recognised as a ground-breaking poet and a leader in the movement to Creolise the canon.[53] Like other early pioneers, Gilroy, Una Marson and Erna Brodber, she was recording stories, opinions and language that were part of an oral tradition of creative expression which would otherwise have been lost. In Paula Burnett's The *Penguin Book of Caribbean Verse in English*, Bennett's work is grouped under the oral tradition of poems, calypsos and anonymous work songs. Una Marson, who had worked with Bennett on a play 'London Calling'(1938), is in the same collection. She was a political activist, poet, dramatist and was editor and compere of the BBC's programme 'Calling the West Indies' during the Second World War years from 1941–45.[54] In this comprehensive collection of poetry, Marson's Creole poem 'Kinky Hair Blues' is collected under 'The Literary Tradition'.[55] This separation of work into the 'literary' and 'oral' is, however, an artificial one, which misses the Creolisation of both forms to produce something new.

Choice of form and content was critical to women's success as writers and, arguably, novels and short fiction about an immigrant's life in England were the most likely to gain the attention of British critics and publishers. My research has discovered very few publications by West Indian women focusing more specifically on their migration and arrival experience during the post-Windrush era. Jamaican Joyce Gladwell's 1969 autobiography, *Brown Face, Big Master*, which depicts, amongst other things, the racism attending her inter-racial marriage is a rare exception.[56] Even when women write about the migration experience, they find it difficult because of a number of factors including patriarchal gate-keeping. Beryl Gilroy writes that her migration novel *In Praise of Love and Children* was 'written in 1959' but lost until 1994.[57] It was rejected by several publishers in the 1960s and Gilroy suggests that *In Praise* 'is the most misunderstood book of mine'.[58]

Misunderstood and under-nourished by fresh critical insights, Gilroy's entry in the *Bloomsbury Guide to Women's Literature* states: 'There has been little criticism of her writing to date'.[59]

Similarly neglected is the novel *The Hills of Hebron* by Cuban-born Sylvia Wynter (1928–) published in London in 1962.[60] *The Hills of Hebron* remains Wynter's only published attempt to fill a void in women's fiction at that time. Wynter lived in London with writer Jan Carew and the impact of this relationship appeared to affect her ambitions as a novelist.[61] His influence may have been a mixed blessing for a West Indian woman novelist in the early 1960s who was trying to find a voice in a male arena. Wynter is best-known as a dramatist and is highly regarded as a postcolonial critic but her achievement as a novelist is often overlooked.[62]

The Hills of Hebron was one of the few literary works by a West Indian woman to receive the critical attention of the influential Kenneth Ramchand, who, however, criticised Wynter's novel for being 'an overloaded work by a West Indian intellectual anxious to touch upon as many themes as possible'.[63] Paul Gilroy has since described 'a common degree of discomfort with the novel and a shared anxiety with its utility as a resource' as a revisionary history of enslaved and post-slave societies'.[64] However, it must be recognised that the West Indian novel had to develop from a European canonical apprenticeship that had voided its history, language and culture. I would argue that *The Hills of Hebron* is the first serious attempt by a West Indian woman to do what Toni Morrison later achieved with *Beloved*, that is, to 'get outside of most of the formal constricts of the novel'.[65] By means of temporal disruptions, Wynter makes connections between strands of history, colonial ruptures of identity, and the relationship of these to patriarchy. We might read this temporal fragmentation quite differently in the light of literary work which has emerged since from African, Caribbean and African-American women. However, Wyntner felt that she should have gone further with her formal invention, writing that:

> I failed with it because I wasn't bold enough to have broken away from the format of the realist novel. The magic realism of say Gabriel Garcia Marquez in Latin America – that's what I should have done with the novel; but at that time, of course, novels like that hadn't been written, so I didn't have it as a model, and I myself was not inventive enough to create such a model.[66]

The situation for white West Indian women writers was equally difficult but for different reasons. The plantocratic Lucille Iremonger was born in 1915 in Jamaica into a family with several generations of French and Scottish Creoles and died in England in 1989. Her autobiography, *Yes My Darling Daughter*, was published in London by Secker and Warburg in 1964, and was favourably reviewed by the *Times Literary Supplement*. By the early 1960s, she had married a politician who was the cousin of Anthony Eden and she had a body of work including historical biographies, autobiographies, children's books and novels. *Yes My Darling Daughter* explores the complex interplay between her own life story growing up in colonial Jamaica and larger family histories, including that of her French aristocratic ancestors who escaped the revolutionary guillotine by travelling to their plantations in Haiti. She writes lucidly and knowledgably about Caribbean history but her work was, and still is, overlooked because it provided an alternative view to that of an Africanist revisionary project.[67] Problematic in terms of her race, privilege and politics, as an object of critical scrutiny she has been avoided. Hence this illuminating material remains out of print and unread. Repeatedly we find that women's work is excluded because it does not meet expectations in relation to form, gender, race and/or class or is buried under the inexplicable criterion of being 'dated'.[68]

Conclusion

This essay has suggested some of the complexities that have rendered the work of many women writers of this period little known. Their careers might have followed a different trajectory had they encountered a degree of openness to multiple forms, stories, perspectives and networks. We have seen that women writers from the Caribbean, Africa and Asia publishing in Britain are often working from a cultural perspective that is alien to the European literary education they received. They may have lacked encouragement and certainly they would find few or no female role models; they may have been struggling to write without any formal or aesthetic paradigms at their disposal; they may have been outsiders in terms of revisionary political agendas. They encounter patriarchal gate-keeping combined with a hostile critical and publishing context in Britain which makes it difficult to fulfil their potential. As colonial and ex-colonial writers, they are implicated in a history of collective trauma resulting from cultural domination and encounter further trauma through metropolitan racism and sexism. The women discussed here were often courageous in their battles to write in spite of all these constraints and were important agents in shaping an emerging post-War British intellectual and cultural scene. They not only produced their own ground-breaking work but inspired a second generation of British-African, British-Caribbean and British-Asian children who went on to win many of the glittering prizes of the late twentieth century.

Notes

1. Homi Bhabha, 'The Vernacular Cosmopolitan' in *Voices of the Crossing* ed. by Ferdinand Dennis and Naseem Khan (London: Serpents Tail, 2000), pp. 133–43 (p. 142).

2. Born in Trinidad, V. S. Naipaul was awarded the Nobel Prize for Literature in 2001. He began his studies at Oxford University in 1950 and his first novel *The Mystic Masseur* was published by André Deutsch in 1957.
3. Frantz Fanon's seminal work on racial psychopathology, *Black Skin, White Masks* was first published in English in 1967 but was originally published as *Peau Noire, Masques Blancs* in 1952 in Paris by Editions de Seuil.
4. Samuel Selvon, *The Lonely Londoners* [1956] (Harlow Essex: Longman Caribbean Writers Series, 1985), p. 142.
5. Bhabha, 'The Vernacular Cosmopolitan', p. 139.
6. Attia Hosain, 'Deep Roots, New Language' in *Voices of the Crossing*, pp. 19–29 (p. 22).
7. Helen Kanitkar, '"Heaven Lies beneath her Feet?" Mother Figures in Selected Indo-Anglian Novels', in *Motherlands: Black Women's Writing from Africa, the Caribbean and South Asia* ed. by Susheila Nasta (London: The Women's Press, 1991), pp. 175–99 (p. 175).
8. Elleke Boehmer, 'Stories of Women and Mothers: Gender and Nationalism in the Early Fiction of Flora Nwapa', *Motherlands: Black Women's Writing from Africa, the Caribbean and South Asia*, pp. 3–24 (p. 7).
9. Desai's early publications in England include: Anita Desai, *Voices in the City, etc.* (London: Peter Owen, 1965); *Fire on the Mountain* (London: Heinemann, 1977); *The Peacock Garden* (London: Heinemann, 1979).
10. Nayantara Sahgal published *The Day in Shadow* with W. W. Norton in London in 1972, otherwise she published her work in the US. *Prison and Chocolate Cake,* her memoir, was published in 1954 by Alfred A Knopf in New York.
11. Sandra Courtman, Interview with Ranjana Ash, London, 1 June 1995.
12. Hosain, 'Deep Roots, New Language', p. 21.
13. Hosain, *Sunlight on a Broken Column* [1961] (London: Virago, 1988), p. 283. For a discussion of the political and social context of this novel and 'the profoundly gendered ways in which nationalism formulates itself,' see A. D. Needham 'Multiple forms of (National) Belonging: Attia Hosain's *Sunlight on a Broken Column*', *Modern Fiction Studies*, 39:1(1993), 93–111.
14. Hosain, *Sunlight on a Broken Column*, p. 15.
15. Hosain, *Sunlight on a Broken Column*, p. 283.
16. Sandra Courtman, Interview with Ranjana Ash, London, 1 January 1995.
17. Kamala Markandaya's early publications in England include: *Nectar in a Sieve* (London: Putnam, 1954); *Some Inner Fury* (London: Putnam, 1955); *A Handful of Rice* (London: Hamish Hamilton, 1966); *The Nowhere Man* (London: Allan Lane, 1973).
18. Courtman, Interview with Ranjana Ash, 1 June 1995.
19. John Gittins, 'Han Suyin Obituary', *Guardian*, 4 November 2012, <http://www.theguardian.com/books/2012/nov/04/han-suyin> [accessed 26 January 2015]
20. Gittins, 'Han Suyin Obituary'.
21. Han Suyin, *A Many-Splendoured Thing* [1952] (London: The Reprint Society,1954), p. 121.
22. Suyin, *A Many-Splendoured Thing*, p. 121.
23. The film *Love is a Many Splendored Thing* starred Jennifer Jones and William Holden and was set in Hong Kong (and partly filmed there) in 1949–50. The book was based on the author's love affair with *Times* correspondent Ian Morrison.
24. Han Suyin, 'Plenary Lecture' in *Asian Voices in English* ed. by Mimi Chan and Roy Harris (Hong Kong: Hong Kong University Press, 1991), pp. 14–21 (p. 21).

25. Bhabha, 'The Vernacular Cosmopolitan', p. 139.
26. Gail Low 'In Pursuit of Publishing: Heinemann's African Writers Series', *Wasafiri*, 37(2002), 31–35, 34.
27. Chadwyck Healey Literature Collections, 'About the African Writers Series', <http://collections.chadwyck.co.uk/marketing/products/about_ilc.jsp?collection=aws> [accessed 30 January 2015]
28. Cited in Low, 'In Pursuit of Publishing', p. 34.
29. As well as these and *The Joys of Motherhood* (1979) Buchi Emecheta's publications include *The Bride Price* (London: Allison and Busby, 1976); *The Slave Girl* (London: Allison and Busby, 1977).
30. Becky Clarke, 'The African Writers Series: Celebrating Forty Years of Publishing Distinction', *Research in African Literatures*, 34:2 (2003), 163–74, 169.
31. Anne Walmsley, *The Caribbean Artists Movement, 1966-1972: A Literary and Cultural History* (London: New Beacon, 1992), pp. 11–12.
32. See *Caribbean Voices Volume I: Dreams and Visions* ed. by John Figueroa (London: Evans Brothers, 1966) and *Caribbean Voices Volume 2: The Blue Horizons* ed. by John Figueroa (London: Evans Brothers, 1970).
33. Sandra Courtman, Interview with Anne Walmsley, London, 14 August 1995.
34. Buchi Emecheta, *Second Class Citizen* (London: Allison and Busby, 1974), p. 181.
35. Emecheta, *Second Class Citizen*, p. 181.
36. Low, 'In Pursuit of Publishing', p. 31.
37. See David Plante, *Difficult Women A Memoir of Three: Jean Rhys, Sonia Orwell and Germaine Greer* (London: Victor Gollancz, 1983) and Diana Athill, *Life Class: Selected Memoirs of Diana Athill* (London: Granta Books, 2010).
38. Athill, *Life Class*, p. 425.
39. Buchi Emecheta, 'A Nigerian Writer Living in London', *Kunapipi*, 4:1(1982), article 11, 114–23, 122.
40. Elaine S. Fido, 'Mother/lands: Self and Separation in the Work of Buchi Emecheta, Bessie Head and Jean Rhys', in *Motherlands* ed. by Nasta, pp. 330–50, (p. 335).
41. Ministry of Labour figures for job vacancies cited in Open University, 'Racism, Employment and the Trade Unions: Migration', *Racism in the Workplace and Community* (Milton Keynes: The Open University Press, 1984), section 9, table 9.2, p. 2.
42. Ron Ramdin, *Reimaging Britain: 500 years of Black and Asian History* (London: Pluto Press, 1999), p. 167.
43. See the *Picture Post* article entitled: 'Thirty Thousand Colour Problems' which discusses the supposed fate of young women arriving in Southampton on 28 May 1956 and disembarking from the SS Irpinia. H. Marchant 'Thirty Thousand Colour Problems', *Picture Post*, 9 June 1956, 38.
44. This term refers to the ex-troop carrier, the MV Empire Windrush, which arrived in Tilbury Docks on 22nd June 1948 and now exists in the national imagination as a symbol of a migrant generation's contributions to the making of a multicultural Britain. The Windrush's summary of British and Alien Passengers lists the number of men, women, and children who are British citizens from the West Indies, alien refugees displaced during the War, stowaways, and members of the forces and crew. There were 941 adult passengers including 257 women.
45. See Sandra Courtman, 'Windrush Women and the Fiction of Beryl Gilroy and Andrea Levy', in Special Issue on Andrea Levy of *ENTERTEXT* ed. Wendy Knepper: an interdisciplinary humanities e-journal, issue 9(2012): 84–105, <http://www.brunel.ac.uk/cbass/arts-humanities/research/entertext/issues/entertext-9>

46. Peter Fraser, 'Obituary for Beryl Gilroy 1924–2001', *Guardian*, 18 April 2001.

47. Sandra Courtman, Interview with Beryl Gilroy, London, 12 June 1995.

48. Sandra Courtman, '"Lost Years": The Occlusion of West Indian Women Writers in the Early Canon of Black British Writing', in *Diasporic Literature and Theory, Where Now?* ed. by Mark Shackleton (Cambridge: Cambridge Scholars Press, 2009), pp. 57–86; Courtman, 'Not Good Enough or Not Man Enough? Beryl Gilroy as the Anomaly in the Evolving Black British Canon' in *A Black British Canon?* ed. by Gail Low and Marion Wynne-Davies (Macmillan Palgrave, 2006), pp. 50–74.

49. Courtman, Interview with Beryl Gilroy, London, 12 June 1995.

50. Beryl Gilroy, *Sunlight on Sweet Water* (Leeds, Peepal Tree, 1994).

51. Louise Bennett, 'Colonization in Reverse', was first published in Louise Bennett, *Jamaica Labrish* (Kingston, Jamaica: Sangsters 1966). *The Penguin Book of Caribbean Verse* ed. by Paula Burnett (London: Penguin, 1986), p. 32.

52. Kenneth Ramchand, *The West Indian Novel and its Background* (2nd edn, Kingston, Jamaica: Ian Randle, 2004), pp. 68–9.

53. 'Although Bennett had published *Dialect Verse* in 1942, it was not until 1967, when Oxford trained critic Mervyn Morris wrote his persuasive essay "On Reading Louise Bennett, Seriously", that attitudes toward the vernacular started to change', D. Jarrett-Macauley, *The Life of Una Marson 1905–65* (Manchester: Manchester University Press, 1998), p. 189. See M. Morris 'On Reading Louise Bennett, Seriously', *Jamaica Journal*, 1(1967), 67–74.

54. Jarrett-Macauley, pp. 144–55. See also British Film Institute, 'West Indies Calling (1944)', YouTube, <https://www.youtube.com/watch?v=ViGwxJlol70> [accessed 5 March 2015] This film, made during the Second World War by the Ministry of Information, shows a group of West Indians, led by Una Marson and Learie Constantine, assemble at Broadcasting House in London. They describe the BBC radio series, 'Calling the West Indies', and speak about how people from the Caribbean are supporting the War effort. Constantine speaks about factory workers, and introduces some war-workers, including Ulric Cross, a bomber navigator from Trinidad.

55. Una Marson, 'Kinky Hair Blues' [1986] in *The Penguin Book of Caribbean Verse* ed. by Paula Burnett (London: Penguin, 2005), p. 158.

56. Joyce Gladwell, *Brown Face, Big Master*, ed. Sandra Courtman (first published by Intervarsity Press, 1969; 2nd edn, Oxford: Macmillan Caribbean Classic Series, 2003). The introduction discusses the conditions which facilitated Gladwell's rare autobiography being published in 1969.

57. Beryl Gilroy, 'In Praise of Love and Children', (Gilroy's private collection of an unpublished paper, n.d.), Beryl Gilroy, *In Praise of Love and Children* (Leeds: Peepal Tree, 1996).

58. Roxann Bradshaw, 'Beryl Gilroy's "Fact-Fiction": Through the Lens of the "Quiet Old Lady"', *Callaloo*, 25.2 (2002), 381–400, (394)

59. *Bloomsbury Guide to Women's Literature* ed. by Claire Buck, (London: Bloomsbury, 1992), p. 578.

60. Sylvia Wynter, *The Hills of Hebron* (London: Jonathon Cape, 1962)

61. See chapter 4, 'Bold Experiments in Form: Novels by West Indian Women Published in Britain' in Sandra Courtman, 'Lost Years: West Indian Women Writing and Publishing in Britain c.1960–1979', digitised doctoral thesis, 'Explore Bristol Research', University of Bristol, 1998. <http://research-information.bristol.ac.uk/en/theses/lost-years--west-indian-women-writing-and-publishing-in-britain-c1960-to-1979(7752595b-71d7-42ef-b25f-4bd8d8c6dd37).html> Section 4.2

specifically discusses the form and reception of Sylvia Wynter's novel and how her collaboration with husband Jan Carew may have negatively impacted on her choice to continue a career as a creative writer, pp. 101–11.

62. Wynter's *The Hills of Hebron* receives no mention in Bruce King's *West Indian Literature* (London: Macmillan, 1995) *The Hills of Hebron* is not placed in Edward Baugh's survey of novels, *Critics on Caribbean Literature: Readings in Literary Criticism* (London: Allen and Unwin, 1978) nor mentioned in *A Reader's Guide to West Indian and Black British Literature* ed. by David Dabydeen and Nana Wilson-Tagoe (London: Hansib, 1988).

63. Ramchand, The West Indian Novel and its Background, p. 41.

64. Paul Gilroy, '"Not a Story to Pass On": Living Memory and the Slave Sublime', in *The Black Atlantic: Modernity and Double Consciousness* (London: Verso, 1993), p. 218.

65. Toni Morrison cited in Gilroy, p. 218.

66. Interview with Sylvia Wynter by Daryl Cumber Dance in his *New World Adams: Conversations with Contemporary West Indian Writers* (Leeds: Peepal Tree, 1992), pp. 275–282, (p. 277)

67. Lucille Iremonger published several works which are now all out of print. She wrote for children as in *West Indian Folk Tales: Anansi Stories retold for English Children* (London: George Harrap, 1956) and for adults including fiction and autobiographies: *It's a Bigger Life* (London: Hutchinson, 1948); *Creole* (London: Hutchinson, 1950); *And his Charming Lady* (London: Secker and Warburg, 1961); *Yes My Darling Daughter* (London: Secker and Warburg, 1964).

68. See chapter 6.5, 'Iremonger's "Child in the Rubble": *And His Charming Lady* and *Yes My Darling Daughter*' in Courtman, 'Lost Years: West Indian Women Writing and Publishing in Britain c 1960–1979', pp. 223–48. <http://research-information. bristol.ac.uk/en/theses/lost-years--west-indian-women-writing-and-publishing-in-britain-c1960-to-1979(7752595b-71d7-42ef-b25f-4bd8d8c6dd37).html>

12
'Witness Literature' in the Post-war Novels of Storm Jameson and Doris Lessing

Elizabeth Maslen

The two novelists I am exploring are of different generations – Storm Jameson born in 1891, Doris Lessing in 1919 – but both share a commitment, in the aftermath of World War Two, to writing novels that engage with the sense of fragmentation, the tragedies and crises, that afflicted the post-war world in the wake of the traumas of trench warfare in World War One, the rise of totalitarian regimes in the interwar years, the scale of the holocaust, and the bombing of Hiroshima and Nagasaki. Inevitably, all these events encouraged writers like Jameson and Lessing to reassess what Western society was about, both at home and abroad. Jameson grew up in the English provinces, Lessing in Southern Rhodesia, yet they share similar concerns. Both had family members who suffered the traumas of World War One: Jameson lost a brother and many friends, while her second husband was not only gassed but, like so many others, emotionally drained by his experiences in the trenches, while Lessing was brought up by parents who were both irreparably damaged by that war. Jameson was very much involved with refugees from Europe during the 1930s, World War Two and the Cold War; Lessing became increasingly aware of the tyrannies imposed by the white colonial powers on the black African communities. So both writers had direct personal experience of twentieth-century traumatic issues that exposed how Western society had mythologised its human image. As Tony Davies comments: 'It is almost impossible to think of a crime that has not been committed in the name of humanity'; and he lists, among other splinter groups that have sought to justify their actions as humanist, '[t]he romantic and positivistic Humanisms through which the European bourgeoisie established their hegemonies ... the revolutionary Humanism that shook the world and the liberal Humanism that sought to tame it, the Humanism of the Nazis and the Humanism of their victims and opponents'.[1]

© The Author(s) 2017
C. Hanson and S. Watkins, *The History of British Women's Writing, 1945–1975*,
History of British Women's Writing, DOI: 10.1057/978–1–137–47736–1_13

The acknowledgement of this fracturing meant that those, like Jameson and Lessing's parents, brought up to believe in a supposedly unified human-ist tradition, were traumatised by the revelations of its tarnished heritage, and suffered what Robert Jay Lifton calls 'an important break in the lifeline that can leave [a survivor] permanently engaged in either repair or the acquisition of new twine'.[2] Lessing's parents and Jameson's husband shared this sense of a broken lifeline with many survivors of World War One and of such subsequent traumatic events as the holocaust or the Vietnam war. Often, such survivors were themselves unable to establish a way forward that made sense of the past, and it would be the task of those closest to them to 'establish ... the lifeline on a new basis'.[3] Of course, as Lifton rightly reflects, in certain historical periods humankind 'has special difficulty in finding symbolic forms within which to locate himself.' One could, he argues, even see this as humankind's 'natural' state. But he also argues that 'there are surely degrees in our sense that the particular time we live in is dis-cordant and "out of joint"'.[4] Which is why, for both Jameson and Lessing, the severity and range of the traumas which overshadowed their lives meant that both felt impelled to evolve such 'inner forms' as would constitute ver-sions of 'witness' literature.

Defining what this undertaking means, Michael Levine builds on Shoshana Felman's assertion that '[t]o testify is ... not merely to narrate but to commit oneself, and to commit the narrative to others: to *take responsibility* ... for something which, by definition, goes beyond the *personal,* in having general (nonpersonal) validity and consequences.'[5] For, as Levine argues, the survivors of traumatic events desperately need

> the listener, interviewer, or reader in the testimonial act. Such a *supple-mentary* witness ... implicitly commits himself to the task of assuming *co*-responsibility for an intolerable burden, for an overwhelming charge, for the crushing weight of a responsibility which the witness had hereto-fore felt he or she ... could not carry out.[6]

Inevitably, in shouldering this responsibility, Jameson and Lessing con-fronted creative problems that faced many like-minded writers of that period. As the Jewish theatre director, Abigail Morris says, referring to the problem of articulating the legacy of the Holocaust:

> there is a danger that we will imprison ourselves in a relentless, uncon-structive pattern of repetition. And if we are not very sensitive to the danger of this treadmill, the images we create may be sentimental and thus actually lessen the importance of the event.[7]

Both Jameson and Lessing show themselves as fully aware of such dangers. The witness each offers in their different ways would be echoed in the revelatory symposium set up by the Swedish Academy in 2002 to celebrate the centenary of the first Nobel Prize.[8] Bringing together writers from many different cultures, the theme of this symposium was 'Witness Literature', underlining the global importance of such writing in the rapidly changing world of the twentieth century. Chinese writers, for instance, discuss the problems of writing 'witness' literature under a totalitarian regime, reminding readers that the 'humanisms' experienced in the West have not necessarily been shared in other places: Li Rui, citing Swedish academicians and Chinese peasants, challenges his audience to consider, 'whether all mortal beings on this earth really live in the same world'.[9] It is in this context that Nadine Gordimer, drawing on her experience in the South Africa of apartheid, makes an important distinction between the reporter's job and that of the novelist: 'Meaning is what cannot be reached by the immediacy of the image, the description of the sequence of events, the methodologies of expert analysis ... Kafka says the writer sees among the ruins "different (and more) things than others ... it is seeing what is really taking place"'.[10]

For her, therefore, the writer has a duty to strive for 'the transformation of events, motives, emotions, reactions, from the immediacy into the enduring significance that has meaning'.[11] And this is the task both Jameson and Lessing set themselves from the late 1940s. Both would experiment with adaptations of realism, but in the process both would confront the problem facing any post-war writer 'committed to realism, who must then wrestle with questions that anticipate poststructuralist notions of the interdependence of language, fictional form, mechanisms of power, subjectivity, and social reality'.[12] For the forms of realism developed in the nineteenth century – the realisms of, for instance, George Eliot or Elizabeth Gaskell – were not designed to address the kind of changes the twentieth century was experiencing. And so realism, the representation of reality, became for Jameson and Lessing a mode that must be reshaped from within, even as 'reality' was being redefined by the global traumas of their age.

For both Jameson and Lessing, given their experiences since World War One, there was, as for many of their contemporaries worldwide, a sense of ongoing crisis, on both a private and public level; there is a sense, in the novels both write in the aftermath of World War Two, that the twentieth century is deconstructing itself. As the political theorist, Waldemar Gurian, wrote in 1946:

> We do not know the significance and the place in history of the second world war which ended with the unconditional surrender of Germany and Japan in 1945. We do not know if this end is a real end or only a pause. We know today that World War I ended only with an extended armistice – and even before the documents of unconditional surrender were signed, the feeling and fear spread everywhere that the series of world wars might be not over yet. All attempts to produce a general confidence in a lasting peace have until now proved vain.[13]

And he goes on to say:

> The shooting war is over, but the humanitarian democratic ideology has not obtained a clear-cut triumph. We observe the old power conflicts reappear intensified by ideological and social differences, so that not a brighter world full of optimism, but a world full of conflicts, fears, and insecurity – even panic – is in the making.[14]

Gurian was himself a Russian Jewish émigré, viewing the conflict from a European perspective, and so fully aware of the many faces of humanism. And importantly, Jameson and Lessing are both writers whose experience goes beyond Britain itself: Jameson travelled widely in Europe and was closely involved, through her work for the PEN, with refugees from the Hitler War, Spain, and the Cold War, while Lessing brought her experience of life in Southern Rhodesia (now Zimbabwe) to bear on what she found in Britain and other countries. For them, as for Gurian and other writers, the post-war world reflected Sartre's description of the existentialist world of the 1930s, where the fabric of society had been torn to shreds, and where each human being was 'condemned to ... a freedom from all authority, which he may seek to evade, distort, and deny but which he will have to face if he is to become a moral being'.[15] Any sense of shared values and principles was severely shaken, bringing with it a crisis in communication. This crisis is voiced early in Jameson's *The Black Laurel* (1947).[16] At a Scottish prisoner-of-war camp, five German prisoners are to be executed for hanging two of their fellow inmates who had betrayed a planned escape. So the reader is faced at the outset of the novel with two opposing 'just' codes: prisoners-of-war had a duty to attempt escape, so betrayal amounted to a treasonable offence worthy of execution, while the British authorities invoke the death penalty for what was deemed to be, under their jurisdiction, straightforward murder. The camp commander recognises the problem and its implications in a world where 'Justice' may have no shared meaning:

> Any bloody thing can be justified, gas chambers, cutting a schoolroomful of Bolshie children's poor little throats, injecting poison into the veins of old girls of sixty or seventy – anything. Once you decide to call a private murder justice you're done for – you and your country are going straight to hell.[17]

This loss of a shared moral perspective lies at the core of Jameson's novel, where at key moments various characters have a private agenda that they see as validating their right to choose a 'just' solution to the problem confronting them. And in Lessing's first novel, *The Grass is Singing* (1950), we find similar concerns about different agendas. When a recent English arrival in Southern Rhodesia tries to voice his home-grown liberal criticism of the white community's response to the murder of a farmer's wife by her black house boy, he is given a sharp lesson about language and how to interpret it if he is to survive in this community:

> When old settlers say, 'One has to understand the country', what they mean is, 'You have got to get used to our ideas about the native'. They are saying, in effect, 'Learn our ideas, or otherwise get out; we don't want you.'[18]

The young man has to be groomed to accept what at first his inherent liberalism rebels against; he is under relentless pressure to conform to a different interpretation of what is acceptable.

So both Jameson and Lessing bring to their post-war writings profound concerns about humankind's potential for violence and cruelty and about the undermining of any faith in shared values. As a result both are intent on bearing witness to a world changed radically by two world wars and the potential for more, and to what this means for the individual. And at the same time both are experimenting with ways to communicate their ideas to their contemporary readership.

***

Jameson had been honing her skills in her novels of the 1930s and 1940s. In a 1938 lecture, 'The Novel in Contemporary Life', she had insisted that writers must strive to separate the key issues in their contemporary world from what was 'dead and done for'[19]; and if they could not encompass the whole in a novel, they must take 'soundings'.[20] She herself had developed this idea throughout the war, mirroring large issues of her time in the relationships and conflicts within small communities, so presenting her readers with situations they could readily comprehend. As the war ended she used this technique in two of her most powerful novels, *Before the Crossing* (1947) and *The Black Laurel* (1947), where individual characters are both fully realised individuals and representatives of aspects of the society evolving around and through them.[21] *Before the Crossing* is set in the summer of 1939, just before war was declared; Jameson looks back from the far side of World War Two and its cruelties, taking characters she had already developed in her 1930s trilogy, 'The Mirror in Darkness' (1934–1936), and showing how all too many of those who, before World War One, had been idealists, are now simply acting for themselves and their own private set of values.[22] But these are not simply acts devoid of context: Jameson shows the power of the *Zeitgeist*, something that Lessing also acknowledges through the experiences of her protagonist, Martha Quest, in the 'Children of Violence' series (1952–1969). In Jameson's novel we are shown, for instance, a moment of partial insight given, ironically, to her 'villain', Hunt, as he contemplates his young victim, Marie: 'He thought confusedly of life fitting its hand in [the girl] as if she were a glove, making its signs with her... And with me?'[23] This image of both villain and victim as glove puppets, tools of the *Zeitgeist*, is of course both insightful and a way for Hunt to deny personal responsibility. But Jameson also shows how easily the passion for justice that drives Renn, her protagonist, as he pursues Hunt, the killer of his friend, can turn to ruthlessness, mirroring the fascism that he set out to oppose. In this he is not unlike Lessing's young Englishman in *The Grass is Singing*, whose inherited liberal views have no chance against the racism and misogyny that surrounds and swamps him in the Southern Rhodesia of that time.

Jameson's Renn is shocked when suddenly confronted with what he has become, and his long quest for personal redemption continues into Jameson's next novel, *The Black Laurel*, where compassion above and beyond the self is constantly shown under siege. This novel takes Renn and other characters from *Before the Crossing* into a post-war Europe not yet at peace, where they meet up with a range of new representative 'soundings' of communities shattered and corrupted by the war: British, German and Jewish. In the ruins of Berlin little Kalb, a Jew returning to his former home, will become the victim sacrificed to the schemes of a group of British and German entrepreneurs: materialism as an ideology assumes the mantle of fascism in the post-war chaos. The novel as a whole embodies the dangers facing a Europe where war has left a legacy of self-interest and corruption, and where casual cruelties have become all too normal. It is worth noting that Jameson was writing this powerful novel even as Orwell was writing *Nineteen Eighty-Four*, a work that contemporary critics from a range of cultures would insist was a realist work about their present, not a futurist fable.[24] It would be comfortable to see Orwell's and Jameson's novels as exaggerations, yet both writers were observing a world where abstract concepts like 'justice' and 'mercy' had lost a meaning that once at least seemed to be shared. Jameson would recall some years later a conversation in 1945 with the Polish poet Czeslaw Milosz, in which he mocked the idea of abstract justice:

> You have just been trying four of my fellow-countrymen; they have been slave-workers in Germany for more than five years, and they robbed and killed a German family. Terrible. They have become beasts. And now, after six years of this life that changed them from human beings into wild animals, you are going to execute them – because they have killed one or two German civilians. I don't understand your people. You have hearts, yes, but do you think with them?[25]

Jameson's two novels were written after visits in 1945 to Poland and Czechoslovakia, where she experienced both the physical devastation and the psychological damage that war inflicts on both society and the individuals who survive it.

Lessing too, in the 'Children of Violence' novels, shows how private and public worlds are interlinked as Martha seeks 'self-definition' in the context of her changing contemporary world. For example, in the second novel of the sequence, *A Proper Marriage* (1954), set in the Southern Rhodesian capital, Martha continues to fight, not only against the conservative pressure of her elders, but against the pressure on her to conform to the image her generation – and especially the men – impose on her; throughout this novel, the image of a wheel keeps intruding, mirroring the mindless cycles of her society.[26] Yet in this novel, World War Two looms in the background, and the arrival of RAF personnel brings ideas that preoccupy war-ravaged Europe, chiming in with Martha's growing sense of social injustice in her own country. As a result, in the third novel of the sequence, *A Ripple from the Storm* (1958), Martha tears herself away from her conventional marriage, seeing for a time her vision of a just society embodied in the Communist group she joins.[27]

The novels of 'Children of Violence' written in the 1950s have within them all the issues that will feed into *The Golden Notebook* (1962), the work that Lessing now wrote, breaking off from the sequence. Here is the gap between what Martha dreams of and the pressures she finds it so hard to resist. Here we have her incoherent life, her need to rebel against family, the men she meets, even as she feels trapped, caged, like the Mary of *The Grass is Singing*. To contain Lessing's sense of a fragmenting world, culturally, politically, and in the home, *The Golden Notebook*, written at the end of the 1950s, moves away from the conventional realism of the three earlier works to experiment with structure.[28] It is still, like the Martha Quest books, set in historical context: this is the post-war world coming to terms with the holocaust, atom bombs, and the depth of brutality inflicted on civilian populations. But *The Golden Notebook* is also a book written by a woman who, like Jameson, does not want us to separate personal relationships from what is going on in the world. It addresses the problem Jameson faced in 1938: for Lessing's protagonist, Anna, is overwhelmed by the sheer scale of crises facing the post-war world, and is finding her own way of taking 'soundings'. The notebooks Anna keeps try, as Lessing herself says, 'to separate things off from each other, out of fear of chaos, of formlessness – of breakdown'.[29] Like Jameson, Lessing shows her acute awareness of the critical dilemma facing the novelist who is trying to create fiction in a chaotic world of newsprint and 'facts', as well as of conventional relationships under pressure; she shows the hypocrisies and self-deceptions that exist within them. Importantly, her protagonist Anna asserts that:

> the function of the novel seems to be changing; it has become an outpost of journalism ... I find that I read with the *same kind of curiosity* most novels, and a book of reportage. Most novels, if they are successful at all, are original in the sense that they report the existence of an area of society, a

type of person, not yet admitted to the general literate consciousness ...
Human beings are so divided, are becoming more and more divided, *and
more subdivided in themselves*, reflecting the world, that they reach out
desperately, not knowing they do it, for information about other groups
in other countries. It is a blind grasping out for their own wholeness ...[30]

What is key here is that she envisages the novel as 'an outpost of journal
ism', not journalism *per se*; Lessing, in *The Golden Notebook*, demonstrates
Kafka's perception, quoted above, that the writer sees 'different (and more)
things than others ... it is seeing what is really taking place.' Like Jameson
before her, Lessing strives for what Gordimer will call 'the transformation of
events, motives, emotions, reactions, from the immediacy into the enduring
significance that has meaning.'[31] Lessing gives us an Anna struggling with
the ways in which language can betray us; reading a political paper, she
finds she can interpret it as:

parody, irony, or seriously. It seems to me this fact is another expression
of the fragmentation of everything, the painful disintegration of something that is linked with what I feel to be true about language, the thin-
ning of language against the density of our experience.[32]

Strikingly, despite the range of issues addressed in *The Golden Notebook*,
it became a flagship for the reawakening women's movement of the late
1960s, and it has continued to be claimed as a classic feminist text. However,
Lessing's concerns, while certainly embracing women's concerns, are never
solely feminist, any more than Jameson's are. Both are primarily concerned
with social justice, with the social constraints on both men and women –
and with the responsibility, the inevitable involvement of the individual
with decisions and actions undertaken by their society.

Jameson, in *The Green Man* (1952), for instance, has as her *leitmotif* characters haunted by the problem of justifying war to ensure a 'just' peace; for
World War Two has done nothing to resolve the dilemma that troubled
Adam Smith and David Hume in the eighteenth century, as they pondered
what the attitude of civilised society to war should be. In Jameson's novel we
hear, for instance, an old intellectual debating with himself responsibility
for the atom bomb. First he blames the scientists, but then:

his passionate belief in human freedom, answered him that, since we are
free, each of us is always responsible for his intentions: the intentions of
the brilliant minds who planned a new form of death – I mean, of dying –
are all theirs: but not only theirs: men created the instrument of a
fiendish cruelty, men gave the order to use it, and used it. Therefore all
men are responsible ... All of us lie under the judgement reserved for
hubris.[33]

This bleak awareness of a responsibility which is too often abused lies at the heart of many novels of the period dealing not only with world war, but with those violated by their families or by their own community; and it is also a major theme in Lessing's work. In *The Four-Gated City* (1969), for example, Mark, the writer of a novel about his vision of a utopian city, covers his walls, like Anna Wulf in *The Golden Notebook*, with factual articles from newspapers and journals about happenings in the world outside, trying to make sense of, and to assume responsibility for, the 'truth' of what has happened. But then there is Jimmy, Mark's scientific colleague, who has written two very successful works of science fiction about 'people who had more senses than are considered normal'; Martha is intrigued by the potential for this theme as he tells her that all science fiction writers were currently playing with these ideas but 'then [he] went on to describe a new machine which he was working on that could stimulate or destroy areas of the brain'.[34] Jimmy, terrifyingly, has insight but no sense of moral responsibility. Mark, on the other hand, uses his writerly skills to attempt to propose a positive human future: Jimmy's failure of responsibility is thus set against Mark's moral integrity.

The post-war period was a time when identity, who we are when set against a constantly shifting context of events and ideas, was a key issue for writers of 'witness literature'. In *A Ulysses Too Many* (1958), for instance, Jameson explores the complex world of exiles with different experiences and expectations of their homeland, Poland: some have sought exile long before World War Two, some have escaped more recently, and Jameson shows how their different paths have shaped them as people and have coloured their perceptions of others of their countrymen.[35] The novel was of course based on Jameson's long associations with refugees from Nazi persecutions, but it also owes a great deal to her close links with Czeslaw Milosz, the eminent Polish poet who defected after the Communist takeover of Poland. In 1951 she had comforted him over abuse he was suffering in Paris from fellow Poles whose allegiance was to a prewar Poland that had vanished for ever:

> They have set up an imaginary Milosz, several imaginary Miloszes (since each of them has a different reason for abusing you), and by drinking his blood they come to life. But you are not any of their imaginary Miloszes.[36]

This insight is at the core of *A Ulysses Too Many*. The novel is set in Nice, where Jameson and her husband had met a group of Poles during a long sojourn in France. In the novel, a number of Polish and Russian exiles from before World War Two form a community in Nice; but gradually, as post-war exiles join them, their different experiences divide rather than unite them. It is the return of the writer Nadzin that stirs them up, each character eventually interpreting Nadzin's life and work differently, each making their own imaginary Nadzin, just as Polish emigrants had each constructed their own Milosz in 1951. Each needed the security of believing in his or her own version of the country they have left behind, and Nadzin's capacity to perceive and comprehend the changes that have occurred throughout the interwar years, World War Two, and the Cold War threaten the mythologised country each holds dear. This is a deeply insightful work about exile from the past as well as from place. As Margaret assured her literary agent, A. D. Peters, it was all too true that Nadzin was suspected by his fellow Poles: 'I have been told such stories by sane people as I could never make feasible in writing'.[37]

Lessing meanwhile, in *In Pursuit of the English* (1960), presents a humorous but equally insightful work that explores, from an outsider's point of view, the ways the English perceived themselves when she first came from Africa to England. This book deconstructs any idea of a shared 'English way of life' – that shared life that was such a comforting propaganda tool in World War Two – very much as the Angry Young Men were doing in the 1950s but in a lighter vein. Lessing brings a fresh perspective to the idea by showing how Englishness was viewed in the Colonies and Dominions of the time; if the term 'English' is tricky in England, she asserts, 'it is nothing to the variety of meanings it might bear in a Colony'.[38] The behaviour of the English whom 'Doris' meets is defamiliarised, since it is seen through the eyes of this outsider, she either misinterprets or interprets in ways not accepted by the particular person or persons she is with. When she takes up Rose's introduction to Flo's family and their house, Lessing sketches in vignettes, anecdotes, and revealing dialogue. We see the people and their behaviour through the narrator's eyes, but also through Rose's: so Flo, according to Rose, is not really English because she had an Italian grandmother, Dan is not really English because he comes from Newcastle, while Rose is a Londoner rather than English. This is no portrait of Englishness across the classes, but the complexities within one boarding house and its group of workers wittily show the impossibility of any satisfactory definition.

In many works of the post-war period, there are those for whom the post-war world is an alienating experience, where identity is permanently under threat. For instance, in Veronica Hull's novel *The Monkey Puzzle* (1958), the protagonist, Catherine, has much in common with Lessing's young Martha, since 'to her, her existence was so tenuous that it needed the thoughts of others to confirm it'.[39] Both Jameson and Lessing explore some of the ways in which characters withdraw from a rapidly changing world which evades definition and challenges ideas of progress. In Jameson's *The White Crow* (1968), the Gothic figures largely, in both tragic and comic guise: [40] in the protagonist's misshapen body, his view of the actual world, and his retreat into the medieval monastery of his inner imaginings. This is a work that responds to Angela Carter's magic realism, and anticipates William Golding's *Darkness Visible*.[41] In the late nineteenth-century, a traveler takes on an orphaned baby with 'two long puckers of skin stretching from the shoulder-blade so far as the third rib, a sort of deformed angel'.[42] Gradually the novel develops this excursion into the Gothic, suggesting that the true Gothic lies at the core of society, for all are judged by how they respond to the appearance of this child. As he matures, Antigua (the nickname the child is given, distancing him from the Western world in which he lives) sees the changing Europe on the brink of World War One, but his observations are increasingly out of tune with 'realist' interpretations of his world and culture, as his mind creates a medieval monastery where he can take refuge, evading the unanswerable questions his experience poses. This gripping work shows Jameson at home with preoccupations that absorbed younger writers: what exactly constitutes, for instance, madness and sanity, something Lessing was exploring in *The Four-Gated City* and *Briefing for a Descent into Hell* (1971)?[43] Aesthetically, too, Jameson was using the Gothic, as other writers have used it, to represent a Europe capable of holocaust. This kind of fiction was not as far from the realities of the post-war world as might be thought. The historian Peter Hennessy, in *The Secret State* (2003), has demonstrated how Gothic horrors of what the future might bring haunted the planning of civil servants during the Cold War; and Adam Piette writes of how the balance of power in wartorn Europe was seen as likely 'to be infected by the Gothic-somatic miasma still oozing from the ruins'.[44] Indeed, the slaughter of World War One, the gas chambers, the refugees still haunt *The White Crow* of 1968. Yet poignantly, Antigua, his physical absurdity a contrast with his extreme delicacy of feeling, reflects the way in which Jameson had increasingly come to see her own role as a writer: as a clownish Quixote, out of step with her contemporary world's preferred view of itself as having moved on from those post-war hauntings.

Lessing for her part explores the inner spaces of the mind as the place where humanity might break free from the crises affecting contemporary society. Jameson's Antigua delved into inner space to find solace for the contemporary problems he could not hope to solve, although for him, this was a retreat rather than an attempt to find a way forward. Lessing however, in the two final works of the 'Children of Violence' sequence, *Landlocked* (1965) and *The Four-Gated City*, would explore the resources of the mind on a different, delicate trajectory between breakdown and breakthrough.[45] But she does not attempt, any more than Jameson does, to divorce inner space from the outside world. Martha, for instance, sees a paradox in herself: 'Martha did not believe in violence', yet she 'was the essence of violence, she had been conceived, bred, fed and reared on violence' by her parents, both 'casualties' of war.[46] Then *The Four-Gated City*, set in a realistic post-war Britain, pits the potential of the human mind against the continuing crises framed in the languages of politics, science, psychology, and literary criticism. The final pages of the novel envisage a post-apocalyptic future, where developments in the mind have ensured humanity's survival. This novel and those Lessing writes over the next decades show how easily idealism can be suffocated by regimentation and rules, how easily society can trap people into conforming, how easily they can be manipulated through shared prejudices and aspirations, so that they fail to develop insightful minds. These are the issues that preoccupied Jameson as well. Both she and Lessing, while engaging with their contemporary world and continually experimenting with ways to present their themes, bear witness to cultural, political and personal issues that have a timeless appeal. What makes them stand out is their skill in creating variations on what Auerbach called 'tragic realism', a province that John Orr has claimed for many postcolonial writers; but, as I have argued elsewhere, what he claims is as applicable for Jameson as for Lessing, and indeed is another way of describing 'witness' literature:

> The disclosures of tragic realism are both contemporary and prophetic, examinations of past and present ... We are thus speaking of worlds *where fiction gets there first*, where it uncovers a world buried or repressed, but where it also imagines events and gives them fictive meanings before they are nailed to the mast-head of fact ... a close reading of tragic realism over the space of the last century offers little scope for liberal complacency. It reveals racism and fascism as the monsters of liberal civilization, just as it reveals Stalinism as the monster of a derailed revolution.[47]

And indeed the problems Jameson and Lessing confronted continue to haunt us today.[48]

Notes

1. Tony Davies, *Humanism* (London: Routledge, 1997), p. 141.
2. Robert J. Lifton, *The Broken Connection: On Death and the Continuity of Life* (New York: Simon and Schuster, 1979), pp. 176–7. Lifton is chiefly known for his studies on the psychological causes and effects of war and subsequent traumas.
3. Lifton, *The Broken Connection*, p. 177.
4. Lifton, *The Broken Connection*, p. 293.
5. Quoted in Michael G. Levine, *The Belated Witness: Literature, Testimony, and the Question of Holocaust Survival* (Stanford: Stanford University Press, 2006), p. 7.
6. Levine, *The Belated Witness*, p. 7.
7. Abigail Morris, 'Beware the Treadmill', *Jewish Quarterly*, 5 (1994/5). And see *Anglo-Jewish Women Writing the Holocaust: Displaced Witnesses* ed. by Phyllis Lassner (London: Palgrave Macmillan, 2008).
8. *Witness Literature: Proceedings of the Nobel Centennial Symposium* ed. by Horace Engdahl (Singapore: World Scientific, 2002).
9. Li Rui 'Cloned Eyes', in *Witness Literature* ed. by Engdahl, pp. 77–83 (p. 78) See also Herta Müller, 'When We Don't Speak, We Become Unbearable, and When We Do, We Make Fools of Ourselves. Can Literature Bear Witness?' in *Witness Literature* ed. by Engdahl, pp. 15–32.
10. Nadine Gordimer, 'Witness: The Inward Testimony', in *Witness Literature* ed. by Engdahl, pp. 85–98 (p. 87). See also, for the subject of 'witness', Mark Rawlinson, *British Writing of the Second World War* (Oxford: Clarendon Press, 2000), p. 11.

11. Gordimer, 'Witness: The Inward Testimony', p. 87.
12. Karen Schneider, *Loving Arms: British Women Writing the Second World War* (Lexington: University of Kentucky Press, 1997), p. 154.
13. Waldemar Gurian, 'After World War II', *The Review of Politics*, 8: 1 (1946), 3–11, 3. See, for a recent perspective, Petra Rau, *Our Nazis: Representations of Fascism in Contemporary Literature and Film* (Edinburgh: Edinburgh University Press, 2013).
14. Gurian, 'After World War II', p. 6.
15. 'Jean-Paul Sartre: Biography', nobelprizeorg, 23 Jul 2012, <http//www.nobelprizeorg/nobel_prizes/literature/lureates/1964/Sartre-bio.html> [accessed 10 November 2015].
16. Storm Jameson, *The Black Laurel* (London: Macmillan, 1947).
17. Jameson, *The Black Laurel*, p. 16.
18. Doris Lessing, *The Grass is Singing* [1950] (London: Fourth Estate, 2013), p. 18.
19. Jameson, *The Novel in Contemporary Life* (Boston: The Writer Inc., 1938), reprinted with some additions in *Civil Journey* (London: Cassell, 1939), pp. 277–309; see also 'Documents' in *Fact*, 4 (1937), 15 July, 9–18.
20. Jameson, *The Novel in Contemporary Life*, p. 24.
21. Storm Jameson, *Before the Crossing* (London: Macmillan, 1947).
22. Storm Jameson, *The Mirror in Darkness* (I Company Parade (London: Cassell, 1934); II *Love in Winter* (London: Cassell, 1935); III *None Turn Back* (London: Cassell, 1936).
23. Jameson, *Before the Crossing*, p. 177.
24. George Orwell, *Nineteen Eighty-Four* (London: Martin Secker and Warburg Ltd, 1949). See Elizabeth Maslen, 'One Man's Tomorrow is Another's Today: The Reader's World and its Impact on *Nineteen Eighty-Four*' in *Storm Warnings: Science Fiction Confronts the Future* ed. by George E. Slusser, Colin Greenland, and Eric S. Rabkin (Carbondale and Edwardsville: Southern Illinois University Press, 1987), pp. 146–58.
25. Storm Jameson, *Journey from the North*, vol. II [1969] (London: Virago, 1984), p. 161.
26. Doris Lessing, *A Proper Marriage* [1954] (London: Harper Collins, 1993).
27. Doris Lessing, *A Ripple from the Storm* [1958] (London: Flamingo, 1993).
28. Doris Lessing, *The Golden Notebook* [1962] (London and New York: Harper Perennial, 2007).
29. Lessing, *The Golden Notebook*, p. 7.
30. Lessing, *The Golden Notebook*, p. 75.
31. Gordimer, 'Witness: The Inward Testimony', p. 87.
32. Lessing, *The Golden Notebook*, p. 273.
33. Storm Jameson, *The Green Man* (London: Macmillan, 1952), p. 675.
34. Doris Lessing, *The Four-Gated City* (London: Harper Collins, 1969), p. 392.
35. Storm Jameson, *A Ulysses Too Many* (London: Macmillan, 1958).
36. Jameson to Czeslaw Milosz, 26 July 1951. Czeslaw Milosz Papers, General Collection, Beinecke Rare Book and Manuscript Library, Yale University.
37. Jameson to A. D. Peters, 8 August 1957. A. D. Peters archive, Harry Ransom Center, University of Texas, Austin.
38. Doris Lessing, *In Pursuit of the English: A Documentary* [1960] (London: Flamingo, 1993), p. 9.
39. Veronica Hull, *The Monkey Puzzle* (London: Barrie, 1958).
40. Storm Jameson, *The White Crow* (London: Macmillan, 1968).
41. William Golding, *Darkness Visible* (London: Faber & Faber, 1979).

42. Jameson, *The White Crow*, pp. 9–10.
43. Doris Lessing, *Briefing for a Descent into Hell* [1971] (London: Flamingo, 1995).
44. Peter Hennessy, *The Secret State: Whitehall and the Cold War* (London: Penguin, 2003); Adam Piette, *The Literary Cold War: 1945 to Vietnam* (Edinburgh: Edinburgh University Press, 2009), p. 21.
45. Doris Lessing, *Landlocked* [1965] (London: Harper Collins, 1993); *The Four-Gated City* [1969] (London: Harper Collins, 1993).
46. Lessing, *Landlocked*, p. 22.
47. Julie Orr, *Tragic Realism and Modern Society: The Passionate Political in the Modern Novel* [1979] (London: Macmillan, 1989), pp. 8–9. See Elizabeth Maslen, '"Someone Should Put it on Record": Storm Jameson and "Witness Literature"', in *Long Shadows: The Second World War in British Fiction and Film* ed. P. Rau (Evanston: Northwestern University Press, 2016), pp.151–175.
48. For fuller discussions of Jameson and Lessing, see Elizabeth Maslen, *Life in the Writings of Storm Jameson* (Evanston, Northwestern University Press, 2014), and Susan Watkins, *Doris Lessing* (Manchester: Manchester University Press, 2010). See also *Margaret Storm Jameson: Writing in Dialogue* ed. by Jennifer Birkett and Chiara Briganti (Newcastle: Cambridge Scholars Publishing, 2007); *British Fiction after Modernism: The Novel at Mid-Century* ed. by Marina Mackay and Lyndsey Stonebridge (Basingstoke: Macmillan Palgrave, 2007); Jane Dowson, *Women's Writing, 1945–1960: After the Deluge* (Basingstoke: Palgrave Macmillan, 2003); Adam Piette *The Literary Cold War, 1945 to Vietnam* (Edinburgh: Edinburgh University Press, 2009) and Lidia Yuknavitch, *Allegories of Violence: Tracing the Writing of War in Late Twentieth-century Fiction*, Literary Criticism and Cultural Theory: Outstanding Dissertations series, ed. W. E. Cain, (New York: Routledge, 2001).

Part IV
Expanding Genres

13

Double Trouble: Helen MacInnes's and Agatha Christie's Speculative Spy Thrillers

Phyllis Lassner

In the past decade, the proliferation of critical attention to middlebrow culture has rescued both detective and spy fictions from being denigrated as formulaic, conservative, and 'just too popular' to deserve a place in the literary canon.[1] This rescue has been supported by the literary historical theory of intermodernism which affirms those writers who don't share the 'values that shaped the dominant English literary culture of their time because they have the "wrong" sex, class, or colonial status'. Although 'intermodernists experiment with style or form ... their narratives ... often resulted in writing that attends to politics ...'.[2] It is now recognised that detective and spy fictions are constructed with complex interplays of innovative aesthetics and political and cultural critique that are critically distinct but also continuous with twentieth and twenty-first cultural history. As Helen MacInnes attests, each genre narrates 'a different point of view' with different 'methods. ... In the detective area the problem is who did this and how and why. In espionage novels you know who's been doing what. This has happened. How can we stop it from becoming a real threat to our society'.[3]

Despite the affirmation of espionage fiction, when it comes to women writers, almost all literary and cultural analysis has been devoted to detective novels. Studies of the interwar golden age of Agatha Christie, Dorothy Sayers and Margery Allingham flourish while critical fame eludes such writers as Helen MacInnes and Ann Bridge.[4] This neglect is especially surprising since the plot designs in both detective and espionage fiction are driven by similar forms of political and emotional mayhem: deception, betrayal and assassination. It is true that spy fiction is most often a man's game and of political import extending beyond the settings that contained golden age fiction with its imagined green and pleasant England replete with country houses and picturesque villages. Yet such venerable women- authored

© The Author(s) 2017
C. Hanson and S. Watkins, *The History of British Women's Writing, 1945–1975*,
History of British Women's Writing, DOI: 10.1057/978–1–137–47736–1_14

detectives as Hercule Poirot, Lord Peter Wimsey, and Albert Campion are frequently called upon to abandon home county troubles in order to save the nation from internal and international security threats. Especially as World War II and the Cold War emerge as subjects, both genres earn their place in the loosely defined category of thrillers.[5]

As I discuss elsewhere, women writers have revised the conventions of spy and detective fiction to construct a hybrid, fluid, intermodern fiction.[6] As studies of intermodern and middlebrow fiction demonstrate, these fictions of political intrigue reveal keen insights into narrative relationships with past and present political concerns and often blur boundaries between home front and battleground. Interestingly varied in narrative approaches, intermodern thrillers also share thematic ground with thrillers by male writers. Like John le Carré's Cold War novels, Helen MacInnes's 1968 novel *The Salzburg Connection* and Agatha Christie's 1970 *Passenger to Frankfurt* are plotted as reassessments of the Allies' victory in World War II. These novels question the lasting possibilities for peace and stability by dramatising anxieties about the reemergence of Fascist principles during the Cold War and its proxy, the Vietnam War. As I will argue, these two novels by MacInnes and Christie complicate the hybridity of detective spy thrillers even further by constructing them as speculative political fantasies.

Both novels dramatise how Cold War tensions, the Vietnam War, and prevailing fears of the resurgence of Nazi power conjoin to inspire revisionary spy fictions. Although Christie and MacInnes deploy prototypical masculine leadership and melodramatic pyrotechnics of double agents, thrilling chases and getaways, they question the genre's constructions of gender. They position women as key to investigating and intervening in international crises rather than characterising them as romantic distractions or sexual sidekicks. Women in their fiction defy the boundaries of their prescribed narrative and social roles. They translate the genre's conventional dismissal of women's domestic and romantic disappointments into political analysis and activism. With revisionary narrative power, these women disrupt the genre's gendered formulas by privileging political concerns over sexual desire. As a result, they create an experimental narrative space.

If, as Gill Plain observes, crime and detection fiction is 'about confronting and taming the monstrous', Christie's and MacInnes's thrillers translate the generic 'unspeakable' into political fantasies expressing anxieties about profound cultural and social change, most often embodied and enacted by women characters.[7] Despite MacInnes's production of more than 20 novels, and winning of the Columbia Prize for literature in 1966, she appears in none of the recent encyclopedias of modern women writers and there is neither a full biography nor much literary criticism to illuminate her writing and activist career. Yet as Mary K. Boyd notes, MacInnes's popularity has remained constant. From her first novel, *Above Suspicion* (1941),[8] she infused her spy thrillers with questions about identity politics, with sophisticated literary allusions, and 'changing standards of social behavior [and] changing fashions in literary style'.[9] Sharing critical ground with modernists who responded with themes of dislocation and disillusionment as the legacy of two world wars, MacInnes departs from them by infusing her social and cultural settings with political propaganda.

Helen MacInnes (1907–1985) was born in Glasgow, received an M. A. from Glasgow University and from University College, London. After her husband, Gilbert Highet, an economic historian, was offered a faculty position at Columbia University in 1937, she moved with him to New York where she began writing fiction. She launched her career by expressing her anti-Nazi politics in her first two novels. As with Phyllis Bottome, Storm Jameson, and Katherine Burdekin in the late 1930s, fiction became her tool to combat British appeasement and American isolationism, and throughout World War II, to lift morale, especially since victory was never assured. As Christine Bold reports, MacInnes and her husband decided that they would use their time in the United States to stimulate 'international resistance', and while Highet wrote 'psychological profiles of Nazi leaders', MacInnes's thrillers of the 1940s exposed the psychological and ethical dangers of collaboration and passivity.[10] In these novels as in later ones, women join the effort to defeat Nazism by responding with incisive political analysis and daring action. A distinguishing mark of these women's fiction is their redefinition of propaganda as an instrument of their own political conviction. In such novels as *Above Suspicion* and *Assignment in Brittany* (1942) MacInnes argued that defeating Nazi Germany was a primary war aim, but as with Bottome's *The Mortal Storm* (1937) and Jameson's *Then We Shall Hear Singing* (1942), sympathy and concern about the fate of Hitler's victims was also paramount, unlike the official Allied position.[11]

MacInnes was inspired to write *The Salzburg Connection* by the news of 'the arrest of a former SS colonel who was posing as a schoolteacher on vacation in Czechoslovakia' and 'the recovery of intelligence material which the Nazis had placed in a chest and dropped into a lake in Czechoslovakia. To me this meant the Nazis intend to come back and they want this material for the future. I was shocked and frightened'.[12] The setting was redolent with memories of the SS encamped in Salzburg with the Nazi Foreign Office whose chief, Joachim von Ribbentrop, found it a pleasant retreat. Her novel evinces the lasting significance of the war that had inspired her activist writing. In 1968, when public memory of World War II had receded into the tensions of containing the Cold War, MacInnes analysed the threat of escalating Soviet oppression as coterminous with ongoing attractions to Fascism and Nazism, the combination of which could 'create international chaos'.[13] Blending the threat of Nazism with that of Communism intensifies the plotting of a thriller that includes Soviet and Chinese agents vying for global power while British and Americans renegotiate the grounds for their 'special relationship'.[14] The resulting novel translates anxieties about the revival of fascist power into a speculative melodrama wherein two Americans, a lawyer, Bill Mathison, and publishing agent, Lynn Conroy, are ensnared in a search for a hidden chest by British, American, and Soviet agents conspiring against each other. Moving between Switzerland and Austria, the novel portrays these countries as more than picturesque backdrops. The neutrality they claim invites deception and betrayal of the moral rectitude associated with the word. Instead of representing peace, neutrality conceals state violence. As the vestiges of World War II bleed into the Cold War, detachment and a refusal to take sides lead to indifference, willful ignorance, and complicity in the fates of innocent victims. The presence of unreconstructed former Nazi officers in Switzerland and Austria attests to the compromised claims for neutrality during World War II and after.

Dangerous women

> Close human relationships ... are sources of danger, comparable to crossing frontiers with false papers. Kipling's Kim was warned that 'by means of women ... all plans come to ruin and we lie out in the dawning with our throats cut' ... and before the First World War Somerset Maugham held the dangerous blonde a cliché.[15]

The women characters in Helen MacInnes's fiction are certainly 'sources of danger', in their intimate relationships with men and as assassins, but they are not victims of formulaic characterisation or plotting. Instead they are portrayed as major actors and analysts of international intrigue. Only one of them is a professional spy. Another carries the unhealed scars of male perpetrated violence. Despite different personal and political concerns, they represent a combined narrative and political threat. Their insights and responses traduce the wishes of the resurgent Nazis and the methods of their own allies. In both cases, the women's critical positions undermine the postwar wish for stability expressed in political discourse and in other contemporary spy thrillers. Lacking desires or skills for domesticity, these women provide neither comfort, nurture, nor sexual relief for the male characters.[16] Instead, they are an unwanted presence in the man's world of comfortable camaraderie and familiar antipathy. The women ask too many critical questions, and they interrogate the political and narrative viability of resolution, victory and peace. In these acts of defiance, these women portend narrative upheaval. For example, although the protagonists in *Above Suspicion* are a married couple, Richard and Frances Myles, and Richard is awarded the conventional male role of rescuer, the novel's 'international resistance', its anti-Fascist critique and argument for British intervention belong to Frances. Her political perorations persistently challenge the silences, innuendo and double messages of espionage conduct. In a genre where plot turns are labyrinthine and follow readers' expectations for tension, suspense, and surprise, MacInnes's women create social, emotional, and narrative havoc.[17] They will not behave. They elbow their way into the men's secret discussions, they insist on sharing responsibilities

Like Frances Myles, Lynn Conroy in *The Salzburg Connection* is a politically astute observer of international tensions. This characterisation, however, is not typical of the period's spy fiction. Indeed, the assertion of Lynn's voice is exceptional in a genre where men's attention to women focuses primarily on their physical attractiveness, vulnerability and expendability.[18] Addressing the implications of this attention, a victim of violent intentions on all sides, Anna Bryant, rejects it as disabling protectiveness:

> "[My brother] thinks women shouldn't know anything that's dangerous. But then Dick [her husband] was like that, too ... Oh, really, you are all so foolish! You only add to any danger, don't you see? How can we recognize it when we have to face it? That is double danger ... And it's terrifying – the feeling of not being able to judge the truth is terrifying".[19]

Whereas terror in spy thrillers is typically propelled by deceiving readers about the source of evil, in this novel, the ineffability of evil also derives from the genre's widespread assumptions about gender roles where women are endangered by the ignorance imposed by men wishing to protect them. A 'double danger' indeed. MacInnes, however, contravenes this conventional construction of women through their resisting voices. As Anna attests, women are only impediments to espionage plotting when they are perceived and treated as constitutionally weak and ignorant. Lynn Conroy's responses to fascist violence, like those of Frances Myles, counter such perceptions. For example, when Lynn admits fear, the emotion represents neither physical nor emotional debility; she is not calling for protection. Instead, the fulcrum of her fear is the responsibility intelligence agents assume for the fates of others.

An agent for an American publishing company, Lynn Conroy also represents MacInnes's ideal reader as spy. She is a close reader of the signs, silences and encrypted rhetoric that forms the discourse of her male colleagues:

> Not much use asking questions, she was thinking, but the trouble was that they kept slipping out. Security at stake, that was what [Mathison] had been willing to tell her this morning, security not only of the United States but of the other non-totalitarian nations as well. And if he didn't answer her questions, then it was only to save him from lying. Lies were easy answers to the unanswerable.[20]

Typical of so many spy thrillers, Lynn Conroy is cast by her male colleagues in an anachronistic and imprisoning role: the sexualised ornament. In defiance she relishes the opportunity to apply her skills as a publisher rather than succumb to a romantic fling. Independent and undomesticated, she recalls her failed marriage and the death of her inadequate husband with unsentimental stoicism. Unlike any of the men on the anti-Nazi mission, she requires more than speculation and conventional procedures to fathom the intricacies of political intrigue. She reads into and between the ellipses, absences, shards, and polysemous nature of intelligence data and decodes them as camouflage, as false and misleading clues. Rejecting the notion that secret intelligence is designed to lead only to the 'unanswerable', she raises questions that lead her to discover where significance hides. Instead of privileging the mission as an unquestionable good, she recognises that there is no security for individuals in the political maelstrom of conflicting national interests. Aware that tragedy looms regardless of victory over the Fascist and Communist enemies, Lynn Conroy's perspective confounds the sense of triumph awarded to male heroes of so many spy fictions.

MacInnes transforms triumph into tragedy through a dual absence. None of the male characters constituting the novel's bevy of American, British, and Austrian agents can protect and save Anna Bryant. Moreover, Anna's victim-isation does not begin and end with violence from Nazis, Communists, or any other antagonists during the novel's time-place nexus. Instead, her story tethers the callousness of espionage plotting to the violence perpetrated against women during wartime. Although only through a brief reference, the story offers a critical commentary on the orthodox meanings of villainy in World War II and Cold War espionage fiction. Anna was raped at the age of fifteen during the Red Army's final advance through the Third Reich. Pregnant as a result, she had no choice but to give up the child.[21] Decades later, when her British husband, Richard Bryant, is killed and threats from all sides envelop her, it is as though the violent past is reanimated, invading the present. As a result, she chooses to commit suicide. Enacting emotional and political protest as well as its decimation, suicide is Anna's angry and hopeless escape from the 'web of deceit' that constitutes her fate.[22] Her sui-cide is also a dramatic departure from women's fates in most popular and literary spy fiction where either assassination or romantic and domestic bliss stonewall women's critical questions. Despite Anna's tragic end, how-ever, like Lynn Conroy, she vocalises the novel's moral consciousness.[23] In response to the cynical declaration that 'rights and wrongs have little to do with' the villainy that surrounds them and that it is merely a reflection of 'a basic injustice in life', Anna asserts her political protest: '"Only if we do nothing about it. Accept what is wrong, and you are forever accepting"'.[24] Anna's rejection of abstract rationalisation constructs a critical voice for women traditionally trapped on the periphery of espionage plotting. Her suicide signifies a critique of mythical portrayals of women in espionage fiction that embed dehumanising and delusive portraits representing oppo-sitional fantasies of compliant or deadly women.

MacInnes complicates the genre's penchant for toxic women with her portrayal of Eva Lengenheim aka Elisabetha or Elissa Lang, a Soviet spy whose ambiguous national origins signify her destabilising presence. Neither Russian patriot nor ideologue, both an embodied and dissolving presence, Eva is an instrument of Cold War anxiety. Her mission is to find the buried chest containing the incriminating list of former Nazis now in hiding or working for the USSR and other nations. Beautiful and seductive, she is also a dedicated professional, 'much too clever to ignore any danger signal. And too important an operator to allow anyone to threaten her mission'.[25] Although she tries to seduce Mathison and to manipulate a besotted lover, Eva is no stock *femme fatale* or sex object. Instead, her character achieves complexity from different narrative perspectives, most importantly, her own. In an extended episode at a crucial juncture in her mission, the narrative switches from third person neutrality to share Eva's fatigued and apprehensive response to her uncertain position. Exposing her consciousness anatomises the genre's classic opposition between ally and enemy to create a narrative coordinate with that of Anna, the victim. Despite Eva's confidence and espionage skills, the novel shows her struggling to assert her authority against a male dominated secret world that offers affirmation at the cost of subordination. While Mathison wonders if the men in her organization would 'have obeyed her', Eva knows that she would have more power if she were a man. On an assignment with her Soviet colleague Lev, she deciphers his taciturnity and petulance as disdain for her while she assumes the burden of keeping 'him safe'. Her words speak louder than her prescribed role.[26]

A long paragraph affirms Eva's indefatigable skills by listing her multi-tasking challenges: 'precipitous' travel, interchanging identities, passports, accents and voices.[27] Exploiting feminine stereotypes, she also disguises her analytical talents as adventurous impulses. Given her transgressions from the narrative norm, Eva could easily be viewed as a romantic fantasy. Yet the historical record reveals more mimesis than romance. Eva's character reflects the emergence of the new woman spy in the 1930s, 'a competent driver, adept at mechanical operations, and usually an efficient photographer'.[28] Her downfall is engineered by her Soviet command, but not because she succumbed to 'a weak moment of romantic nonsense ... 'a foolish impulse to meet a man again.' Understanding, however, that her cover is blown, she nonetheless resolves, '"there is a mission to complete"'.[29] Eva is destroyed when her handlers decide to eliminate her by removing the time delay on a bomb she is supposed to trigger. Assuming that a woman's folly will betray the mission, her handlers deceive her. They eliminate the time delay and obliterate Eva. Had she not been betrayed, the mission might have succeeded: eradicating the woman spy destroys both the Soviets' mission and a role for the ambitious and canny woman spy.

This plot move would certainly satisfy readers' expectations of defeating the enemy. The question remains, however, whether the novel also conforms to the formulaic destruction of the woman who transgresses her prescribed role as subservient if lethally attractive. To address these questions, we need to consider that the novel's premise is based on the apocalyptic threat of

Nazi revival and Communist domination. Yet both powers are constituted as shadowy presences, barely visible or audible in a five hundred page novel. In stark contrast, the woman spy overwhelms the narrative power of the villains. The consequences are indeed explosive, as her death suggests. In concert with the critical questions posed by Lynn Conroy and Anna Bryant, Eva's talents and desire for her own authority repudiate the genre's restrictive roles for its women characters 'as peripheral romantic interest, domestic background, or ambiguously androgynous companionship for the hero'.[30] MacInnes's women storm the barricades of an exclusionary masculinist secret world, challenging its stability and ability to fulfill readers' expectations for heroic protection of hearth, home and nation.

Apocalyptic parody

Agatha Christie (1890–1976) has been a bestselling novelist since her first publication, *The Mysterious Affair at Styles* in 1920, which introduced her Belgian detective, Hercule Poirot and critical relationships between the search for justice and restoration of a stable British social culture. Athough Agatha Christie wrote spy thrillers early in her career, including *The Secret Adversary* (1922), *The Man in the Brown Suit* (1924), *The Big Four* (1927), and *The Seven Dials Mystery* (1929), her 1971 speculative spy fantasy, *Passenger to Frankfurt*, is a departure. Set far beyond the village green and entangled legacies, eschewing purloined government documents and secret agents, the novel is also bereft of bodies in the library as well as the self-effacing Miss Marple and self-important Hercule Poirot. This is neither a detective story nor a crime fiction. It is a dystopian thriller: a creative adventure for the author and for her amateur investigators. While the past is as lethal as always in Christie's oeuvre, the threat in this novel extends her favored time-place nexus into a hypothetical global future. As with *The Salzburg Connection*, this novel raises the spectre of a resurgent Nazism but one that depends on uniting the world's youth. Promises of glory and heroism inspire them to overthrow their nations' governments and redeploy national resources to support a self-appointed oligarchical master race.

Passenger to Frankfurt features a trio of women characters who embody, enact, and respond to the political and social upheavals on which the plot is predicated.[31] Although the narrative and political plots are set in motion by a cadre of Britain's powerful men, their momentum is driven by women. While the men debate international intrigue and national strategies with customary oppositional discourses, the women embody and activate critiques of mythic archetypes of wisdom, villainy, and heroism. A speculative fable of neo-Nazi ideology and conquest, the novel also parodies the figuration of women in popular spy fiction as sex objects, damsels in distress, or domesticated sidekicks. Here, the secret world of espionage is exposed as morally and representationally vacuous by the political acuity of one woman, the drive for domination of another, and the intrepid adventurousness of a third. The authority of Christie's women contrasts sharply with the spyscapes in male-authored Cold War espionage fictions, including those by John le Carré, Ian Fleming, Frederick Forsyth, and Len Deighton. In these novels, the genre's convention of doubling is deployed to expose the male-dominated moral authority of the British Secret Service as undermined by its public school codes of class-bound antagonisms that create resemblances between its own methods and those of the enemy.

Like Bill Mathison, the male protagonist of *Passenger to Frankfurt* is an amateur spy. A 'disappointment in diplomatic circles', Sir Stafford Nye drifts into a plot to prevent a global coup by neo-Nazi oligarchs from overturning the world order of sovereign states.[32] Although Nye's centrality and the genre's conventions prefigure his transformation into a hero, the power that drives him and the narrative belongs to a woman, Countess Renata Zerkowska. Cloaked in a panoply of shifting identities and ambiguous loyalties, she disrupts the stability of the secret world as well as the thriller's gender order. While the inner sanctum of 'the dear old sleepy Foreign Office' dithers in response to the ominous forces threatening Britain and its spheres of interest, the Countess, a.k.a. Mary Ann, intuitively seizes an opportunity for action. Spying Sir Stafford dozing in the Frankfurt airport lounge, she targets his constitutional boredom and offers him respite in adventure.[33] With 'a deep contralto voice, almost as deep as a man's', with an uncanny resemblance to Nye, the mysterious Countess challenges the complacency of masculine heroism.[34] Eschewing prototypical feminine wile or fragility, the Countess asks for Nye's help by challenging him to identify with her: 'I think you are a man who is ready to take risks. Just as I am a woman who takes risks'.[35] Her plan to travel safely from Frankfurt to London would dissolve their gender differences if she borrows his hallmark crimson lined cloak and passport and impersonates him.

Compounding this melodramatic gender spin, the novel adds a parodic gloss to Nye's response: '"You know what you're talking like? A beautiful spy in a thriller"'.[36] And, one might add, considering Renata's polysemous nature, a mythological thriller. Suspected of being a 'dedicated killer', compared to the Biblical women assassins Jael and Judith, the Countess has everyone fooled: 'There's been too much coincidence about the way she has been turning up in different places' in the company of powerful politicians, scientists, and even the suspected villain.[37] The combination of mythology, apocalyptic fantasy and parody is set in motion the moment the Countess and the diplomat reverse roles and she leads the charge against global neo-Nazism. A female 'Virgil', taking her 'Dante ... down into hell', she initiates her male sidekick into a 'romantic adventure'.[38] Like Dante's odyssey through the nine circles of hell, Christie's odd couple embarks on a mythic descent into escalating dangers from which the only escape is into the knowledge of good and evil. In the face of a fascist apocalypse, Christie's sojourners are positioned to question whether the world can be renewed and good resurrected.

Christie demonstrates the liminal status of the thriller, as middlebrow entertainment and cultural critique, with a double-edged gloss on the genre. This spy thriller engages its weighty political issues and its readers with the light hand of parody. Deploying a favorite trope of the genre, the novel figures the quest for political knowledge as a labyrinth. But unlike the hapless Pamela, handcuffed and hauled across Scotland in Hitchcock's version of John Buchan's *The Thirty-nine Steps,* the savvy Countess knows her way around an allegorical hell.[39] More talked about than seen, she resists the ontological status confining women characters in spy thrillers. Instead, she exploits her protean nature to maneuver among antagonists and produce knowledge that will thwart the new Reich, which with its 'drugs and sadism and the love of power and hatred' will annihilate what is left of individuality and a democratic social and political order.[40]

The novel leaves no doubt that Hitler's creed of power is about to be reignited and represents a global threat. Nye's great-aunt Lady Mathilda, the novel's fount of political wisdom, warns: '"It's so frightening, this same idea that always recurs. History repeating itself. The young hero, the golden superman that all must follow ... The young Siegfried"'.[41] In response to her nephew's focus on the recognisable dangers of Russia and China and dismissal of neo-Nazism, Lady Mathilda expounds:

"They're not only fancies, my dear boy. That's what people said about Hitler ... and the Hitler Youth. But it was a long careful preparation. ... It was a fifth column being planted in different countries all ready for the supermen. The supermen were to be the flower of the German nation. That's what they thought and believed in passionately. Somebody else is perhaps believing something like that now. It's a creed that they'll be willing to accept – if it's offered cleverly enough".[42]

With a different generational axis than *The Salzburg Connection,* no unreconstructed members of Hitler's old guard threaten the world order in Christie's novel. Instead, as though responding to the brigades of revolutionary youth in the late 1960s, Christie locates danger in the apathy of the older generation as youth in all hemispheres riot and violently overthrow their governments and all semblances of progressive and even traditional conservative social cultures. Evocations of 'Guevaras, the Castros, the Guerrillas' are tethered to 'the rules of Himmler and Hitler' and the Holocaust to intensify the sense of totalitarian terror coalescing into an apocalyptic fantasy.[43] The cooptation of the 'golden supermen' into a new 'Children's Crusade' is the result of their parents' and grandparents' failure to do more than restore an archaic political order barren of even whiggish notions of progress.[44]

That Stafford Nye is discovered dozing in the Frankfurt airport is not an incidental narrative choice. Instead the diplomat's political nonchalance recalls the audience to which Phyllis Bottome addressed her despairing question about the appeasement of Nazi Germany in the 1930s: 'Has England gone Nazi in its sleep?'[45] The danger for Christie lies in the lack of democratic vitality on the part of young and old, creating an ideological and political void filled by 'lov[ing] destruction for its own sake,' whereupon 'evil leadership gets its chance"' to propel causes and crusades through inflaming rhetoric, 'capable of communicating to others a wild enthusiasm, a kind of vision of life and of happening' that even devoid of content, is a 'magnetic power'.[46]

In their quest to stop this fascist crusade, Nye joins the Countess Renata to investigate its power source and in so doing, they travel from late 1960s Britain to a Schloss built in the late eighteenth century and located 'not far from Berchesgaden', Hitler's mountain lair (*PF* 168). Like Hitler's retreat, the Schloss is a place where strategies for world domination lead to the dissolution of the human subject and national sovereignty, a place where individuals are transformed into an undifferentiated robotic mass. This is a collective force that destroys community. However ominous the setting, it is also redolent with the parody that impels the novel's style, evoking swashbuckling costume romances like *The Prisoner of Zenda*, with its neat split between 'the hero Rudolf Rassendyll' and villainous 'King of Ruritania'.[47] The doyenne of this castle fortress is also constructed as commingling malevolence and mockery: the Gräfin Charlotte von Waldsausen, 'a whale of a woman', 'wallowing in fat', whose crude expressions of omnipotent power are exceeded only by her turgid metaphorical representation.[48] That the Gräfin's family name is really 'Krapp' is a scathing pun; it indicts Krupp, the massive industrial power that helped Hitler's war machine produce its human waste.[49]

A figurative parody, the portrait of the Gräfin is anti-mimetic, a monumental mockery of the outsize planetary power of villains in Ian Fleming's spy romances. It occurs to Nye that this 'masquerade' is 'ridiculous', 'like a super production of a period historic play', and that 'Such things can't happen nowadays'.[50] Signifying a nexus of critical relations, this comedy of omnivorous appetites is accompanied by the sounds of political dystopia as an 'Elite Corps' of 'golden-haired boys' shout '"Heil! Heil!"' and sing new versions of Wagnerian strains.[51] The Siegfried corps becomes the model of exploiting adolescent rebelliousness worldwide, a self-replicating force that would unite the Nazi past, the Cold War and other insurgent enemies, and an apocalyptic future. A *danse macabre*, the scene represents anxious memory traces of the Nazis' translation of feudal sovereignty into their supremacist mythology. That this mythology became a recipe for conquest and the Holocaust is recalled in the Gräfin's approval of 'the deaths in gas chambers, the torture cells' – 'a great tradition'.[52] The reference to the specific atrocities that comprise the Holocaust overwhelms the meanings of 'romantic adventure' and Dante's hell with cold irony. As Terrence Des Pres warned, to allegorise the camps, to see 'the SS as satanic monsters and the prisoners as condemned souls' evades the experiential actualities of torture, starvation, beatings, and gassing.[53]

The visual portrait of the Gräfin can easily be read as representing Christie's misogynist views of women who achieve powerful positions. The Gräfin rules over men as though her power would devour them and take over the entire planet, the size and shape of which she grotesquely resembles. Reading the novel's structure as apocalyptic parody, however, produces a different conclusion. This depiction of women's desire for power can also be seen as reflecting and mocking Nazi sexist ideology and policies.[54] During the Nazi era, women who had worked in the public sphere, including the law, science, and business, were coerced to return home to fulfill their responsibility to build the Master Race through motherhood. Although we're not told whether the Gräfin is a biological mother, she has birthed a monumental size battalion, an 'Elite Corps' of physical perfection that has been trained to achieve 'mastery of a new world which the young Siegfried came to conquer ... Myth, heroes, resurrection, rebirth, it was all there. His beauty, his strength, his incredible assurance and arrogance'.[55] The Gräfin's gargantuan size and ugliness embody the political and social consequences of Nazi gender policies. The power of women in Nazi ideology lies in sacrificing their bodies so as to transform a fantasy of biological alchemy into a reality of global conquest and domination. Women's work consists of the boundless labor of birthing the new world order. No wonder the Gräfin is huge and ugly. Her body is a mockery of the denaturalising implications of Nazi maternal ideology. In extremis, the Nazi myth of the maternal disfigures women's biological capacity for producing life by transforming it into an industrialised birthing and killing machine. In her incarnation as the mother of the new Nazism, the Gräfin's power to produce countless legions of warriors is a personified metonym for the exploitation of overabundant natural resources: 'She's oil. Copper. Goldmines in South Africa, Armaments in Sweden. Uranium deposits in the north. Nuclear development, vast stretches of cobalt. She's all those things'.[56] By the end of the novel, this triad of superfluity implodes, as though the woman's drive for power has engorged itself and instead of global dominance, its only product is her self-consuming narrative.

MacInnes and Christie create speculative spy thrillers that ponder the future arising from a present still troubled by the unresolved violent past. The timescape is both politically and narratively inflected. Men retain their prototypical roles as protagonists, but their political and narrative power is eclipsed by women. Demonstrating their own political and narrative authority, women embody and give voice to concerns unprofessed by their male leaders, including recognising a continuum of persecution and violence, and offering alternative responses to global warfare and the failure of revolutionary promises. Lynn Conroy, Anna Bryant, Renata Zerkowska, and even the villainous Eva and the Gräfin recognise the intertwined instability of the past, present, and future because they confront their own position in social, political, and literary culture as a continuum of displacement and lack of agency. However spy thrillers have been classified, analysed, and historicised, women characters have been dismissed as narrative asides, as negligible irritants or necessary ornaments.

The triadic figures of women as thinkers, spokespersons, and villains created by Helen MacInnes and Agatha Christie disturb the traditional gendered formations of the genre. They abandon domestic spaces and overturn sexualised objectification to intervene in the narrative spaces created for them, representing a speculative power to revivify the genre by revising stereotypical images. Although both novels end with the triumph of romantic love, Lynn Conroy and Renata Zerkowska are positioned as partners in building the future, not as returning to domestic spaces. As they assert their presence in fictional secret worlds and insist on being heard, these women offer alternative perspectives and critical voices through which to represent the international crises on which spy fiction depends for its thrills.

Notes

1. See *Reading Sideways: Middlebrow into Modernism*, special issue of *The Space Between: Literature and Culture 1914–1945*, 9: 1 (2013), and *Middlebrow Literary Cultures: the Battle of the Brows 1920–1960* ed. by Erica Brown and Mary Grover, (Basingstoke: Palgrave, 2012).
2. Kristin Bluemel, *George Orwell and the Radical Eccentrics: Intermodernism in Literary London* (Basingstoke: Palgrave, 2004), p. 5.
3. Joy Stilley, 'Violence Normal, Necessary in Books and Life', *Ashland (KY.) Daily Independent*, 9 February 1969, 38.
4. The MLA bibliography confirms this conclusion; however, novels by Helen MacInnes and Ann Bridge have recently been reprinted.
5. Andrew Hammond sees the 1945–89 period as 'expressly Cold War', including the Soviet threat, 'nuclear annihilation', powerful secret services, diminished British influence, and emerging 'US global supremacy', *British Fiction and the Cold War* (Basingstoke: Palgrave, 2013), p. 1. His claim that 'The left-liberal tradition of thriller writing' was superseded by Ian Fleming's 'right-wing thriller' (p. 113) is refuted by MacInnes and other women writers challenging the genre.
6. See Phyllis Lassner, 'The Mysterious New Empire: Agatha Christie's Colonial Murders', in *At Home and Abroad in the Empire* ed. by Robin Hackett, Freda Hauser, and Gay Wachman (Newark: University of Delaware Press, 2009), pp. 31–50; 'Under Suspicion: The Plotting of Britain in World War II Detective Spy Fiction' in *Intermodernism: Literary Culture in Mid-Twentieth Century Britain* ed. by Kristin Bluemel (Edinburgh: Edinburgh University Press, 2009), pp. 113–30.
7. Gill Plain, *Twentieth Century Crime Fiction: Gender, Sexuality and the Body* (Edinburgh: Edinburgh University Press, 2001), p. 3. Alison Light analyses Christie as politically conservative, but narratively innovative in her *Forever*

England: Femininity, Literature and Conservatism Between the Wars (London: Routledge, 1991).

8. Helen MacInnes, *Above Suspicion*, (Boston: Little, Brown, 1941).
9. Mary K. Boyd, 'The Enduring Appeal of the Spy Thrillers of Helen MacInnes', *Clues*, 4 (1983), 66–75, 66, 68.
10. Christine Bold, 'Domestic Intelligence: Marriage and Espionage in Helen MacInnes's Fiction', *Paradoxa*, 24 (2012), 31–53, (31).
11. Writers such as Muriel Spark and Elizabeth Bowen supported the war effort by gathering intelligence or like Leslie Howard, broadcasting propaganda messages to North America and in feature films, such as *Pimpernel Smith* and *Parallel 149*.
12. R. Morehouse, 'Gentle Queen of Spy Story Writers', *St. Louis Globe-Democrat*, 19 February 1969, 17A.
13. Helen MacInnes, *The Salzburg Connection* [1968] (London: Titan, 2012), p. 200.
14. For discussion of the Anglo-American alliance and its tensions, see Tony Judt, *Postwar: A History of Europe Since 1945* (New York: Penguin, 2005), pp. 299, 302.
15. Jeanne Bedell 'A Threatening World: Suspense in Espionage Fiction', *Clues*, 13: 2 (1992), 115–26, (122).
16. Julie Wheelwright examines a 'long tradition of espionage writers' who depict women spies as the archetypal '*femme fatale*', undomesticated, 'sexually independent, usually childless', and so 'represents a deeply-embedded anxiety in contemporary western culture' in 'Poisoned Honey: The Myth of Women in Espionage', *Queen's Quarterly*, 100: 2 (1993), 291–309, 294–5.
17. For discussion of spy thrillers' labyrinthine plots, see John Gardner, 'The Espionage Novel', in *Whodunit?: A Guide to Crime, Suspense, and Spy Fiction* ed. by Henry R. F. Keating (New York: Van Nostrand Reinhold, 1982), pp. 70–80. Bedell analyses the narrative shaping of suspense.
18. The classic example is Ian Fleming's James Bond series and their film adaptations, where women enemy agents are portrayed as grotesque lesbians, like Rosa Kleb, unless their beauty warrants political transformation, like Tatiana, both in *From Russia with Love*, Dir. Terrence Young, United Artists, 1963.
19. MacInnes, *The Salzburg Connection*, p. 384.
20. MacInnes, *The Salzburg Connection*, p. 371.
21. MacInnes's inclusion of this history anticipates feminist research over the last decade that exposes the widespread occurrences of rape during World War II. A searing account of relentless rape of German women by Soviet soldiers is *A Woman in Berlin, Anonymous* (New York: Henry Holt, 2005). Studies of rape in the concentration camps, including sexual slavery and exploitation include *Sexual Violence against Jewish Women during the Holocaust* ed. by Sonia M. Hedgepeth and Rochelle G. Saidel, (Waltham, Mass.: Brandeis University Press, 2010). Anna's decision fits Lawrence Langer's term for the double bind imposed on Holocaust prisoners, 'choiceless choice', that between worse and worst: 'whatever you choose, somebody loses – shorn of dignity and any of the spiritual renown we normally associate with moral effort', *Admitting the Holocaust* (New York: Oxford University Press, 1995), p. 46.
22. MacInnes, *The Salzburg Connection*, p. 350.
23. Liz Gold in le Carré's *The Spy Who Came in from the Cold* also serves this purpose but she is assassinated.
24. MacInnes, *The Salzburg Connection*, pp. 247–8.
25. MacInnes, *The Salzburg Connection*, p. 282.
26. MacInnes, *The Salzburg Connection*, pp. 301, 368.
27. MacInnes, *The Salzburg Connection*, pp. 358–9.

28. Wheelwright, 'Poisoned Honey', p. 305. Wheelwright notes that despite the indomitable courage of Allied women spies during World War II, during the Cold War 'the spy-courtesan resurfaced – this time as a handmaiden to the godless communists', p. 308.

29. MacInnes, *The Salzburg Connection*, p. 456.

30. Christine Bold, '"Under the Very Skirts of Britannia": Re-reading Women in the James Bond Novels', *Queen's Quarterly*, 100: 2 (1993), 311–27, 314.

31. M. Vipond delineates Christie's women characters as resisting the 'stereotypes and caricatures' demanded by detective fiction; even those who seek marriage as a life goal are often 'self-sufficient, capable and courageous', 'Agatha Christie's Women', *International Fiction Review* 8: 2 (1981), 119–23, 119, 122. See G. Plain, *Twentieth Century Crime Fiction*, for Christie's gender critique.

32. Agatha Christie, *Passenger to Frankfurt* (London: Harper Collins, 1970), p. 20. Imagining the restoration of Nazi or Fascist power also forms the plot of Frederick Forsyth's *The Odessa File* (N.Y. The Viking Press, 1972). See Laurence Baron's study 'Holocaust Iconography American Feature Films about Neo-Nazis', *Film & History*, 32: 2 (2002), 38–47.

33. Christie, *Passenger to Frankfurt*, pp. 103–4.

34. Christie, *Passenger to Frankfurt*, p. 25.

35. Christie, *Passenger to Frankfurt*, p. 27.

36. Christie, *Passenger to Frankfurt*, p. 30.

37. Christie, *Passenger to Frankfurt*, p. 330.

38. Christie, *Passenger to Frankfurt*, pp. 102, 200.

39. Alfred Hitchcock, Gaumont films, 1935; John Buchan, *The Thirty-nine Steps* (New York: Doran, 1915).

40. Christie, *Passenger to Frankfurt*, p. 286.

41. Christie, *Passenger to Frankfurt*, p. 106.

42. Christie, *Passenger to Frankfurt*, p. 105.

43. Christie, *Passenger to Frankfurt*, pp. 283, 284.

44. Christie, *Passenger to Frankfurt*, p. 305.

45. Phyllis Bottome, *The Goal* (New York: Vanguard Press, 1962), p. 259.

46. Christie, *Passenger to Frankfurt*, pp. 109, 149.

47. Christie, *Passenger to Frankfurt*, p. 101.

48. Christie, *Passenger to Frankfurt*, pp. 174–5.

49. Christie, *Passenger to Frankfurt*, p. 239. The Nuremberg Military Tribunal convicted Alfred Krupp for using slave labour during the Hitler era. He was sentenced to twelve years in prison and was released in 1951, taking over once again in 1953. See P. Hayes, *From Cooperation to Complicity: Degussa in the Third Reich* (Cambridge: Cambridge University Press, 2004).

50. Christie, *Passenger to Frankfurt*, pp. 176, 183, 176.

51. Christie, *Passenger to Frankfurt*, pp. 186, 184.

52. Christie, *Passenger to Frankfurt*, pp. 183, 260.

53. Quoted and discussed in R. Franklin, *A Thousand Darknesses: Lies and Truth in Holocaust Fiction* (Oxford: Oxford University Press, 2011), p. 133.

54. See Gisela Bock, 'Racism and Sexism in Nazi Germany: Motherhood, Compulsory Sterilisation, and the State' in *When Biology Became Destiny: Women in Weimar and Nazi Germany*, ed. by Renate Bridenthal, Atina Grossman, and Marion Kaplan (New York: Monthly Review Press, 1984), pp. 162–85.

55. Christie, *Passenger to Frankfurt*, p. 186.

56. Christie, *Passenger to Frankfurt*, p. 192.

14
Historical Fictions

Diana Wallace

In 1961 the historian Helen Cam noted the contemporaneous vogue for historical fiction, quoting approvingly John Raymond's comment that, 'We must all agree ... that there is no time like the present for the historical novel in all its variety and richness.'[1] Yet by 1969 Ursula Brumm was stating that, 'In our time, which is postrealistic in that realism has been superseded by other literary conventions, the historical novel has almost disappeared.'[2] And in *The English Historical Novel: Walter Scott to Virginia Woolf* in 1971, Avrom Fleishman argued that Woolf's *Orlando* (1928) and *Between the Acts* (1941) 'bring the tradition of the English historical novel to a self-conscious close.'[3] Why is it that, while Cam sees a thriving literary field, Brumm and Fleishman see a dead tradition?

The years between 1945 and 1975 are, in fact, extraordinarily rich in historical fiction by women. Indeed, this period has some claims to be regarded as a golden age of 'popular' historical fiction by writers such as Eleanor Hibbert (writing as 'Jean Plaidy' and 'Victoria Holt'), Georgette Heyer, Margaret Irwin, Anya Seton (a British writer who lived mainly in the US and often wrote about British subjects), Norah Lofts, Doris Leslie, Mary Stewart and Catherine Cookson. The period is equally rich in 'serious' historical fictions, many of which have yet to be widely discussed: major historical novels include Naomi Mitchison's multi-levelled *The Bull Calves* (1947), Sylvia Townsend Warner's convent novel *The Corner That Held Them* (1948), and *The Flint Anchor* (1954), H. F. M. Prescott's *The Man on a Donkey* (1952) – 'widely held to be the best historical novel of our days,' according to Cam,[4] Mary Renault's rewriting of the Theseus myth in *The King Must Die* (1958), and the first two novels in her Alexander trilogy, *Fire From Heaven* (1970) and *The Persian Boy* (1972), and Jean Rhys's radically revisionary *Wide Sargasso Sea* (1966). All are formally innovative, although in very different ways.

© The Author(s) 2017
C. Hanson and S. Watkins, *The History of British Women's Writing, 1945–1975*,
History of British Women's Writing, DOI: 10.1057/978–1–137–47736–1_15

It's not that contemporary relevance is missing either. The novels of Bryher (Winifred Ellerman) frequently function as political allegories (what Georg Lukács in *The Historical Novel* calls 'parables of the present'[5]): her Foreword to *This January Tale* (1966), for instance, draws a pointed parallel between 1066 and 1940.[6] Then there are what might be labelled the 'middle-brow' historical fictions, such as Dorothy Dunnett's sixteenth-century Lymond Chronicles, beginning with *The Game of Kings* in 1961. Or Margaret Kennedy's Regency *Troy Chimneys* (1953) which, like Dunnett's series and Warner's *The Flint Anchor*, explores the damaging splits at the heart of patriarchal masculinity. Even more difficult to categorise is Daphne du Maurier who hated her reputation as a writer of 'romance', a label which is in any case belied by the crippled heroine of *The King's General* (1946), or the bleak ending of *My Cousin Rachel* (1951), both novels which experiment with unreliable first person narration.

The critical neglect of mid-century women's writing is particularly acute in relation to the historical novel, a genre which is problematically hybrid, yoking together fiction and history. This is exacerbated by the fact that in the early twentieth century historical fiction had become associated with women writers and readers to damaging effect. Cam was in no doubt that historical fiction 'is not only a respectable literary form: it is a standing reminder of the fact that history is about human beings.'[7] It was, however, the particular tendency of post-war historical fiction to assert that history is 'about' *gendered* human beings – through questioning the values which shaped accepted historical, cultural and mythical accounts of men, women and civilisation – which contributed to its marginalisation.

The variety of these mid-century historical fictions is striking. While Fleishman and Brumm focus on the tradition of 'realist' historical fiction which Lukács traced from Walter Scott through a male and European canon, post-war women writers are reworking the genre in many different ways. Their work often crosses and blurs the accepted categories – 'realist', 'Modernism', 'popular', 'middlebrow', 'romance'. Moreover, many of the older writers discussed here – Mitchison, Heyer, Warner, Rhys, du Maurier, Renault – began publishing in the 1920s and 1930s. While some of them have been usefully situated in those contexts (for instance, discussions of Warner and Mitchison as 1930s writers or of Warner and Rhys in relation to Modernism),[8] the relevant mid-century context for their later work is often under-researched.

We need a critical account which both links these historical fictions to the wider mid-century literary context and inserts them into the history of the historical novel as genre which stretches back to the proto-realism of Walter Scott and forward to the postmodern 'historiographic metafictions' identified by Linda Hutcheon. Hutcheon placed the historiographic metafiction, a mode characterised by its 'theoretical self-awareness of history and fiction as human constructs' and exemplified by texts such as John Fowles's *The French Lieutenant's Woman* (1969), at the centre of postmodernism. However, her assertion that this is 'not just another version of the historical novel' comes at the cost of obscuring the ways in which earlier realist and modernist historical novels also problematise history.[9] The tendency to leap from either realism or modernism to postmodernism ignores some of the most formally innovative and politically radical writing by women in the mid-century. It also erases the continuities represented by the influence of, for instance, Georgette Heyer on A. S. Byatt, or Mary Renault on Sarah Waters.

Frequently stigmatised as 'escapist', historical fiction offered release from present-day anxieties in a post-war world which was, despite the hope offered by the Coronation and the Festival of Britain, still shadowed by the Bomb and increasingly aware of internal fractures, decolonisation and the decline of Britain as a global power. By centralising female characters such as Elizabeth Tudor or Anne Boleyn, historical novels could offer what Alison Light has called compensatory 'fantasies of power' to women who were being pushed back into home and family by the coercive domestic ideology of the 'feminine mystique'.[10] Equally, historical fiction could enable political intervention through a range of techniques, including formal experimentation and allegorical commentary (what Elizabeth Maslen has called 'Aesopian' techniques).[11]

Interestingly, Cam saw historians and novelists as mutually indebted, arguing that the 'generally high standard of [historical] fiction today corresponds with the widening of the field of history'.[12] Women's historical fiction made imaginative use of the work of historians such as Eileen Power on medieval convents and Margaret Murray on witches, anthropologists such as Jane Harrison and J. G. Fraser, and archaeologists such as Sir Arthur Evans, who excavated the Minoan palace on Crete. The popularisation of Freudian psychoanalysis was equally important. It provided a way of interpreting the motives and characters of historical personages which paid attention to the formative nature of childhood experiences and which foregrounded the importance of sexuality and gender. While sometimes crude, such psychological analyses of the past allowed an understanding that gender was constructed and historically contingent.

Royal Tudor women: fantasies of power?

The popular historical fiction of this period is particularly associated with biographical historical novels or romantic biographies focusing on royal women by writers such as Plaidy, Seton, Lofts and Irwin. This centralisation of a female point of view in history is in itself a proto-feminist assertion. As Anya Seton pointed out in the Author's Note to *Katherine* (1954), there is frequently a paucity of information about or interest in women in either contemporary sources or standard histories, and yet, as she writes, Katherine Swynford, mistress and then wife of John of Gaunt and thus ancestress of the Tudor dynasty, 'was important to English history'.[13] Tudor women, particularly Elizabeth I and Anne Boleyn, are especially important to this genre, because their stories crystallise crucial issues around the place of female agency and desire in history. The true story of the Bluebeard King who went through six wives and transformed England into a Protestant country in his search for a male heir, only to have his despised daughter surpass him as the greatest monarch Britain has ever known, has the quality of myth or fairy tale. As well as sensational incident, it includes a varied cast of female characters who are self-evidently 'important to English history'.

Margaret Irwin (1889-1969) was singled out as 'perhaps the most brilliant of the novelists who are mainly concerned with historical personalities' by Cam.[14] Educated at Clifton School, Bristol, and Oxford University, Irwin began writing fantasy novels in the 1920s but then turned to historical fiction. Mainly depicting Elizabethan and early Stuart subjects, she gained a reputation for her historical accuracy. Cam especially praised Irwin's trilogy, *Young Bess* (1944), *Elizabeth, Captive Princess* (1948), *Elizabeth and the Prince of Spain* (1953), for its 'psychologically convincing portrait'.[15] Although Irwin's psychological realism is twentieth rather than sixteenth century, it was a strong part of the appeal for contemporaneous readers. The eager twelve-year-old princess in the opening scene of *Young Bess*, who 'may become anything',[16] is a figure for the reader to identify with. She comes to symbolise England itself. Alison Light has importantly explored the attractions of these novels, both reactionary and radical. Although recognising that they 'fed a conservative vision' for her as a young girl, she argues, they are also 'compensating registers of profound discontent.'[17] Whilst not 'feminist' as such, then, these novels have proto-feminist elements.

Irwin's trilogy traces Elizabeth's development from vulnerable young adolescent in an England threatened with invasion (as it was in the early 1940s) to a crowned queen who will bring stability to her country (echoing the accession of Elizabeth II in 1953). The problems of female identity are played out on a national scale. While *Young Bess* is structured around Bess's attraction to Tom Seymour, it offers a quasi-Freudian explanation for Elizabeth's famed reluctance to marry. Family life is 'a difficult affair with a father who had repudiated two of his six wives, beheaded two others, and bastardised both his daughters.'[18] For Elizabeth, as for the reader, Henry's wives symbolise the dangers for women in a society where men hold the power. As she remarks, "I've learnt about marriage from my stepmothers."[19] At the end of *Young Bess*, sexual desire is sublimated into a wider fantasy of power as Bess wants 'with all the wild excitement of a young lover's desire, to live, and to be Queen'.[20]

The final volume, *Elizabeth and the Prince of Spain*, was published in the year of the coronation. Like Elizabeth II, the young wife and mother held up as a symbol of 'New Elizabethan' womanhood, her Tudor predecessor is now presented as 'a smart modern woman, symptom of this modern England'.[21] The novel culminates in a lengthy coronation scene which is, like that of Elizabeth II, designed to be 'a show to be remembered for generations to come'.[22] Irwin emphasises that the 'meaning in the heart of the ... ceremonial' is the monarch's contract with her people – 'she was here to serve her countrymen; they were her charge, for God had charged her with them.'[23] – an interpretation with obvious appeal in 1953. This concern with the nature of 'kingship' unexpectedly links Irwin's novel with the work of Renault which is discussed below.

Even more than Elizabeth, Anne Boleyn is an enigmatic figure who has become a screen onto which historians, novelists and readers can project their own fantasies. As Jerome de Groot notes, the many novels about Boleyn 'tell a similar narrative with slightly different inflections.'[24] Each novelist has to make decisions in the face of gaps in the historical evidence. Thus Anne may be presented as a romantic heroine, a tragic victim, an astute politician, a vengeful harpy, or a feminist icon. Jean Plaidy's *Murder Most Royal* (1949), for instance, presents Anne as ambitious rather than in love with Henry VIII. It is broadly sympathetic to her, while Henry is depicted as a lascivious, narrowly religious man who 'murders' Anne.[25]

In contrast, *The Concubine* (1963), by Norah Lofts (1904–1983), which takes its title from the name used for Anne Boleyn by the Spanish Ambassador, self-consciously foregrounds the problems of historiography when the past can only be known through textual fragments. Born in Norfolk, Lofts gained a teaching diploma from Norwich Training College and taught English and History before she turned to writing, publishing over 50 books during her lifetime. Often (mis)labelled a romance writer, Lofts's novels are notable for her concern with economic and social issues, particularly in relation to women, whether queens or gypsies. As she said herself: 'most of my people are concerned with earning a living, achieving an ambition, holding their own in a harsh world.'[26]

The Concubine is divided into sections (rather than chapters) which act as vignettes, each prefaced by a quotation from a historical source: letters from Henry, court papers, Cavendish's *Life of Cardinal Wolsey*. These epigraphs simultaneously connote authenticity and point to the instability of historical evidence. This metafictional quality is thrown into further relief by a section headed '*I do not say that this is how it happened: I only say that this is how it could have happened. Your author.*'[27] In this section three masked balls are held by Anne at which 43 of her ladies pay her the compliment of dressing as her. Among 'Forty three versions of her[self], of varying validity', Anne is able, anonymously, to conceive the second child Henry now cannot give her but which she then miscarries.[28] The 43 versions of Anne vividly suggest the proliferation and circulation of her image, and its 'varying validity', in both contemporaneous documents and later fictions. Despite being pigeonholed as a writer of 'popular romance', Loft's sensitivity to the constructed and partial nature of women's representation within male-authored histories anticipates the historiographic metafictions analysed by Hutcheon.

'Playing games with the comedy of manners': Georgette Heyer's Regency Romances

While the biographical historical novels of Irwin, Plaidy and Loft focus on a real female personage, Georgette Heyer (1902–1974) established a new genre, the Regency romance, which set invented characters against a minutely-detailed historical background. Heyer attended Westminster College, London, and published her first historical novel, written to amuse her ill brother, when she was just 19. She went on to become a hugely successful author of bestsellers. While her early novels were historical adventure stories, she found her metier with *Regency Buck* (1935) – in which the spirited Judith Taverner meets her match in the Earl of Worth, a noted whip, gamester and friend of Beau Brummell. Judith's selection of *Sense and Sensibility* from the lending library at one point not only acts as a historical marker but sends a signal as to the kind of book Heyer is writing.[29]

In the 1940s, Heyer's novels became increasingly Austenesque comedies of manners – except that Austen, writing about her own time, gives us very few descriptions of clothes, interiors or carriages and rarely refers to public events or figures, whereas Heyer is self-consciously 'historical', using period detail to create and distance the effect of 'reality' which makes possible a fantasy of romance. In *Arabella* (1949), for instance, there is an orgy of costume detail when the heroine and her sisters look through the trunks of their mother's past finery to make it over for Arabella's debut:

> There were unimagined delights in the trunks: curled ostrich plumes of various colours; branches of artificial flowers; an ermine tippet ...; a loo-mask; a tiffany cloak ...; several ells of ribbon of a shade which Mamma said was called in her young day *opéra brull*, and quite the rage ...[30]

It is primarily through language that Heyer evokes a sense of the past: through narrative prose which is self-consciously, as Heyer noted, 'a mixture of Johnson and Austen',[31] with period terminology for costume and carriages and so on, and dialogue which is loaded with Regency slang ('take a damper', 'a man-milliner', to 'make a cake of oneself').[32]

By the late-1940s, Heyer had created a fictional world, a highly stylised and artificial version of the Regency period, which was so well established that she could begin to mock her own conventions. In *Arabella* the heroine, from a modest background, is provoked by the hero's disdain into pretending to be an heiress; in *The Grand Sophy* (1950) the tall, independent and unconventional Sophy is able to cry at will, her '*only* accomplishment!', as she informs the discomforted hero;[33] in *Sylvester* (1957) Phoebe has caricatured the hero in a Gothic novel, casting him as a villain named Count Ugolino, recognisable by his distinctive soaring black eyebrows.[34] The psychological drama of these novels is developed through verbal sparring between hero and heroine, adding another level to their linguistic playfulness.

Writing in 1969 well before feminist critics began to acknowledge the subversive possibilities of romance as a form for women, A. S. Byatt pinpointed the reasons for Heyer's success not only in her wealth of detail but also in the way in which she is 'playing romantic games with the novel of manners'.[35] One of Heyer's best novels, *A Civil Contract* (1961), self-consciously upends the romance plot, starting with the marriage of Adam Deveril to plain and sensible Jenny, the daughter of a wealthy Cit, rather than to the beautiful and sensitive Julia with whom he is in love.[36] While Adam has made this marriage to save his ancestral estate the novel develops into an exploration of the values of 'sense' and 'sensibility', 'reality' and 'fantasy'. Ultimately, it is Jenny, the wife who knows how he likes his tea and that he hates muffins, who ends by winning Adam's love. The 'balance' Byatt identifies in Heyer's novels 'between romance and reality, fantastic plot and real detail'[37] is produced through this kind of metafictional game-playing with conventions. Thus the influence of this consummate stylist can be traced in Byatt's own historiographic metafiction in the late twentieth century, particularly in *Possession: A Romance* (1990), providing an important but often unrecognised continuity in women's historical fiction.

The economics of realism: Sylvia Townsend Warner's *The Flint Anchor* (1954)

Belatedly recognised as a major writer, the later work of Sylvia Townsend Warner (1893–1978) is still under-discussed.[38] This neglect can be attributed to her politics, her sexuality and the fact that five of her seven novels were historical fictions during a period when this was an unfashionable genre. The daughter of a history master at Harrow, she was privately educated and initially became a musicologist, working as the only female editor of the ten-volume *Tudor Church Music* (1925–30). Both she and her partner of 40 years, the poet Valentine Ackland, were members of the Communist party and visited Spain during the Civil War. A fine poet, Warner also wrote short stories, publishing regularly in *The New Yorker*.

Warner described her final novel, *The Flint Anchor*, a family saga set in the early nineteenth century, as 'my work on Hypocrisy: neglected, I can but suppose, because by 1954 the worm of McCarthyism had got into English critical fashion as well and corrupted it.'[39] Like her earlier *The Corner That Held Them* (1948), it is a novel written on then unfashionable Marxist principles in order to expose the economics of realism. Warner lays bare the stony economic base which underpins the nineteenth-century realist novel and the ways in which this is 'authorised' by the damaging ideologies of imperialism, capitalism and heteronormativity which intersect in the domestic space of the home. Thus *The Flint Anchor* delineates the price paid for the hypocrisies involved in the making of a *pater familias*.

The novel opens with the inscription on the tombstone of John Barnard (1790–1863) which lauds him as a nineteenth-century ideal: 'a devoted husband and father, an example of industry, enterprise and benevolence to his native town, and for seventy years a regular worshipper in this Church.'[40] Yet, as his son Wilberforce recognises, Barnard was a hypocrite and domestic tyrant:

> There he lay, the author (under God, as he would be the first to point out) of Wilberforce's being and of the being of four other sons and five daughters, five of them dead, two self-exiled; and of untold mischief, fear, and discouragement: a man who had meant no harm, who had done his best for his family ... and who had spread around him a desert of mendacity and discomfort.[41]

Barnard's wife Julia is a drunkard, whose empty rum bottles symbolically fill the cellar of Anchor House; his son Joseph has escaped to the West Indies where he fathers illegitimate children – 'sooty little Barnards';[42] his daughter Euphemia joins the Moravians; Ellen, defaced by a birthmark, remains a spinster; and the 'angelic' Mary, the daughter Barnard loves to idolatry, is a manipulative hypocrite; Wilberforce himself is supremely selfish.

The family home, Anchor House, named after the anchor made of cut flints embedded in its brickwork, is surrounded by a 'wall of dark flint, twelve feet high, surmounted with a criss-cross of iron spikes', originally set up to deter Jacobins.[43] These symbolise the rigid boundaries of class, gender and race which keep the working classes out and the bourgeois family in. They also figure the structures of the realist novel which Warner is undermining. The novel has no chapters, no sympathetic central protagonist, and no plot. The disjunction between text and reality opened up by the inscription on the gravestone is reinforced by a range of intertextual references, including Moliere's study of hypocrisy, *Le Tartuffe* (1664), Daniel Defoe's *Robinson Crusoe* (1719); Jane Austen's *Mansfield Park* (1814); and Thackerary's *Vanity Fair* (1847). In a telling moment Julia interrupts Barnard's reading of Scott's *Old Mortality* (1816), exclaiming 'Murder!' and, taking issue with his rendering of a 'Scotch accent', reads it herself, following it with a dramatic rendition of Robert Burns's 'Tam o'Shanter' (1791) with its economically apposite 'moral': *'Think, ye may buy the joys o'er dear,/ Remember Tam O'Shanter's mare.'*[44]

The price of conformity for Barnard himself is a life spent in bad faith. A man who should never have married, he is made miserable by family life: Julia has to resort to 'unwomanly prompting' to rouse 'a brief lust' which ensures the begetting of children.[45] Contrasted with this is the camaraderie his son-in-law, Thomas Kettle, finds with the fishermen of Loseby. Confronted by the words 'Thomas Kettle goes with Dandy Bilby' written on a wall, Thomas tells their author, '"For a man to love a man is a crime in this country, Crusoe."'[46] Crusoe, openly declaring his love for Thomas, responds:

'"Not in Loseby, Mr Thomas, ... Nor in any sea-going place that I've ever heard of. ... in Loseby we go man with man and woman with woman, and nobody think the worse.'[47] This fluidity is contrasted with the flinty anchor and with the frozen lake on which Barnard escapes briefly from his married self, 'a truant from fatherhood' as he skates in 'luxurious isolation'.[48] For Barnard himself, as the description of him through the eyes of the Loseby fishermen as 'romantically handsome ... the image of a man's young man' suggests,[49] may be read as the 'apparitional' homosexual of this novel.[50]

Warner's publisher asked her to censor the Crusoe passage: 'I felt sorry for Ian,' Warner recorded, 'breathed on by all this howdydo about homosexuality (though my heart laughed him to scorn when he said so artlessly that no one could call it provocative, and it was a period story – like Forever Amber, no doubt).'[51] Radically different from Kathleen Winsor's Restoration bodice-ripper, *Forever Amber* (1944) *The Flint Anchor* may be, but Warner was right in recognising that both would be pigeonholed, and at best dismissed, as 'period stories'. It's perhaps not surprising that in the climate of 1950s McCarthyism and homophobia (in October 1953, for instance, the actor John Gielgud had been tried for homosexual soliciting) and with critical emphasis focused on the documentary social realism of the 'Angry Young Men', *The Flint Anchor* was Warner's last novel. As she told Arnold Rattenbury: 'Nothing big enough was left to say. We had fought, we had retreated, we were betrayed, and are now misrepresented.'[52]

Gothic Histories: Jean Rhys's *Wide Sargasso Sea* (1966) and the 'modern Gothic'

In 1966 an author many people had assumed dead, Jean Rhys (1890–1979), published a book, *Wide Sargasso Sea*, which has much more in common with *The Flint Anchor* than might at first appear.[53] Born in Dominica, Rhys came to England in 1907 and trained as an actress. After her first husband was imprisoned for fraud she had an affair with Ford Madox Ford who encouraged her to write. Her novels of the 1920s and 1930s, set in London and Paris, are now recognised as powerful explorations of the predicament of modern women financially and emotionally adrift in a brutally uncaring patriarchal society.

A revisionary prequel to *Jane Eyre*, *Wide Sargasso Sea* gives a voice and a history to the madwoman in the attic, the first Mrs Rochester.[54] Rhys uses modernist techniques – indeterminacy, symbolism, dreams, interior monologue, psychic fragmentation and multi-voicedness – to put into question the forms of realism and the ideologies of gender and race they support. Although Hutcheon does not include it in her discussion of historiographic metafiction, *Wide Sargasso Sea* is a crucial hinge or intertext between modernism and postmodernism. While it fits into Kristin Bluemel's definition of 'intermodernism' as a period, [55] its alignment with the 'middlebrow' or 'mass' genres recuperated under that umbrella is particularly complex. It offers a powerfully suggestive interface between the bestselling 'modern Gothic' of the 1960s and the 'serious' historical novel. Indeed, it arguably paves the way for the feminist literary theory of the 1970s, notably Ellen Moers's *Literary Women* (1976) and Sandra M. Gilbert and Susan Gubar's *The Madwoman in the Attic* (1979) both of which position the Gothic at the centre of women's writing.

The 'modern Gothic' or 'drugstore Gothic' craze began when Eleanor Hibbert, writing as 'Victoria Holt', published *Mistress of Mellyn* in 1960. This rewriting of *Jane Eyre* mediated through du Maurier's *Rebecca* (1938) – governess falls in love with her employer, only to fear that he has murdered his first wife – set a template for dozens of imitations. Holt herself wrote over 30. As well as the first person narrative voice borrowed from *Jane Eyre* via *Rebecca*, Holt's novels also use a vaguely 'Victorian' setting, thus displacing the plots of Brontë and du Maurier's novels (both set in what was then the contemporary) and making them explicitly 'historical' for the twentieth-century reader. By 1971, *Time* magazine was hailing this as one of the 'few boom areas in a generally depressed publishing industry' with paperback sales for 'top Gothics' running 'into the millions'.[56] Their formulaic nature, indicated by the ubiquitous cover image of a young woman with a looming Gothic house or castle, undoubtedly helped to give women's historical fiction a bad name. The obsessive repetition of plot motifs, both inter- and intra-textually, as critics have noted, suggests the ways in which these texts are enacting a psychic drama: a version of the Freudian family romance, whereby the 'daughter' must compete with the 'mother' for the love of the 'father'.[57]

The Gothic motif of the captive or imprisoned woman recurs repeatedly in women's writing during the 1960s: in historical fictions such as Irwin's *Elizabeth, Captive Princess*, or Jean Plaidy's *The Captive Queen of Scots* (1963), for instance, and in feminist studies such as Hannah Gavron's *The Captive Wife: Conflicts of Housebound Mothers* (1966). Holt's novels usually culminate with the heroine imprisoned in a tomb/womb-like space from which she is released by her husband/lover who reveals the real villain to be another woman: in *Mistress of Mellyn*, for instance, Martha is rescued from the crypt into which she has been locked with the decaying body of her husband's first wife.[58] The ubiquity of this motif suggests that these texts were articulating intense anxieties about the constricting role of 'housebound' women in this period. The modern Gothics, however, look to the husband for liberation.

Reading *Wide Sargasso Sea* against these other mid-century Gothic-historical fictions makes it look both less of a one-off and more radical. While the rewriting of *Jane Eyre* was a common strategy,[59] Rhys's stated motive was to correct the representation of the Creole Bertha Rochester, 'the "paper tiger" lunatic': 'For me', Rhys wrote, 'she must be at least *plausible with a past.*'[60] Thus Rhys rewrites *Jane Eyre* through a prequel which is an explicitly *historical* novel, situating it precisely in time and place to examine the conditions which shaped Antoinette and Rochester. A reference to the Emancipation Act on the opening page situates the action in Jamaica after 1833, a period of disorientation for the white Creole former slave-owning class, while a sampler stitched by Antoinette in school is dated 1839.[61] As Gayatri Chakravorty Spivak notes in an important post-colonial reading:

> In the figure of Antoinette ... Rhys suggests that so intimate a thing as personal and human identity might be determined by the politics of imperialism. Antoinette, as a white Creole child growing up at the time of Emancipation in Jamaica, is caught between the English imperialist and the black native.[62]

Antoinette's indeterminate position – stigmatised as a 'white cockroach' by the black former slaves and as a 'white nigger' by the English – makes her psychically vulnerable: 'Between you I often wonder who I am and where is my country,' she says, 'and where do I belong and why was I ever born at all'.[63] Married for her money to a man who both desires and fears her, and eventually locks her up in an attic in England, she descends into madness.

In making Antoinette/Bertha Mason the protagonist and giving her the voice she is denied in *Jane Eyre* (and which Rebecca is denied in du Maurier's novel), Rhys, like Warner, shows us the underside of the nineteenth-century realist novel, the violent and messy histories of racial and gender oppression which underlie the coherent surface of the text. Antoinette narrates the opening and ending of the novel, thereby framing and under-cutting the central section related by the Rochester figure (who is never named in the text). His renaming of Antoinette as 'Bertha' is a desperate attempt to control her. But, tellingly, he finds in the house where he and Antoinette spend their honeymoon a selection of canonical books, including novels by Walter Scott, 'and on the last shelf, *Life and Letters of* ... The rest was eaten away,'[64] suggesting that the grand narratives of Western culture have no explanatory power for women or the colonised. 'There is always the other side, always,' as Antoinette tells him.[65] Her dreamlike, fragmented and indeterminate narrative disrupts and displaces the violently oppressive hegemonic narrative he attempts to impose upon her. Rhys' novel is thus, to borrow Brumm's phrase, a 'postrealistic' text which uses modernist techniques to deconstruct the traditional historical novel. But it also exposes the con at the ending of the modern Gothic with its promise of a husband who will release the protagonist from captivity.

Performing gender, performing race: Mary Renault

At the end of *The English Historical Novel*, Fleishman briefly notes the emergence of Mary Renault (1905–1983) as a writer whose novels about classical civilisation represented one possible 'liberating trend' in post-Woolfian historical fiction.[66] Having studied English at Oxford, Renault trained as a nurse at the Radcliffe Infirmary where she met her lifelong partner, Julie Mullins. Her early novels used contemporary settings and included characters who were gay, bisexual or sexually unorthodox. Like Warner, however, Renault faced censorship in a climate where prosecutions for 'homosexual offences' had risen five-fold between 1939 and 1953.[67] Her American publishers refused to publish her sixth novel, *The Charioteer* (1953), with its frank depiction of a young soldier's homosexual awakening, for fear of prosecution. Renault, her biographer writes, 'never doubted that their decision sprang from McCarthyism, which had placed "sexual perverts" on a level with Communists.'[68] Set just after Dunkirk, *The Charioteer* uses classical texts, particularly Plato's *Phaedrus*, to explore the ideal of a love between men which is not damagingly stigmatised but accepted as an honourable relationship in a society where bisexuality was regarded as a norm. This experience of censorship explains why after 1953 all Renault's novels were historical, set in an ancient world which allowed her freedom to explore taboo issues of gender, sexuality and race and, by implication, to contrast this with more constricted contemporaneous mores.

Renault has become particularly associated with depictions of male homosexuality and this laid her open to criticism from, for instance, Carolyn Heilbrun who argued that she failed to imagine autonomous female characters.[69] More recently the development of theories of gender as performance, particularly those of Judith Butler, has allowed criticism to respond in more nuanced ways to Renault's work. Noting Renault's fascination with performance and her use of 'masks', for instance, Caroline Zilboorg argues that Renault occupies

> a predominantly constructionist position, which is at once conservative ...
> and radical, based on her own experiences of both heterosexual and lesbian desire, and on her historical and intercultural awareness that same-sex desire and same-sex acts have different meanings at different times and in different places.[70]

Ruth Hoberman, in *Gendering Classicism*, goes further in arguing that Renault, through a process of 'masquing the phallus', suggests that 'gender is itself more masquerade than biological essence and that the phallus, crucial indicator in Western culture of sexual difference, may not be as clear a gender marker as it seems.'[71] Hoberman's study importantly locates

Renault's work in relation to a wider tradition of reworking classical material in historical novels by Mitchison, Bryher, H.D. and Mary Butts.

A sense of the complexities of Renault's destabilising of the certainties of both gender and race can be gained by comparing two key figures in her work: the mythical Greek hero Theseus, reimagined as a short, slender bull-dancer in *The King Must Die* (1958) and *The Bull From the Sea* (1962), and the Macedonian Alexander the Great, who appears first as a boy in *Fire from Heaven* (1970) and then as seen through the eyes of the eunuch, Bagoas, in *The Persian Boy* (1972). Like Irwin's *Young Bess,* these are *Bildungsromans* which are concerned with the maturation of a leader and the notion of 'king-ship'. Both Theseus and Alexander are, like Elizabeth, shaped by their early experience of particularly fraught versions of the Freudian family romance and by their perceived 'illegitimacy' or difference. Brought up by his mother amid rumours that he has been sired by Poseidon himself, Theseus discovers his real father is Aigeus, king of Athens. Similarly, Alexander, caught in a bit-ter feud between his parents, Olympias and Philip, is rumoured to have been fathered by Zeus in the form of 'fire from heaven'.[72] Both men have power-ful mothers who are priestesses in the cult of the mother-goddess (Olympias is further associated with the Freudian 'phallic' mother by her habit of shar-ing her bed with snakes). In both cases they mature into exceptional leaders characterised by a mature openness to the difference of others.

Renault's achievement is to flesh out the source material – whether legend-ary myth or fragmentary, inconsistent histories – to reimagine a man who is historically plausible and psychologically realistic because he is a product of his environment. Reading Robert Graves's *Greek Myths* (1955), she wrote, she could 'begin to guess at the way Theseus's mind was furnished', specifically 'the tensions between victorious patriarchy and lately-defeated, still power-ful matriarchy' which underlay his relations with women.[73] Studying new archaeological evidence that the tribute to the Minotaur must have been conscripts to the bull-dance, she came to see 'the kind of man [Theseus's] conditioning might produce if his mind and aspiration had been that of a Helladic prince, but his body that of a [light, slender and wiry] bull-leaper.' Crucially, both Theseus and Alexander, who, as she notes, 'was not tall,'[74] can be seen as being like women in having to overcome the perceived limita-tions of their bodies and an 'illegitimate' or marginal position within their society.

By retelling Theseus's story in his own voice Renault is able to offer rational explanations for mythic happenings. The novels are structured as a series of encounters with 'kings', both male and female, who offer him possible role models. Thus his victory over the matriarchal Queen of Eleusis in *The King Must Die* can be read against his love of Hippolyta, the Amazon queen who is his equal in *The Bull From the Sea*.[75] The problem with the Eleusian queen's rule is not that it is matriarchal per se but that it suppresses men: 'Fathers were nobody in Eleusis, and could not choose wives for their own sons, or leave them a name, let alone property.'[76] This reversal of the patriarchal status quo we take for granted implicitly asks us to question the more usual norm where women are 'nobody' and cannot bequeath a name or property to their children. In the story of Alexander (written when she was living in South Africa) Renault develops her thinking about 'kingship' more specifically in relation to race. The love relationship between Bagoas, the Hellenised Persian eunuch who is both 'male' and 'female', and Alexander, the Asianised bisexual Macedonian king who attempts to unite East and West, radically destabilises essentialised categories. Not only gender, Renault suggests, but race is historically contingent and 'performed'.

Conclusion

As Barbara Caine has remarked, 'the importance of history within the British Women's Liberation can hardly be overestimated.'[77] While she is thinking of the work of historians such as Sheila Rowbotham, women's mid-century historical fiction, too, has a central place in feminism. Bringing together historical research with imaginative insight it explored and anticipated many of the issues which were to occupy second-wave feminists: the recovery of women's past, the confinements of family life, and the place of female desire and agency in the public and private worlds. A concern with the psychology of gender, often drawing on Freudian theories, is one theme that links many of these novels. It is notable that even the 'popular' texts – such as Irwin's Elizabeth trilogy or Heyer's romances – strive for psychological realism. In the work of Renault, Rhys and Warner, however, an understanding of the formative nature of early experience and the damage which can be done within family structures where gender roles are rigidly enforced frequently leads to an understanding of gender, race and sexuality as socially and historically constructed. Though an imaginative recreation of the psychologies of people in the past, these fictions also suggest the roots of our own fantasies and desires in history. We have, however, barely started to appreciate the range and complexity of these texts or to disentangle the reasons for their neglect in critical accounts.

Notes

1. Helen Cam, *Historical Novels* (London: Routledge & Kegan Paul, 1961), p. 3.
2. Ursula Brumm, 'Thoughts on History and the Novel', *Comparative Literature Studies*, 6 (1969), 327.
3. Avrom Fleishman, *The English Historical Novel: Walter Scott to Virginia Woolf* (Baltimore and London: Johns Hopkins Press, 1971), p. 233.
4. Cam, *Historical Novels*, p. 17
5. Gyorgy Lukács, *The Historical Novel*, trans. Hannah and Stanley Mitchell [1936/7] (Lincoln and London: University of Nebraska Press, 1983), p. 338.
6. Bryher, *This January Tale* (New York: Harcourt, Brace and World, 1966), p. viii.

7. Cam, *Historical Novels*, p. 4.
8. See Jan Montefiore, *Men and Women Writers of the 1930s: The Dangerous Flood of History* (London and New York: Routledge, 1996), Chapter 5; Chris Hopkins, *English Fiction in the 1930s: Language, Genre, History* (London: Continuum, 2006); *The Gender of Modernism: A Critical Anthology* ed. by Bonnie K. Scott (Bloomington and Indianapolis: Indiana University Press, 1990), pp. 372–92.
9. Linda Hutcheon, *A Poetics of Postmodernism: History, Theory, Fiction* (New York and London: Routledge, 1988), p. 5.
10. Alison Light, '"Young Bess": Historical Novels and Growing Up', *Feminist Review*, 33 (1989), 61; Betty Friedan, *The Feminine Mystique* [1963] (Harmondsworth: Penguin, 1982).
11. Elizabeth Maslen, 'Naomi Mitchison's Historical Fiction' in *Women Writers of the 1930s: Gender, Politics and History* ed. by Maroula Joannou (Edinburgh: Edinburgh University Press, 1999), pp. 138–50.
12. Cam, *Historical Novels*, p.18.
13. Anya Seton, *Katherine* [1954] (London: Hodder, 1961), p. 9.
14. Cam, *Historical Novels*, p. 16.
15. Cam, *Historical Novels*, p. 16.
16. Margaret Irwin, *Young Bess* [1944] (London: Allison and Busby, 1988), p. 4.
17. Light, '"Young Bess"', 58, 66.
18. Irwin, *Young Bess*, p. 8
19. Irwin, *Young Bess*, p. 189.
20. Irwin, *Young Bess*, p. 264.
21. Margaret Irwin, *Elizabeth and the Prince of Spain* [1953] (London: Allison and Busby, 1999), p. 191.
22. Irwin, *Elizabeth and the Prince of Spain*, p. 310.
23. Irwin, *Elizabeth and the Prince of Spain*, p. 321.
24. Jerome de Groot, *The Historical Novel* (London: Routledge, 2010), p. 75.
25. Jean Plaidy, *Murder Most Royal* [1949] (London: Pan, 1966)
26. *Twentieth-Century Romance and Historical Writers* ed. by Leslie Henderson, second edition (Chicago and London: St James Press, 1990), p. 403.
27. Norah Lofts, *The Concubine* (New York: Doubleday, 1963), p. 224.
28. Lofts, *The Concubine*, p. 226.
29. Georgette Heyer, *Regency Buck* [1935] (London: Pan, 1959), p. 113.
30. Heyer, *Arabella* [1949] (London: Arrow, 1999), p. 28.
31. Jane A. Hodge, *The Private World of Georgette Heyer* (London: Pan, 1985), p. 158.
32. Both A. S. Byatt and Hodge note the extensive private library Heyer acquired for her research and her notebooks of Regency vocabulary. Hodge, *The Private World of Georgette Heyer*, pp. 78–9.
33. Heyer, *The Grand Sophy* [1950] (London: Arrow, 1991), p. 245.
34. Heyer, *Sylvester* [1957] (London: Mandarin, 1992), p. 47–9.
35. A. S. Byatt, 'An Honourable Escape: Georgette Heyer' in *Passions of the Mind* [1969] (London: Vintage, 1993), p. 261.
36. Heyer, *A Civil Contract* [1961] (London: Arrow, 2005).
37. Byatt, 'An Honourable Escape', p. 265.
38. See Maud Ellmann, 'The Art of Bi-Location: Sylvia Townsend Warner' in *The History of Women's Writing, 1920–1945* vol. 8 ed. by M. Joannou (Basingstoke: Palgrave Macmillan, 2013), pp. 78–93.
39. Arnold Rattenbury, 'Plain Heart, Light Tether', 'Sylvia Townsend Warner 1893–1978: A Celebration', ed. Claire Harman, *PN Review* 23(1981), 8:3, 47.

40. Sylvia Townsend Warner, *The Flint Anchor* [1954] (London: Virago, 1997), p. 1.
41. Warner, *The Flint Anchor*, p. 241.
42. Warner, *The Flint Anchor*, p. 207.
43. Warner, *The Flint Anchor*, p. 2.
44. Warner, *The Flint Anchor*, p. 236.
45. Warner, *The Flint Anchor*, p. 243.
46. Warner, *The Flint Anchor*, p. 177.
47. Warner, *The Flint Anchor*, p. 183.
48. Warner, *The Flint Anchor*, p. 79.
49. Warner, *The Flint Anchor*, p. 5.
50. See Terry Castle's influential reading of Warner's *Summer Will Show* in *The Apparitional Lesbian: Female Homosexuality and Modern Culture* (New York: Columbia University Press, 1993), pp. 66–91.
51. Warner, *The Diaries of Sylvia Townsend Warner*, ed. Claire Harman (London: Virago, 1994), pp. 205–6.
52. Rattenbury, 'Sylvia Townsend Warner 1893–1978: A Celebration', p. 47.
53. For a rare comparison see J. P. Nesbitt, 'Rum Histories: Decolonising the Narratives of Jean Rhys's *Wide Sargasso Sea* and Sylvia Townsend Warner's *The Flint Anchor*', *Tulsa Studies in Women's Literature*, 26: 2 (2007), 309–30.
54. Peter Widdowson describes *Wide Sargasso Sea* as 'perhaps the best-known and prototypical re-visionary novel' in 'Writing back: contemporary re-visionary fiction', *Textual Practice* 20: 3 (2006), 497.
55. K. Bluemel, 'Introduction', in *Intermodernism: Literary Culture in Mid-Twentieth-Century Britain* ed. by Kristin Bluemel (Edinburgh: Edinburgh University Press, 2011), pp. 1–18.
56. Maureen Duffy, 'On the Road to Manderley', *Time*, 97(1971), 12 April, 65.
57. See for instance Joanna Russ, 'Somebody's Trying to Kill Me and I Think It's My Husband: The Modern Gothic', *Journal of Popular Culture*, 6 (1973), 666–91; T. Modleski, *Loving with a Vengeance* (London: Routledge, 1982).
58. Victoria Holt, *Mistress of Mellyn* [1960] (London: Fontana, 1963).
59. See Patsy Stoneman, *Brontë Transformations: The Cultural Dissemination of* Jane Eyre *and* Wuthering Heights (London: Prentice Hall, 1996), on *Jane Eyre* as an archetypal text which is repeatedly transmitted and transformed.
60. Jean Rhys, *Letters 1931–1966*, ed. Francis Wyndham and Diana Melly (London: Andre Deutsch, 1984), p. 262, p. 157, emphasis added.
61. Jean Rhys, *Wide Sargasso Sea* [1966] (London: Penguin, 2000), p. 5, p. 11. The setting of *Jane Eyre* is vague – a reference to Scott's *Marmion* (1808) as a new publication suggests the early nineteenth century but later references to riots suggest the Chartist unrest in 1839 and 1840.
62. Gayatri C. Spivak, 'Three Women's Texts and a Critique of Imperialism' in *Feminisms* ed. by R. R. Warhol and D. P. Herndl (Basingstoke: Macmillan, 1997), p. 901.
63. Rhys, *Wide Sargasso Sea*, p. 64.
64. Rhys, *Wide Sargasso Sea*, p. 46.
65. Rhys, *Wide Sargasso Sea*, p. 82.
66. Fleishman, *The English Historical Novel*, pp. 255–6.
67. Caroline Zilboorg, *The Masks of Mary Renault: A Literary Biography* (Columbia and London: University of Missouri Press, 2001), p. 86.
68. David Sweetman, *Mary Renault: A Biography* (London: Chatto and Windus, 1993), p. 145.

69. Carolyn Heilbrun, *Reinventing Womanhood* (London: Victor Gollancz, 1979), p. 75.
70. Zilboorg, *The Masks of Mary Renault*, p. xi.
71. Ruth Hoberman, *Gendering Classicism: The Ancient World in Twentieth-Century Women's Historical Fiction* (New York: State University of New York Press, 1997), p. 74.
72. Mary Renault, *The Alexander Trilogy* (London: Penguin, 1984).
73. Renault, 'Notes on *The King Must Die*', in *Afterwords: Novelists on Their Novels* ed. by T. McCormack (New York and London: Harper and Row, 1968), p. 83.
74. Renault, 'Notes on *The King Must Die*', p. 84.
75. Renault, *The King Must Die* [1958] (London: Four Square, 1961); Renault, *The Bull from the Sea* [1962] (Harmondsworth: Penguin, 1973).
76. Renault, *The King Must Die*, p. 68.
77. Barbara Caine, *English Feminism from 1780–1980* (Oxford: Oxford University Press, 1997), p. 257.

15

Children's Literature: Ideologies of the Past, Present and Future

Catherine Butler

British children's literature after the second world war

In 1945 the state of British children's literature was not a particularly healthy one. The United Kingdom was not only emerging from a shattering conflict, it was also in the midst of an extended period of austerity, one aspect of which – paper rationing – had had a particularly direct effect on the publishing industry. At the end of the war there was only one specialist children's publisher in the country, the Brockhampton Press.[1] Even Penguin's Puffin imprint, founded in 1940 and destined to be a dominant force in shaping the priorities and canon of modern British children's literature from the 1960s, initially published a mere dozen books per year. In the immediate post-war years publishers' output was dominated by reprints of pre-war favourites, and by newer books that tended to replicate almost exclusively their comfortably middle-class settings and norms.[2] By the end of the period covered by this volume the situation had been transformed, and British children's literature was in the middle of what would become known as its second Golden Age (the first being at the turn of the twentieth century). This transformation was due in part to a growing economy more able to support a flourishing industry, in part to a number of energetic and enlightened publishers and editors, and in part to a new generation of writers with a determination and vocation to produce high-quality literature for children and to reject the view of children's books as works of secondary merit.

The Second World War itself might seem to offer a rich subject matter for literature. Before 1945 numerous women writers had used the war as a setting for novels, these primarily being set on the Home Front. However, although a few books with wartime settings were published in the immediate aftermath of the war, such as Noel Streatfeild's *Party Frock* (1946),

© The Author(s) 2017
C. Hanson and S. Watkins, *The History of British Women's Writing, 1945–1975*,
History of British Women's Writing, DOI: 10.1057/978–1–137–47736–1_16

the subject remained virtually unaddressed by British women writers for children in the succeeding 20 years. Male authors were a little less reticent, especially once the war had become a staple subject of boys' comics such as *War Picture Library* (from 1958), *The Victor* (from 1961) and others;[3] however, it was to be several decades before a substantial body of works of British children's literature emerged with the Second World War at its heart. When such books did come, in the 1960s and particularly in the 1970s, they would largely be written by authors who were themselves children at the time of the conflict and were writing through the prism of their own childhood experience, as in Jill Paton Walsh's *The Dolphin Crossing* (1967) and *Fireweed* (1969), Susan Cooper's *Dawn of Fear* (1970), Jane Gardam's *A Long Way from Verona* (1971), Judith Kerr's *When Hitler Stole Pink Rabbit* (1971) and Nina Bawden's *Carrie's War* (1973). In the years immediately after the war, however, women writers were primarily working in very different genres: domestic fiction and adventure stories (both fantasy and realist), historical fiction, contemporary school stories, and some more specialised genres such as pony stories.

Many of these genres had already flourished for a considerable time before 1945. The girls' boarding school story, for example, had arguably been at its zenith in the early decades of the twentieth century, although 'classic' authors such as Elsie Oxenham and Elinor Brent-Dyer would continue to publish their long-established Abbey and Chalet School series well into the post-War period. Domestic fantasy had been a staple of British children's literature since Mrs Molesworth and Edith Nesbit at the turn of the century, while historical fiction was one of children's literature's foundational genres, albeit hitherto most notably in the work of male writers. A further continuity lay in the largely homogeneous class perspective of most children's writers. The vast majority of children's books in the 20 years after the war were set within a bourgeois milieu, in which private education, cars, domestic help and holidays in rented cottages were the norm. This, too, was in direct continuity with pre-war literary models. Even though Eve Garnett had won the Carnegie Medal in 1937 for her sympathetic portrayal of working-class life in *The Family from One End Street*, her perspective (while affectionate) was distinctly anthropological and her implied readership was clearly not expected to identify with the book's protagonists. Equally, while Mary Norton's depiction of the Clock family in *The Borrowers* gave a prominent place to a 'working class' family (albeit one parasitic on their bourgeois hosts for the necessities of life) it did so only within the context of a fantasy that portrayed them as diminutive and largely unseen. It would not be until the 1960s that a substantial number of books representing contemporary British working-class life from 'within' would be written for children. Black British children would have to wait even longer for their experience to be given a central place within fiction, in Beryl Gilroy's Nippers series (from 1970).

Despite these continuities, many of the books produced in the decades following 1945 exhibited a shift in tone and emphasis, reflecting some of the fundamental changes in post-war Britain. The decline of Empire and the physical destruction by bombing of much of the fabric of the country's major towns and cities were accompanied by the advent of a reforming Labour government, increasing social mobility and widespread technological advances. While many saw in these changes opportunities for greater freedom and equality, others were ambivalent at best, viewing the conservation of the past (in both its physical and less tangible forms) as an urgent cultural necessity, concerns that were repeatedly rehearsed in children's literature. Gender roles too were deeply implicated in many of these developments and in the reaction to them. As after World War I, despite women's widespread participation in war work the cessation of hostilities signalled a cultural lurch to the *status quo ante* and to an emphasis on housewifery as the natural vocation of women and of mothers in particular. Not for nothing were the BBC's afternoon radio (and later television) programmes for children called *Listen with Mother* (from 1950) and *Watch with Mother* (from 1953). The latter title, according to the British Film Institute, 'was intended to deflect fears that television might become a nursemaid to children and encourage "bad mothering"'.[4] Children's books too, in their frequent depictions of domestic life, were a key cultural arena in which such norms might be either reinforced or challenged.

In the remainder of this chapter we shall explore some of these tensions as they existed in the first half of this period, as well as some of the later developments within children's literature from the 1960s onwards, through the work of Philippa Pearce (1920–2006), Rosemary Sutcliff (1920–1992), Joan Aiken (1924–2004) and Enid Blyton (1897–1968), among others.

Philippa Pearce and fantasies of the past

If any single novel from the first half of this period can be said to have achieved an iconic status, it is probably Philippa Pearce's second novel, *Tom's Midnight Garden* (1958).[5] Tom Long, the book's protagonist, is sent for reasons of quarantine (his brother having contracted measles) to spend the summer in his childless aunt and uncle's stuffy flat, which is part of what was once a large house – the building being based on the mill house in Great Shelford in Cambridgeshire where Pearce spent her own childhood. There he suffers days of overheated boredom and stodgy food before discovering that every night the old grandfather clock in the downstairs hall strikes an impossible thirteen hours, at which moment the back door of the house opens onto not a concrete yard but the beautiful garden that existed in the Victorian age, before the house was divided and its land sold off. Repeated visits reveal the garden and house of the past in their various seasons, and introduce Tom to Hatty, a young Victorian girl who is the only person (other than Abel, the gardener) able to see him there. This central part of the book is an idyll, as Tom and Hatty share adventures together in the garden; but Hatty grows older with each nightly visit, eventually becoming a young woman to whom Tom is barely visible, and for Tom this increasingly painful experience is ameliorated only by the eventual discovery that the Victorian child Hatty is now the flats' aged landlady, Mrs Bartholomew, whose nightly dreams of her childhood were the key through which he gained access to the past.

In some ways *Tom's Midnight Garden* is a familiar and even conventional work. Within children's literature stories of time travel date back to E. Nesbit's *The Story of the Amulet* (1906), though a more precise precursor is Alison Uttley's 1939 classic, *A Traveller in Time*, which uses the same device of a modern child making repeated 'visits' to a point in the past and forming deep emotional bonds with the people there. Both books also owe much to another venerable genre, in which lonely children, often isolated by illness, bereavement or enforced separation from parents, discover themselves through exploration of a large and initially forbidding house or garden. At the head of this tradition stands Frances Hodgson Burnett's *The Secret Garden* (1911), but it is prominent too in such post-war classics as Elizabeth Goudge's *The Little White Horse* (1946), Mary Norton's *The Borrowers* (1952) and Lucy M. Boston's *The Children of Green Knowe* (1954). As Humphrey Carpenter observes, in many of these books the themes of self-discovery and discovery of the past are explicitly linked:

> A very large number of good books for children were written in England between the 1950s and the 1970s, so it is all the more striking that the greater part of children's fiction produced in this period has the same theme: the discovery or rediscovery of the past.
>
> A typical plot from this period is likely to concern one or two children who stumble across some feature of history or mythology which concerns their own family or the place where they are living or staying, and which often involves magic or supernatural events. The children become drawn into it, usually at their own peril, and in consequence achieve some kind of spiritual, moral or intellectual growth.[6]

In Boston's and Pearce's treatments particularly, the past becomes the touchstone by which the present may be validated or against which it is found wanting. It is also presented as the taproot that permits present-day growth, the cutting of which threatens to leave the modern world sterile and spiritually dead. In *The Children of Green Knowe*, Boston's deracinated child protagonist, Tolly, discovers in the company of his wise great-grandmother Mrs Oldknow and of the seventeenth-century child-ghosts who haunt her ancient house (which, like the house in *Tom's Midnight Garden*, is closely modelled on a real place, the mediaeval manor house in Cambridgeshire where Boston lived) a sense of belonging and identity he has not known before, and is able not only to find physical refuge but to take his place more or less unproblematically in the great trans-historical community of masters and servants who inhabit Green Knowe's grounds, moated from modernity by the fenland flood.

Pearce's Tom Long enjoys no such landed inheritance, and in *Tom's Midnight Garden* the depredations of the twentieth century are no distant threat but rather an established fact that defines the setting of the story. Significantly, at the time of the novel's composition the mill house where Pearce had spent her childhood was under threat of being divided into flats, much like the house in the book. *Tom's Midnight Garden* has long been recognised as a work offering profound insights into time, personal growth and the nature of friendship, particularly across the generations, but beyond these broad human concerns it also situates itself firmly within a particular historical perspective. The loss of the garden to small plots and ugly houses, like the conversion of the grand house into flats, is cast by Pearce in a wholly negative light, and forms part of a wider picture of contemporary Britain as drab, diminished and subject to what Linda Hall has dubbed 'an epidemic of modernity'.[7] By contrast, the Victorian past is idealised. The labour that maintains the affluent existence of the big house and its family remains largely invisible; Abel, the gardener who is the only named working-class character, is characterised as a simple, devout, child-like man, and (like Burnett's Dickon Sowerby before him) floats free of any real socio-economic context. Hatty's is a lost world, and while Pearce's novel encourages the reader to come to terms with that loss it makes little attempt to show any positive aspect to the more egalitarian present inhabited by Tom Long. In *Tom's Midnight Garden* the consolation of individual human relationships appears to be the only compensation for a more general decline. To this extent Pearce's is a conservative book: however, time slip and time travel fictions need not involve this presentation of the past as preferable to the present, and in later novels such as Penelope Farmer's *Charlotte Sometimes* (1969), Penelope Lively's *The Driftway* (1972) and Jill Paton Walsh's *A Chance Child* (1978), such comparisons would be more nuanced.

Rosemary Sutcliff, Joan Aiken and historical fiction

Similar questions are, of course, also implicated in realist historical fiction, a genre that notably flourished in the period 1945–1975, with Rosemary Sutcliff, Cynthia Harnett, Hester Burton and Barbara Willard amongst its foremost female British practitioners. Of these, Sutcliff is probably the most celebrated, especially for her novels set before, during and in the centuries after the Roman occupation of Britain, of which the first to be published was *The Eagle of the Ninth* (1954).[8] Sutcliff's recurring interest in military stories may reflect her family background (her father was an officer in the Royal Navy), but the Roman invasion and occupation in particular received attention from numerous children's writers in the 1950s. This is understandable at a time when questions of empire and imperial decline were prominent in British life. The British Empire was beginning the long process of dismantlement, and the Cold War had redrawn the political and ideological map in ways that left the United Kingdom a far more marginal place. The country was having both to deal with the legacy of its own empire and to find a way to accommodate itself to its new and diminished position, learning to align itself with larger political blocs centred elsewhere, primarily in the United States. The Roman period offered a conveniently ambiguous setting,[9] in which authors could either place their implied readers in the position of the Romans, cast (as the imperial British had cast themselves) in the role of bringers of literacy, luxuries and the other trappings of civilization to benighted savages, or else emphasise the experience of the invaded Britons, a group living near the edge of the map whose independence, culture and religion were subjected to unprovoked attack by a foreign power intent on subjugating the land and looting its resources. Again and again in children's books of the 1950s, authors such as Henry Treece, Lawrence Garde du Peach and Lydia Eliott play out these debates, typically landing firmly on the side of 'progress' in the form of Rome, the benefits of which are seen easily to outweigh the drawbacks of military occupation.

From the beginning, Sutcliff's approach was far more sophisticated. While acknowledging the importance of cultural background in shaping individuals' beliefs and values she refused to reduce her Roman and British characters to simple 'representatives' of their respective cultures, instead showing the complexity with which cultural factors combined with individual personalities in the new world that followed the Claudian invasion. In *The Eagle of the Ninth* influence runs in both directions, not just from Rome to Britain, and there are in any case commonalities between the worldviews of figures such as Marcus (the young invalided Roman officer who is the book's primary protagonist), and his British slave Esca, the relationship between whom forms the backbone of the novel. In later books, set in the succeeding centuries of Roman Britain and in the aftermath of Roman withdrawal, both the political situation and the blending of cultural and personal lives are still more complex.

Sutcliff created some memorable female characters, including Marcus's young admirer Cottia in *The Eagle of the Ninth*, but it is notable that after her two early works, *The Queen Elizabeth Story* (1950) and *The Armourer's House* (1951), it would be another 28 years (and more than 20 novels) before she gave a children's novel a female protagonist – in her story of Boudicca, *Song for a Dark Queen* (1978). In part this reflects her subject matter, which often carries the action into public and military arenas where it would be harder to find plausible ways to give a female figure a central role; but it also reflects a more general tendency in British children's publishing of the time to favour male protagonists, at least outside certain well-defined genres such as pony books and girls' boarding-school stories. It is true of course that there are numerous important female-centred novels from this period that lie outside these fairly tight generic boundaries, including family and coming-of-age stories such Dodie Smith's *I Capture the Castle* (1949) and Jill Paton Walsh's *Goldengrove* (1972), and supernatural and fantasy stories such as Catherine Storr's *Marianne Dreams* (1958) and Joan G. Robinson's *When Marnie was There* (1967). Nevertheless, in this period (and since) there was a general deference to the received marketing wisdom that, whereas girls will willingly read stories about boys, the reverse is not the case. While prominent female writers such as Sutcliff (and indeed Philippa Pearce) typically placed boys centre-stage, their male counterparts were far less likely to do the same for girls, and the overall result was a situation in which boys became the default protagonists of children's books, especially in stories of adventure.

The Sussex-based writer Joan Aiken's series of quasi-historical novels beginning with *The Wolves of Willoughby Chase* (1962) illustrates one alternative approach.[10] These books are set in an alternative nineteenth century, in which the Stuart king James III is on the throne (though under continual threat from Hanoverian pretenders), and packs of wolves roam Britain, having migrated from the Continent by way of the recently constructed Channel Tunnel. *The Wolves of Willoughby Chase* itself is a lively melodrama, concerning the attempt of the villainous Miss Slighcarp to take over Willoughby Hall through forgery and subterfuge, ousting the young cousins Bonnie and Sylvia and consigning them to an orphanage – a predicament they overcome with the aid of their friend, the cave-dwelling goose boy, Simon. It is only in the second book, *Black Hearts in Battersea* (1964), which tells of Simon's later adventures in the capital, that we meet the girl who went on to become the series' central character, the ever-resourceful working-class Londoner Dido Twite. Aiken, who had not intended to base the series around Dido, appeared to drown her at the end of that book, only to revive her by popular demand in several subsequent novels, in most of which she is instrumental in thwarting villainous (not to say ludicrous) Hanoverian plots.[11]

The use of an alternative-history setting allows Aiken many kinds of freedom not permitted to a traditional historical novelist, and Dido, whose self-confidence and warm heart allow her to converse with everyone from street urchins to royalty with equal ease, is given a leading role in national events. At the same time, the novels' use of exaggeration and absurdity, such as the Hanoverian scheme to put St Paul's Cathedral on wheels and roll it into the Thames, may prompt us to question how seriously we are to take Aiken's attribution of extraordinary agency and influence to this humbly-born girl. Aiken wrote that her subversion of historicity in these books offered a release that unfettered her imagination in other ways, too:

Have you ever noticed how peculiarly liberating it is to follow a conventional pattern in nearly all respects, but to include one odd factor? ... At a sticky children's party, if you simply paint a blue nose on every guest the effect is very uninhibiting. One step aside from the normal and you're away…Having a Stuart king and a few wolves in the middle of the nineteenth century somehow set me free to enjoy myself.[12]

This aspect of Aiken's novels is ambiguous, as is typical of the carnivalesque. The subversion of conventional power relations in her books is counterbalanced by the fact that Dido is loyal to the Stuart dynasty, while Simon for his part turns out to be of royal blood. Equally, Dido's centrality to high politics and the ease with which she assumes leadership may be undermined by the suspicion that the presentation of a young girl in these terms is itself an aspect of Aiken's absurdism; nevertheless, Dido Twite models a variety of empowered girlhood that was in short supply elsewhere in British children's literature.

Enid Blyton and the children's publishing scene

We have noted that the default setting of post-war British children's literature was middle-class. Much of it was also self-consciously literary, in that the criteria for publication and for awards tended to favour books featuring and demanding a sophisticated breadth of cultural, literary and linguistic reference. This orientation reflected the didactic imperatives that have always underlain children's literature, but in the 1960s and 1970s, as Lucy Pearson has shown in her study of British children's publishing in this period,[13] that post-war consensus concerning what children's books should do and be began to break down. Pearson takes as representative and contrasting case studies the publishers Kaye Webb, head of Puffin from 1961, and the novelist and educationalist Aidan Chambers, who founded Macmillan's Topliner imprint in 1968. In the early 1960s the Puffin imprint was devoted exclusively to the paperback republication of existing titles, and from the beginning of her tenure Webb sought to remake Puffin's hitherto eclectic list in order to reflect her commitment to literary quality. Almost all the authors so far mentioned in this chapter were at some point published by Webb, something that came to be seen as denoting their having met a certain 'standard' defined in terms of traditional literary culture.

With Topliners, Aidan Chambers took a different approach, seeking to inspire a love of books in reluctant readers, and commissioning writers and titles with the intention of meeting such readers halfway rather than demanding they be already acculturated to canonical tastes and norms. The experience of ethnic-minority and working-class children was also reflected far more widely in Topliners books than in Puffins. Many featured first-person narrators using non-standard English, and dealt with urban city environments rather than the villages, small towns and grand houses that had provided the settings of much classic British children's literature. Although there was no British equivalent of the American writer Judy Blume, who from the early 1970s tackled such taboo subjects as menstruation, masturbation and birth control in books such as *Are You There God? It's Me, Margaret* (1970), *Deenie* (1973) and *Forever* (1975), the Topliners imprint was also part of the wider 1960s cultural movement to reduce inhibitions regarding the reality of young people's sexuality, and helped to entrench young adult literature as a distinct generic and marketing category. Nevertheless, while his tactics differed from Webb's, Chambers shared with her a desire to induct child readers into the reading of canonical adult literature.

> Teenage books as a bridge between children's and adult literature was the initial impelling idea between Topliners and the beginning of my accidentally acquired career as an editor. As one Topliner reader wrote, explaining why he liked them, 'It is a big step up from Blyton to Dostoevsky'. If you haven't made it by the time you are twelve you need help.[14]

Chambers may have been more active than traditional publishers such as Webb in looking beyond the traditional constituency of child readers, but classic adult literature was still his ultimate destination.

I have spent a little time sketching out this context, in part because it is necessary to understand the anomalous position of the bestselling British children's writer of the period, Enid Blyton. Blyton had been a famously (perhaps notoriously) prolific writer since the 1920s, and in 1938 her commercial success had enabled her to buy Green Hedges, the house in Buckinghamshire that became a symbol of the kind of middle-class wholesomeness she promoted in her work, and where she would go on to produce many of her best-known books in the post-War years. These include the six instalments of her popular boarding school series, Malory Towers, which follows schoolgirl Darrell Rivers and her friends through their education at a seaside school in Cornwall; and all but three of the 21 titles in the Famous Five series, which recount the adventures of siblings Julian, Dick and Anne, their cousin George (officially Georgina) and George's dog Timmy, as they hike and camp their way through various rural locations, solving mysteries and foiling thieves and smugglers along the way.

Blyton died in 1968, but the popularity of her books continued unabated through the 1970s and beyond, with her sales to date reportedly totalling more than 600 million books. Nevertheless, she has been a curiously marginal figure in critical accounts of British children's literature. John Rowe Townsend's classic *Written for Children* (1974), for example, while it laments the absence of L. Frank Baum from some authoritative American histories of children's literature, attributing the omission to 'unconscious snobbery',[15] itself omits all mention of Blyton. There are numerous possible reasons for this, as we shall see, but one is that in the world of British children's publishing Blyton fell between two stools. On the one hand, she did not fit the criteria for literary quality demanded by an editor such as Kaye Webb, who decided against publishing Blyton under the Puffin imprint on the grounds that she was insufficiently demanding.[16] Webb, as we have noted, favoured sophisticated authors, who challenged readers to share in the creation of worlds rather than stopping to explain events or tell the reader what to think and feel about them. Blyton's work, by contrast, was limited in terms of both vocabulary and grammatical and stylistic variety, and laced with narratorial interventions designed to direct readers' responses in quite an explicit way: '"Good-bye, Darrell and Sally and the rest. We'll meet you again soon. Good luck till then!"'[17] One might imagine that Blyton would have found greater favour with the new wave of editors represented by Aidan Chambers, whose imprint catered especially for readers lacking the literary and cultural fluency assumed by Webb, but such was not that case. Chambers wished to lead readers *from* Blyton and the kind of reading she represented; indeed, he described a liking for Blyton as 'a symptom of arrested development'.[18] Moreover, Blyton's intensely middle-class world view, along with her dubious representations of race and gender, made her co-option by figures such as Chambers highly unlikely.

In addition to the doubts about Blyton expressed from within the publishing industry there has been no shortage of educationalists, librarians, parents, and pundits ready to condemn various aspects of her work. Besides her perceived technical inadequacies, which extend to plotting and characterization as well as style, she has been the object of considerable political and social criticism. The fact that her protagonists, such as the Famous Five and the pupils at Malory Towers, are white and staunchly middle-class does not distinguish them from the vast majority of protagonists in British children's books of her era; more problematic is the extent to which class is sometimes used by Blyton as a moral marker, with an urban accent or a 'scruffy' appearance tipping off both characters and reader that a person may be untrustworthy. That such indications are sometimes subverted does not alter the fact that they are part of the books' structure of expectation, any more than the existence of 'good' working-class characters, such as the rural women who supply the Five with hearty meals in farms and cafés, or the lean countrymen who are able to furnish them with natural lore or local knowledge. The attitude of the Five (or at least of the four human ones) is essentially tribal, and the reader is implicitly asked to share the perspective of that tribe.

The question of gender is a more complex one. Both the Malory Towers and Famous Five series have been criticised in terms of their representation of femininity in particular. In Malory Towers, the school's ethos is explicitly devoted to turning the schoolgirls into helpful young women and only secondarily to their academic education, as the headmistress's annual welcome talk makes clear:

I do not count as our successes those who have won scholarships and passed exams, though these are good things to do. I count as our successes those who learn to be good-hearted and kind, sensible and trustable, good, sound women the world can lean on.[19]

We catch a glimpse of what this means in practice in the second book, *Second Form at Malory Towers* (1948), when one of the girls rashly practises her talent for caricature, to the humiliation of one of her subjects:

"I'll never draw anyone again!" said Belinda dismally.
"Oh yes you will!" said Miss Linnie. "But you'll probably draw kinder pictures in future. Don't be too clever, Belinda – it always lands you in trouble sooner or later."[20]

The lesson that being 'too clever' inevitably leads to trouble reinforces the sense that education at Malory Towers has more to do with socialization into such 'feminine' qualities as helpfulness and the prioritization of others' needs than with book learning.

In the Famous Five books, the figure of Anne – the youngest of the group, and as much a housewife by vocation as Wendy Darling – is the usual focus of feminist misgiving. Her elder brother Julian, the group's self-appointed leader, has a tendency to patronise her (although she is far from the sole victim of his arrogance), and it is taken for granted that, as a girl, she will not take part in the group's more perilous adventures. Moreover she generally welcomes and confirms that view, being happy to take charge of the group's base camp and to supply its domestic needs. Anne, however, has a powerful counterpart in the form of her cousin George, who dresses as a boy and insists on being addressed as one, and who from her first appearance frequently expresses the wish that she were a boy herself: "'I hate being a girl. I won't be.'"[21] Characters with a desire for boys' activities and freedoms had been a staple of girls' literature since Jo March in *Little Women* (1868), and George is usually read accordingly as a tomboy, although the text leaves open the possibility of a more fundamental identification with the male gender. Despite frequent put-downs from Julian, George is frequently successful in showing that she can be as brave, athletic and resourceful as the boys, and in that respect demonstrates an alternative model of girlhood from that provided by Anne.

In creating Anne and George, Blyton takes advantage of a longstanding tradition of children's books with multiple protagonists, whether in the form of tight friendship groups like those often featured in school stories, or of the various combinations of friends and relations who embark on joint adventures in the work of E. Nesbit, Arthur Ransome, Hilda Lewis, C. S. Lewis and many others. Combining a mixture of sexes, ages and personality types provides readers with a 'selection' from which they are implicitly invited to choose. Sometimes, indeed, the invitation is explicit, as in the final lines of Noel Streatfeild's *Ballet Shoes* (1936): '"I wonder" – Petrova looked up – "if other girls had to be one of us, which of us they'd choose to be?"'[22] If Anne were the only girl of the Five, her devotion to traditional femininity would be obviously regressive; if George were, her desire for boyhood might be read as an admission that to be a girl is to be inferior. However, as part of a larger group engaged in a continual dynamic negotiation of what is appropriate behaviour for boys and girls and the limits of their natures and capabilities, their joint presence serves (as David Rudd puts it) to 'put the whole debate about sexism on the agenda'.[23] Similarly, while the ethos of Malory Towers is certainly far from being feminist, one can argue that with this, as with other series in the same genre, the existence of an all-female society allows girls to explore roles and spaces that in a mixed setting are more usually reserved to boys, and encourages readers to question the culturally-bound limits placed on female behaviour and character.

Conclusion

In so far as Blyton's books were sexist they were far from unique in that respect. By the end of our period feminists were paying serious attention to the representation of girls and women in children's books, and research carried out on both sides of the Atlantic by scholars such as Lenore J. Weitzman, Wilma Pyle and groups such as the Children's Rights Workshop demonstrated that girls were still grossly under-represented in children's books for all ages, especially in active and protagonist roles – a situation that more recent research suggests has been only partially remedied.[24] By the mid-1970s Blyton's style of adventure story was in any case largely outmoded, and a new generation of female British writers had begun to take children's literature in fresh directions. Diana Wynne Jones was producing ingenious fantasy novels that crossed the lines of class and race; Joan Lingard was dealing with contemporary political issues such as the Troubles in Northern Ireland; Jan Mark was bringing a writerly seriousness to the realist depiction of the lives of 'ordinary' children; and Gene Kemp was providing a searching interrogation of gender norms and assumptions.

As one brief example of how things were changing we may point to Penelope Lively's *The House in Norham Gardens* (1974).[25] This book is aimed at a slightly older readership than those discussed so far in this chapter, and concerns teenaged Clare Mayfield, the great-granddaughter of a member of the Cooke-Daniels expedition of 1905. Clare discovers a trophy of that expedition in the attic of the Victorian house in Oxford where she lives with her two aunts – a building redolent of 'hymns and the Empire, Mafeking and the Khyber Pass'.[26] The object is a tamburan (or ceremonial shield), and Clare becomes increasingly concerned with the moral obligation to return it to the isolated New Guinea tribe that created it, for whom such objects were a way of memorializing the souls of their ancestors. In this sense the book assumes (without ever leaving Oxford) the nature of a quest narrative, but this is an unconventional quest in which the destination is vague and perhaps no longer extant, so corrosive has the influence of Western culture been in the 70 years since her own ancestor's voyage. As Clare's friend, the Ugandan student John Sempebwa, puts it: '"They stop making tamburans ... as soon as they've jumped into the twentieth century. They seem to forget how, or why they did it."'[27] This is a sophisticated story that deals with numerous issues largely ignored in the first half of our period: colonial guilt, cultural appropriation, the constructed nature of historical truth and the cultural biases inevitably involved in its telling, immigration and multiculturalism and of course the functions of personal and cultural memory, all of which are explored with the subtlety and deftness that would later become the trademark of Lively's adult novels.

One could easily multiply such examples. Overall, the range of subject matter and genres available to children's writers at the end of our period was far broader than it had been at the beginning, and although the default settings of British children's literature remained white, middle class and centred on the traditional nuclear family, writers and publishers were increasingly attentive to the growing proportion of young readers with different experiences and interests.

Notes

1. Lucy Pearson, *The Making of Modern Children's Literature in Britain* (Farnham: Ashgate, 2013), p. 3.
2. Nicholas Tucker, 'Setting the Scene' in *Children's Book Publishing in Britain since 1945* ed. by Kimberley Reynolds and Nicholas Tucker (Aldershot: Scolar Press, 1998), pp. 1–19 (pp. 1–3).
3. Brian Edwards, 'The Popularisation of War in Comic Strips 1958-1988', *History Workshop Journal*, 42 (1996), 180–9.
4. Alistair McGown (n.d.) 'Watch with Mother', *Screen Online*, British Film Institute: <http://www.screenonline.org.uk/tv/id/445994/> [accessed 1 October 2014].
5. Philippa Pearce, the daughter of a flour miller, was educated at the Perse Girls' School in Cambridge and won a state scholarship to read English and History at Girton College, Cambridge. She worked for the civil service from 1942 to 1945 and then as a producer and scriptwriter in the BBC's schools broadcasting department.
6. Humphrey Carpenter, *Secret Gardens: A Study of the Golden Age of Children's Literature* (Boston: Houghton Mifflin, 1985), pp. 217–18.
7. Linda Hall, '"House and Garden": The Time-Slip Story in the Aftermath of the Second World War' in *The Presence of the Past in Children's Literature* ed. by Ann L. Lucas (Westport CT: Praeger, 2003), pp. 153–8 (p. 154); see also Catherine Butler and Hallie O'Donovan, *Reading History in Children's Books* (Basingstoke: Palgrave Macmillan, 2012), pp. 173–5.

8. Rosemary Sutcliff was brought up in a naval family. As a child she contracted Still's disease, a form of juvenile arthritis, which led to long spells in hospital, a broken education and was life affecting. Sutcliff was a painter of miniatures who exhibited at the Royal Academy before she began writing.

9. Butler and O'Donovan, pp. 15–47; also Butler, 'The "Grand Tour" as Transformative Experience in Children's Novels about the Roman Invasion' in *Heroes and Eagles: The Reception of Ancient Greece and Rome in Children's Literature* ed. by Lisa Maurice (Leiden: Brill, 2015), pp. 257–79.

10. Born into a writing family (her father, mother, sister and brother were all writers) Joan Aiken worked as an information officer, and later as the librarian at the United Nations' London information centre between 1943 and 1949. She subsequently worked as a journalist, including five years as features editor at Argosy magazine (1955–60), and as a copywriter.

11. Lizza Aiken, 'Dido Twite – the Ever Hopeful Heroine', *Joan Aiken Website*, 2014, <https://joanaiken.wordpress.com/2014/04/21/dido-twite-the-ever-hopeful-heroine/> [accessed 21 April 2014].

12. Joan Aiken 'A Thread of Mystery', *Children's Literature in Education*, 1: 2 (1970), 30–47, 39.

13. Pearson, *The Making of Modern Children's Literature*.

14. Aidan Chambers, 'Alive and Flourishing: a Personal View of Teenage Literature' in *Booktalk: Occasional Writing on Literature and Children* (Stroud: Thimble Press, 1995), pp. 84–91 (p. 87); qtd. in Pearson, *The Making of Modern Children's Literature*, p. 127.

15. John R. Townsend, *Written for Children: an Outline of English-Language Children's Literature*, 2nd Edition (Harmondsworth: Kestrel, 1974), p. 109.

16. Pearson, *The Making of Modern Children's Literature in Britain*, p. 91.

17. Enid Blyton, *First Term at Malory Towers* [1946] (London: Dean, 2004), p. 169.

18. Aidan Chambers, *The Reluctant Reader* (London: Pergamon Press, 1969), p. 22; qtd in David Rudd, *Enid Blyton and the Mystery of Children's Literature* (Basingstoke: Palgrave, 2000), p. 60.

19. Blyton, *First Term at Malory Towers*, p. 23.

20. Blyton, *Second Form at Malory Towers* [1948] (London: Dean, 2004), p. 83.

21. Blyton, *Five on a Treasure Island* [1942] (London: Hodder & Stoughton, 2012), p. 15.

22. Noel Streatfeild, *Ballet Shoes* [1936] (London: Puffin, 2011), p. 235.

23. Rudd, *Enid Blyton*, p. 116.

24. Lenore J. Weitzman, Deborah Eifler, Elizabeth Hokoda, and Catherine Ross, 'Sex-Role Socialization in Picture Books for Preschool Children' in *Sexism in Children's Books*, ed. Children's Rights workshop (London: Writers and Readers Publishing Cooperative, 1976), pp. 5–30; Wilma J. Pyle, 'Sexism in Children's Literature', *Theory into Practice*, 5: 2 (1976), 116–19; Janice McCabe et al, 'Gender in Twentieth-Century Children's Books: Patterns of Disparity in Titles and Central Characters', *Gender and Society*, 25 (2011), 197–226.

25. Penelope Lively (1933–) is a well-known writer of fiction for both children and adults. She won the Booker Prize in 1987 for *Moon Tiger*. She spent her early childhood in Egypt before being sent to boarding school in England at the age of 12, and read Modern History at Oxford.

26. Penelope Lively, *The House in Norham Gardens* [1974] (London: Pan, 1977), p. 7.

27. Lively, *The House in Norham Gardens*, p. 100.

16
Science Fiction

Susan Watkins

In 1972, US science fiction writer Joanna Russ famously argued that science fiction (sf) should be 'the perfect literary mode in which to explore (and explode) our assumptions about "innate" values and "natural" social arrangements ... about differences between men and women, about family structure, about sex, about gender roles'. She continues 'but speculation ... about gender roles, does not exist at all.[1] Russ's pessimism about the possibilities offered by sf is echoed in commentaries on the history of the genre in the UK, such as the following by Colin Greenland: 'Any survey of sf before 1970 would show that, by an overwhelming majority, it was written by men for men – or, some would say, adolescent boys. Female writers are memorable because they were exceptional, often using ambiguous names or male pseudonyms like women novelists of the nineteenth century.[2] The views expressed here might imply that the flowering of women's sf writing was in fact to take place from the mid 1970s onwards, outside the scope of this volume.[3]

In fact, the period 1945–1975 saw the publication of a substantial number of interesting sf works by British women writers, and their establishment or consolidation of key themes or sub-genres within sf. They wrote 'lost race/tribe' and 'ruined earth' novels, fictions of invasion, post-apocalyptic novels and 'inner space' fiction. In a number of texts, there is a growing suspicion of the US as the Cold War is established, and the threat of nuclear annihilation looms large. If sexual and gender roles are not questioned in all of this work, there are some important books where, as Russ suggests should be the case, the social arrangements concomitant upon heterosexuality and patriarchy are challenged. This chapter will discuss each of the key sub-genres in which women were writing during the period 1945–1975, and will also examine the field of cultural production in which they can be situated, including issues raised by the use of pseudonymity, the significance

© The Author(s) 2017
C. Hanson and S. Watkins, *The History of British Women's Writing, 1945–1975*,
History of British Women's Writing, DOI: 10.1057/978-1-137-47736-1_17

of magazine and paperback publication and the importance of editorial work. I also want to examine the attitudes to technology explored in their work and the relevance to women writers of familiar narratives about the development and periodization of sf in the period 1945–1975, which often organises discussion of the field into the era of the 'Golden Age', followed by the 'New Wave'.

This examination of the field of production of science fiction begins, however, with a brief discussion of three key critical works of the period by male writers: C. P. Snow's *The Two Cultures and the Scientific Revolution* (1959), Raymond Williams's 'Science Fiction' (1956) and Kingsley Amis's *New Maps of Hell* (1961). These three texts establish some of the struggles taking place in the field during the mid-1950s and into the 1960s. In his well-known argument about the gulf that exists between the literary and scientific establishments – the two cultures of the book's title – C. P. Snow says nothing at all about science *fiction*. By ignoring sf he refuses it admission to the field of literature: in fact he does not see sf as literature at all. Snow argues that 'literary intellectuals are totally lacking in foresight' and are only concerned with 'the existential moment'.[4] For Snow, only scientists have 'the future in their bones'.[5] If literature could be more forward looking, then it might have more in common, he implies, with science. It is noteworthy, however, that in his imagining of an ideal world in which the clash of the two cultures ought to produce the 'most creative chances' he uses a metaphor of 'two subjects, two disciplines, two cultures – of two *galaxies*, so far as that goes' [emphasis mine].[6] The allusion to *galaxies* plural is noteworthy, since according to the Oxford English Dictionary:

> [t]he existence of galaxies as separate systems analogous to and outside of the Milky Way system was proposed in the 19th cent. but not proved until the first meaningful determinations of the distances of galaxies by E. P. Hubble in the 1920s. Before Hubble's work many astronomers considered galaxies to be star clusters or 'nebulae' within the Milky Way system.

Even Snow's range of available metaphors, then, is marked by the development of scientific knowledge, demonstrating more interpenetration of the scientific and literary fields than he admits.

By the time of publication of *New Maps of Hell: A Survey of Science Fiction* in 1961, Kingsley Amis describes himself as 'grateful that we have a form of writing which is interested in the future, which is ready ... to treat as variables what are usually taken to be constants, which is set on tackling those large, general, speculative questions that ordinary fiction so often avoids'.[7] In a clear development from Snow, science fiction is now acknowledged as a forward-looking mode able to tackle the big questions, and its status in relation to literary fiction also begins to alter. At the start of the book Amis makes a clear distinction between the sf reader's 'addictive' enjoyment and what he calls 'ordinary literary interest';[8] by the end of the book he admits that 'at least a dozen current practitioners' have attained 'the status of the sound minor writer whose example brings into existence the figure of real standing'.[9] If the 'sound minor sf writer' is still not a major literary figure, there is an awareness of more fluidity of definition and interpenetration between these roles.

Raymond Williams's 'Science Fiction' of 1956 predates both the previous works, but is far in advance of either in the serious attention it gives to sf. Although beginning by dismissing what is referred to as 'magazine fiction', Williams then isolates three key sub-genres of the sf mode, which he terms 'putropia' (the dystopian novel), 'doomsday' (the post-apocalyptic novel) and 'space anthropology' (the lost/new tribe novel). Williams here identifies sub-genres that were of significance in the period 1945–1975. He then surprises us by picking the 'space anthropology' novel as the most interesting. For him, the 'putropia' is dominated by the 'myth' of the 'isolated intellectual' against the 'masses, who are at best brutish, at worst brutal'.[10] Williams's attention to an oft-overlooked aspect of dystopian imaging of the future – the prevalence of an under-class of proles, or epsilons – is suggestive of other elisions. Although the three essays discussed above are valuable attempts to create a rapprochement between literature and science, determine the value and place of sf writing in relation to the wider field of literary production, and identify some of the significant sub-genres characteristic in the sf mode, they do not discuss women, either as producers or consumers of sf; nor do they consider issues of gender and sexuality.[11]

If we follow Roger Luckhurst and view science fiction as a 'literature of technologically saturated societies ... a popular literature that concerns the impact of Mechanism (to use the older term for technology) on cultural life and subjectivity' then the exclusion of women (as both producers and consumers of sf) and questions of gender and sexuality is even less warranted than it might appear to be on common-sense grounds of equality.[12] It is certainly surprising in Snow's essay, which focuses on what he refers to as 'the application of real science to industry' and the changes that resulted from that application.[13] Technological changes that particularly affected women in the period 1945–1975 included transformations of both the domestic and office space as well as of women's relations to their bodies, reproduction and sexuality. Not only the era of Sputnik, the space race and the Cold War, this was also the era of the contraceptive pill, which gave women the ability effectively to control their fertility independently of men. It was also the period when the electric typewriter and automated telephone became commonplace in the office environment, and the refrigerator and vacuum cleaner in the home. As producers of scientific knowledge, feminist scientists also effected 'potent transformations' in the 'institutions, professions and disciplines of science', including work in fields as varied as developmental biology, archaeology, medicine, psychiatry and primatology.[14] Women like Jacquetta Hawkes (1910–1996), for example, whose novel *Providence Island* (1959) will be discussed shortly, were deeply embedded in both the scientific and cultural life of their times. An archaeologist and writer, Hawkes was the first woman to read archaeology and anthropology for the new Cambridge undergraduate degree. During her writing life she produced poetry, plays, journalism, fiction, biography, popular guide books, as well as books and academic papers about archaeology.[15]

One of the most significant technological changes to affect the production of science fiction was the gradual move away from magazine to paperback publication in the 1950s. The lifting of paper rationing in 1953 led to the increasing dominance of the paperback. British reprints of US magazines and the two key UK magazines, *New Worlds* and *Science Fantasy*, were gradually replaced by paperbacks published by firms such as Scion, Curtis Warren and Hamilton's (who published the Panther imprint). The Science Fiction book club, organised by Sidgwick and Jackson, released its first titles in 1953 and published six books per year. The prominence of magazine publication in the early days, the overlap between US and UK publication and the practice of frequent reprinting (from magazine to anthology and sometimes to paperback novel) had particular consequences for ideas of authorship. Initially it was customary for magazines to acquire *all* rights, which meant that authors lost out when their stories were reprinted in anthologies. As time went on, magazines acquired all *serial* rights, but not *book* rights, which meant that authors could sell these subsequently. The very notion of authorship was rather flexible. A number of publishers had 'house pseudonyms' which several different authors used. Mike Ashley argues that 'pseudonymity was not helpful to the field. It meant that good sf became indistinguishable from bad sf, because if readers exercised any discrimination they would probably not buy the next novel bearing the same by-line as one they had disliked'. Clearly, novels with the same 'by-line' might not have been written by the same person. He continues: '[pseudonymity] also meant that most science fiction rapidly became tarred with the same brush, the lowest common denominator being the worst sf around'.[16] I would suggest that pseudonymity was not, therefore, merely a matter of gender, but also a marker of the low status of the sf mode.

The editorial work done by women is another important element of their involvement in the production of sf in the period 1945–1975. A case in point is the writer and editor Hilary Bailey (1936 –). Bailey is perhaps best known to literary critics for her reworkings of *Jane Eyre*, *Frankenstein* and *The Turn of the Screw* as well as her more recent dystopian fiction and co-written work with Emma Tennant.[17] However at this time she was married to Michael Moorcock (sf novelist and editor of *New Worlds* throughout the 1960s) and authored in the period under discussion a number of short stories, including 'The Fall of Frenchy Steiner' (1964) (a well-known 'Hitler Wins' story). She was also the co-editor throughout the 1970s of several issues of *New Worlds Quarterly* (an anthology series taking over occasional publication from the journal of the same name after it folded). She also co-authored *The Black Corridor* (1969) with Moorcock (although at time of publication she was credited in the Acknowledgements rather than as co-author).[18] The range of different positions women like Bailey occupied in the sf production of the period is striking: whether as editors, authors, or co-authors their involvement is central, but as with the broader history of sf publication this questions the relevance of ideas of authorship imported from literary fiction.

Michael Moorcock's efforts to revalue sf writing and begin to associate it with *avant garde* or experimental literary fiction have been well documented. Greenland argues that Moorcock's aim was 'to publish a more ambitious and flexible kind of science fiction which would no longer subscribe to the narrative conventions established in American pulp'.[19] The distinction being drawn here between the 'Golden Age' and the 'New Wave' is frequently made.[20] Undoubtedly there are a number of key texts published in the late 1960s and early 1970s by women which can be read in terms not only of the new wave, but also in relation to the other key framework established within *New Worlds* by J. G. Ballard. Ballard's designation 'inner space fiction' has been equally influential.[21] The different metaphors here – of the wave and the space – are certainly interesting ways of understanding the relation between writing, time and space. Whereas the wave suggests linear progression and forward movement in historical time, the inner space metaphor understands literary change in terms of a movement inwards which is also an opening out.[22] The changes in sf writing over time and space being implied in these metaphors are clearly partly about national identity (an attempt to distinguish between US and British traditions of writing) and also partly about cultural value. By implication, 'serious' British sf writers were trying to separate themselves from US pulp fiction, and they were trying to make their writing more respectable in literary circles. However, we must be clear about whether women sf writers' experience can be understood in terms of conventionally elitist, nationalistic and patriarchal frameworks. Luckhurst claims that '[t]he *New Worlds* experiment ... was not a project to elevate sf from a ghetto, to plea bargain for its status as "serious" literature. Instead, it was one manifestation of a wider move to question the very categories and values of "high" and "low" culture'.[23] He thus places the new wave as part of a broader postmodernist experiment that began to value popular and elite art forms alike. Using the prism of gender and focusing on the sub-genres in which women sf writers worked allows us to see the continuity between supposedly 'pulp' and 'literary' works and undoubtedly re-situates the fiction discussed in this chapter at a tangent to some of the key historical, national and evaluative frameworks discussed above.

Two novels of the 1950s: Margot Bennett's *The Long Way Back* (1954) and Jacquetta Hawkes's *Providence Island* (1959) are a good case in point. We can see a suspicion of growing US dominance and even an attempt to challenge western imperialism and technoscience in both texts, which could be broadly defined as 'lost race', or 'ruined earth' novels. The term 'ruined earth' is used in the Encyclopedia of Science Fiction for:

> the longer range sf aftermath of disaster and holocaust scenarios. First comes the cataclysm, then the Post-Holocaust struggle with a general emphasis on survival and adaptation. If humanity avoids extinction, the details of past technology and the fall of civilization are apt to become increasingly blurred – and often mythologized – with each new generation of survivors. Beneath such cultural Amnesia lies the promise of rediscovery via a potentially moving Conceptual Breakthrough.[24]

According to the Encyclopedia of Science Fiction the 'lost race' theme 'goes hand in hand with that of the Lost World; there are few lost worlds ... which do not come equipped with one or more indigenous races ripe for First Contact and perhaps displaying interesting quirks for the student of Anthropology'.[25]

Bennett's novel was first published in 1954 by John Lane Bodley Head, but a 1957 edition was published 'for sale to members only' of the Science Fiction book club (proprietors Sidgwick and Jackson). Bennett (1912–1980) was a Scottish crime fiction writer who had worked as an advertising copywriter in Sydney and London and as a nurse in the Spanish Civil War. *The Long Way Back*, though now little-read, has become relatively well-known in sf circles. The book imagines a technologically advanced African society sending an expedition to England: a country that has been ruined by some unspecified long-distant disaster and is now occupied by primitive tribes. The book is surprisingly violent, with most of the expedition killed off gruesomely by the mutated wildlife they find. When they eventually find the native inhabitants of Britain they speak a variant of the African language but are otherwise brutal cave-dwelling 'savages'. One of the more likeable native Britons is befriended by the expedition team, and points out the similarity between the green stone in his wife's necklace and the female expedition leader's pendant. Valya, the team leader, refuses to see the resemblance, arguing that her necklace comes from Africa, where she knows it is a by-product of nuclear fusion. The novel concludes, however, with the realisation that the green stone in Britain is a result of the same atomic process. Valya laments: '"if the Britons ever knew so much, how could they be only a poor tribe today?"'[26] What is of interest in the book is how Bennettt discusses change. What Clare Hanson refers to as 'the refiguring of the genetic landscape which took place in the period between 1945 and 1975' allows Bennettt to parallel ideas about change caused by genetic mutation with ideas about changes in human culture and civilisation.[27] The impact of past nuclear destruction in Britain has been to generate genetic mutations that cause a reversion to primitive, atavistic and violent characteristics in the flora and fauna. This has been accompanied by the loss of 'advanced' or 'developed' traits of human civilisation consequent on the nuclear disaster, such as the ability to read, write, perform simple mathematical operations, and build dwellings.

The novel is deeply ironic. The majority of the expedition team is not significantly shaken by the discoveries they make; they plan to colonise Britain and reintroduce coal-mining, arguing that '"you can't stop development. Once it's started, it goes on. It's a law."'[28] The final lines of the novel show us the native Briton, Brown, 'dream[ing] of the future when Britain might raise itself, generation by generation, to become a nation that would conquer the earth'[29] Only Grame, the protagonist, represents a different viewpoint. For him, change is something fluid and is in fact non-narrative:

> Grame looked at civilisation retreating before the forest, and thought of cities and trees and desert, rising and falling in immense waves through time for ever. No separate human life had any importance in this infinite movement; the most any man could hope for was that he might learn a little of the immensity he lived in.[30]

Grame's vision of flux in nature and culture stands as a rejoinder to both the atavism of the representation of Britain in the novel and the expedition's sense of the necessity of colonial progress. The title of the novel itself suggests this paradox: narratives of progress are not in fact the opposite but the inverse of narratives of degeneration.

The representation of women in *The Long Way Back* is fairly unremarkable. Valya, the team leader, is a member of the 'spinster class', who, after a brief relationship with Grame, decides at the end of the novel to remain as a bride of the state on her return to Africa. Far more interesting is the treatment of Dr Alice Cutter in Jacquetta Hawkes's *Providence Island*. The novel concerns the discovery of a 'lost race' or tribe on a previously undiscovered island in the Pacific. The tribe has sophisticated 'psi powers' or ESP, which have allowed it to remain untouched by civilization, but it is threatened by planned US nuclear testing.[31] The plot of the novel develops around the subterfuge engaged in by the expedition of British academics in order to prevent this, see off the US forces and allow the islanders to remain undiscovered. Alice Cutter is fascinated by the tribe and its culture and she takes part in a fertility rite with an islander that restores her sense of herself as a sexual being. This is presented entirely positively, and is viewed as such by her love interest, an American anthropologist of Chinese French ancestry who accompanies the US forces, but is quickly convinced to support the British academics' efforts to prevent the discovery of the tribe and the nuclear testing of the island. When Alice tells Jean that she took part in the rite and doesn't know who her sexual partner was he merely admires her confidence and erotic aura. Here we can see contemporary sexual mores questioned by an apparently more 'enlightened' anthropological awareness of different cultures' sexual arrangements. Both of these lost race/ruined earth novels are satirical visions attacking the potential end result of techno-scientific development. Both are willing to dislodge Britain from its place as an imperial power.

The anxiety about American neo-imperialism in a Cold War context is clear not only in *Providence Island* but also in a number of other fictions of invasion, including Marghanita Laski's 1954 play *The Offshore Island* and Daphne du Maurier's *Rule Britannia* (1972).[32] Laski's play imagines a post-nuclear UK where small groups of survivors exist in pockets where the local weather conditions have prevented the spread of fall-out, surviving by subsistence farming. The arrival of US forces at the end of Act One is closely followed by the arrival of Russian forces at the end of Act Two. The alliance between the former cold war enemies means that a small bomb will be dropped to destroy any remaining uncontaminated UK land so that it can't be used by either side. Any people living on this land are 'contaminated persons' who will be sterilised, and put to work in camps outside the UK for the war effort. The US Captain argues that '[y]ou've got to have an enemy because that's the condition of mankind', but the usual enemies are shaken up by the truce, so the 'real' enemy becomes the British survivors.[33] The play romanticises the British attachment to rural life, to family and to independence, as the daughter, Mary, who has yearned throughout the play for civilization, excitement and companionship, decides at the very end to go to another local small-holding which neither the US nor Russian forces knows about, rather than being air-lifted off to the CP camp in the US.

This British self-reliance and independence undoubtedly draws on clichés of the national character, and the critique of the 'special relationship' between the US and the UK loses its force somewhat as a result. This is arguably not entirely the case in *Rule Britannia*, by Daphne du Maurier (1907–1989) in which US invasion of the UK after Britain abruptly leaves the European Union is countered by pockets of regional resistance in Cornwall and Wales. Published in 1972, the novel was a huge flop, but can now be read not merely as a jingoistic anti-American rant, but as part of a tradition of regionalism.[34] The novel pits an elderly actress, her granddaughter and adopted family of boys against the USUK alliance, which is supported by her son, a banker working closely in London with international financiers and politicians. When freedom of movement is restricted and rationing is introduced in Cornwall, some of the locals, helped by a Welsh man known as the beachcomber, begin a series of subversions and insurrections against the US forces. This Celtic alliance is what saves the day, and eventually the US forces withdraw. The victory of localism against the metropolitan alliance of international bankers and politicians is a late example of the puzzling mixture of radical and conservative sympathies that Alison Light refers to as 'romantic Toryism'.[35] This romantic Toryism is equally apparent in du Maurier's better-known novels *Jamaica Inn* (1939), *Rebecca* (1940),

Frenchman's Creek (1944), *Hungry Hill* (1946) and *My Cousin Rachel* (1951). Du Maurier is now acknowleged as a writer whose immense popularity is intrinsically related to her complex consideration of issues of sexuality, desire and gendered identity, although those issues are not to the forefront of *Rule Britannia*.[36]

At one point in *Rule Britannia* the heroine is terrified that either a nuclear bomb or a chemical weapon has been dropped. Although this apocalyptic scenario does not take place in this novel the post-apocalyptic novel is a staple of the period 1945–1975. Whether caused by plague, chemical attack, a rupture in the earth's core, or some unspecified physical and social break-down of society, writers including Penelope Gilliatt, Polly Toynbee, Emma Tennant, Josephine Saxton, Doris Lessing and Angela Carter all produced work in this genre in the 1960s and 1970s. *One by One* (1965) by the journalist and writer Penelope Gilliatt (1932–1993) has a young married couple torn apart by the spread of plague.[37] The book really seems, however, to be about the threat of homosexuality, as it is revealed that Joe, the husband, was arrested for indecency with a friend when he was a school-boy. Although his wife is not upset by this, the newspapers get hold of the story and publish an exposé, as Joe is working long hours in a hospital and has previously been built up as a public-spirited figure fighting the outbreak. In the end he becomes depressed and anxious and kills himself. The odd analogy here between male homosexuality and plague makes for an unsettling read.[38]

The journalist Polly Toynbee's *Leftovers* (1966), written when she was studying for the Oxford Entrance Exam, imagines gas and germ warfare vaporising the majority of humanity. The young people that remain spend their time driving fast around London, choosing whether to sleep in Buckingham Palace or a castle or country house outside the city, and generally living lives of pleasure. They make a pathetic attempt at self-sufficiency and building a perfect society, but in the end return to London. The novel ends with a curious turn towards suburban living, traditional family values, domestic bliss and the language of advertising, prompted by the birth of several babies. The death of teenage rebellion and the counter-culture is here seen as a depressing inevitability after the collapse of civilization.

Some of the more interesting post-apocalyptic novels do use the catastrophic scenario to challenge the status quo. Despite the fact that *Ice* (1967) by Anna Kavan (1901–1968) was not originally published under an sf label, it was voted by Brian Aldiss the best science fiction novel of the year, with 'all the virtues and very few of the vices – the pretension or the obscurity – of the sort of high-SF novel that many of the more ambitious writers in the speculative field were then striving to achieve'.[39] The term 'high-SF' here clearly suggests an attempt on Aldiss's part to situate Kavan's novel as literary fiction, or as part of the new wave. Kavan was a writer and painter who began writing increasingly experimental work, influenced possibly by her own heroin addiction and frequent suicide attempts. The *novum* of the novel, as the title suggests, involves encroaching ice overtaking the earth, but this is merely the backdrop to an eerie fable involving a man who is eternally locked in the chase of a girl (probably not the same girl) from country to country, rivalled by another man, who is also a double or *doppelganger* figure. The book makes a number of important innovations typical of the best women's sf writing towards the end of the period, for which Ballard's designation 'inner space' is arguably more appropriate. There is a breakdown of distinctions between good and evil (the doppelganger is not the 'evil twin' of the protagonist and both figures are morally compromised); the catastrophic device of encroaching ice affects the writing mode, which becomes highly experimental, and there are disruptions in the treatment of time and place: the novel has a repetitive quality associated with the protagonist's obsessive behaviour towards the girl. Writers such as Kavan, Angela Carter, Doris Lessing and Emma Tennant perceive that both ideas about time and ways of writing have to change after the apocalypse. For these women, the move into sf is part of a broader creative questioning of realism that generates other generic innovations as well in their work in this period (for example the use of gothic, fairy-tale and magic realist modes).

Doris Lessing's *The Four-Gated City* (1969) starts out in realist mode, but its appendix stages a series of nuclear and chemical accidents that destroy the 'civilised' world. The heroine is one of a new generation of people with ESP or psi powers, which, as in Hawkes's *Providence Island*, are seen as offering future alternatives to the destructiveness of techno-scientific society before the disaster. More importantly, however, the grafting of this sf appendix onto the fifth novel in a sequence of realist *bildungsromane* creates a disruption in the literary field and in the reading experience which is startling but productive.

Published in the same year, Angela Carter's *Heroes and Villains* is a *tour de force* that is also deliberately difficult to categorise. The text is clearly set in a post-apocalyptic environment, where people have divided into two groups: the Professors and the Barbarians. The rational, intellectual world of the Professors is threatened by the outbreak of irrational violence both from within and from without (by the Barbarians). Marianne, the heroine, moves outside the cloistered community of the Professors to live with the Barbarians, where she undergoes a profound sexual and spiritual awakening with Jewel, the Barbarian leader. This awakening process establishes that the tendency to think in terms of binary oppositions (for example between rationality and irrationality, Professors and Barbarians, or the Heroes and Villains of the title) is destructive. More importantly, in terms of its form and mode the novel also successfully breaks down the distinctions between realism and its 'others' such as fable, Gothic and science fiction. This categorical disruption generates a breakdown in Marianne's sense of chronometric and historical time.

Like Carter's novel, *The Time of the Crack* (1973) by Emma Tennant (1937 –) plays with the idea of division. The device of a crack in the earth's surface appearing along the river Thames generates a fantastic Swiftian diatribe which pits South and North London against each other in Manichean terms.[40] Doris Lessing's *Memoirs of a Survivor* (1974) is an even more fully-developed example of what might be called 'inner space' fiction. In this novel generic dislocation and disruption of time and space are present throughout. In the apparently day-to-day world of the novel 'civilised', industrialised society is collapsing, as is the nuclear family. A bureaucrat brings a young girl, Emily, to live with the middle-aged narrator. Emily is partly a daughter-figure, but also a kind of double, and she appears in some of the painful scenes (mixtures of memories, fantasies, and dreams) that take place in the alternative world the narrator discovers existing beyond the living room wall. In the 'everyday' world, Emily and her boyfriend Gerald (somewhat reminiscent of Jewel) try to take charge of the large numbers of vagrant children roaming the streets and living underground, but the children have become feral. Again (as with Bennett's *The Long Way Back*) we can see a questioning of narratives of historical time that seek to understand behaviour either in terms of development or degeneration. The breakdown in conventional domestic and social arrangements does not represent some kind of reversion to primitive atavism, but nor is it viewed as a 'new' development. The novel's conclusion offers a utopian alternative to the collapsing external world, when all the characters are miraculously offered escape into the world beyond the wall. Here questions about time and ways of writing also become questions about space and the constraints of the novel form altogether.

The extent to which women writers of this period were able to speculate about gender roles varies. *Future Imperfect* (1946), by Bridget Chetwynd (1910–1970) is set in the mid-1960s, but flashes back to the 1940s and 1950s. It is a satirical imagination of a world where gender roles have been entirely reversed. Women have taken over the public sphere and men are confined to the home, childcare and decorative roles. Childbirth has been outsourced to machines. The novel is clearly a response to the changes brought to gender roles by WWII, but what particularly interests is its early recognition that merely reversing gender stereotypes, particularly ones that exist in a hierarchy, is insufficient to make meaningful change, and will only generate the 'imperfect' world of the title.

Naomi Mitchison's two novels are a good point on which to conclude this chapter. Throughout her life Mitchison (1897–1999) was deeply embedded in a scientific culture and one of her abiding interests was biology and particularly genetics: it is these interests that enable her critique of conventional gender and sexual roles.[41] Hilary Rubinstein's introduction to the SF Master Series edition of *Memoirs of a Spacewoman* (1962) comments on the book's scientific credibility, noting that 'it is one of the relatively few sf novels to be written from within the scientific community and to communicate to the reader an absolute confidence in the scientific infrastructure of the story'.[42] Mary, the spacewoman of the title, is heterosexual, but has children by a number of fathers who are deliberately and carefully chosen for the role. Family arrangements are inevitably affected by time travel, which requires that space explorers are put into time blackouts in order to survive long journeys to other worlds. Those Terrans who are not explorers and are 'time-bound' are looked down on. Mary's role on expeditions is communication, including via telepathy, which is highly valued. One of the absolute rules of space exploration is non-interference in other worlds, but as the novel progresses she begins to wonder whether the logical outcome of this directive would be the end of space exploration.

Mary's ability to be self-critical is one of the most striking aspects of the novel. Specialising in communications with alien cultures makes her alert to changes in her own thought process and to the fact that other cultures think entirely differently (she becomes aware of how important binary thinking is to humanity, but also how limited). The novel's treatment of other species, including Terran animal species is striking: Mary is able to communicate with them and they are treated as equals and even friends. The two episodes where alien grafts are grafted onto Mary as host are particularly memorable. The first graft dies abruptly, shortly after separating from Mary, and she is grief-stricken. However, this does not prevent her from taking part in a second experiment, although this is terminated when she begins to have self-destructive impulses under the influence of the graft. The descriptions of these experiments are brutal and the reader certainly questions the motives of the human scientists, even if Mary does not, feeling that she had been 'somebody else. Somebody, from a scientific point of view, delinquent'.[43] Clare Hanson demonstrates the extent to which Mitchison was 'deeply embedded in the eugenic problematic and the belief that an understanding of biology holds the key to social advancement' and argues that 'her fiction demonstrates little interest in the social and political structures that might provide an alternative to this goal'.[44] It could be argued, however, that at this point in the novel Mitchison successfully engineers a critique of the scientific values of the spacewoman's culture, which does not in fact practice what she preaches.

Solution Three (1975) develops a similar critique of conventional scientific method and, again, this is intimately related to the sexual and gender roles in the novel. The title of the novel refers to the scientific and cultural response to overpopulation and food shortages post catastrophe. Crops are genetically engineered and humans are cloned, both of which processes, it is believed, will prevent dangerous random mutation. The cultural and social response that goes in tandem with this is the privileging of homosexuality, which, if not exactly compulsory, certainly becomes normative.

The plot of the novel involves the growing awareness that continued genetic engineering is causing crops to fail, and that there are outbreaks of social unrest emerging in 'less developed' parts of the world. A number of characters wish for more diverse sexual arrangements too: not merely a re-privileging of heterosexuality but an acknowledgement of a variety of sexual possibilities and sexual object choices. Again, Mitchison's broad insight is about the importance of social and biodiversity, and even more importantly, the acknowledgement of diversity within scientific method. As Susan M. Squier suggests in her Afterword to the Feminist Press edition of the novel, '[f]lexibility rather than competition, the acknowledgement that paradigms not only can but must shift in response to new voices and new needs: these qualities characterize the model for feminist scientific practice that Mitchison dramatizes'.[45]

This chapter has demonstrated that by concentrating on the sub-genres in which women sf writers worked ('lost race/tribe' and 'ruined earth' novels, fictions of invasion, post-apocalyptic novels and 'inner space' fiction) we can see that in the period 1945–1975 women's sf writing existed at a tangent to some of the key historical, national and evaluative frameworks discussed in other accounts of sf. Partly these accounts are about cultural value, and an attempt to make sf more 'literary' in the 1960s and 1970s, but there is clear continuity between women's supposedly 'pulp' and more 'literary' works. The attempt to distinguish between the British 'new wave' or 'inner space' fiction and US 'golden age' pulp is a clear attempt to mark the superiority of British over US national identity, but women sf writers of the time were suspicious of British colonial desires as well as US ones. Mitchison's critique of conventional scientific methods is perhaps the foremost example of women writers using the sf mode to make thoughtful interventions in science itself, but the challenge to the frameworks and methods of the 'science' in science fiction is also present in other work of the period.

Notes

1. Joanna Russ, 'The Image of Women in Science Fiction' in *Images of Women in Fiction* ed. by Susan C. Cornillon (Bowling Green: Bowling Green Popular Press, 1972), p. 94 (p. 80).
2. Colin Greenland, *The Entropy Exhibition: Michael Moorcock and the British 'New Wave' in Science Fiction* (London: Routledge and Kegan Paul, 1983), p. 26.
3. Much feminist criticism of women's sf writing considers for the most part work that is outside the historical scope of this chapter, or is not by British writers, for example: Lucie Armitt, *Where No Man Has Gone Before: Women and Science Fiction* (London: Routledge, 1991); Marleen Barr, *Alien to Femininity: Speculative Fiction and Feminist Theory* (London: Greenwood, 1987) and *Lost in Space: Probing Feminist Science Fiction and Beyond* (Chapel Hill, N.C: University of North Carolina Press, 1993); Justine Larbalestier, *Daughters of Earth: Feminist Science Fiction in the Twentieth Century* (Middletown: C. T: Wesleyan University Press, 2006); Sarah

LeFanu, *In the Chinks of the World Machine: Feminism and Science Fiction* (London: Women's Press, 1988); Hilary Rose, 'Dreaming the Future', in *Love, Power and Knowledge: Towards a Feminist Transformation of the Sciences* (Cambridge: Polity Press, 1994); Jenny Wolmark, *Aliens and Others: Science Fiction, Feminism and Postmodernism* (London: Harvester, 1993).

4. C. P. Snow, *The Two Cultures and the Scientific Revolution* (Cambridge: Cambridge University Press, 1961), p. 6.
5. Snow, *The Two Cultures*, p. 11.
6. Snow, *The Two Cultures*, p. 17.
7. Kingsley Amis, *New Maps of Hell: A Survey of Science Fiction* (London: Victor Gollancz, 1961), p. 156.
8. Amis, *New Maps of Hell*, p. 16.
9. Amis, *New Maps of Hell*, p. 156.
10. Raymond Williams, 'Science Fiction' in *Tenses of Imagination: Raymond Williams on Science Fiction, Utopia and Dystopia* ed. by Andrew Milner (Bern: Peter Lang, 2010), pp. 13–19 (p. 16).
11. Amis does consider the treatment of sex by male writers in his first chapter on Utopia in *New Maps of Hell* but all his chosen texts are by male writers. See pp. 87–110.
12. Roger Luckhurst, *Science Fiction* (London: Polity Press, 2005), p. 3. Luckhurst considers 'Feminism and Science Fiction' on pages 180–97 at the end of his chapter on the 1970s.
13. Snow, *The Two Cultures*, p. 31.
14. Angela Creager, Elizabeth Lunbeck, and Londa Schiebinger, *Feminism in Twentieth-Century Science, Technology and Medicine* (Illinois: University of Chicago Press, 2001), p. 4.
15. See Christine Finn, 'Jacquetta Hawkes', *Oxford Dictionary of National Biography*, <http://www.oxforddnb.com.ezproxy.leedsbeckett.ac.uk/view/article/61934> [accessed 13 March 2015].
16. Mike Ashley, *Transformations: The Story of the Science Fiction Magazines from 1950 to 1970* (Liverpool: Liverpool University Press, 2005), pp. 81–2. Much of the information about magazine and paperback publication in this chapter comes from Ashley's book.
17. Bailey's novels include *Frankenstein's Bride* (1995), *Miles and Flora* (1997) *Mrs Rochester* (1997) *Fifty-First State* (2008) and with Tennant *Balmoral* (2004) *The Autobiography of the Queen* (2007) and *Hitler's Girls* (2014).
18. See entry on Bailey in the Science Fiction Encyclopedia <http://www.sf-encyclopedia.com/entry/bailey_hilary> [accessed 13 March 2015]. Also Greenland, *The Entropy Exhibition*, pp. 20–1. See also the Fantastic Fiction website where both Bailey and Moorcock are credited as joint authors of *The Black Corridor*, <http://www.fantasticfiction.co.uk/> [accessed 13 March 2015].
19. Greenland, *The Entropy Exhibition*, p. ix.
20. The distinction between the 'Golden Age' of US magazine 'pulp' sf and more literary, experimental, British 'New Wave' sf is made in a number of key critical books, including Adam Roberts's *Science Fiction* (London: Routledge, 2000); also see Luckhurst, *Science Fiction*, pp. 141–8.
21. J. G. Ballard, 'Which Way to Inner Space?', *New Worlds*, 118 (1962), 2–3, 116–18.
22. The metaphors of waves and spaces may also draw on R. D. Laing's understanding of inner space and time as a valid alternative to outer space and time for those labelled schizophrenic (see R. D. Laing, *The Politics of Experience and The Bird of*

Paradise (London: Penguin, 1967), p. 103 and discussion in chapter 7) and also Albert Einstein's insights in his general theory of relativity that 'space and time were interwoven into a single continuum known as space-time. Events that occur at the same time for one observer could occur at different times for another' - N. T. Redd, 'Einstein's Theory of General Relativity', *Space.com*, 10 April 2015, <http://www.space.com/17661-theory-general-relativity.html> [accessed 12 May 2015].

23. Luckhurst, *Science Fiction*, p. 146.
24. See <http://www.sf-encyclopedia.com/entry/ruined_earth> [accessed 19 March 2015].
25. See <http://www.sf-encyclopedia.com/entry/lost_races> [accessed 19 March 2015].
26. Margot Bennett, *The Long Way Back* (London: Sidgwick and Jackson, 1957), p. 191.
27. Clare Hanson 'Reproduction, Genetics, and Eugenics in the Fiction of Doris Lessing', *Contemporary Women's Writing*, 1 (2007), 1–2, 171–84.
28. Bennett, *The Long Way Back*, p. 167.
29. Bennett, *The Long Way Back*, p. 206.
30. Bennett, *The Long Way Back*, p. 182.
31. US nuclear testing in this region took place throughout the 1950s, including the explosion of the first H-bomb in 1952. See http://whc.unesco.org/en/list/1339. Jaquetta Hawkes was a founder member of the Campaign for Nuclear Disarmament.
32. Storm Jameson's *The Moment of Truth* (1949) is concerned with an imagined Soviet invasion, although the characters who are waiting for evacuation to the USA do also express concerns about American culture and values.
33. Marghanita Laski, *The Offshore Island* (London: The Cresset Press, 1959), p. 57.
34. The UK joined the EEC on 1 January 1971 and voted to remain in the EEC in 1975.
35. Alison Light, 'Daphne du Maurier's Romance with the Past' in *Forever England: Feminity, Literature and Conservatism between the Wars* (London: Routledge, 1991), pp. 156–207 (p. 156).
36. Du Maurier's own issues with her ambivalent place in English establishment culture, as well as with her sexuality and gender identity, are discussed well in Nina Auerbach, *Daphne du Maurier: Haunted Heiress* (Philadelphia: University of Pennsylvania Press, 1993); Margaret Forster, *Daphne du Maurier* (London: Chatto and Windus, 1993); and Avril Horner and Sue Zlosnik, *Daphne du Maurier: Writing, Identity and the Gothic Imagination* (Basingstoke: Macmillan, 1997).
37. Penelope Gilliatt wrote for the *New Statesman*, *The Guardian*, *The Spectator*, *Queen*, *Encounter*, the *London Review of Books*, and many other newspapers, magazines, and journals. She was also the features editor of *Vogue* and alternated as film critic with Kenneth Tynan in *The Observer* (1961–5 and 1966–7). She was the second wife of the playwright John Osborne and author of the screenplay for *Sunday Bloody Sunday* (1971). See K. Whitehorn, 'Penelope Gilliatt' *The Oxford Dictionary of National Biography*, <http://www.oxforddnb.com.ezproxy.leedsbeckett.ac.uk/view/article/52076?docPos=1> [accessed 2 June 2016].
38. The Sexual Offences Act of 1967 legalised sexual acts between consenting males over the age of 21 in private.
39. Brian Aldiss, 'Introduction' to Anna Kavan, *Ice* (London: Pan Books, 1973), pp. 5–10 (pp. 7–8).
40. Emma Tennant is perhaps now better known for her reworkings of and sequels to classic literary fiction, such as *Two Women of London: The Strange Case of*

Ms. Jekyll and Mrs. Hyde (1989), *Pemberley: A Sequel to Pride and Prejudice* (1993), *Emma in Love: Jane Austen's Emma Continued* (1996).

41. Mitchison was the daughter of John Scott Haldane, a physiologist. Her brother was the geneticist J. B. S. Haldane, who also wrote popular science books and was a frequent guest on the radio. Her sons Denis and Murdoch were biologists and her son Avrion was a zoologist. See chapters 10 and 14 for discussion of her historical novels set in classical or pre-classical times. See Hanson, 'Reproduction, Genetics, and Eugenics', p. 172, and E. Maslen, 'Naomi Mitchison', *Oxford Dictionary of National Biography* <http://www.oxforddnb.com.ezproxy.leedsbeckett.ac.uk/view/article/50052> [accessed 27 March 2015].

42. Hilary Rubinstein, 'Introduction' to Naomi Mitchison, *Memoirs of a Spacewoman* (London: New English Library, 1976), p. 8.

43. Mitchison, *Memoirs of a Spacewoman*, p. 159.

44. Clare Hanson, *Eugenics, Literature and Culture in Post-war Britain* (Abingdon: Routledge, 2013), p. 131.

45. Susan M. Squier, 'Naomi Mitchison: The Feminist Art of Making Things Difficult', Afterword to Naomi Mitchison, *Solution Three* (New York: The Feminist Press, 1995), pp. 161–79 (p. 175).

Electronic Resources

Doris Lessing Society https://dorislessingsociety.wordpress.com/ A selection of useful materials for Lessing scholars

Literary Encyclopedia https://www.litencyc.com/ A reliable online encyclopedia

National Poetry Archive http://www.poetryarchive.org/ A collection of recordings of poets reading their own works, with texts

Orlando Project: http://orlando.cambridge.org/ Integrated online resource for British Women's Writing in the British Isles

Oxford Dictionary of National Biography http://www.oxforddnb.com/ Exhaustive collection of biographical material

Paris Review Interviews http://www.theparisreview.org/interviews Searchable electronic resource including interviews with many post-war women writers

The Middlebrow Network http://www.middlebrow-network.com/Home.aspx Covers the period 1920 – 1950 and has useful resources for studying mid-century middlebrow writers

University of Bristol Theatre Collection http://www.bristol.ac.uk/theatre-collection/ An accredited museum and one of the world's largest archives of British theatre history and live art

Women's Library http://digital.library.lse.ac.uk/collections/thewomenslibrary Extensive resources in women's history with online catalogue

© The Author(s) 2017
C. Hanson and S. Watkins, *The History of British Women's Writing, 1945–1975*,
History of British Women's Writing, DOI: 10.1057/978-1-137-47736-1

Select Bibliography

Primary Sources

Adcock, Fleur, *Selected Poems* (Oxford: Oxford University Press, 1983)

Alvarez, A. L. (ed.), *The New Poetry* (Harmondsworth: Penguin, 1962)

Arden, Jane, *Vagina Rex and the Gas Oven* (London: Calder and Boyars, 1971)

Arendt, Hannah, *Eichmann in Jerusalem: A Report on the Banality of Evil* (London: Faber and Faber, 1963)

—— *The Life of the Mind* (New York: Harcourt Brace, 1981)

Athill, Diana, *Stet* (London: Granta, 2000)

Bainbridge, Beryl, *The Bottle Factory Outing* [1974] (London: Abacus, 2011)

—— *English Journey* [1984] (New York: Carroll & Graff Publishers, Inc, 1997)

—— *Harriet Said* [1972] (Harmondsworth: Penguin Books, 1992)

—— *Sweet William* (London: Gerald Duckworth & Co. Ltd, 1975)

Bedford, Sybille, *As It Was* (London: Picador, 1990)

Beer, Patricia, *Collected Poems* (Manchester: Carcanet, 1990)

Behan, Brendon, 'The Captains and the Kings', Brendan Behan Sings Irish Folk Songs and Ballads (Arran Records, 2008)

Bennett, Louise, *Jamaica Labrish* (Kingston, Jamaica: Sangsters, 1966)

Bennett, Margot, *The Long Way Back* (London: Sidgwick and Jackson, 1957)

Blyton, Enid, *First Term at Malory Towers* [1946] (London: Dean, 2004)

—— *Five on a Treasure Island* [1942] (London: Hodder & Stoughton, 2012)

—— *Second Form at Malory Towers* [1948] (London: Dean, 2004)

Boland, Eavan, *Collected Poems* (Manchester: Carcanet, 1995)

Bottome, Phyllis, *The Goal* (New York: Vanguard Press, 1962)

Bowen, Elizabeth, *The Heat of the Day* [1948] (New York: Anchor Books, 2002)

Brooke-Rose, Christine, *The Christine Brooke-Rose Omnibus* [1964] (Manchester: Carcanet, 1986)

—— 'Illiterations' in *Stories and Things* (Cambridge: Cambridge University Press, 1991) pp. 250–264

Bryher, *This January Tale* (New York: Harcourt, Brace and World, 1966)

Burnett, Paula (ed.) *The Penguin Book of Caribbean Verse* (London: Penguin, 1986)

Byatt, A.S., *The Shadow of the Sun* [1964] (London: Vintage, 1991)

—— *Still Life* [1985] (London: Vintage, 1995)

Carter, Angela, *Fireworks: Nine Profane Pieces* (London: Quartet Books, 1974)

—— *Heroes and Villains* [1969] (Harmondsworth: Penguin Classics, 2011)

—— *The Infernal Desire Machines of Doctor Hoffman* [1972] (Harmondsworth: Penguin Classics)

—— *Love* [1971] (London: Vintage, 2006)

—— *The Magic Toyshop* [1967] (London: Virago, 2003)

© The Author(s) 2017

C. Hanson and S. Watkins, *The History of British Women's Writing, 1945–1975*, History of British Women's Writing, DOI: 10.1057/978–1–137–47736–1

—— *Several Perceptions* [1968] (London: Virago, 1995)

—— *Shadow Dance* [1966] (London: Virago, 1994)

Christie, Agatha, *Passenger to Frankfurt* (London: Harper Collins, 1970)

Churchill, Caryl, *Caryl Churchill: Shorts* (London: Nick Hern Books, 1990)

—— *Churchill: Plays* 1 (London: Methuen, 1985)

Cornford, Frances, *Poems* (Melbourne: Leopold Classic Library, 2014)

Couzyn, Jeni (ed.) *The Bloodaxe Book of Contemporary Women Poets* (Newcastle upon Tyne: Bloodaxe, 1985)

Dane, Clemence, *Call Home the Heart: A Play in Two Acts* (London: Heinemann, 1947)

Delaney, Shelagh, *A Taste of Honey* [1959] (London: Methuen, 1982)

Desai, Anita, *Fire on the Mountain* (London: Heinemann, 1977)

—— *The Peacock Garden* (London : Heinemann, 1979)

—— *Voices in the City, etc.* (London : Peter Owen, 1965)

Drabble, Margaret, *Jerusalem the Golden* [1967] (Harmondsworth: Penguin Books, 1969)

—— *The Millstone* [1965] (London: Weidenfeld and Nicolson, 1981)

—— *A Summer Bird-Cage* [1963] (Harmondsworth: Penguin Books Ltd, 1967)

—— *The Waterfall* [1969] (Harmondsworth: Penguin Books, 1986)

Duffy, Maureen, *The Microcosm* [1966] (London: Virago, 1989)

—— 'Rites' in Michelene Wandor (ed.) *Plays by Women, Vol 2* (London: Methuen, 1983)

—— *Wounds* [1969] (London: Methuen, 1984)

Dunn, Nell, *Poor Cow* [1967] (London: Virago Press, 1988)

—— *Up the Junction* [1963] (London: Virago Press, 1988)

Emecheta, Buchi, *The Bride Price* (London: Allison and Busby, 1976)

—— *The Joys of Motherhood* (London: Allison and Busby, 1979)

—— *The Slave Girl* (London: Allison and Busby, 1977)

Fainlight, Ruth, *New and Collected Poems* (Tarset: Bloodaxe, 2010)

Feinstein, Elaine, *Children of the Rose* (Harmondsworth: Penguin, 1975)

—— *Collected Poems and Translations* [1966] (Manchester: Carcanet, 2002)

Forrest-Thomson, Veronica, 'Through the Looking Glass', *Collected Poems and Translations* (Bristol: Shearsman Books, 2008)

Gallie, Menna, *The Small Mine* [1962] (Dinas Powys: Honno, 2000)

—— *Strike for a Kingdom* [1959] (Dinas Powys: Honno, 2003)

—— *You're Welcome to Ulster* [1970] (Dinas Powys: Honno, 2010)

Gershon, Karen, *Collected Poems* (London: Papermac, 1990)

Gilroy, Beryl, *In Praise of Love and Children* (Leeds, Peepal Tree, 1996)

—— *Sunlight on Sweet Water* (Leeds: Peepal Tree, 1994)

Gladwell, Joyce, *Brown Face, Big Master*, ed. Sandra Courtman (London: MacMillan Caribbean, 2003)

H.D. (Hilda Doolittle), *Helen in Egypt* (New York: New Directions, 1961)

—— *Trilogy* [1946] (New York: New Directions, 1998)

Hall, Radclyffe, *The Well of Loneliness* [1928] (Ware: Wordsworth, 2014)

Hawkes, Jacquetta, *Providence Island* (London: Chatto and Windus, 1959)

Heyer, Georgette, *Arabella* [1949] (London: Arrow, 1999)

—— *A Civil Contract* [1961] (London: Arrow, 2005)

—— *The Grand Sophy* [1950] (London: Arrow, 1991)

—— *Regency Buck* [1935] (London: Pan, 1959)

—— *Sylvester* [1957] (London: Mandarin, 1992)

Holt, Victoria, *Mistress of Mellyn* [1960] (London: Fontana, 1963)

Hosain, Attia, *Sunlight on a Broken Column* [1961] (London: Virago, 1988)

Hull, Veronica, *The Monkey Puzzle* (London: Barrie, 1958)
Iremonger, Lucille, *West Indian Folk Tales: Anansi Stories retold for English Children* (London: George Harrap, 1956)
Irwin, Margaret, *Elizabeth and the Prince of Spain* [1953] (London: Allison and Busby, 1999)
—— *Young Bess* [1944] (London: Allison and Busby, 1988)
Jameson, Storm, *Before the Crossing* (London: Macmillan, 1947)
—— *The Black Laurel* (London: Macmillan, 1947)
—— *The Green Man* (London: Macmillan, 1952)
—— *Journey from the North* [1969] (London: Virago, 1984.
—— *The Mirror in Darkness* (I *Company Parade* (London: Cassell, 1934); II *Love in Winter* (London: Cassell, 1935); III *None Turn Back* (London: Cassell, 1936))
—— *A Ulysses Too Many* (London: Macmillan, 1958)
—— *The White Crow* (London: Macmillan,1968)
Jellicoe, Ann, *The Knack and The Sport of my Mad Mother* (London: Faber and Faber, 1985)
Jennings, Elizabeth, *New Collected Poems* (Manchester: Carcanet, 2002)
Joseph, Jenny, *Rose in the Afternoon and Other Poems* (London: Dent & Sons, 1974)
Johnston, Jennifer, *The Captains and the Kings* [1972] (London: Coronet, 1979)
Kavan, Anna, *Ice* (London: Pan Books, 1973)
Kerr, Judith, *When Hitler Stole Pink Rabbit* [1971] (London: Collins, 1974)
Laski, Marghanita, *Little Boy Lost* [1949] (London: Persephone Books, 2001)
—— *The Offshore Island* (London: The Cresset Press, 1959)
Le Guin, Ursula K, *The Left Hand of Darkness* (New York: Ace Books, 1969)
Lehmann, Rosamond, *The Echoing Grove* [1953] (Glasgow: William Collins Sons & Co, 1984)
Lessing, Doris, *Briefing for a Descent into Hell* [1971] (London: Flamingo, 1995)
—— *The Children of Violence* series: *Martha Quest* (1952), *A Proper Marriage* (1954), *A Ripple from the Storm* (1958), *Landlocked* (1965), *The Four-Gated City* (1969), reprinted in Harper Perennial editions (New York: Harper Perennial, 1995)
—— 'Each His Own Wilderness' in E. M. Browne (ed.) *New English Dramatists: 1* (Harmondsworth: Penguin Books, 1959)
—— *The Golden Notebook* ([1962] (London: Paladin, 1972)
—— *The Grass is Singing* ([1950] (London: Fourth Estate, 2013)
—— *In Pursuit of the English* (New York: Harper Perennial, 1960)
—— *Memoirs of a Survivor* (London: Octagon, 1974)
—— *Play with a Tiger* in V. Sullivan and J. Hatch (eds) (1974) *Plays By and About Women* (New York: Vintage Books, 1958)
Levertov, Denise, *Collected Earlier Poems, 1940–1960* (New York: New Directions, 1979)
—— *Selected Poems* [1961] (New York: New Directions, 2004)
Lively, Penelope, *The House in Norham Gardens* [1974] (London: Pan, 1977)
Lofts, Norah, *The Concubine* (New York: Doubleday, 1963)
Loy, Mina *The Lost Lunar Baedeker*, ed. Roger Conover (Manchester: Carcanet Press, 1997)
Macaulay, Rose, *The World My Wilderness* [1950] (London: Virago, 1983)
MacInnes, Helen, *Above Suspicion* (Boston: Little, Brown, 1941)
—— *The Salzburg Connection* [1968] (London: Titan, 2012)
Manning, Olivia, *The Balkan Trilogy* (Harmondsworth: Penguin, 1981)
—— *The Levant Trilogy* (Harmondsworth: Penguin, 1982)

Markandaya, Kamala, *A Handful of Rice* (London: Hamish Hamilton, 1966)
—— *Nectar in a Sieve* (London: Putnam, 1954)
—— *The Nowhere Man* (London: Allan Lane, 1973)
—— *Some Inner Fury* (London: Putnam, 1955)
Marson, Una, *Selected Poems* (Leeds: Peepal Tree Press, 2011)
Mayer, Gerda, *Prague Winter* (London: Hearing Eye, 2005)
McNeill, Janet, *Tea at Four O' Clock* [1956] (London: Virago, 1988)
Miller, Betty, *Farewell Leicester Square* [1941] (London: Persephone Books, 2000)
—— *On the Side of the Angels* [1945] (London: Virago, 1985)
Mitchison, Naomi, 'The Hill Modipe' in T. A. Dunn (ed.) *Scottish Short Stories 1975* (London: Collins, 1975)
—— *Memoirs of a Spacewoman* (London: Victor Gollanz, 1962)
—— *Return to the Fairy Hill* (London: Heinemann, 1966)
—— *Solution Three* [1975] (New York: The Feminist Press, 1995)
Mitford, Nancy, *Love in a Cold Climate and Other Novels* [1949] (London: Penguin, 2000)
Mortimer, Penelope, *Daddy's Gone A-Hunting* [1958] (Persephone: London, 2008)
—— *The Home* [1971] (Harmondsworth: Penguin Books Ltd, 1973)
—— *The Pumpkin Eater* [1962] (London: Bloomsbury Publishing, 1995)
Murdoch, Iris, *The Nice and the Good* [1968] (London: Vintage, 2000)
—— *Under the Net* [1954] (London: Vintage, 2002)
Nwapa, Flora *Efuru* [1966] (Long Grove, IL: Waveland Press, 2013)
Philippa Pearce, *Tom's Midnight Garden* (Oxford: Oxford University Press, 1958)
Pitter, Ruth, *Collected Poems* (London: Enitharmon, 1996)
Plaidy, Jean, *Murder Most Royal* [1949] (London: Pan, 1966)
Plath, Sylvia, *The Bell Jar* (London: Faber and Faber, 1963)
—— *Collected Poems*, ed. Ted Hughes (London: Faber, 1981)
Pym, Barbara, *Excellent Women* [1952] (Harmondsworth: Penguin Books, 1983)
—— *Jane and Prudence* [1953] (London: Virago, 2007)
Quin, Ann, *Berg* [1964] (London: Marian Boyars, 2009)
Raine, Kathleen, *Collected Poems* (Ipswich: Golgonooza Press, 2008)
Reid Banks, Lynne, *The L-Shaped Room* [1960] (London: Vintage Books, 2004)
Renault, Mary, *The Alexander Trilogy: Fire From Heaven* [1970], *The Persian Boy* [1972] *Funeral Games* [1981] ed. Sarah Dunant (London: Penguin, 1984)
—— *The Bull from the Sea* [1962] (Harmondsworth: Penguin, 1973)
—— *The Charioteer* [1953] (London: Vintage, 2003)
—— *The King Must Die* [1958] (London: Four Square, 1961)
—— *The North Face* [1948] (London: Virago, 2014)
—— *Return to Night* [1947] (London: Virago, 2014)
Reznikoff, Charles, *Holocaust* (Los Angeles: Black Sparrow Press, 1975)
Rhys, Jean, *Wide Sargasso Sea* [1966] (London: Penguin, 2000)
Ridler, Anne, *Some Time After and Other Poems* (London: Faber, 1972)
Roberts, Kate, *Te yn y Grug (Tea in the Heather)* (Denbigh: Gee, 1959)
—— *Tegwch y Bore (Fairness of Morning)* (Llandybïe: Christopher Davies, 1967)
—— *Y Byw sy'n Cysgu (The Living Sleep)* (Denbigh: Gee, 1956)
Rook, Jean, *Rook's Eye View* (Worthing: Littlehampton Books Services, 1979)
Sahgal,Nayantara, *The Day in Shadow* (London: W.W. Norton, 1972)
—— *Prison and Chocolate Cake*, (New York: Alfred A Knopf, 1954)
Seton, Anya, *Katherine* [1954] (London: Hodder, 1961)
Smith, Stevie, *Collected Poems* (London: Allen Lane, 1975)

—— *The Collected Poems and Drawings of Stevie Smith*, ed. William May, (London: Faber & Faber, 2015)
—— *The Holiday* [1949] (London: Virago, 1979)
Spark, Muriel, *The Comforters* [1957] (London: Virago, 2009)
—— *The Complete Short Stories* (London: Penguin, 2001)
—— *Doctors of Philosophy* (New York: Alfred A. Knopf, 1966)
—— *The Driver's Seat* [1970] (London: Penguin, 1974)
—— *The Go-Away Bird and Other Stories* [1958] (Harmondsworth: Penguin, 1963)
—— *The Mandelbaum Gate* [1965] (London: Penguin, 1967)
—— *The Prime of Miss Jean Brodie* [1961] (London: Penguin, 1965)
—— *Voices at Play* (Harmondsworth: Penguin,1961)
Stevenson, Anne, *Correspondences: A Family History in Letters* (London: Oxford University Press, 1974)
—— *Travelling Behind Glass: Selected Poems* (Oxford: Oxford University Press, 1974)
Stott, Mary, *Forgetting's No Excuse* [1973] (London: Virago, 1989)
Streatfeild, Noel, *Ballet Shoes* [1936] (London: Puffin, 2011)
Suyin, Han, *A Many-Splendoured Thing* [1952] (London: The Reprint Society, 1954)
Taylor, Elizabeth, *At Mrs Lippincote's* [1945] (London: Virago, 2000)
—— 'The Devastating Boys' in *The Devastating Boys* [1972] (London: Virago, 1984)
—— *A Game of Hide and Seek* [1951] (London: Virago, 2009)
—— *A View of the Harbour* [1947] (London: Virago, 2013)
—— *A Wreath of Roses* [1949] (London: Virago, 2011)
Townsend Warner, Sylvia, *The Flint Anchor* ([1954] (London: Virago, 1997)
Wandor, Michelene (ed.) *Strike While the Iron Is Hot* (London: The Journeyman Press, 1980)
Weldon, Fay, *Down Among the Women* (Harmondsworth: Penguin Books Ltd, 1973)
—— *The Fat Woman's Joke* ([1967] (London: Flamingo, 2012)
West, Rebecca, *A Train of Powder* (New York: Viking, 1955)
Wynter, Sylvia, *The Hills of Hebron* (London: Jonathon Cape, 1962)

Secondary Sources

Amis, Kingsley, *New Maps of Hell: A Survey of Science Fiction* (London: Victor Gollancz, 1961)
Ashley, Mike, *Transformations: The Story of the Science Fiction Magazines from 1950 to 1970* (Liverpool: Liverpool University Press, 2005)
Ballard, J. G., 'Which Way to Inner Space?', *New Worlds*, 118 (1962), 2–3, 116–18
Bassnett, Susan, 'A Commercial Success: Women Playwrights in the 1950s' in M. Luckhurst (ed.), *A Companion to Modern British and Irish Drama 1880–2005* (Oxford: Blackwell, 2006), pp. 175–87
Beavoir, Simone de, *The Second Sex* [1949] (London: Vintage, 1997)
BBC, 'A Short History of the BBC' (2002) <http://news.bbc.co.uk/1/hi/entertainment/1231593.stm>
Bergonzi, Bernard, *The Situation of the Novel* [1970] (Basingstoke: Macmillan, 1979)
Bhabha, Homi, 'The Vernacular Cosmopolitan' in F. Dennis and N. Khan (eds), *Voices of the Crossing* (London: Serpents Tail, 2000), pp. 133–43
Bluemel, Kristin (ed.), *Intermodernism: Literary Culture in Mid-Twentieth-Century Britain* (Edinburgh: Edinburgh University Press, 2009)

Bock, Gisela, 'Racism and Sexism in Nazi Germany: Motherhood, Compulsory Sterilisation, and the State', in R. Brienthal, A. Grossman and M. Kaplan (eds), *When Biology Became Destiny: Women in Weimar and Nazi Germany* (New York: Monthly Review Press, 1984), pp. 271–96

Booth, Martin, *British Poetry 1964–84: Driving Through the Barricades* (London: Routledge & Kegan Paul, 1985)

Bos, Pascale Rachel, 'Women and the Holocaust: Analyzing Gender Difference', in E. R. Baer and M. Goldenberg (eds), *Experience and Expression: Women, the Nazis, and the Holocaust* (Detroit: Wayne State University Press, 2003), pp. 23–52

Brooke, Stephen, 'Gender and Working Class Identity in Britain during the 1950s', *Journal of Social History*, 34 (2001), 773–95

Brown, Erica and Grover, Mary (eds), *Middlebrow Literary Cultures: the Battle of the Brows* (Basingstoke: Palgrave Macmillan, 2011)

Butler, Catherine, and O'Donovan, Hallie, *Reading History in Children's Books* (Basingstoke: Palgrave Macmillan, 2012)

Byatt, A. S., *Passions of the Mind: Selected Writings* (London: Chatto & Windus, 1991)

—— 'Soul Searching', *The Guardian*, 14 February 2004, <http://www.guardian.co.uk/books/2004/aug/15/summerreading2004.summerreading3>

Byers, Margaret, 'Cautious Vision: Recent British Poetry by Women' in M. Schmidt and G. Lindop (eds), *British Poetry Since 1960: A Critical Survey* (Manchester: Carcanet, 1972), pp. 74–84

Cam, Helen, *Historical Novels* (London: Routledge & Kegan Paul, 1961)

Carpenter, Humphrey, *Secret Gardens: A Study of the Golden Age of Children's Literature* (Boston: Houghton Mifflin, 1985)

Carter, Angela, 'Notes from the Front Line' in J. Uglow (ed.), *The Collected Angela Carter, Shaking a Leg: Journalism and Writings* (London: Chatto & Windus, 1997), pp. 36–43

Chambers, Aidan, 'Alive and Flourishing: a Personal View of Teenage Literature' in *Booktalk: Occasional Writing on Literature and Children* (Stroud: Thimble Press, 1995), pp. 84–91

—— *The Reluctant Reader* (London: Pergamon Press, 1969)

Chambers, Deborah, Linda Steiner, and Carole Fleming, *Women and Journalism* (London: Routledge, 2004)

Cheyette, Bryan, *Muriel Spark* (London: Northcote House, 2000)

Cook, Hera, *The Long Sexual Revolution: English Women, Sex, & Contraception 1800–1975* (Oxford: Oxford University Press, 2007)

Cooke, Rachel, 'Shelagh Delaney: the Return of Britain's Angry Young Woman', *The Observer*, 25 January 2014, <http://www.theguardian.com/stage/2014/jan/25/shelagh-delaney-angry-young-woman-a-taste-of-honey>

Creager, Angela, Elizabeth Lunbeck, and Londa Schiebinger, *Feminism in Twentieth-Century Science, Technology and Medicine* (Illinois: University of Chicago Press, 2001)

de Groot, Jerome, *The Historical Novel* (London: Routledge, 2010)

Di Cenzo, Maria, ''Militant Distribution: Votes for Women and the Public Sphere', *Media History*, 6: 2 (2010), 115–128

Dorney, Kate and Francis Gray, *Played in Britain: Modern Theatre in 100 Plays* (London: Methuen, 2013)

Dowson, Jane, *Women's Writing, 1945–1960: After the Deluge* (Basingstoke: Palgrave Macmillan, 2003)

Drabble, Margaret, 'Women Writers as an Unprotected Species' in Judy Simons and Kate Fullbrook, (eds), *Writing: A Woman's Business* (Manchester: Manchester University Press, 1998), pp. 163–175

—— 'Writing *The Millstone*', *Guardian*, 18 March 2011, <http://www.theguardian.com/books/2011/mar/19/book-club-margaret-drabble-millstone>

Duncker, Patricia, *Sisters and Strangers: An Introduction to Contemporary Feminist Fiction* (Oxford: Blackwell, 1991)

Eagleton, Mary, 'The Anxious Lives of Clever Girls: the University Novels of Margaret Drabble, A. S. Byatt, and Hilary Mantel', *Tulsa Studies in Women's Literature*, 33: 2 (2014), 103–21

Engdahl, Horace (ed.), *Witness Literature: Proceedings of the Nobel Centennial Symposium* (Singapore: World Scientific, 2002)

Emecheta, Buchi, 'A Nigerian Writer Living in London', *Kunapipi*, 4: 1 (1982), 114–23

Feather, John, *A History of British Publishing*, 2nd edition (London: Routledge, 2005)

Felski, Rita, *Beyond Feminist Aesthetics: Feminist Literature and Social Change* (Cambridge, MA: Harvard University Press, 1989)

Fraser, Nancy, 'Rethinking the Public Sphere: A Contribution to the Critique of Actually Existing Democracy', *Social Text*, 25/26 (1990), 56–80 <http://my.ilstu.edu/~jkshapi/Fraser_Rethinking%20the%20Public%20Sphere.pdf>

Friedan, Betty, *The Feminine Mystique* [1963] (London: Penguin Modern Classics, 2010)

Fleishman, Avrom, *The English Historical Novel: Walter Scott to Virginia Woolf* (Baltimore: Johns Hopkins University Press)

Gale, Maggie B., *West End Women: Women and the London Stage 1918–1962* (London: Routledge, 1996)

Gasiorek, Andrzej, *Post-War British Fiction: Realism and After* (London: Edward Arnold, 1995)

Grant, Linda, 'Profile: Marjorie Proops', *The Independent*, 3 January 1993, <http://www.independent.co.uk/voices/profile-marjorie-proops-marjes-mirror-image-britains-most-famous-agony-aunt-has-been-as-unhappy-as-her-readers-linda-grant-explores-a-pretence-that-deceived-millions-1476382.html>

Greenland, Colin, *The Entropy Exhibition* [1983] (London: Routledge, 2013)

Greer, Germaine, *The Female Eunuch* (London: Paladin, 1971)

Guppy, Susha, 'Beryl Bainbridge, The Art of Fiction No. 164', *The Paris Review*, No. 157 (2000) <http://www.theparisreview.org/interviews/561/the-art-of-fiction-no-164-beryl-bainbridge>

—— 'Interview with Sybille Bedford', *Paris Review*, 126 (1993), 230–49 (239)

Habermas, Jurgen, *The Structural Transformation of the Public Sphere* (Cambridge, Massachusetts: MIT, 1989)

Hall, Lesley, *Sex, Gender and Social Change in Britain since 1980* (Basingstoke: Macmillan, 2000)

Hanson, Clare, *A Cultural History of Pregnancy: Pregnancy, Medicine and Culture, 1750–2000* (Basingstoke: Palgrave Macmillan, 2004)

—— *Eugenics, Literature, and Culture in Post-War Britain* (London: Routledge, 2012)

—— *Hysterical Fictions* (Basingstoke: Macmillan, 2000)

—— 'Reproduction, Genetics, and Eugenics in the Fiction of Doris Lessing', *Contemporary Women's Writing*, 1, 1–2 (2007), 171–84

Hartley, Jenny, *Millions Like Us: British Women's Fiction of the Second World War* (London: Virago, 1997)

Hartley, John, *Understanding News* (London: Methuen, 1982)

Hayman, David and Keith Cohen, 'An Interview with Christine Brooke-Rose', *Contemporary Literature*, 17 (1976), 1–23

Head, Dominic, *Modern British Fiction, 1950–2000* (Cambridge: Cambridge University Press, 2002)

Hechter, Michael, *Internal Colonialism: The Celtic Fringe in British National Development, 1536–1966* (London: Routledge, 1975)

Hennessy, Peter, *The Secret State: Whitehall and the Cold War* (London: Penguin, 2003)

Hoberman, Ruth, *Gendering Classicism: The Ancient World in Twentieth-Century Women's Historical Fiction* (New York: State University of New York Press, 1997)

Hosain, Attia, 'Deep Roots, New Language' in *Voices of the Crossing* ed. Ferdinand Dennis and Naseem Khan, pp. 19–29

Humble, Nicola, *The Feminine Middlebrow Novel, 1920s to 1950s: Class, Domesticity and Bohemianism* (Oxford: Oxford University Press, 2001)

Humm, Maggie, *Border Traffic: Strategies of Contemporary Women Writers* (Manchester: Manchester University Press, 1991)

Hutcheon, Linda, *The Politics of Postmodernism*, 2nd ed. (London: Routledge, 2002)

Jameson, Storm, *The Novel in Contemporary Life* (Boston: The Writer Inc., 1938)

Joannou, Maroula, *Contemporary Women's Writing: From* The Golden Notebook *to* The Color Purple (Manchester: Manchester University Press, 2000)

—— *Women's Writing, Englishness and National and Cultural Identity: the Mobile Woman and the Migrant Voice, 1938–1962* (Basingstoke: Palgrave Macmillan, 2012)

Kiernan, Kathleen, Hilary Land and Jane Lewis, *Lone Motherhood in Twentieth-Century Britain: From Footnote to Front Page* (Oxford: Oxford University Press, 1998)

Lassner, Phyllis, *Anglo-Jewish Women Writing the Holocaust: Displaced Witnesses* (Basingstoke: Palgrave Macmillan, 2008)

—— *British Women Writers of World War II: Battlegrounds of their Own* (Basingstoke: Palgrave Macmillan, 1998)

—— *Colonial Strangers: Women Writing the End of the British Empire* (New Brunswick: Rutgers University Press, 2004)

Lifton, Robert Jay, *The Broken Connection: On Death and the Continuity of Life* (New York: Simon and Schuster, 1979)

Light, Alison, *Forever England: Femininity, Literature and Conservatism between the Wars* (London: Routledge, 1991)

Lodge, David, 'The Novelist at the Crossroads', *Critical Inquiry*, 11 (1969), 105–32

Low, Gail, '"Finding the Centre?" Publishing Commonwealth Writing in London: The Case of Anglophone Caribbean Writing 1950–65', *Journal of Commonwealth Literature*, 37: 2 (2002)

—— 'Publishing Histories', in S. Chew and D. Richards (eds), *A Concise Companion to Postcolonial Literature* (Chichester: Wiley-Blackwell, 2010), pp. 204–228

—— *Publishing the Postcolonial: Anglophone West African and Caribbean Writing in the UK 1948–1968* (London: Routledge, 2012)

Lukács, Gyorgy, *The Historical Novel*, trans. Hannah and Stanley Mitchell [1936/7] (Lincoln and London: University of Nebraska Press, 1983)

Lucas, Ann Lawson (ed.), *The Presence of the Past in Children's Literature* (Westport CT: Praeger, 2003)

Luckhurst, Roger, *Science Fiction* (London: Polity Press, 2005)

MacKay, Marina and Stonebridge, Lindsey (eds), *British Fiction after Modernism: the Novel at Mid-Century* (Basingstoke: Palgrave Macmillan, 2007)

MacKay, Marina, *Modernism and World War II* (Cambridge: Cambridge University Press, 2007)

Maslen, Elizabeth, *Life in the Writings of Storm Jameson* (Evanston, Northwestern University Press, 2014)

McCabe, J., '50 years of the Guardian's womens' pages', *the F word blog: Contemporary UK Feminism*, 18 July 2007, <http://www.thefword.org.uk/blog/2007/07/50_years_of_the>

Mellor, Leo, *Reading the Ruins: Modernism, Bombsites and British Culture* (Cambridge: Cambridge University Press, 2011)

Mitchell, Caroline (ed.), *Women and Radio: Airing Differences* (London: Routledge, 2000)

Mitchell, Juliet, *Women: The Longest Revolution: Essays in Feminism, Literature and Psychoanalysis* (London: Virago, 1984)

Morris, Abigail, 'Beware the Treadmill', *Jewish Quarterly*, 41: 4 (1994), 4

Murdoch, Iris, 'Against Dryness' in M. Bradbury (ed.), *The Novel Today* [1961] (London: Fontana, 1990)

Nairn, Tom, *The Break-Up of Britain: Crisis and Neo-Nationalism*, 2nd expanded edition (London: Verso, 1981)

Nasta, Susheila (ed.), *Motherlands: Black Women's Writing from Africa, the Caribbean and South Asia* (London: The Women's Press, 1991)

Orr, Julie, *Tragic Realism and Modern Society: The Passionate Political in the Modern Novel* [1979] (London: Macmillan, 1989)

Pearson, Lucy, *The Making of Modern Children's Literature in Britain* (Farnham: Ashgate, 2013)

Philips, Deborah, *Women's Fiction 1945–2005* (London: Continuum, 2006)

Philips, Deborah and Ian Haywood, *Brave New Causes: Women in British Postwar Fictions* (London: Leicester University Press, 1998)

Piette, Adam, *The Literary Cold War: 1945 to Vietnam* (Edinburgh: Edinburgh University Press, 2009)

Plain, Gill, *Literature of the 1940s: War, Postwar, and Peace* (Edinburgh: Edinburgh University Press, 2013)

—— *Twentieth Century Crime Fiction: Gender, Sexuality and the Body* (Edinburgh: Edinburgh University Press, 2001)

—— *Women's Fiction of the Second World War: Gender, Power and Resistance* (New York: St. Martin's Press, 1996)

Plath, Sylvia, *The Journals of Sylvia Plath* ed. by Ted Hughes (New York: Dial Press, 1982)

Rabinovitz, Rubin, *The Reaction Against Experiment in the English Novel, 1957–1960* (New York: Columbia University Press, 1967)

Radner, Hilary, *Shopping Around: Feminine Culture and the Pursuit of Pleasure* (Abingdon: Routledge, 1995)

Raine, Kathleen, 'Love, Cambridge, Poetry: Extracts from an unpublished essay' in Grevel Lindop, 'Kathleen Raine: The Tenth Decade', *PN Review*, December 2008

Rau, Petra, *Our Nazis: Representations of Fascism in Contemporary Literature and Film* (Edinburgh: Edinburgh University Press, 2013)

Rawlinson, Mark, *British Writing of the Second World War* (Oxford: Clarendon Press, 2000)

Rebellato, Dan, *1956 and All That: The Making of Modern British Drama* (London: Routledge, 1999)

Renault, Mary, 'Notes on *The King Must Die*', in T. McCormack (ed.), *Afterwords: Novelists on Their Novels* (New York and London: Harper and Row, 1968), pp. 84–86

Reynolds, Kimberley, and Nicholas Tucker (eds), *Children's Book Publishing in Britain since 1945* (Aldershot: Scolar Press, 1998)

Rhys, Jean, *Letters 1931–1966*, eds Francis Wyndham and Diana Melly (London: Andre Deutsch, 1984)

Riley, Catherine, 'The Intersections Between Early Feminist Polemic and Publishing: How Books Changed Lives in the Second Wave', *Women: A Cultural Review*, 26: 4 (2016), 384–401

Rose, Hilary, 'Dreaming the Future' in *Love, Power and Knowledge: Towards a Feminist Transformation of the Sciences* (Cambridge: Polity Press, 1994)

Rowbotham, Sheila, *Promise of a Dream: Remembering the Sixties* (London: Allen Lane, 2000)

Rowbotham, Sheila, *Woman's Consciousness, Man's World* (London: Penguin, 1973)

Russ, Joanna, 'The Image of Women in Science Fiction' in S. C. Cornillon (ed.) *Images of Women in Fiction* (Bowling Green: Bowling Green Popular Press, 1972), pp. 79–94

Sage, Lorna, *Women in the House of Fiction: Post-War Women Novelists* (Basingstoke: Macmillan Press Ltd, 1992)

Schneider, Karen, *Loving Arms: British Women Writing the Second World War* (Lexington: University Press of Kentucky, 1997)

Sebba, Anne, *Battling for News: The Rise of the Woman Reporter* (London: Hodder and Stoughton, 1994)

Sierz, Aleks, *In-Yer-Face Theatre* (London: Faber and Faber, 2001)

Spivak, Gayatri C.,'Three Women's Texts and a Critique of Imperialism', in R. R. Warhol and D. P. Herndl (eds), *Feminisms* (Basingstoke: Macmillan, 1997), pp. 896–912

Steedman, Carolyn, *Landscape for a Good Woman: A Story of Two Lives* (London: Virago, 1986)

Steiner, Linda, 'Newsroom Accounts of Power at Work', in C. Carter, J. Branston and S. Allan (eds), *News, Gender and Power* (London: Routledge, 1998), pp. 145–159

Stevenson, Anne, 'Writing as a Woman' in M. Jacobus (ed.), *Women Writing and Writing About Women* (London: Croom Helm, 1979), pp. 159–76

Stevenson, Iain, *Book Makers: British Publishing in the Twentieth Century* (London: The British Library, 2010)

Stewart, Victoria, *Narratives of Memory: British Writing of the 1940s* (Basingstoke: Palgrave Macmillan, 2006)

Stonebridge, Lyndsey, *The Judicial Imagination* (Edinburgh: Edinburgh University Press, 2011)

Suleiman, Susan Rubin, 'The 1.5 Generation: Thinking about Child Survivors and the Holocaust', *American Imago*, 59: 3 (2002), 277–95

Taylor, D. J., *After the War: the Novel and English Society since 1945* (London: Chatto & Windus, 1993)

Todd, Janet (ed.), *Women Writers Talking* (New York: Holmes & Meier, 1983)

Townsend, John Rowe, *Written for Children: an Outline of English-Language Children's Literature*, 2nd Edition (Harmondsworth: Kestrel, 1974)

Townsend Warner, Sylvia, *The Diaries of Sylvia Townsend Warner*, ed. Claire Harman (London: Virago, 1994)

Tredell, Nicolas,'A. S. Byatt in Conversation', *P. N. Review*, 17: 3 (1991), 24–8

Tucker, Nicholas, 'Setting the Scene', in K. Reynolds and N. Tucker (eds), *Children's Book Publishing in Britain since 1945* (Aldershot: Scolar Press, 1998), pp. 1–19

Tweedie, Jill, *Eating Children: Young Dreams and Early Nightmares* (London: Penguin, 1994)

Wandor, Michelene, *Look Back in Gender: Sexuality and the Family in Post-War British Drama* (London: Methuen, 1987)

Watkins, Susan, *Doris Lessing* (Manchester: Manchester University Press, 2010)
Waugh, Patricia, *Feminine Fictions: Revisiting the Postmodern* (London: Routledge, 1989)
Whitehorn, Katharine, *Selective Memory: An Autobiography* (London: Virago Press, 2007)
Wieviorka, Annette, *The Era of the Witness* (Ithaca: Cornell University Press, 2006)
Williams, Raymond, *The Long Revolution* (Harmondsworth: Pelican Books, 1965)
Wilson, Elizabeth, *Only Halfway to Paradise: Women in Postwar Britain: 1945–1968* (London: Tavistock Publications Ltd, 1980)
Zilboorg, Caroline, *The Masks of Mary Renault: A Literary Biography* (Columbia and London: University of Missouri Press, 2001).

Index